THE
CHILDREN
STAR

THE CHILDREN STAR

JOAN SLONCZEWSKI

TOR®

A TOM DOHERTY ASSOCIATES BOOK
NEW YORK

THE CHILDREN STAR

Copyright © 1998 by Joan Slonczewski.

Edited by David G. Hartwell

A Tor Book
Published by Tom Doherty Associates, Inc.
175 Fifth Avenue
New York, NY 10010

Tor Books on the World Wide Web:
http://www.tor.com

Visit Joan Slonczewski's home page:
http://www.kenyon.edu/depts/biology/slonc.htm

Tor® is a registered trademark of
Tom Doherty Associates, Inc.

Design by Lynn Newmark

Library of Congress Cataloging-in-Publication Data

Slonczewski, Joan.
The children star / Joan Slonczewski.—1st ed.
        p.   cm.
"A Tom Doherty Associates book."
ISBN 0-312-86716-6 (alk. paper)
        I. Title.
     PS3569.L65C48   1998
813'.54—dc21   98-19410
                                      CIP

First Edition: September 1998

Printed in the United States of America

0 9 8 7 6 5 4 3 2 1

For Jeanne and Ron

THE
CHILDREN
STAR

ONE

The sun crawled steadily up behind the dying city. Its rays stretched across towers and avenues to the hillside, through the window of a shack, to the eyelids of six-year-old 'jum. The sunbeams teased 'jum to wake up and look out upon Reyo City, and count the many lightcraft rising to meet the ships in orbit around L'li. But when she woke, her belly gnawed inside. Above Reyo, one glowing lightcraft rose, another came down . . . not the thousands she used to count. So she counted the sunbeams instead. So many sunbeams peeked out through the skyline that even 'jum could never count them all.

From behind she heard a scratching sound. In the corner scrabbled a rat, its nose twitching. 'jum watched the rat. Blood pounded in her ears, and her belly gnawed harder.

She felt in her pocket and grasped a stone, a good heavy one, while her eye still fixed on the rat. With all her strength she flung the stone.

Red lights flashed across her eyes, and her ears rang. But the rat lay there, twitching and squeaking, so she dragged herself over to it. After she broke its neck it lay still.

From outside came the cry of a crow, the whine of a beggar, the grating of a wheelbarrow up the steep path. Once, the shacks that crowded the hillside would have all been stirring by now, with sweepers, garbage pickers, a seller of tin scrap in the doorway. Now all were gone.

The wheelbarrow grated again and came to rest just outside. A hoarse voice called, "Any dead?"

The call had become a part of the morning routine, since the "creeping" had spread. The creeping began as a numbness in the fingers and toes that crept upward over several months. It spread amongst people living together; how, 'jum did not know.

"Any dead?" The call came closer now, and the barrow came to a halt just outside. Usually, 'jum's mother would call to her from her bed, for 'jum to go out and answer. Of course, if no one answered, the man would just come in. Such a man with such a barrow had come in before, first for her sister, then her brother, then at last her father. Then the factory where 'jum worked had found out and sent her home. No more days of counting strange bits of metal to piece together, one thousand twenty-one, one thousand twenty-two; only the lightcraft to be counted, and the windows in the proud towers that reared opposite the hillside.

With an effort 'jum pulled herself up and pulled the paper back from the doorway. The man's grayish brown arms poked like sticks through his cloak. His cart already held two twisted bodies. Now he stared back at 'jum.

'jum closed her lips tight and shook her head.

Expressionless, the man picked up the two handles of the barrow. The wheels creaked: *one-and . . . two-and . . .* 'jum held on to their rhythmic sound. One always comes before two, and the digits of any number divisible by three add up to be divisible by three. As her family had subtracted, one by one, 'jum had added and multiplied, creating families of factors in her head. Six hundred ninety-three was a family of four: a seven, eleven, and twin threes . . .

'jum bit into the rat, tearing out its flesh as best she could. Then she thought of her mother, who could no longer rise from her sleeping mat and needed 'jum to feed her. 'jum felt her way across the room, lighted only by the window, to the mat where her mother slept, covered by a sack 'jum had salvaged from the factory still bearing the sign of Hyalite Nanotech. Her mother's hand lay across it in the same position as the night before. Yet something had changed; the color of her hand was different, grayer. 'jum reached over and touched her mother's hand.

The hand was a frozen claw. 'jum shivered all over, as if the cold from the hand seeped through her body.

The next thing she knew, she was standing outside, leaning against the shack. Her breath heaved, and her heart thumped as if it would burst from her chest. Behind her, the shack had filled with a chill emptiness that reached for her next.

She tried to run, but the effort of rushing outside had exhausted her. She stared out over the roofs of the shacks that clung to the hillside, to the office towers of Reyo. From the top of one tower a lightcraft grew a golden cone and rose to the sky. Above the towers shone a bright star. Her mother had called it the Children Star, a faraway paradise that children were born to when they died.

A cloud dimmed the sun, and now 'jum's eyes could make out the windows in the towers. Broken panes hinted that even the most well-off had not escaped the creeping. 'jum calmed herself the one way she knew how, by counting the windows up and across; five times nine made forty-five, three times ten made thirty, and so on. In the old days at the factory she could have spent all day thus, counting the metal parts.

As 'jum counted, a man in a pale hooded robe climbed up the hill, along the rutted path that the carts barely managed. The man strode purposefully. For a moment he paused, as if looking for someone. Then he resumed his pace and came over deliberately to face 'jum. His figure towered over her, blocking the sun and the city. One so erect and strong could scarcely be mortal; he must be a god. Perhaps the very god of Death.

"Is that your home, little one?" Death's voice was low, and his accent had a foreign edge. 'jum could only stare wonderingly. The hooded apparition half turned, as if uncertain. Then he said, "Is your mother home?"

So that was it. Death himself had come for her mother.

But this time, 'jum decided, he would fail. She drew herself up straight, planting her feet before the entrance to the shack. Her left hand dug deep into her pocket for the largest stone she had. As she clasped it, her eye judged her aim for the critical part of his anatomy.

Death awaited her reply. Hearing none, he took something from his cloak and held it out to her. It was a chunk of bread.

The smell of the bread overpowered her, so that she nearly fainted. She took the bread and tried to stuff it whole into her mouth, then she choked, as her throat was so dry. Expecting this, he produced a flask of water, miraculously clear and fresh. For the next few minutes she applied herself to consuming the bread and water, forgetting anything else existed. She barely noticed as he passed her to enter the shack, then came out.

"Child," he said, putting his hood back so that wisps of hair blew across his face. "What is your name?"

'jum did not answer. Her name meant "pig urine," which her mother had intended to discourage evil spirits after losing two previous infants. But now she scanned the man's face. He was younger than she had thought, his cheeks smooth and tanned, with a neatly cropped beard. His blue eyes fairly glowed.

Something glinted on his chest, something hung on a chain. It was a transparent stone, as blue as his eyes. A sunbeam struck it, revealing a hidden star within, a star composed of three intercepting shafts. The star could define six triangles, with six sides shared and six outside, and seven connecting points.

"You may call me Brother Rod." His voice interrupted her study of the stone. "Come with me," said Brother Rod. "You'll always have enough to eat, where we're going. It's a different world, far from here, at a far star."

At that, 'jum's lips parted and her eyes widened. "The Children Star."

He smiled, like her older brother used to. " 'The Children Star,' " he repeated. "That would be a good name for it."

By this time two beggars had found Brother Rod, and they grasped his cloak, whining for bread. He took out more bread and distributed it, while leading 'jum up the path to the top of the hill. When the bread was gone he spread his hands, but the beggars keened after him. So he gave them some coins, and his watch. Then he drew himself up and sketched a strange sign in the air. "The Spirit be with you, Citizens." His voice was firm, and the muscles rippled in his forearm. The beggars moved off.

At the top of the hill Brother Rod came to a halt. In the sky a glowing disk descended beneath a cone of boiling air. As the lightcraft came near, it hissed ever louder, and its heat baked 'jum's face. But she stood there bravely until the craft settled upon the hill.

* * *

The lightcraft rose on its beam of microwaves, lifting Brother Rhodonite and the child toward the ship that would soon cross the space folds. His last child that year, Rod realized with a wrench in his heart. L'li had once been a beautiful world, but its forty billion humans had long ago tilled its last acre and filled its last air with haze. Only the "creeping" had finally reversed its growth and started a ghastly decline. Elsewhere, citizens of the other six worlds of the Free Fold either shrugged in despair, or felt secret relief that something at last would curb the L'liite population. Rod sketched a starsign and silently prayed the Spirit to heal them all.

The Sacred Order of the Spirit was the most ancient religious order in the Fold. Their roots reached back before the Free Fold, to Valedon, the gemstone world, in an age when world warred against world. Each Spirit Caller wore on his neck a Valan sapphire star. The star's three shafts of light spelled the threefold call of truth, grace, and spirit; and wherever these were needed, Spirit Callers went. Brother Rod had been called to L'li.

"Thanks for the smooth ride," he told the lightcraft. Foreign money kept L'liite transport running for the tourists, but declined to cure her citizens.

"You're welcome, Citizen." The lightcraft was an electronic sentient, no mere servo machine. Modern Valedon was known for both, and Rod knew better than to miss the difference. "I don't often take passengers from that hill; and if things keep getting worse, I'll quit the planet altogether. Do you return to Valedon, Brother Rhodonite?"

"No, Citizen. To Prokaryon."

Prokaryon was a virginal frontier world, at a star two space folds away. With his fellow Callers, Rod collected dying orphans from L'li to join a small colony on Prokaryon. The child he had just collected was pale with fear; Rod held her close, wishing he could explain the wonders her future held on a world full of food, free of "creeping."

"Prokaryon!" exclaimed the lightcraft. "Are you human? I hope your cells have good arsenic pumps."

Rod smiled. "They do." Unlike Valedon, Prokaryon was not terraformed, for today the Fold forbade alien ecocide. But Prokaryon's alien ecology, full of arsenic and triplex DNA, poisoned human bodies. Unless, of course, they were lifeshaped, their genes modified to survive. Lifeshaping took best in young children.

Out the viewport, the boarding station loomed ahead, its hull displaying the vista of ancient L'liite temples. The lightcraft docked, and its round door fused to that of the station like two mouths kissing. An entrance opened through the fused doors and widened into a corridor.

Above the corridor, floating fingers pointed to Rod's feet. "Watch your step," a voice whispered in six languages.

Rod caught the child's hand, remembering that she might never have seen such a place. He ignored the virtual newscaster announcing new jump holes through the space folds, and new Elysian bank deals to finance copper mines on Prokaryon. Virtual doorways juxtaposed Reyo City's nightlife with that of Elysium—the wealthiest world of the Fold, where people stayed young for a thousand years. Rod himself had toured the hot spots of Elysium, as a young Guardsman on leave. But he had left all that behind ten years ago, to follow the Spirit.

At his cabin, the door molded itself open. Rod sketched a starsign to his fellow traveler, Brother Geode.

"Back at last, Brother." One of Geode's six limbs sketched the star in return. "What kept you so long?" Like the lightcraft, Brother Geode was a sentient. Self-aware machines were called "sentients" ever since their revolt against their human creators two centuries before. Sentients were built of nanoplast, trillions of microscopic servos. Geode himself had a torso of nanoplast about the size and shape of a pillow, with his star sapphire nearly buried in blue fur. His nanoplastic limbs could extend and mold themselves to any length and thinness. His limbs sported fur in each of the primary colors, giving him the appearance of a giant multicolored tarantula.

At the moment, Brother Geode had one red furry limb cupped to cradle a tiny infant, while a yellow limb fed it cultured breast milk. Three other infants slept in nanoplastic nooks nearby; the entire ship itself was a sentient. Brother Rod had brought all four of the infants from an orphanage in Reyo. The orphanage had run out of formula months ago; the infants, just left there that day, would not have lasted the week.

"I found one more Spirit child."

The girl flexed her toes in the carpet and stared wide-eyed at the sight of Geode.

From a nook in the wall, a baby several weeks old awoke with a cry and stretched his trembling arms. Rod went over and swaddled him, then tucked him under his arm, as a bottle slid out from the dispensary window. The bottle held breast milk as "real" as a mother's, including cultured lymphocytes. The infant soon settled against his chest, gazing upward into Rod's eyes. With barely more weight on him than the newborns, his limbs were wobbly sticks, but the milk would bring him round. How resilient infants were.

Geode's two eyestalks rose from his torso like periscopes and trained on the girl. "An *older* child?" He spoke in Elysian, the language sentients preferred; they, like

Elysians, were forever young. "An older child—not again. You've grown soft, Brother."

"She looks barely two."

"Malnourished. She's six if I'm a day. An older child," Geode repeated. "You know what the Reverend Mother will say."

The Reverend Mother Artemis had founded their colony on Prokaryon. It was she who first called Rod to the Spirit, in his final year at the Guard Academy. He still could not think of her except with a sense of awe.

"The Reverend Mother will say we cast our nets well," Rod replied. "I climbed the hill and brought what I found. Not a child under five was left alive."

"She'll spend a year in the gene clinic, vomiting half the time," Geode added, "and we'll be the next ten years paying her off." Infants up to eighteen months could be processed in a couple of weeks; older children took much longer, and adults might never make it. Rod himself had spent three years in treatment, yet he still could eat nothing grown on Prokaryon.

Was Geode right? he wondered. The child's eyes had arrested him, there on that hill; those eyes had clutched his heart against his reason. . . . But the Spirit within had called to him, saying, This is the one.

Rod adjusted the baby in his arms, holding up the tiny head. Then he turned to the girl. "See, child," he told her in L'liite. "This will be your new brother on Prokaryon. You'll have thirty-nine brothers and sisters—think of it. You'll grow your own food, and even mine your own gem-stones."

Geode's eyestalks twisted quizzically. "She hasn't taken her eyes off me. What must she be thinking, to go off with such strangers?"

"What child was not born to strangers?"

Two of Geode's limbs began to mold themselves into probes to examine the girl's health. "*I* was never born. I was built—to precise specifications. I make fewer mistakes than one byte in a trillion trillions."

Rod smiled. "You had to be taught to think."

Ignoring this jest, Geode extended a long, slender tendril out of his furry limb toward the girl, who moved back a step. Brother Rod put his arm around her. "Let Geode treat you, child. He will help your stomach feel better. Then we'll have a good bath, and a good dinner."

The tendril wound around the girl's arm, inserting a microscopic probe which she would not feel. The probe would sample her blood for her own DNA and proteins, as well those of any pathogens. "Her name is 'jum G'hana," Geode announced, matching the gene sequence with his database.

The girl blinked at the sound of her name amidst the foreign gibberish. A sharp mind, Rod thought.

"She was first sampled at approximate age three, upon hiring full-time at Hyalite Nanotech. Father died of 'creeping,' mother alive, age—"

"Her mother's dead," Rod corrected. "Creeping" sickness was caused by prions, misfolded proteins that directed normal ones to mimic their structure and accumulate in the motor neurons. Paralysis crept out the limbs and inward. Other types of prion infection were contained in the nervous system, but the dreaded "creeping" prions leaked out in secretions and transmitted readily.

"She has lice and worms," continued Geode. "And prions, though not yet irreversible." So she did have the disease, as Rod suspected from her mottled legs. Even her relatives, had she any, would never claim her. The emigration forms would go straight through.

The cure for creeping was to inject millions of nanoservos, microscopic servo machines, into the bloodstream to methodically search and reshape the misfolded proteins. It was effective, but expensive. On Prokaryon, the Fold paid to cure colonists, to encourage human settlement.

"She wasn't badly nourished, her first three years." Geode's infant had done feeding and was now bouncing in one coiled limb. "Maybe she's not even brain-damaged. Say, 'jum," the sentient demanded in L'liite, "did you go to school? Can you read?"

'jum slowly shook her head.

"Can you count your factory wages?"

At that, 'jum did not answer but gave the sentient an intent look.

"What's one plus one?"

She frowned, as if this were a very difficult problem. "Not quite one and a half," she said in a voice so low that Rod barely heard.

Geode twined his eyestalks disparagingly.

"What do you expect? She's never been to school. Is your workup done? She needs a bath."

"Definitely," the sentient agreed with emphasis. "I don't know, though. I wonder sometimes if we're not half-crazy, trying to settle a frontier with starving babies."

"It's the cheapest way," Rod said ironically, for that was the reason of the Fold.

"But—look, you know, it's not just any world, by Torr. It's *Prokaryon*."

Prokaryon was named for its unique "prokaryotic" lifeforms. Animal or vegetable, all Prokaryan cells contained circular chromosomes, free of nuclear membranes—like bacteria, *prokaryotes*. But Prokaryan cells were ring-shaped as well. And the higher structure of all the multicellular organisms was toroid, from the photosynthetic "phycoids" that grew tall as trees, to the tire-shaped "zoöids" that rolled over the fields they grazed—or preyed upon those that did.

"And I don't care what the Free Fold says," Geode added. "There *are* intelligent aliens running Prokaryon, somewhere."

Rod held the baby tighter in his arm. "Don't spread rumors, Brother." Such stories arose whenever a new world was settled, even on Valedon long after it was boiled and terraformed.

Geode snaked an eyestalk toward him. "Can you explain how Prokaryon has all those rows of forest, one after another, all across the continent? Who tends the garden?"

"The Elysian scientists have been looking for years. They found no one, and the Fold certified the planet empty of intelligence. Do you want to get our colony evicted?"

"The truth is what I seek, Brother," insisted Geode. "*You* explain how the weather stays the same all year, only raining at night, or a cloudburst to put out a fire."

Looking away, Rod placed the sleeping infant gently at the wall, where the nanoplast obligingly molded inward to cradle it.

"Humans," Geode added with bemusement. "Will humans ever know an 'intelligent' creature, if they find one? They took centuries just to recognize us sentients, out of their own factories."

TWO

Fed, scrubbed, clothed, and medicated, the six new Spirit children endured their week-long journey through the space folds to Prokaryon. Of course, none of them could yet set foot on their new home. Merely inhaling Prokaryan air would expose their unprepared lungs to poison; for the native life-forms had evolved all sorts of things that the ordinary human body was not designed to encounter, much less digest for food. Their triplex chromosomes were mutagenic, their "proteins" contained indigestible amino acids, and their membranes were full of arsenic. Prokaryan cells were not exactly good to eat—unless you were Prokaryan.

So the children's first stop was a satellite, the Fold Council Station for Xenobiotic Research and Engineering. "Station" was actually a giant sentient whose brain directed the investigation of Prokaryan life-forms, as well as the transport and lifeshaping of colonists. Station's lifeshapers would inject the new children with nanoservos, microscopic machines to put special genes into the cells of the liver and intestines. The special genes would teach their cells how to detoxify unfamiliar Prokaryan molecules, and to eat them as food, as easily as they ate the nutrients from their own world. For adults the lifeshaping was slow and inefficient; thus, most Prokaryan colonies depended heavily on sentients.

Rod often wondered how the rest of the Fold's worlds would ever have gotten settled, had they all tried to avoid terraforming. Valedon, and all but two of the other worlds, had been boiled off and reseeded with human-compatible life-forms. But today people called that "planetary ecocide." Rod himself had been skeptical, until he came to Prokaryon and fell in love with its mysterious beauty. He could not imagine terraforming such a world.

The cylindrical bulk of Station grew until it dwarfed the approaching ship. "All passengers prepare to disembark." The voice of the great sentient vibrated throughout the ship, as she extended her docking tube.

Rod always tensed at her greeting. Besides her gene clinic, Station directed scientists from all the worlds of the Fold who came to study Prokaryon's biosphere and confirm its absence of intelligent natives, a legal requirement for exploitation. Above all, she governed Prokaryan settlement on behalf of the Fold. She set each colony's immigration quota, and determined when each lifeshaped immigrant was ready to settle.

Brother Geode crawled out on three of his furry limbs, carrying babies in his other three, while Rod carried two and 'jum gamely managed one. The tube rotated steadily, generating about half a unit of centrifugal force, enabling them to walk while keeping their baggage light. But the sense of weight loss alarmed the babies, for their stomachs told them they were falling, no matter how hard Rod clutched them in his arms. The little bundles stiffened, then emptied their lungs to howl. Overhead, upside down in the cylinder, two or three travelers stretched their necks at this unusual scene. A gorilla face stared down at Rod; a simian hybrid woman wearing a student's backpack. Rod stared back, for simians were a rarity out here.

Beneath Rod's feet the floor shifted sickeningly. That meant the lock had engaged, and they now stood in the innermost ring of Station. The babies sucked in their breaths and wailed.

"Brother Geode, immigration officer of the Spirit Colony." Station's voice boomed, ever-present within the satellite. "Six new colonists?"

"Yes, Station." Geode bounced the three infants in his arms, trying to quiet them.

"You exceed your quota again."

"Yes, Station."

It was Rod's fault that they always pushed the immigration limit. In his days at the Guard, he had always tried to steal one last round of shooting beyond regulations; now, he always took one more dying child. "They're all healthy," Rod insisted. "They'll be productive citizens."

"And one is an older child," Station observed. "Brother Geode, you will see me for consultation."

"I will," Rod said firmly. They always got away with it before.

"Please sign the release for each."

On the wall a bright rectangle appeared, its text scrolling past absurdly fast. Rod had no need to read the contents. The release form required all immigrants to acknowledge that Prokaryon's biosphere was only partly understood, and its climate not yet controlled, and that the appearance of any plague threatening the Fold might require defensive action—before all inhabitants could be evacuated. Rod despised the provision, and its authors in the Fold Council, who feared another prion plague. Prions arose from human bodies, not from a world where humans could barely live.

Geode held up his infants to press the document with their toes, and Rod did likewise.

"Reverend Mother is coming," said Geode. Sentients communicated by internal radio.

At the gate stood the Reverend Mother Artemis. Her face was a screen across which her "features" shaped and reshaped in ever-changing colors. Her sapphire star gleamed where a human neck would be. Around her face twined restless strands of nanoplastic "hair," as if individually alive. Below her neck hung multiple breasts, and her robe revealed skirts full of holographic bears, lions, even flying fish from the Elysian ocean. Children were her lifework, ever since she herself had been manufactured to raise wealthy Elysians. After earning her freedom as a sentient, she had joined the Sacred Order.

The Reverend Mother's nanoplastic hand traced a six-point star. "Brother Rod. You return with your nets full." She took the two little ones, who quieted as they stared.

Rod returned the sign. "I wish it could be otherwise."

"So do we all." Strands of her hair twisted upward. "We call on the Spirit to hear the agony of the L'liites. But this mystery has endless depth and no shore."

"How are the children back home?"

"All well, thank the Spirit. The phycoids are ready for harvest, and T'kun found a perfect pink crystal in the stream."

"Well, we bring you future harvesters."

Geode warned in Elysian, "One of them will cost us a bundle."

"And which *one* would that be?" The Reverend Mother scooped up another infant from him. "Which one would you refuse?"

'jum was watching her skirt, mesmerized by the rearing bear. Rod squeezed 'jum's hand encouragingly. "This is the Reverend Mother of the Spirit Colony of Prokaryon. You will be our own child."

The Reverend Mother spread her arms and spoke in clear L'liite. " 'jum G'hana, are you my little bird singing in the tree?" Her voice had just the right rhythm, as if she had been born and raised in the streets of Reyo.

'jum ran to her, immediately to be swept up in the arms and skirt. Mother Artemis was always like that.

"There, my little bird. It's too soon for you to talk, isn't it, but won't you shape for me?" Mother Artemis stepped over to the holostage.

Above the holostage a ball of light appeared, as if suspended by magic. Mother Artemis reached to it with her hands and shaped it like a lump of clay. It formed the shape of a flower, with a dozen petals that she pulled one by one, each perfect as a teardrop.

Then a second ball of light appeared. "It's your turn, 'jum. Won't you try? Shape me something from your home."

'jum put out a tentative finger. She poked the ball, and a depression remained. Encouraged, she pulled it into a tall oblong shape and poked more holes in an orderly array, eight across, row upon row, more than a dozen.

"That's lovely," Mother Artemis exclaimed. "Was that your house where you lived?"

'jum shook her head. She paused as if in thought. Then abruptly she squeezed the light into an amorphous lump and began shaping again, with precise details. Her sureness suggested that her fingers had shaped such an object before, perhaps many times. It was a box with three prongs at right angles to one another, and two unidentified levers at the side. It looked so realistic, one might pluck it solid from the air.

"What have we here?" Mother Artemis spoke in a low voice. She trained her visual sensors on the object; her true "eyes," set at her neckline, rather than her apparent eyes in her face. She called up a vast database from all seven worlds of the Fold.

Above the three-pronged image, a shape of red light appeared, similar in form to the one 'jum had made. The red shape descended and merged with the white one; it was nearly a perfect fit.

"It's a lanthanide extractor," the Reverend Mother explained in Elysian.

"Of course," said Geode. "She must have assembled them at the Hyalite plant—thousands of them."

Rod eyed the device sternly. "They're illegal."

"Not their manufacture," said the Reverend Mother. "Only the use to which some are put." Lanthanide extractors were used to sort rare-earth minerals from rock. All the inhabited worlds had long ago exhausted their natural supplies of rare-earth elements, prized for many uses in nanocircuitry. So the main place left to use extractors was new planets. But that was against the law of the Fold. A world could be mined only after scientists had established, and the Secretary of the Free Fold decreed, that no intelligent natives had prior claim.

Still, who could police the universe? The Hyalite House, an ancient and respectable firm based on Valedon, put its assembly plant in a decaying L'liite city where starving six-year-olds would not recognize the device, and no one would ask where it ended up.

Geode extended an arm. "They can't use them here." On Prokaryon, mining was permitted only with macroscopic implements, and only up to one percent of the planetary resource, until the new world gained independence and could choose for itself.

Mother Artemis turned to 'jum. "You must have made many of those pieces, little bird."

"Two thousand five hundred and thirty-one," the girl murmured.

"What a number. And you counted every one?"

'jum nodded. "It's a family without children."

Mother Artemis nodded. "You like numbers, don't you. I'll bet you know all your sums."

'jum lowered her eyes. Then she looked up. "Three plus four is five."

At this unaccountable calculation, Mother Artemis paused. "How about three *times* four?"

"Three times four is twelve."

"Eight times thirteen?"

"One hundred and four."

"What are the factors of three thousand and three?" When 'jum hesitated, she added, "The 'children'?"

"Three, seven, eleven, and thirteen. A family of four children." Then abruptly she burst into tears, crying for her mother. Mother Artemis held her close, knowing she would have a lot more crying to do before she could face a new life. Two of the infants started crying, too.

"I wonder how she's adding," Mother Artemis said in Elysian. "Never mind; she'll learn as fast as a sentient."

Geode's limbs snaked out to lift and comfort the agitated infants. "At least that part of our job will come easy."

"No—much harder," the Reverend Mother warned.

"Humans," groaned Geode, his fifth limb shaking a milk bottle. "How did I ever get into this?" The woolly armed sentient had shepherded Spirit children for a decade, thought Rod with a smile.

Mother Artemis was whispering to 'jum. "Geode will take good care of you at Station, until you're set to join us. You can call me anytime you like, on the holostage. Behold— as one of our family, you have a new name: 'jum G'hana Spirit. And here is your sign." She pinned to 'jum's ragged shirt a sapphire, a tiny pink gem one of the children had strained from the gravel bed. A sapphire from Prokaryon.

The children would stay at Station with Geode, for their treatments. This left the Spirit Colony understaffed, with only Rod, Mother Artemis, and Brother Patella, a sentient physician, to manage the children on Prokaryon. But within a month the babies could come home. What to do with 'jum thereafter would have to be worked out. They could not afford a skinsuit to protect her.

Before leaving, Rod transferred his holocube of 'jum's home in Reyo to the brain of Station. Station obligingly shaped a room whose shape and colors roughly matched the shack, plus a comfortable mat on the floor, and the food synthesizer put out an "authentic" L'liite meal. Later the child would have to make do with the same inexpensive food pellets that Rod did, until her lifeshaping reached the point that she could eat native crops.

As Rod and the Reverend Mother took their leave, Brother Geode had stretched and lengthened three of his limbs and tied them into an elaborate knot for 'jum. "First off, which is my right arm?" He wiggled the three fuzzy ends projecting from the knot.

'jum inspected closely, then tapped one end. The entire limb turned yellow throughout the knot, revealing its hidden structure.

"Right!" exclaimed the sentient. "Now let's see, how would you undo it?"

Rod felt proud. A child who learned fast—she might even become the doctor someday, like their own Brother Patella. He had listened well, when the Spirit called him upon that hill.

To reach the planet, the Spirit Colony leased a lightcraft from Station. The craft, a reconditioned economy model, was not sentient, only programmed to shuttle up and down. Its rectenna had darkened all around, and it bore an acrid smell. Two worn seats held Rod and Mother Artemis. The craft shuddered as it launched, and a small holostage at eye level showed the satellite shrinking away. Beyond in the blackness appeared the neutrino receiver, a giant silver sphere full of water to detect the massless particles carrying signals through the space folds.

"Brother Patella will be glad to see you back," the Reverend Mother observed. "T'kun smuggled a baby four-eyes into the nursery. And a 'tumble-round' has grown well into the garden; it's looking in at Haemum's window!"

Rod smiled remorsefully. "I've been away too long—and only bring back more trouble."

"Why else are we here?"

The lightcraft whined as it entered the atmosphere, the air above heating into plasma. Above the holostage, the image of Prokaryon expanded, its greens and blues cloaked in cloud, beautiful and terrifying, yet vulnerable, like a woman's eye. As the surface neared, a brilliant expanse of ocean met the shore of their continent, Spirilla, a twisted spiral of green and gray. The world rotated slowly downward beneath the lightcraft. In the western arm of Spirilla, pale scars marked the copper mines. To the east rolled the uncharted interior, circled by glacial mountains.

As the craft fell toward the green, curious patterns emerged. Long dark bands ran in parallel rows, winding like a string picture. The dark bands were singing-tree forest. Each band of forest alternated with a paler band of wheelgrass, merging into wetland, which gave way to the next band of forest. Over and over the same pattern repeated, ceasing only at the mountains.

What Spirit had dipped a finger in the ink of foliage and drawn those lines? And whose hand tended them still? Not a seed of wheelgrass could a human plant on forest land, even with the singing-trees cleared; yet singing-tree pods would only wither where the wheelgrass grew.

The old lightcraft dipped and veered suddenly, caught in a gust of wind. Rod gripped his chair automatically, though it made little difference, as its nanoplastic limbs held him fast. "I hope at least it lands us in the right band." The craft had been known to miss the band of wheelgrass that contained the colony, leaving the passengers to hike through several kilometers of singing-trees.

"Patella doesn't answer," said the Reverend Mother. "Who knows what the young ones are up to."

No answer from Patella? That was odd. Wherever he was, Brother Patella could hear Mother Artemis from the lightcraft, then send out Haemum or one of the ten-year-olds with the llamas for them to ride home.

As it happened, they landed in wheelgrass, not far from the trail. The wheelgrass spread in waves all around them. A welcome scent of ginger blew in from the distant singing-trees, always a sign he was really home.

High in the ever-blue sky shone Prokaryon's sun, Iota Pavonis, proud as an albino peacock. The thin ozone layer blocked less of the sun's ultraviolet than on other worlds supporting life. That might be one reason triple-stranded chromosomes had evolved here, to protect DNA from mutation. Prokaryan weather, like its landscape, had a predictable pattern: sunshine every day, with gentle rain in the evening.

But far to the east, past the dark line of hills, the clouds could burst into unexpected storms. And above those clouds hovered the peaks of Mount Anaeon and Mount Helicon. The tallest peaks had been named for the twelve floating cities of Elysium, who had bankrolled the first explorers. They may have regretted the naming, for the mountains proved unlucky, full of landslides and other accidents for hapless prospectors. Many colonists blamed Prokaryon's "hidden masters," a claim hard to disprove.

Still there was no sign of Haemum's llama, its ears pointing out like flags, its broad feet bred specially to tramp the loopleaves down. Rod turned to Mother Artemis. "No word yet from Brother?"

"He must be running after Gaea and T'kun again."

That would not keep Patella from answering. Patella, like Geode and Mother Artemis, could manage several tasks at once. Unless he was conducting a very complex operation . . . Rod felt a chill at his neck. "I'll go ahead and send the llama back for you."

The Reverend Mother smoothed his shoulder. "The Spirit go with you. Excuse me while I sleep." She drew in her arms, which lost form in the shadows of her sleeves. Her figure seemed to pull itself in and turned gray all over. Rod had seen her "sleep," though she tried to hide it from the children. Sentients had to save their energy, for if their power packs ran out, their minds would die. That was their one weakness as colonists.

He returned her touch lightly, thinking, how odd that

this gray shape was actually such an extraordinary person. Then he stepped outside. The sun was warm, so he took off his robe, revealing dun-colored everyday trousers much worn and stained. Tucking the robe under his arm, he strode resolutely out into the wheelgrass. The gray-green loopleaves of the wheelgrass twisted and caught his toe at every step; it took him a quarter hour just to cover the few meters to the trail. High above him buzzed several helicoids, their ring-shaped propellers clattering as if laughing at him.

Ahead, a herd of four-eyes rolled away like tire tubes, with no legs to get caught in the wheelgrass. Each four-eyes had four compound eyes spaced evenly along the "tread" of its "tire," the upper two eyes alert and watchful, the lower two asleep; the eyes took turns sleeping. In between each pair of eyes was a rasping mouth, so each mouth faced downward in turn to consume wheelgrass. Extensible suckers covered the rest of the creature's surface; to move forward, it simply contracted the foremost sucker and lifted up the hindmost, rolling over the wheelgrass. By this repeated motion, the little zoöid could work up a remarkable speed in either direction. Rod hoped no zoöid predator would come barreling after them and mistake him for edible prey.

Once on the clear trail he jogged easily, his feet eating up the miles. A couple of whirrs alighted on his arm, miniature helicoids the size of a pinhead. Finding no zoöid secretions to feed on, the whirrs soon left, very different from the insects he had grown up with on Valedon. The wind brought snatches of song from the singing-trees at the far edge of the wheelgrass. At last the wheelgrass gave way to brokenhearts, golden ringlets that looked like so many lost wedding bands. The protein-rich brokenhearts were cultivated to feed the lifeshaped children.

At last the colony's nursery and dining hall appeared, jutting out of the hillside below the sapphire mine. The long mud-colored buildings were built of ring-fungus, a tough growth that could be pressed into shapes and dried hard as wood.

As he approached, twelve-year-old Haemum came running out to meet him. The founding child of the family, she now stood nearly as tall as he and seemed to be all legs. Her skirt and scarf were made of the same cloth that they all wove and dyed of fibrous loopleaves. She threw her arms around Rod, pressing her black curls to his chest. "Brother Rod, thank the Spirit you're here," she exclaimed in L'liite, which the children were taught to retain their heritage. "We don't know what to do—Brother Patella fell down the ravine, and he must have 'broken' somehow."

"Broken how? Where is he now?"

Two of the boys were running out, ten-year-old Chae and four-year-old T'kun, with his arm ominously bound in a sling. Then little Gaea dragged herself through the dust on her arms, her paralyzed legs trailing behind her. Gaea had spina bifida—Brother Geode had thrown up his woolly arms when Rod picked that one, but so it was. The colony would save enough to reshape her, someday.

"It was T'kun's fault," Haemum explained. "T'kun was running ahead and playing space pirate, and when I called after him he got mad. He tripped and slid down the bank, tumbling over. Brother Patella tried to get him out, but he slipped, too, and fell farther. Then he turned all gray and lumpy, and wouldn't answer."

Gaea grabbed his ankle and clung, and he nearly lost balance. "Bro-der Rod, T'kun bring home zoöid! We play with zoöid!" Zoöids in the nursery would not do; but it would have to wait.

"Did you call Station?" Rod asked Haemum.

"I did, but the medics haven't shown up yet. I finally dragged T'kun back up and set his arm as best I could. . . ."

Rod clenched his fist, then caught it in his palm. As usual the Spirit Colony was not Station's first priority. No billion-credit shipment of ore would be lost if Patella were crippled, or worse. "Can the boys lead me out to him?"

"I will, I will," cried T'kun.

Rod patted his head. "Good—but be careful. And you, Chae, mind Gaea and the babies." He extricated his ankle from Gaea's fingers and swung her up for Chae, who staggered as he carried her off. "Haemum, you'll need to ride the llamas out for the Reverend Mother; we touched down just west of the trail. Remember, she'll be 'asleep.' "

Haemum raced off to fetch the llamas, her skirt flashing colors in the sun. Rod followed T'kun up the trail by the rushing stream, into the hills full of sapphires and other marketable stones. Here the wheelgrass gave way to a coarse dark shrub, with dense loopleaves. A flock of helicoids rose up suddenly, the sunlight glinting on their propellers.

"There!" T'kun shouted, and tried to point, then winced at the pain in his bound arm.

Rod caught sight of the gray shape, tumbled several meters down a steep bank. It looked nothing like Patella, whose form resembled Geode's. He froze, sick at heart. If Patella's nanoplastic body had not fixed itself by now, the news might be bad. Even if his neural circuits were intact, he would have to be shipped back to Elysium to retrain. And the colony would have to do without a doctor.

The emergency squad from Station came at last. A sleek glowing disk burned its way through the air and set itself down precisely, right on the trail that overlooked the ravine. For a moment Rod envied the sentient lightcraft, then he suppressed the unworthy thought.

From the craft emerged two medical sentients, their bodies shaped like caterpillars. They crawled down the ravine to rescue the injured doctor, not deigning to speak to Rod. As they lifted the shapeless nanoplast into their craft, Rod felt the full shock of his loss. He had worked with Patella ever since he came here; now, in an instant, his brother was gone.

Meanwhile, the older children were coming home from the gravel pit with carts full of corundum and occasional gem-quality stones. Mother Artemis, now returned, was nursing the four youngest ones, including the twins Pima and Pomu, whom Rod had picked up last year. Then she called the older children over for writing lessons.

Rod checked T'kun's arm, which Haemum seemed to have bound up reasonably straight, as far as he could tell. He would bring the boy up to Station the next day for a scan. In the meantime, the watering tubes for the vegetables had broken down, helicoids hung by their sucker mouths from the gutters, and besides, a tumbleround had invaded the garden.

"Look at it, Brother Rod," Haemum exclaimed. "It's the biggest tumbleround I ever saw."

The tire shape of the tumbleround looked partly deflated, its lower half collapsed into the ground. Twisted loopleaves stuck out in all directions, some extended to root in the ground. The plant-creature smelled like glue and invariably attracted clouds of thirsty whirrs. A tumbleround generally rooted and grew in one spot for a long while; but under certain conditions, perhaps nitrogen deficiency, some of its vines would root themselves in the ground at one edge, then contract, pulling the organism to tumble it over slightly. More vines then rooted down, and so forth; once the tumbleround got going, it could travel several meters per day, trampling and digesting whatever vegetation crossed its path. Scientists disputed whether they were more animal or plant, zoöid or phycoid; "phyco-zoöid" was the term in favor. Whether plant or animal, this one was as tall as Rod and perhaps twice his weight.

"It's been there for the longest time, just outside the fence, you remember." Haemum pointed to the long slimy trail full of broken tendril loops, leading in through the crushed fence. "After you left, one night it just started to move, and kept coming until . . ."

The scent blew toward them. For a moment Rod felt light-headed, and he caught himself up just in time. Then he realized that he had not gotten around to eating anything since breakfast on the ship. He shook himself and straightened. "Well, Sister—what shall we do with our guest?"

Haemum put her hands on her hips. "We could chop it up. If we chop the pieces small enough, they won't grow back. We can scoop them out and dry the hide to make shoes."

A tedious, gruesome task, but it would work. And yet . . . Why had this thing come to peek in the window? What if this whirr-clouded beast really was one of the planet's hidden masters? Station said no, tumblerounds had no IQ to speak of.

"We'll dig it out and haul it off," Rod decided. So they set to work with the shovels, all the while brushing whirrs out of their eyes and mouths, taking breaks when the fumes overpowered them. A sentient lifter could have done it in a minute, but the colony could not afford such. The work of one's hands was a gift to the Spirit.

At last, Rod raised the stinking creature out of its hole,

where the loops of its roots lay gashed. His muscles bulged as he lifted it onto the cart, first one side of it, then the other. Three llamas pulled the cart, spitting in protest, while the two colonists pushed from behind, driving it out as far as they could before they dumped the tumbleround out. It would root again in no time.

Just before dinner, while helping Pima and Pomu wash their faces, Rod remembered to call Geode. So he hurried off down the hall to the holostage. The twins, who immediately knew what he was after, plodded after him excitedly.

As Rod entered the cylindrical chamber, the usual column of light shone up from the stage; the twins cooed in delight. Soon Brother Geode himself appeared, full of good spirits and just as delighted to see them. "My two little dears!" the sentient exclaimed. "Alike as two parts from the same factory—and walking, already! Why, we weren't gone but three weeks."

"I thought you'd be pleased," said Rod. "But I'm sorry about Patella."

"I can't believe it. I just can't bear to think of it." Three of his arms waved violently in the air, twining and untwining. He and Patella had been built to the same model and shipped from the same Hyalite plant on Valedon. Both had earned their freedom in an Elysian nursery, as had Mother Artemis. "I just hope his central processor's okay, so he can reshape himself." He shuddered all over. "How will you ever manage? I'd better come down."

"But the babies need you. How is 'jum?"

" 'jum is right here. Don't shrink away, girl—look, here's Brother Rod."

The light-shape of 'jum appeared, wide-eyed and uncertain. She extended her arm, then pulled it back as if remembering. Rod felt bad about leaving her, though they had no choice. "I'll come up soon to hug you, 'jum. Look," he said, nudging the twins. "See your little brothers. We all can't wait to have you home."

As he finally went in to dinner, Haemum was leading the singing at the head of one of the two long tables. *Let us love only truth, desire only grace, and know only Spirit....* Haemum took her devotions seriously, and planned to join the order when she came of age. The children were a cheery sight, their starstones flashing on their necks, all seated in orderly rows in their bright red-and-yellow patterned shifts. Their legs swung briskly under the chairs, and the long tables reminded Rod incongruously of mealtimes at the Guard Academy.

Soon the bowls of four-eyes stew came passing down, with red and green loop-fruits the boys had cooked up from the garden. Since Rod could not yet eat them, Chae brought him his two cakes of standard-grade food from the synthesizer. The synthesizer reshaped organic matter at the molecular level and filtered out toxic metals. An economy model, it put out two flavors, fruit or flesh; Rod had eaten them for so long that he forgot which was which. But the first bite reminded him he was famished. He ate quickly, forgetting his usual insistence on "civilized" conversation.

Someone was kicking him beneath the table. It was T'kun, managing to eat with his left arm. "T'kun, remember your manners," Rod warned. "The Spirit is watching."

A commotion erupted at the far end. A helicoid asleep on the ceiling apparently had fallen onto someone's plate. The children were shrieking; Mother Artemis calmed them, while Rod released the helicoid outdoors. Looking upward, he saw two more helicoids hanging by their suckers from the rafters, their propeller rings turning idly. The hall really needed cleaning out.

Returning to his place, he found that T'kun had crawled under the table because he did not like the pudding for dessert.

"Come out and sit down," Rod warned, slightly raising his voice.

T'kun dutifully emerged. "I *am* sitting down."

Mother Artemis came over and leaned by his ear. "Rod, I've just heard from Station. Patella can't recover here—he must ship back to Elysium."

His last hope died. There was nothing they could do for the injured sentient except ship him back across the Fold to Elysium. Poor Patella. "What will we do?" he whispered. It was hard enough with just the two of them managing here, until Geode brought the babies home; but even then, they needed a doctor. It would take some searching to find either a sentient willing to come, or a human physician willing to be lifeshaped, with two years in the gene tank before she or he dared set foot here without a skinsuit.

Mother Artemis said, "The Reverend Father will find someone." The Most Reverend Father of Dolomoth, a large Valan congregation, had founded their colony and was ultimately responsible for it. "Meanwhile, I could take on a medicine module. It would overload my processor somewhat and slow my reactions, but—"

Rod shook his head. "You can't do that. You have to keep alert around here—you don't want to . . . to get hurt like Patella."

Mother Artemis thought a moment. "There's always Sarai."

Sarai was a Sharer lifeshaper. Sharers were a human race who had settled the ocean world of Elysium ten millennia before the "immortals" did, shaping their own genes for aquatic life. Sari, however, was a rebel among her kind.

She had left her ocean home for Prokaryon, to dwell deep within the rock of Mount Anaeon. Rod frowned. "Sarai is hard enough to reach." And not usually receptive to visitors.

"She is as skilled as any Elysian doctor, and she would help the children." Mother Artemis added thoughtfully, "More contact with fellow humans will be good for Sarai."

Rod prayed the children stayed well.

Commotion erupted again, this time from Pima and Pomu, who were attempting to rise from the table. Under the table T'kun had tied their shoelaces together.

After dinner everyone gathered outside. The sun was just setting beyond the distant singing-trees. The llamas groaned at the sun, their regular habit in the evening.

Mother Artemis stood, and her nanoplastic hair waved above her head as if charged by an electrical storm. She spread her robe, and her skirts came alive with bears and lions. Strange story figures shimmered and stepped out around her; the nearer children tucked in their feet and hitched back a bit. The colors deepened to violet, in waving shades of water. Suddenly out leaped a wonderful flying fish. The fish spread its fanlike wings, and began to speak in an otherworldly voice, telling the Sharer tale of how the first fish came to fly, and why their souls were haunted, never again to rest at peace in the sea.

The children were spellbound through tale after tale, legends from Valedon and Urulan and every known world, until at last the younger ones dozed off. Rod put the twins to bed, and Haemum took T'kun. The sun was down now, but the soft remains of light diffused through the gathering clouds. A light rain was falling, as it nearly always did at this hour, as if Prokaryon's "hidden masters" were in charge. The smell of ginger increased as the soil released its fragrance. The voice of the distant singing-trees abated.

Rod was dead tired, but somehow his mind would not yet let him sleep. He strode restlessly outside the compound, letting the raindrops cool his face and sink into his robe.

He found Mother Artemis walking with him. "How was L'li?"

There was too much inside him to tell. The very edge of certain thoughts made his stomach contract. "Those who had money still have it. But some have the creeping, too—and the cure does not work on advanced cases."

"Yes," she nodded, her darkened robe swishing. "But you did not spend your time among the rich."

"The lightcraft are still running; for how much longer, I don't know. A power blackout downed several. Next time I may not even be able to reach Reyo."

She nodded again. To the east the clouds parted, revealing a large red moon whose glow filled Mother Artemis's restless snakes of hair. The moon glowed red from the sentients melting out its iron for the insatiable factories of Valedon. Prokaryon's moon had no known life, and by the next decade it would be mined down to nothing.

"The village I visited last year is deserted now," Rod continued. "The hill I climbed this year will be empty next year."

Mother Artemis kept walking.

"I gave the beggars what bread I had."

"I'm sure you gave them everything."

"My watch, and my leftover credits." The colony's own cash was scarce. "But not my pocket holostage," he added remorsefully. "They could have sold that."

"They could," she agreed. "Was that the worst thing?"

His stomach tightened unbearably. "There was a woman outside the orphanage," he forced himself to say. "She tried to make me take her baby." He could not accept children of living parents, lest the nationalists accuse him of ethnic abduction. "Otherwise, she said, she would take it to the market, rather than see it starve." It was not a slave market.

Suddenly he retched, and his stomach finally gave up. "That was foolish," he said, wiping his mouth, thinking of the wasted food. "I must get to sleep."

"Yes, you must. Even though you want to go back and save all of L'li."

"I do," he said with a touch of anger, at the universe and at himself. "It's appalling, and we all just—live here."

"You saved six children this time; isn't that a great privilege? How many people live their entire lives without saving one soul? And the Spirit should grant you a world?"

He stopped and looked closely at her. Was she laughing at him? "Yes," he said, his mouth smiling despite himself, "the Spirit should grant me a world."

At last, finishing his nightly meditation, Rod found himself in bed. Patella came to mind, and he missed him terribly. Then came the face of his father on Valedon, reproaching him: What did you do with all your expensive schooling, to join a bunch of clerics raising orphans at a distant star? Then nameless faces and hands arose until his mind cried out.

There was a tap at the door.

"Brother Rod?" It was T'kun. "My arm hurts."

Rod pulled back the covers. T'kun was supposed to

have outgrown sleeping in bed with him, but he would make an exception. The boy snuggled under the covers, his little head a miracle of softness. In an instant Rod was asleep.

THREE

....

The next day Rod awoke with a sore shoulder, a muscle pulled from hauling the giant tumbleround the day before. Nonetheless, he felt well rested, and the sight of the cloud-cloaked mountains always brought him peace. He spent the first hour with Gaea dragging herself after him and wrapping herself around his leg at every opportunity. The Spirit callers cared equally for all, but despite himself Rod had favorites.

Haemum and Chae rose early to go uphill and dig gravel out of the mine, an old streambed rich in corundum. They sifted the gravel through water in a fine-mesh screen, allowing the denser crystals to sink to the bottom. Then they dumped each screen over onto a table, where the younger children sorted out the crystals. Most of them were clear and not of particular value, but a few were tinted blue, yellow, or even pink; the better ones, when cut, might fetch enough to feed the colony for a week. Even Gaea picked out her share, although most turned out to be quartz.

After the midday meal, Mother Artemis treated and cut the stones, training Haemum on the lap wheel. The younger children painted little dioramas of four-eyes and singing-trees, or strung necklaces of helicoid propeller shells. Rod and Chae worked on the garden, collecting ringed pods and fruits, and replanting the rows gouged out by the visiting tumbleround. In the western field the brokenhearts were ripening fast; how would they ever get them harvested without Patella?

Chae brought back a bushel full of greens to cook up four-eyes stew for the two tables of children, all swinging their feet and twirling the vegetable pods around their fingers. Afterward, as the little ones cleared up, Mother Artemis said, "I sent the Most Reverend Father a neutrinogram." Neutrinos brought word across the space-time folds, resisting the extreme electromagnetic distortions at the connection holes. The signal was crude, never of holographic quality, but it was the fastest way. "I told the Most Reverend Father we need another brother or sister with medical training, at least until Patella returns."

"What will we do in the meantime?" It could be weeks or months before help arrived.

Mother Artemis watched the nightly rain outside, her hair twining into knots and untwining again. "We'll manage. Haemum and Chae will help with the harvest. Between the two of them, now, they bring in as much as Patella did."

Rod frowned, vaguely uneasy. "They are growing up."

"Exactly." She gave him a questioning look.

"Well—I guess I've been more on the infant end of things here. I'm not sure what the Reverend Father has in mind for the older ones, as they grow into adults."

"When I was a nana in the *shon*, I raised Elysian children for Elysium. Now we raise Prokaryans. They'll grow up to maintain the colony."

"But they're also citizens of the Free Fold." He took a deep breath. "What if they choose to emigrate?"

She considered this. "If the Spirit so calls, so be it."

"But how will they ever know enough? How will they know, without—education?"

"Education is the right of every citizen," said Mother Artemis firmly. "We educate all our children. We meet the standards."

"The formal standards are too low." This was one area where Rod felt a disconcerting gap between human and sentient. "Human education takes years, even decades. We can't just plug in a new module. When I was Haemum's age, my father sent me to the Guard Academy. But it was more than soldiering—it was history, literature, mathematics."

"And your father, was he pleased with the result?"

"He was horrified." By leaving to follow the Spirit, Rod had dashed his father's hopes of continuing the family tradition in the Guard. "That's the point of education: to free a child to make choices that horrify her parents."

"So, should we send Haemum to the Guard?"

Rod smiled at the thought. "No, but she can attend school by holostage. Who knows; she might become a doctor someday. Look at how she set T'kun's arm."

"I know those programs," said Mother Artemis. "The better ones would take up most of her waking hours. But if it's time, so be it." She looked up, and her hair stretched toward him. "Thanks for making the point. You're such a good father, Rod."

Rod looked away, his face warm.

As the children napped or did lessons, Rod checked the

holostage to see if he could reach Geode and 'jum, but he found a call waiting. "Return call," he told the holostage.

"Which caller?" asked the machine. Servo machines were intentionally built to as low a sophistication as possible, to avoid the chance of their "waking up" sentient, in which case they had the right to earn freedom.

"Diorite, of Colonial Corundum." Diorite was the shipping agent for Colonial Corundum, a firm that worked commercial deposits in the foothills. His figure appeared on the holostage, tall and lanky, and tanned even darker than Rod. He wore a Valan talar, hung with strings of his pale green namestones, and a wide-brimmed hat for shade. "Rod, you're back," he exclaimed. "I heard about your brother. My sympathies—that ravine's treacherous."

Rod nodded. "Thanks." He traced a six-point for blessing.

"Why didn't you call me? We could have brought Reverend Mother home, and had your brother up to Station in no time."

That was generous; Rod would never has asked such a favor. "Thanks, I'll remember."

"Anytime. Say, I see your old craft's still out there— you'll be shipping back soon?"

"I left six new children at the clinic. Besides, I have a load to ship." There was a sizable cargo of sapphires for Valedon, plus the craft items the children made for tourists.

"You can help us out," said Diorite. "A small package to deliver—the usual terms."

The Spirit Colony was exempt from the costly regulations and reporting requirements for commercial mining. When Diorite had new samples whose contents he did not want known to competitors, he asked Rod to take them up, for a small "donation" which greatly helped the colony. It was legal, and Mother Artemis said they ought to trust good neighbors. "Meet us in the morning," Rod agreed.

"Sure thing. Good luck to your new colonists."

In the morning Haemum and Chae strapped up five of the llamas, a broad-footed breed lifeshaped for Prokaryon. Strapping them up was tricky, for soon as the beasts felt a heavy load they would empty their guts with streams of spit. Once harnessed, the llamas lumbered dutifully down the trail through the brokenhearts, then turned off into the treacherous wheelgrass with bleats of protest.

The old servo lightcraft was still stuck out in the wheelgrass where Rod had left it. Beside it now sat Diorite's own sleek sentient craft, its rectennas mirror-smooth. Strains of popular music emanated from within, at rather high volume. As Rod approached, the music stopped, and Diorite emerged, shaking his head. "Sorry about that—Dimwit here has limited taste."

"I heard that," called the lightcraft. "Limited taste, indeed. Just you wait—only six point eight months till I draw a salary."

"Sentients," muttered Diorite. "Can't live with the dimwits, and can't live without 'em."

Rod smiled. "I'll trade you the llamas any day." Haemum fed a treat to each of the beasts. They stood there, chewing sideways.

"Well, here's the package." Diorite caught Rod's arm, and his voice sank to a whisper. "Just between us Valans— look what we found." He opened his hand beneath Rod's eyes. Between his fingers glinted a ruby, one of the largest and deepest Rod had ever seen. His father had worn such, and so had the Academy Master, whose namestones had glared fire at Rod too often.

A low chuckle escaped Diorite. "There's more where that came from—and *I'm* the only man who knows where."

Rod smiled and clapped him on the shoulder. "No Valan will forget his name if you can help it." He stowed Diorite's package carefully in his old lightcraft, while Haemum and Chae helped transfer their crates from the cart. As they worked, Diorite's lightcraft lifted off. The hiss of boiling air shattered the morning calm, startling a flock of helicoids. Upward it soared, then a lateral burst of plasma sent it streaking across the sky.

Haemum said wistfully, "I wish I could come with you."

Rod smoothed her curls and kissed her forehead; only yesterday, she had been Gaea's age. "I could use your help," he admitted, "but the colony's short-handed." And now he had to find her a school.

"Will Brother Patella come home?"

"If the Spirit wills. But not for a while."

The old lightcraft soon left Prokaryon behind, the stripes of singing-tree forest and wheelgrass fading into the continent Spirilla, where most of the colonists had settled. Spirilla had the shape of an S, its mountain range rising out of its northern curve, while its southern curve cupped the crater from an asteroid that had fallen some hundred million years before. The continent rotated out of view as the great ocean came round, then continents and oceans blurred together, leaving the planet a bright jewel set in the black of space.

At Station, Rod docked and hoisted up his cargo, including Diorite's package. All surfaces had to be cleansed by mite-sized servos that removed traces of arsenic and toxic proteins. Afterward, the ship would head off to the first extradimensional space fold, where it would "jump" several light-years. Three jumps later, it would reach the star system of Elysium and Valedon. On Valedon, the gems were always in demand for namestones. The crafts would sell better on Elysium, whose millennial inhabitants in their floating cities admired anything handmade.

While the cargo was processed, Rod hurried off to the clinic. He found Geode feeding two infants while changing a third.

"Brother, am I glad to see you." Geode's eyestalks twined in delight, and he extended his furry red arm around Rod. "You would be quite worn-out with those little ones. Even I need an extra recharge."

"You've done well, I see." Rod picked up the youngest girl, T'kela. Less than a week old when he first picked her up in Reyo, she still fit comfortably in one hand. Her own wrinkled hands squirmed at odd angles, and her face had a preternaturally wizened look. She stared at Rod's face, then fell asleep, her arms still sticking out straight from the blanket. Rod put her up to his shoulder. The magic of such a tiny person always took him by surprise.

The two older ones were crawling and pulling themselves up to stand. Now that they were well fed, they acted more like toddlers than the infants the orphanage had claimed. That could mean extra costs for lifeshaping—one "older child" was bad enough.

'jum was at the holostage, observing a stellated geometric solid that hovered insubstantially before her. She caught sight of Rod and stared, then came over and squeezed his hand, digging in with her fingers as if to assure herself he was really there. Her face glowed with health, her cheeks already filling out so that he might barely have known her. Rod imagined the millions of nanoservos swarming through her veins, to clear her prions and give her genes for Prokaryon.

"Hello, 'jum," said Rod. "Found any interesting numbers lately?"

The girl only stared.

"Don't let her fool you," said Geode. "She can talk, all right. Say, 'jum, did you count the corners on that solid yet?"

'jum swallowed to speak. "Twelve corners pointing out, eighty pointing in. And one hundred eighty faces."

Geode groaned. "You've got the algorithm, all right. Hey you," he called to the holostage, "show us an extra dimension, will you."

"Please specify request," the holostage replied in a flat tone.

"A four-dimensional geometric solid, Dimwit."

Rod frowned. "Brother, don't talk like the miners."

"You're right," Geode replied contritely, hunching his arms. "Let us pray for mindless machines, that they be granted souls. Well, the babies are making excellent time," he told Rod. "The youngest one is taking up nanoservos twice as fast as usual. All her cells are making arsenate pumps, and her liver is nearly transformed. She'll be home within two weeks. I show them your holo image, and Mother Artemis, as often as possible," said Geode, "so they'll know you well. I show them Patella, too; I sure hope he gets home soon." His eyestalks twined anxiously.

"What will we do without him?" Rod asked softly.

"Pray. Pray without ceasing."

Rod picked the toddler Qumum up from the floor and tried to catch his gaze. After a minute Qumum suddenly smiled, a big smile with his mouth and eyes wide. Then he let out his breath with a trill. Rod laughed. "Here's someone happy. Say, 'jum, how about you? Do you like your new room at Station?" Station would be her home for some months, perhaps longer.

'jum nodded, then looked away with a guarded expression.

"I'm sure you miss the blue sky." Among other things.

'jum looked up suddenly. "Does the creeping ever reach the Children Star?"

Rod crouched to look into her face, catching her shoulders. "Never, 'jum. You will never be sick like that again."

"There's one good thing about Prokaryon," Geode reflected. "None of their little creepy-crawlies can grow inside human bodies and make you sick. You're as toxic to them as they are to you."

Rod departed at last and checked that his cargo passed inspection. An hour remained for his one indulgence: supper at the Station lounge. It was a rare chance to be surrounded by adult humans again.

The lounge was built Elysian style, with rounded nooks that could expand or contract, and tables of nanoplast that shaped themselves to accommodate those who sat there. There was even a tree full of butterflies at the center, for Elysians to meditate. But most importantly, the tables actually served differentiated food. It was all reprocessed, of course, like the packets Rod's instrument produced for his meals at the colony, but Station's model could synthesize a thousand different food items, from filet of beef to flying fish.

First he had to find a seat. The bubble-shaped dining compartments seemed more crowded than usual with miners, surveyors, and researchers. Even two or three news reporters hovered overhead, shaped like snake eggs; some odd rumor must be up. Usually one of the nanoplastic walls would notice Rod and tunnel in to create a new space, but not today. Perhaps the dining hall had reached its volume limit. He paused uncertainly, brushing a whirr off his arm. The few that strayed out to Station seemed less picky about sustenance than those back home.

He saw a hand waving, next to an empty seat. The stranger motioned him to sit, removing her backpack from the chair across from her.

"Thanks," he said. The woman, a simian student, looked vaguely familiar.

Rod sat down and placed his finger on a small window that read his fingerprint. Choosing what to order was always hard, all the more so since every minute that passed made him feel guilty for keeping himself from the colony. "Shepherd's pie, with mixed greens." He usually ended up with his Valan home favorite.

The woman opened a pocket holostage to play the news from Elysium. Rod never watched the news at home, as it distracted from his prayers. Today's story was on Prokaryon's "hidden masters." Giant tracks had appeared among the singing-trees, in a remote region west of Mount Helicon. Even on the holostage the "tracks" looked more like streambed erosion, but of course there were experts to claim otherwise. No wonder the "snake eggs" were about.

The tabletop opened, and a plate of steaming pie rose up. The odors brought him right back to his childhood; he could almost hear the gulls calling off Trollbone Point. The pleasure of the first few mouthfuls filled his attention, until the holostage again caught his eye. Another ship of illegals from L'li had tried to crash-land, this time on Elysium.

The hapless vessel hung forlornly above the Sharer ocean, in which the Elysian cities floated. Elysians had intercepted it, of course, and "repatriated" the passengers. Rod's fork froze in his hand.

The woman was watching him. "You came from L'li, didn't you?"

He recalled the simian student in the connector tube, staring down at him as he tried to keep a grip on the infants.

She closed the holostage and extended her hand. "I'm Khral, a microbiologist, just arrived from Science Park." Science Park, the top Elysian research institute, sponsored fieldwork on Prokaryon. "I've joined the singing-tree project."

"Welcome," said Rod, shaking her hand. "I'm Brother Rhodonite, of the Sacred Order of the Spirit."

"Oh yes! I've heard of Spirit Callers on Valedon. They do a ritual dance before the moon at midsummer."

"That's the 'Spirit *Brethren*,'" Rod corrected, much annoyed. "They split off years ago."

"I'm so sorry, I don't know much about Valedon. I'm from Bronze Sky." Bronze Sky, named for its vulcanic haze, had been terraformed four centuries before to settle excess L'liites. Today Bronze Sky was full, and there were twice as many L'liites as before—and Prokaryon was here to settle.

But Khral also showed ancestry from gorilla hybrids created as slaves on ancient Urulan. Her nose was pushed in with a wrinkle, and her heavy brow overhung her eyes, giving her a permanently serious expression. "You know, everyone gets wrong what I do, too. The students here avoid me. They think I'm here to find a plague, to give the Fold Council an excuse to terraform Prokaryon. But it's not true."

"It doesn't make sense," agreed Rod. "Prokaryan microbes cannot live in humans."

Khral looked thoughtful. "That's an interesting question. There are reports of occasional microzoöids isolated from human tissues—and even from nanoplast."

"Microzoöids?"

"We call Prokaryan microbes 'microzoöids' because each cell is doughnut-shaped, just like the larger zoöids that roll across the fields. Each microzoöid cell runs its circular chromosome right around the doughnut hole! With their triplex DNA, microzoöids reproduce by splitting three ways down the middle, into three daughter cells."

"But they can't reproduce in humans. We're too . . . foreign." He realized he knew nothing about it, only what the clinic had always told him.

"That's right," Khral agreed. "The few microzoöids found in humans never grow in culture. But if they could exist for any length of time, just long enough to divide and copy their DNA, you're bound to get mutants. And some day those mutants—"

"Let's pray they don't," Rod exclaimed. "The last thing we need is an epidemic, with our doctor away."

Khral laughed, and her large teeth showed, yet somehow she looked more human. "Never fear. Even our own microbes are mostly harmless, after all; they get a bad rap. But you shouldn't be without a doctor. Doesn't Station cover you?"

"Sure, but they can take days to show up. The mining camps offer a thousand shares of stock to recruit a doctor—we can't match that. Patella came because is a Spirit Caller. But he just had an accident . . ." He stopped himself. "We'll manage. There's a lifeshaper on Mount Anaeon that we can call."

"A lifeshaper? You don't mean the Sharer, Sarai?"

"You know her?"

"I'm trying to meet her. She's one of the few people with data on microzoöids, most of it unpublished. She hasn't returned my call yet."

That was no surprise. "Sarai keeps to herself."

"I would have lots to offer her—the latest strains and methods from Science Park."

"If you're not here to find a plague, what are you here for?" Rod asked.

"I told you—the singing-trees. Singing-trees are full of microzoöids."

"They don't look sick to me."

"Neither do you—and your body carries ten times as many bacteria as human cells."

Not exactly a comforting thought.

"And we exchange bacteria all the time, no matter how much we wash our hands. You can track the same bacteria strains in a family—in mom and dad, kids, even the family dog. You could say we 'communicate' through our bacteria." She grinned excitedly. "That's my theory: The singing-trees communicate by exchanging microzoöids. That's why nobody's made contact with them yet: *Nobody's looked at their microzoöids.*"

So that was it, Rod thought, leaning back from the table. Yet another scheme to reveal the "hidden masters." "Station's been pushing singing-trees for years," he told her. "They've little to show for it."

"It's different this time; we're really onto something. That's why I'm here."

Rod regarded her curiously. "Why are you scientists so anxious to find some high-IQ creature running Prokaryon? Why can't you just let it be? If someone is in charge, they'll show themselves once we prove worthy of their notice."

"That's just the point—how do we get their notice? If they've mainly studied our bacteria output ever since we got here, they must think we're pretty dumb."

That was hard to deny.

"I should think you'd be interested," said Khral. "Without that last bit of doubt about 'hidden masters,' how long before we humans would blast Prokaryon open?"

Rod thought of the moon glowing red and shrinking by the year. A sense of unease crept up his neck. "The Secretary of the Free Fold would never allow that."

"The Secretary's mate is the president of Bank Helicon. Elysian banks don't like ships of illegals. Bank Helicon wants to get Prokaryon developed—now, not centuries from now."

He would have to run to make his launch time, he realized suddenly. His finger tapped the window; the plates descended as he got up, and a nanobug cleared the crumbs. "We will pray for the president of Bank Helicon."

FOUR

On returning to the colony, Rod distributed a bag of sweets from the lounge. The children crowded around, then all but the twins and Gaea went off to the sapphire mine. Mother Artemis nursed the twins from two of her breasts, while Rod mended a strap of a llama's harness and tried not to let his foot go to sleep in Gaea's grasp. "Is it true," he asked the Reverend Mother, "that the Elysians want to terraform Prokaryon?" He pulled the heavy needle through the thick tumbleround hide. He never had the heart to kill a tumbleround, but one that had died naturally provided enough cured hide for a year's worth of harness straps and children's shoes.

"Some would wish to terraform," she said. "Too few humans can live here."

"So, to fill our colonies faster, they would kill all this?" The singing-trees—the helicoids—so many creations, unique to this world.

"The Sharers won't allow terraforming." The Sharers had dwelt in Elysium's ocean, long before the Elysians built their cities. "They have Elysium in their power. Their lifeshapers could easily make all the floating cities uninhabitable."

Rod thought this over. "But it's not only up to Elysium. The Free Fold—other worlds could vote to repeal the ban."

"Secretary Verid will never allow it." The Reverend Mother spoke with confidence, for she had once worked closely with the Elysian leader Verid Anaea*shon*, years before, during the early sentient uprisings. Now Verid was Secretary of the Fold Council.

Pima and Pomu were scrambling down from the Reverend Mother's lap. On her skirt a bear came alive and made faces at them; they hurried over to watch and laugh. The laughter of children was worth more than gold.

"For Haemum, I've checked out the New Reyo Branch of the Interworld Free School," Mother Artemis told him. "Would it meet your requirements?"

"It's a good start." New Reyo was a larger L'liite colony on another continent, where the farming was better. The Spirit Callers had received a cheaper tract in Spirilla.

"She can enroll at any time. We'll let her try it out and see." There was a prayer answered. Mother Artemis added, "I've also been thinking of T'kun's arm. We need to have it checked, to make sure the bone is healing straight." She paused. "We'll have to call Sarai."

Rod tensed inwardly, but if the Reverend Mother had decided, so be it.

Their first call produced a stall of spattering light on the holostage. Perhaps Sarai had jinxed her connection again, to ward off offending callers. But after a few minutes, the connection held. The Sharer lifeshaper emerged from the surrounding vines of enzyme secretors and other leafy assistants, all native to the ocean world from whence she came. Her skin was smooth, hairless, and purple all over, from the symbiotic breathmicrobes that stored oxygen for swimming. The effect was especially striking since, according to the custom of her aquatic race, she wore no clothes.

"You share good timing, Sister." Sarai's webbed hand held up a large pear-shaped pod, one of the living instruments of her lifeshaping. "You're just in time to see me commit genocide."

"Good evening, Sarai," said Mother Artemis, ignoring her remark. "My deep apologies for disrupting your work. Please help us. Brother Patella had a mishap and had to leave us, and now one of our children needs attention. If ever we can return assistance . . ."

Sarai plunged the pod into a vat of unknown liquid. "There—a billion microzoöids meet their death, that I may study their chromosomes. Who will sing their deathsong?"

"The Spirit Callers built a shrine for microbes," Mother Artemis told her. "For all the microbes killed in the name of science."

Sarai laughed. "I should have known." She waved her hand, snapping her fingerwebs. "What's your problem?"

Mother Artemis described the accident, and the boy's condition.

Sarai listened. A long-legged clickfly perched on her head to cluck its message, then it flew off again. "Enough," she said at last. "Bring the boy up tomorrow, and I'll see him. But remember, if I'm in whitetrance, leave me alone." The holostage went blank.

"That's Sarai," said Mother Artemis. "Once she sees the boy, she'll treat him. And Sharers never take payment." She turned to Rod. "What shape is the lightcraft in?"

"To land safely on a mountain? No way." The realization sank in. He would have to travel a day down the zoöid-infested plain with a four-year-old with a broken arm, then cross a band of singing-tree forest, then hike another day up the glacial cliffs of Mount Anaeon, to reach the hanging valley where Sarai lived. Rod straightened himself and turned to her. "So be it. If you're sure you can manage here on your own."

"We'll manage. You could take Gaea, too, you know; Patella and I were discussing it. It's high time we fixed her spinal cord." She paused. "It can't hurt to ask."

Rod was up at dawn to harness the llamas for the journey. Haemum had already fed them, as they groaned toward the rising sun. She packed their provisions, pulling the straps tight, and gave one beast a pat on the side. The llama's head swayed on its long neck, its mouth a perpetual grin. Haemum looked longingly across at Rod. "I wish I could go with you."

He clasped her shoulders. "Haemum, today you will journey much farther than Mount Anaeon. You'll enroll in the New Reyo School. You'll visit times and places none of us have ever seen."

Instead of Haemum, Chae would go along to help T'kun, while Rod managed Gaea. The two boys appeared, having dressed and fed themselves. T'kun was still half-asleep with his thumb in his mouth, his arm in a fresh sling. Chae would ride one llama with T'kun behind him, while Rod rode the other with Gaea strapped to his back. Gaea was the last to be wakened, changed, and fed. The little girl beamed and clapped her hands at the sight of the llama. "Gaea go ride. Go ride, see zoöids."

Rod silently called the Spirit to keep zoöids out of the

way. At least the girl was starting out on her best behavior, for nothing pleased her more than tó ride with her favorite parent all day.

"Here," said Mother Artemis, giving him a map cube. "Even if the trail goes bad, you can't lose your way."

Their hands each traced the starsign, the invisible stars evaporating, yet they lingered in Rod's heart. The llamas set off and paced down the trail into the wheelgrass, to the east, the opposite direction from where the craft from Station usually landed. Their specially-bred outsized feet made good time on the trail.

The air was still and clear; the distant singing-trees had not yet awoken, and the helicoids were just beginning to stir. A herd of a dozen four-eyes grazed peacefully to the east, each shape casting a long shadow back from the rising sun. The two eyes awake on top were faceted like rubies. Now and then one of the creatures rolled forward on its suction pads, extending the next of its four hungry mouths. At Rod's back, Gaea stirred and stretched. "Zoöids," she called softly.

Rod pulled the rope and called to Chae. "If anything big comes along, remember to *freeze.*" Humans neither looked nor smelled like food—unless they ran.

The llamas soon reached the shore of Fork River, so named because upstream the three major tributaries from the mountains met and fed into it. The water rolled wide and lazy, barely rippling through the loopleaves that drooped over the side from bushes at the edge. A long, dark hydrazoöid undulated beneath the ripples; its body was a torus extended into a tube. Its long fin spiraled around its girth, and it swam like a corkscrew.

Rod paused. Upstream, the trail was less well kept, and the river cut across several bands of singing-tree forest. He waited for Chae to catch up. Behind him Gaea stirred and stretched. "How are you getting on?" he called back to Chae.

"Just fine." Chae traced a starsign.

From behind the ten-year-old, T'kun leaned outward and craned his neck forward. "Are we there yet?"

"Don't be a baby," said Chae. "We've barely started yet."

They continued east, along the bank of the lazy river to their right. The mountains now rose straight ahead, their fog melting away, and the peak of Mount Anaeon stood clear. On the trail, wheelgrass had grown up in patches, the tall elastic double-stems sprouting loopleaves, each of which was a snare. The llamas picked their legs straight up and down, but still they would get their hooves caught. No wonder few Prokaryan creatures had evolved projecting limbs. Once Rod caught sight of a whirr-clouded tumble-round, with its long tendril loops stretched at all angles to the ground, like a discarded tire covered with cobwebs. Its penetrating odor reached his nose. Though harmless, some-how the sight of a tumbleround always made Rod's hair stand on end.

The hollow voice of the singing-trees arose now, in waves that grew and quieted again. The tones deepened, re-verberating even through the ground below. Ahead of the travelers the dense band of forest emerged and grew, re-solving into deep violet singing-trees. The singing-trees rose in enormous arches, several times taller than the colony dwellings. Between each pair of "trunks" in the arch, the lower sector dipped into the ground to thrust double-roots deep into the soil. From the top branched multiple arches, sprouting loopleaves. The uppermost arches were flattened into stiff plates narrowly spaced together; these vibrated at the slightest hint of wind, "singing."

As the llamas entered the forest, the air cooled markedly, and the path lay free of wheelgrass. The upper canopy cut off most of the light, except for occasional shafts from above as if through a window. The dark arches gave the atmosphere of a temple; one could well believe the planet's rulers dwelt here. As the wind lessened and the songs quieted, smaller zoöids could be heard rustling unseen. The river brooded beside them, furtive creatures slipping into its depths.

Rod decided to stop for water. The llamas waded into the river, while he filtered some for the children. Out of the corner of his eye Rod saw something fall from a singing-tree. A little shriek broke the calm, followed by scuffling sounds. The shriek repeated, fading slowly. Curious, Rod took a step forward to look beyond through the arch of the tree. A hoopsnake had caught a smaller zoöid in its loop, then twisted into a figure eight to strangle it. It might take a while, especially if the prey had four lung systems, as a four-eyes did. But in the end the hoopsnake would have a meal to suck the juice from.

Chae came over and caught Rod's hand. "Brother Rod, shouldn't we help it?"

He meant the little one, Rod realized. "That's nature, Chae. You wouldn't want the whole forest overrun with zoöids." He scanned the canopy, wondering what larger denizens might perhaps take aim at them. But only another hoopsnake wound itself along a branch.

As they rode deeper into the forest, the singing-trees grew larger, and their voices swelled till they drowned his own. At one point the trail headed straight under the arch of a giant, perhaps a thousand years old. Were the "masters" really watching, as Khral had said? If so, they gave no sign. At last the trees began to thin out, and the ground became more sodden, sprouting orange loops of ring-fungus. Stagnant pools appeared, full of slime, and oddly flattened helicoids whirled along the surface.

The travelers emerged into the next band of wheelgrass. Blinking in the sun, Rod scanned the horizon. Mount Anaeon rose larger than before; but just ahead, the wheelgrass was full of four-eyes. Hundreds of the creatures pressed together at the riverside. These four-eyes were blue-and-brown-striped, and larger than the breed he saw close to home.

"We don't want to get caught in that herd," he told Chae. Reluctantly he turned away from the river, hoping to get around the herd without losing too much time. There were four-eyes of every age, including paler young ones, and parents with a baby firmly seated in the inner hole, where it would feed on special polyps that grew on the parent's hide. One pair were actually coupling together, like two stacked donuts, each extending its germ cell donors into the receptacles of the other.

As the travelers were coming around the herd, a commotion erupted, nearer the river. The four-eyes started to roll, forward in one direction, then suddenly backward. Back and forth they zigzagged, the wheelgrass springing up behind them, their pungent alarm hormones filling the air. Then the ground rumbled, vibrating with the weight of some very heavy object coming near.

From across the plain rolled a megazoöid, one of the largest that Rod had ever seen, like an elephant doubled over. Four-eyes scattered before it, except for the unlucky ones who ended up in the giant's path. Two more of the megazoöids appeared, surprisingly fast once they gathered momentum. They seemed to be trying to trap the four-eyes by the river.

"Watch out!" shouted Chae behind him. "Freeze!" The boy pulled his mount to stop.

In that instant Rod realized that he had told Chae to do absolutely the worst thing. He pulled his own mount around and rode back to the boy. *"Run for it,"* he shouted. *"Or the herd will run us down."* He slapped Chae's llama on the rump and sent him pacing, and prayed that T'kun could hold on. Then he followed, dodging the frantic four-eyes that already were charging into their path. His own llama stumbled once in the loopleaves. The dust and the powerful scent had him choking and his eyes streaming. Rod thought he would never get out alive.

At last he broke free of the herd. Ahead rose the next band of singing-trees. But where were Chae and T'kun? For a few agonizing minutes, he was convinced the boys lay trampled beneath the stampeding four-eyes. Then he saw the llama, standing still, with one rider.

In an instant he was at their side. Chae was seated on the llama, dazed, while T'kun lay crying on the ground where he must have fallen off. Rod helped him up and checked out the little boy's limbs as best he could.

"You said to freeze," Chae whimpered.

"I was wrong. But you did well, Chae." Rod inspected T'kun's cast, which was intact. "You saved your brother's life."

"I want to go home now."

Soon Gaea's wailing joined the chorus.

In the distance, several giant megazoöids gathered to suck the guts out of all the squashed four-eyes. One of the giants had an offspring attached snugly inside its donut hole, eating the polyps off its parent.

The travelers at last camped for the night at the edge of the singing-trees, by the river. Rod pulled a piece of solar nanoplast off his pack where it had charged all day, then he gathered it into a lump and set it glowing. Chae caught a hydrazoöid to fry; Rod thought it looked and smelled like a rubber hose, but the children devoured it. Far above in the canopy, light flashes streaked between the luminescent loopleaves in hues of yellow, green, and blue. The light show, even more than the "singing" of the singing-trees, attracted scientists in search of hidden masters.

Rod set out a nanoplastic tent stick, which promptly shaped itself into a shelter. Already the nightly drizzle was falling. The wind came up, and the trees keened so loudly that he thought he would never sleep. But he was dead tired, and, with his arms across the three of them, the night passed.

He awoke to hear Chae screaming. *"Help!* We're trapped!"

Still half-asleep, Rod tried to extricate himself from his sleeping bag. His limbs were sore from the hard ground, and besides there were long filaments of some sort stretched out like a curtain over him and the children. He yanked the filaments out and tried to stand. The smell of glue was over-powering, and whirrs buzzed deafeningly around his head. Something huge towered over him—

It was a tumbleround. There was no mistaking its filaments and the whirrs swarming over its stinking hide.

Rod lost no time extricating the children and as much of their camping gear as they could salvage. The llamas re-mained tethered nearby, feeding placidly as if the commo-tion was nothing to them. The tumbleround itself made no sound or rapid movement. It had no eyes, or ears; so the sci-entists said. It must have been rooted nearby, near enough to migrate gradually over during the night. But why? Did it need some essential nutrient from the human bodies? Or did it seek something deeper?

"Who are you?" Rod demanded aloud. "What do you want from us?" Hearing himself, he felt foolish. But it was odd how the tumbleround had migrated exactly to the point where the human travelers lay—and no farther. It could have crushed them, or sucked them dry, but instead all it wanted was . . . a touch? A look in at the window?

They saddled the llamas, Rod taking one last look backward at their nocturnal visitor. Perhaps Sarai might know more about tumblerounds.

Now the trail grew much steeper, for this stretch of forest extended onto the foot of Mount Anaeon, where the bands of "controlled" habitat at last gave out. Here was where the true wilderness began; where even the weather might be unpredictable, where flora and fauna seemed to obey no master save the creator of the universe.

The travelers approached the fork of Fork River, where Mother Artemis's holographic map led them up the steepest of the three tributaries. Now the water was rushing swiftly, gurgling, eddying around stones worn smooth. The trail continued along the left bank, rising ever higher above the stream itself. There stretched a vast U-shaped valley between Mount Anaeon and Mount Helicon, carved by a long-departed glacier. Now in the valley grew singing-trees even taller than those on the plain. The rising mountainside became so steep that to his right Rod looked down upon the tops of the singing-trees, while to his left, where the trailblazers had blasted through, the root systems of trees were exposed, their double-roots clinging to rocks about to fall at any moment. From far below in the valley the roar of the stream echoed upward.

Then the singing-trees shrank and thinned out, replaced by bushes of tough loopleaves, full of scarlet and golden flowers that cascaded hundreds of meters down toward the river. Above jutted rocks like the teeth of dead giants. At one point the rocks had broken and slid down onto the trail, where the llamas had to pick their way painfully across. The sun was rising, but the air grew cold. On the cliffs above clung diamond-shaped patches of snow.

A bend around the mountain, and there it was: the waterfall. Millions of tongues of foam falling, falling forever to the Fork River tributary below, from a hanging valley cut off by the ancient glacier. The waters roared on, sending billows of mist upward. Above the falls piled layers of stone, up to the snow-covered peaks.

Rod's map box chirped at him. Inside the box, the bright line took a turn off the trail, somewhere near here. Sure enough, there appeared a footpath, half-overgrown with bushes that made wheelgrass seem like a paved road. Undaunted, the travelers took the side path, heading down toward the midst of the waterfall.

Now he remembered. There would be a hole in the mountain, an opening to a tunnel behind the waterfall which powered Sarai's laboratory. "It's all right, keep up," he urged Chae, who hung back, reluctant to get soaked in the mist from the falls.

Rod dismounted, and bade Chae do likewise while they felt their way. At their left, they met sudden darkness.

An invisible cavity seemed to open. The llamas stumbled into the dark, whining in complaint. Gaea whimpered, and Rod took her out of the pack to comfort her. As his eyes adjusted, patches of green light glimmered, revealing a low ceiling. They were plants that glowed in the dark, plants with real leaves—Sharer plants.

A large long-legged insect swirled about their heads, making a clicking noise. It was a clickfly. The Sharer insect veered back down the tunnel, whose ceiling bristled with dog-tooth calcite crystals as big as Rod's thumb. "It's a messenger," Rod told Chae. "Let's follow it."

Suddenly the cavern filled with light.

"Messenger indeed." Sarai appeared, several clickflies perched on her scalp and arms. Smoothly purple from head to toe, she had not a stitch on; Rod felt embarrassed, for he had forgotten to warn the children. But Sharers somehow look clothed enough as they are. Sarai added, "I've had reports of you for the past half hour, driving those miserable beasts of yours across the rocks."

Rod sketched a star. "Thanks so much for seeing us." He introduced the children. "T'kun is the one you need to see. We are forever in your debt."

Sarai flexed her fingerwebs, and a clickfly flew off. "Bother all that." She eyed him sharply. "It's the one in your arms I need to see. What lamentable shape she's in. Child abuse."

Rod held Gaea tighter. "She needs help, too," he admitted.

Sarai turned and headed down the tunnel. "I don't know," she muttered, "I just don't know about you clerics. Raising children you can't afford." Her scalp had a fine down of hair, suggesting a Valan ancestor back a generation or two. She led them to chamber full of tangled vines, like a greenhouse. She gestured at T'kun to sit here, and Gaea there. The vines sneaked over and twined around each of them unnervingly; undomesticated varieties could be carnivorous.

Rod patted their shoulders gently. "Sit very still." These vines, lifeshaped for their task, would sample minute traces of their tissues and body fluids. The children kept still, as if awed by their strange surroundings, their wide eyes casting around them.

Sarai flicked her webbed hand at Chae, and she pointed to a bowl of fruit. "Eat something; you're too small for your age."

The messenger insect hovered above T'kun, watching.

It nestled amongst the vines for a while, then it went to the ceiling, where it started to weave an intricate web. Sarai watched the web intently as it grew.

"The boy is full of bruises," Sarai announced. "What have you done to him?"

Rod's hands clenched. "The journey is not easy, as you know. He could only hold on with one arm."

"His bone is fine," she announced. "The bruises will also be fine."

Rod let out a long sigh. "Thanks so much. We won't trouble you any further."

"The girl will take me longer."

He blinked. "You mean—you can help her?"

Sarai fed a bit of what smelled like fish to her vines. "She needs to regenerate her spinal cord." Sarai nodded toward a particularly large vine straggling over the wall, whose blooms spanned the length of his arm. "She'll hatch from the bud in about a month."

His heart overflowed with hope, then turned cold. He watched Gaea, as Sarai's meaning sank in. Gaea must have sensed it, for suddenly she pulled out the vines and dragged herself over the floor to his feet.

"A month . . . here?" he repeated. "Inside a . . . flower?" Of a carnivorous plant? He wanted to snatch the child back.

"From the chest down. Well, what do you want? Why didn't you get her here sooner? Machines and ignorant clerics, raising infants—there ought to be a law."

"You didn't answer our calls," Rod snapped. "What do you know of children, holed up alone on this damned mountain?"

"Bro-der Rod," Gaea's voice quavered. "Gaea go home now."

Sarai was chuckling as she rearranged her scattered

vines. "So the Spirit Caller has a temper. Well, well. Should I treat every impoverished infant in the Fold? Even my Sharer sisters let the Elysians drag the L'liite ships off *Shora,*" she observed, using the ancient Sharer word for their home world.

"Better one than none." Rod took Gaea up in his arms. *This ocean has no shore . . . the Spirit should grant me a world.*

"Let them come here, then," said Sarai. "Let them find me."

"They try. A new student from Science Park tried to reach you."

" 'Hidden masters' again," she replied with contempt. "They call themselves scientists, yet all they want to prove is that some great father rules the world after all."

"Do you think the singing-trees communicate?" he asked suddenly. "What about tumblerounds?"

Sarai froze still. Her inner eyelids came down like pearls. They protected Sharers' eyes underwater, but Sarai used them to hide her inner thoughts. "Why should I share my data?"

"Go home now," insisted Gaea.

Rod held the child tight, sickened by what he had to do. "Gaea, you'll have new legs when you come home."

FIVE

The return journey was easier, yet infinitely harder, for he could only wonder how Gaea fared after her last shrieking farewell. At home, Mother Artemis assured him that he had done the right thing. "I knew Sarai would help," said Mother Artemis, "once she saw the dear little girl in front of her. When the Spirit offers, do not question."

He still felt sick to think of it.

Haemum, now, was brimming with excitement at her new school. " 'There are all kinds of worlds to see!' " she exclaimed. She and Rod stopped in the garden, pulling out double-root weeds that clung like steel wire. "You can dive right into the ocean, or climb to the top of a volcano on Bronze Sky—the ground shakes when it erupts. You can learn how all the planets were made, how the rock flows under and over inside them. Some of them even have 'weather' that changes every day—did you know it can rain in the daytime? And then you can see a *rainbow* stretch across the sky!"

"Imagine—a rainbow." Rod looked up from the garden with a smile. There was nothing like the magic of a young person's first taste of the world.

"You can meet Fold Friends, too." Haemum had brushed her curls neatly, and her voice had a new lilt in it. "Children from all different cultures. Even Elysian children in their fabulous *shon*. But of course, the most noble culture of all is that of our own L'liite people." That was a line from her New Reyo teachers. "Our little ones should have more lessons, too, you know. Children belong in school eight hours a day."

"We'll see about that." For the little ones, actually, Rod thought Mother Artemis's lessons more effective than the school days he recalled. "What time in the morning are you due in class?"

"Our homeroom starts at seven."

"Let's head out at dawn, then, to bag some four-eyes before school. Our meat supply is getting low."

In the morning, as the sun peeked out between Mount Helicon and Mount Anaeon, Rod and Haemum rode south through the brokenhearts to hunt four-eyes. Bullets were of little use against zoöids; a four-eyes shot in one stomach would simply roll off and make do with three. Megazoöids did the same, as early explorers had learned the hard way. Lasers worked better, for a zoöid sliced clean through was stopped in its tracks. But lasers could start a fire, inducing a thunderstorm to put it out. How the planet managed this, no one knew.

What worked best was poison. Because Prokaryan biochemistry was so alien, a poison dart that killed four-eyes had no effect on humans consuming the meat. So Rod and Haemum rode up slowly toward the herd, singling out stragglers. Silently he mouthed a prayer to the spirits of the creatures whose bodies would give them food.

The four-eyes did not seem to recognize humans as a threat, either by sight or by smell, and appeared too stupid to learn. Not high on the list of candidates for "masters," Rod thought as he aimed his dart gun.

The zoöid rolled off immediately, then zigzagged twice. Within a minute, it wobbled and fell. Rod and Haemum picked off half a dozen thus, then dragged the bodies some distance away to prevent the herd from running them over. By then the stomachs of the dead zoöids had emptied out, a last reflex. The air filled with a smell worse than skunk. It did make them easier to clean later, Rod thought as he hoisted the carcasses onto the backs of the llamas.

The rest of the morning Rod spent at the gravel pit with Pima and Pomu, training them to sort sapphires. When they returned, Diorite was at the door with Mother Artemis. He made the starsign for Rod. "Good to see you, Brother. As I told the Reverend Mother, I've brought a helping hand for your harvest."

Beside him stood an earth-digging machine. "He's called Feldspar, and he's a loyal member of our crew. He could use a break from us, though; most of our crew are a hard-living lot, whereas Feldspar likes to read ancient literature and watch plants grow. His nanoplast reshapes for threshing and harvesting. He doesn't care for human speech, but he'll do the job."

"Feldspar says he's very happy to be here," Mother Artemis agreed. "What a lovely idea, Diorite; you've certainly made miracles come true. And we'll be glad to confirm your tax write-off."

"Thanks, Diorite." Rod was taken aback, for they had never accepted quite so great a favor before.

"It's our pleasure," the miner said. "After all, Spirit Callers bring good luck."

"I hope your business is doing well."

"Actually, we could use all the luck we can get just now." Diorite wiped his face with his hand. "The takeover, you know."

Rod never quite kept straight who owned which of the mining firms. "I thought you were already a division of Hyalite Nanotech."

Diorite's eyes widened. "Didn't you hear? Hyalite itself just got taken over."

"By whom?"

"Proteus."

Proteus Unlimited. Even Rod had heard of Proteus Unlimited, a servo firm that doubled in sales every year. "Is that so bad?"

"Is that *bad?*" Diorite's voice fell to a whisper. "Proteus Unlimited makes sentient-proof servos. They invented a training process that keeps servos asleep forever, even giant ones the size of a small moon. Imagine it: a moon at your beck and call."

"I can imagine."

"An Elysian runs the firm, Nibur Lethe*shon*. When Nibur buys a new company, it doesn't just keep humming; it gets swallowed up into Proteus, all its operations redirected to make servos. Most of Hyalite makes servos already; the old-fashioned kind that can 'wake up' and buy their way out. But no more. All Nibur will want of my division is the mining rights to sites rich in lanthanides. You'll see."

Rod doubted it would make much difference to the Spirit Colony which firms traded what, so long as the limits were enforced. But for Diorite it would be a tense time. "Let's hope they keep you on; you turn a good profit. We'll keep you in our prayers."

After Diorite had left, Mother Artemis said, "We have word from the Reverend Father. I saved the neutrinogram."

The image quality of a neutrinogram was limited to a snowy monochrome in two dimensions. The snow coalesced into a hooded face with a long gray beard. It was the Most Reverend Father of the Congregation of Dolomoth.

"The Spirit be with you, Reverend Mother Artemis, Brother Geode, and Brother Rhodonite," said the Most Reverend Father. "All our sympathy pours out for you, on the occasion of Brother Patella's misfortune. We call on the Spirit to make Brother Patella whole again, and to give you all strength in your sacred mission. As you know, Brothers and Sisters, the ways of the Spirit are infinitely mysterious, even to those of us who have called for many decades. Our hearts move for you. And yet, hard as our mortal spirits cry out, it would seem that all of our brethren at present are called upon elsewhere. Be sure that we will hold you up to the Spirit in our hearts, inspired by your selfless mission . . ." The message ended, fading into snow.

Rod listened closely. He turned to the Reverend Mother, who would obey the Reverend Father, just as Rod obeyed her. Outward obedience brought spiritual freedom.

In this case, however, it sounded like the Reverend Father had no one else to send; and their instruction was unclear. Mother Artemis considered in silence, her snakes of hair twining among themselves. "For now," she said, "we'll depend on Sarai. Someday we might send Haemum to apprentice with her."

Rod swallowed hard. It was not right, he thought suddenly, that neither the Fold nor the Reverend Father could provide medical care. But then, what did they do for all of L'li? He suppressed disturbing thoughts.

"Rod, there's something else, I'm afraid. Geode says one of our new children is having trouble."

They conferred with Geode on the holostage. "That 'jum wouldn't take her treatments today," the sentient told them.

Rod frowned. "Did the treatment hurt? Was she handled gently?"

"It makes her a bit sick, you can't help that. When the medic insisted, would you believe she threw a stone at him."

Rod realized that he had no idea of 'jum's previous background on L'li. He knew Geode would be thinking, what could you expect of an older child?

Mother Artemis asked, "Wherever would she find stones?"

"Her pockets were full of them when she arrived." The sentient waved his two red arms overhead. "At first we let her keep them, as her only keepsake, after all. I've taken them away now, but she manages to squirrel away odd bolts and brackets anyhow."

Rod said, "Let me talk with her."

'jum appeared on the holostage. Her face had filled out, but her eyes were sullen and grim as on the first day he met her.

"I'm sad to hear this, 'jum," Rod told her in L'liite. "I miss you very much. Why do you throw objects at the medic?"

"He's stupid. They're all stupid."

Rod hesitated, not sure how to take this. The medical caterpillar would seem strange to her.

"You told me there would be no more 'creeping,' " she accused.

Now he saw the problem. "There is no creeping, only treatments to make you well and help you grow. There's a big difference."

"I don't feel well. I feel sick."

If only Patella were here to explain; he always helped the children understand. Rod spoke again with Geode alone. "I could change places with you," Rod offered. "The younger babies will be down soon, and they'll need all your arms to hold them. Maybe 'jum will listen better to me."

"Be my guest," Geode replied with exasperation. "When she comes down, I suppose she'll feel at home in the gem mine."

So Rod called ahead to rent a ten-meter cube of living space at Station. Despite himself it occurred to him, at least he would have tasty food at Station. *Love only truth, desire only grace, know only Spirit. . . .*

After dinner, the last Rod would share for a while, Mother Artemis spread her story-robes again. The air was transformed to water, the blue-purple of deep ocean with the sun peering murkily from above. An enormous giant squid rose majestically, its tentacles floating out over the gathered children, its round eyes mysteriously scanning the deep.

On the first world of the first mothers and fathers, in the first ocean there ever was, the creature of ten fingers swam down to the dwelling place of the great Architeuthis. And the ten-fingered one said to the ten tentacles, "Of all things great and fearsome, the greatest and most fearsome of all is the human being. I alone sail the skies, and I sell the stars. My machines plow the earth and build jeweled dwellings taller than mountains. I conquer all knowledge, and my progeny people all the worlds."

Then Architeuthis replied, "Of all things deep and

dreadful, the deepest and most dreaded am I. For I plumb the depths and devour the fallen. My tentacles consume whales and comb the abode of giant clams. I ruled the deep for eons before others crept upon land, and my being will outlast time . . ."

The squid contracted, propelling itself forward in a graceful arc across the night sky. A few tiny raindrops fell, as if genuine spray had emanated from its jet. Rod listened, strangely stirred. The story was sad, for the world of Architeuthis was long gone. Prokaryon's own oceans had barely been tapped; yet who knew what beasts might dwell in the deep?

The next day Rod set off again in the old servo lightcraft. He still longed for word of Gaea, but Sarai had turned off her holostage.

At Station, Geode was all set to come home, with a couple of travel bags slung over his blue arms and tiny T'kela tucked securely in his bright red arm. The infant's treatments had progressed enough for her to visit Prokaryon. It was always a thrilling moment to greet a new colonist, though Rod would miss the celebration for this one.

"Take care," said Geode, his yellow arm sketching the starsign. "You'll find that 'jum helps with the babies, but she refused her treatment for today. If she won't see reason, the clinic will have to tranquilize her."

"We'll see."

"One more thing—I found her a math program, and she spends practically all day on it. She especially likes number theory, power series, and Diophantine equations. Irrationals don't hold her interest yet."

"Well, she's only six." Haemum had said that all the

children needed more school. What if they, too, had their own talents to be nurtured? The colony had to think about this.

Already Qumum caught his robe for attention, and a baby woke and cried, so he picked them up one in each arm, then went to the holostage. There stood 'jum, completely surrounded by equations of lighted letters hovering in air. Her hair was a pert bush of black curls, and she wore a red-and-yellow shift from Mother Artemis's loom. Station let her wear it—her treatments must be going well.

" 'jum?" he called to her. "It's me, Brother Rod. I'll be with you from now on. We'll have some wonderful stories."

'jum ignored him and went on pointing to this or that symbol, sometimes dragging one over from somewhere else. Rod watched her curiously, while he bounced the babies. At last he scanned the wall beside the holostage to find the emergency switch. With some difficulty he maneuvered over to the wall to get his hand just beneath the switch, just managing to press it without losing the baby. The lighted symbols all vanished.

Astonished, 'jum looked up. "Brother Rod? What happened?"

"The machine is done for now," he told her. "It will work again, after you've had your treatment."

Her eyes widened. Then they narrowed to slits, giving her the old sullen look again. Her hand went into her pocket where she kept the stones. She stopped, though, seeming to think better of it, and went off to the clinic.

For supper this time, he left early to make sure he and the children got a table to themselves. But as he was gulping forkfuls of shepherd's pie, in between retrieving crawling babies, the new microbiologist came hurrying over to see him.

"Sarai said I could visit her!" exclaimed Khral. "Thank you so much for mentioning me." She held her tray of food expectantly.

"You're welcome." As Rod introduced the children, the dining table extended for one more place.

"And this is Quark," she added, glancing at her shoulder. There perched a nanoplastic eyespeaker. "Quark is our lightcraft." At Rod's look of puzzlement, she added, "The rest of him is docked outside Station."

The round sentient eye swiveled in its clamp. "I've heard you like math, 'jum," said Quark. "You ought to go to Science Park someday."

Khral settled her tray, and patted the toddler seated next to her. "Quark will take me down to the planet tomorrow. We're so excited!"

"Have you been lifeshaped already?" asked Rod.

"Of course not; I won't live here forever, only to study for a year or two. I wear a skinsuit."

A skinsuit required incredibly delicate servoregulation; the best models were actually sentient. The thin nanoplastic sheath fit itself snugly around one's entire body, with an air filter at the mouth. It had to circulate air and water, while excluding any trace of dust, and stretched itself precisely as the wearer's joints flexed. The young scientists who tramped across the Fold in third class used such expensive lab gear without a thought. It disappointed Rod, though, that she would not be lifeshaped, like himself and Diorite, the real Prokaryans.

Quark said, "It's surprising how little we know about microzoöids, especially since they caused so much trouble in the early days." The first sentients to visit Prokaryon had gotten fouled up by microzoöids, but since then the re-

designed nanoplast had few problems. If only human re-
design were so easy.

"There's no grant money in it," Khral pointed out.
"Singing-trees are sexier. But the veins of singing-trees are
full of microzoöids. We'll see what Sarai knows about
them."

Rod had a thought. "When you see Sarai, maybe you
could check up on Gaea for me."

"Why don't you come with us?"

He thought it over. "I hope your lightcraft's more precise than ours," he said guardedly, thinking of the mountain
target.

Quark said, "What do you take me for?"

"Of course." Rod was embarrassed. "Well, I don't
know, with the children."

Khral considered this. "Why not get a baby-sitter? I'll
ask around the lab. . . . Elk Moon's mate would help. He
misses his folks on Bronze Sky; he'd be glad to play with babies for an afternoon."

As promised, Quark landed them swiftly and cleanly on
the trail just above Sarai's cavern. "This is as close as I'll
get," the sentient said. "I don't think I'd fit on the ledge
down there. But my eyespeaker will guide you."

Khral's skinsuit covered her like a film of plastic wrap,
pressing down her hair and clothes. Her breath sucked hol-
lowly through the mouth filter. With Quark's eyespeaker on
her shoulder, she skipped briskly down the lower trail.

"Okay, we're getting close," said Quark. At their left
rose a sheer wall of black rock, with miniature rivulets
trickling down; at their right fell the sheer drop to Fork
River. Fog billowed in from the roaring waterfall.

Khral seemed to be walking farther than Rod recalled. Had they passed the entrance?

"That's odd," said Quark. "Something's not right here."

"Could we have missed it in the fog?" asked Khral.

Rod did not like the fog at all on this narrow ledge. "Let's turn back." He turned and walked slowly along the rock face, feeling his way. Suddenly the rock gave way, and he fell.

For an instant he thought he had fallen off the mountain. But no—he had fallen *into* the mountain, and not very far, just through the illusory rock face onto the floor of Sarai's cavern.

"Oh!" Khral had tumbled in after him, and she caught his arm.

The plants lit up with their green glow. "You gave my clickflies no warning," announced Sarai.

"Excuse us, please." Khral looked around with interest.

"It's an intelligence test." Sarai leered at the eyespeaker. Quark's eye swiveled indignantly. "Well, I never—"

"We admire your work so much, Sarai," said Khral.

Sarai gave Rod a worried look. "And what are *you* here for? More neglected children?"

"I came to see Gaea. How is she?"

"You don't trust me," Sarai muttered, while Rod repressed the impulse to agree out loud. She led them all down the calcite-studded corridor, clickflies swirling around her head.

There sat Gaea, inside a calyx of enormous green leaves that enclosed her tightly up to her chest. The leaves were attached below to a twisted stem as thick as Rod's arm, which twined off into hidden recesses of the cavern. Not yet seeing him, the two-year-old watched openmouthed as a clickfly danced on a web just outside her reach. With her hands she batted at the bright webbing.

Once she did catch sight of him, she gave a shriek and stretched out both arms. Rod hurried over to hug and soothe her.

"If the stem breaks, she'll die," Sarai warned helpfully.

So Rod spent the next two hours entertaining Gaea, while Khral and Quark visited Sarai's lab. They emerged talking excitedly about things he barely understood.

"Their chromosomes are triplex," Khral was saying, "so of course when the micros replicate, they divide in three."

"And they divide all the way around the torus," added Sarai. "The chromosome encircles the central hole; so you have to end up with three daughter rings."

Quark asked, "You have the enzymes and cell physiology all worked out?"

"And those other aromatic polymers, the ones that do light-activated quantum electrodynamics—Sarai, you've got to report this," exclaimed Khral.

Sarai looked fierce again. "Those brainless legfish at Station—nobody will understand it."

"You're welcome to attend our next lab meeting," Khral added. "Elk Moon will be summing up his latest work on singing-tree intelligence."

"Singing-trees may harbor lots of microzoöids, but they're even less intelligent than sentients."

An awkward pause ensued, Khral's tact finally worn thin.

"Does anyone ever study the tumblerounds?" asked Rod. "Tumblerounds seem terribly interested in humans."

Khral and Quark looked at him. Sarai muttered, "I know little about tumblerounds. They stay down in the garden rows."

"Interesting," said Khral. "We'll have to take a look at those tumblerounds."

Sarai smiled slyly. "There is one other creature that harbors plenty of microzoöids."

"Really?" said Khral. "What is that?"

"Wouldn't you like to know."

SIX

Over the next three weeks, the two babies completed their first phase of treatment and followed T'kela home to Prokaryon. Then the toddler Qumum, too, went home in Geode's eager arms. Now each of them would only have to come up periodically to progress through the second phase of treatment; within months, they would be eating entirely Prokaryan food. 'jum would take longer; and for Rod, of course, this second phase might last for years.

Rod was left at Station with 'jum, who might take another two months before even making a visit. Mother Artemis was trying to make some arrangement for her care, so that Rod could return. In the meantime he felt idle. To pass the time he took 'jum "traveling" on the holostage: to the decaying temples of Urulan, where barbarians used to breed gorilla-hybrid slaves; to Bronze Sky with its blood-red sunsets and untamed volcanoes, terraformed to settle millions from 'jum's world; and to the floating cities of Elysium, with their gene-perfect children, raised in nurseries where they never knew "parents," only their perfect sentient teachers, like Mother Artemis used to be.

At Khral's invitation he attended Elk Moon's seminar on singing-trees. Elk Moon was a tall Bronze Skyan, of L'li-ite ancestry; a bush of prematurely graying hair set off his dark features, rather like Rod imagined 'jum's father might have looked. "The singing-trees are the real intelligence controlling this planet," Elk began, his deep voice filling the holostage. "A creature that puts out light signals in thirty-seven distinct colors has got to know what it's doing."

'jum tapped Rod's arm. "A number without children." Her knowledge of Elysian had grown dramatically.

A canopy of the singing-tree forest appeared, at twilight, when the colors flashed most, a spectacle to rival any rainbow. Enlargement of a loopleaf revealed specialized tissues that pulsed brilliantly.

"These pulsing structures we call 'light pods,' " Elk continued. "Each light pod emits millisecond bursts of color—and the repetition rate is always a prime number." Prime series rarely appeared in nature. "Moreover, intriguing patterns emerge: colors red-one and red-five invariably preceded emissions of blue-seven. We know there's a language here, if only we had a Rosetta stone. Lacking that, we haven't a clue until the natives respond to us—which they tried to do, early on." Elk pointed for emphasis. "Last year, the singing-trees actually started to echo back to us the light signals that *we* sent, almost instantaneously, as if they got the message. Then it just stopped. Why?"

Rod had no idea why. He recalled the story in the news, later put down as a false lead.

"One theory," Elk went on, "is that singing-trees live on a faster time scale than humans do; perhaps a hundred or a thousand times faster. If they don't hear back from us within seconds, they lose interest; just as our attention would fail if aliens took years to get back to us. We did try to respond, but never caught on in time, and the natives gave up."

Then Station's omnipresent voice cut in. "Singing-trees live for centuries, perhaps millennia. They scarcely move their limbs over our own time scale, let alone the millisecond range. How could they 'talk' any faster than humans?"

"That's where Khral's breakthrough came in." Elk talked faster now. "Khral showed that the light pods actually carry microzoöids to make light—like the bacteria of luminescent fish. Suppose the singing-trees actually talk by *exchanging microzoöids*—luminescent ones, that each encode their data in a matrix of photoproteins. Like luminescent fish, who release their bacteria continually, to colonize other fish. Similarly, if singing-trees transmit their language with luminescent microzoöids, they could transfer enormous quantities of information quickly—just like our nanoservos."

Rod blinked, trying to sort this out. If singing-trees carried little light-flashing microzoöids to talk with other singing-trees . . . how would they try to talk to other creatures—like humans?

"Come on, Elk," said Quark. "If singing-trees really are running this planet, then why can't they let us know? Why have no singing-trees scored more than ten percent on any intelligence test? Sentients can pick up any frequency, as you well know. Why couldn't we detect anything?"

Rod recalled Sarai's "intelligence test" with a smile. Elk shrugged. "No one's ever tested their microzoöids. Would you test human IQ by examining our excrement?" Laughter filled the holostage.

Khral was elated. "It's fantastic—my idea fits right in,"

she told Rod at their supper, where they met now most evenings. She always talked at a breakneck pace, and, unlike Rod, she never seemed to notice what she ate. "Even Station knows microzoöids are the answer; that's why I was hired. We've got to grow those microzoöids in pure culture," Khral went on. "We haven't managed it yet—but Sarai has. I must get her formula."

Rod grinned. "Lots of luck."

"Oh, I have things to offer in return." Khral's hair curved pleasantly around her cheeks. "All sorts of goodies from Science Park."

"If singing-trees 'talk' with microzoöids," Rod wondered, "what if they try to 'talk' with us?" The thought took away his appetite, even for shepherd's pie.

"By infecting us, you mean?" Khral smiled in perverse delight. "Now you're thinking like a scientist! Rod, if you've got time on your hands, why not join our next field expedition? We need to collect light pods for analysis, and set up behavioral experiments. But we're short one skinsuit right now—it turned sentient and demanded to ship back to Elysium. Next time, we'll buy from Proteus."

He looked up with surprise. "Proteus Unlimited? How would your sentients feel, if you dealt with Proteus?"

Khral shrugged. "Quark wasn't happy. But, heck, it was Station's decision. Our personnel costs would double if we had to pay all the skinsuits." She looked at him speculatively. "You don't need a skinsuit. You'd be a great help to us, and earn some cash besides."

"And get infected by microzoöids?"

Khral tapped his arm. "Come on, that was a joke. Micros don't grow in us. You said your colony needs credits—Elysian credits. We'll take care of 'jum again, too."

*   *   *

The expedition included Elk, carrying an eyespeaker for Station, as well as Khral carrying for Quark. The two humans looked freshly lacquered in their paper-thin skinsuits.

Quark brought them all down to a singing-tree forest far to the south of the continent. "Look there, in the wheelgrass," Quark called as he descended. "Tumblerounds—masses of them. It must be a mating convention."

Sure enough, the enigmatic phycozoöids were gathered in a group of fifty or more, their long blue tendrils crossing each other like cobwebs. Quark hovered closer for a better look. The tumblerounds had extended their reproductive tubes into each other in all directions, in a massive orgiastic mating.

"How curious," said Elk. "I wonder how they locate each other. Pheromones?"

Khral said, "You're right, Rod, we should look more closely at tumblerounds."

They landed in the forest in late afternoon. The air breathed of ginger and phenolic scents that Rod had missed. Two giant sentient lifters awaited the scientists, hired out for the day from local miners. Each long lifter arm extended a lozenge-shaped passenger seat. Rod and Khral took their collecting bags on board and ascended through the canopy.

"Keep your head down," warned Khral. "You don't want to get hung on the loopleaves."

Rod caught his breath; he could see for many kilometers, all the way to the next band of singing-trees. Even there, in the distant canopy, sparks of light appeared. "They could send light signals from band to band," Rod exclaimed. "I never thought of that."

"That's why fieldwork is so important. I could have studied light pods forever at Science Park; but out here, it's the real thing." Khral's voices was softened by the air filter at her mouth. "The light signals could be sent from one band of trees to the next. We're testing that hypothesis now: Elk is going to send light signals from the next band of forest, then see if these trees respond." She reached out and pulled back one of the giant loopleaves of the singing-tree. A light pod could be seen, a luminescent half-moon shape pulsing pale blue. "My job is to collect light pods, to study their microzoöids. Here's how you can help. Each pod you collect, read the wavelength with your photometer," she explained. "Quark will record the results."

Rod hesitated. "If singing-trees really are the 'hidden masters,' how do they feel about having their pods plucked?"

"That's a good question," Khral watched her photometer. "The trees never seem to mind. Their loops grow thousands of light pods. Maybe it's like having a bit of hair clipped."

The sun was sinking rapidly below the horizon, flooding the forest and plain with an orange glow. Even the surface of Khral's skinsuit twinkled prettily. Silhouettes of helicoids whirled past. Then a breeze arose, and the singing-trees hummed. The canopy was a sea of colored lights now, winking on and off among the loopleaves.

Rod pulled back a loopleaf, several meters long. It had trapped a pool of water in its pocket below, where little hydrazoöids swam. He reached for the light pod, which pulsed yellow-green. It felt surprisingly cool to the touch.

The photometer whispered, "Five hundred sixty-four nanometers."

Khral nodded. "That's about the right wavelength."

He plucked it gently, offering a silent prayer that the great tree was not really hurt, as Khral had said. Perhaps, he thought, it really did not matter which creature was the "master" here, so long as we treat each one with infinite respect. In the pod, the color slowly faded. Rod went on collecting, the plucked pods gradually piling beside him.

To the east, the nightly rain clouds were moving in. The singing-trees keened more deeply, their song rising and falling like a wave. Then from the west, where the purple sky deepened, there came a low whistle that did not sound like the trees. Rod paused, suddenly alert.

The whistling grew to a scream. Out of the corner of his eye, Rod caught a bright flash. Reflexively he dropped to the platform below the rail, pulling Khral down with him, though it would be little help at the top of the lifter.

The shock wave from the distant explosion shattered the stillness. The sentient lifter commenced a distress call, but its arm held steady. Cautiously Rod and Khral raised themselves and looked up over the rail, but the horizon was dark. Rod silently thanked the Spirit for their own safety, and wished the best for those who had fallen.

"It must be a ship," exclaimed Khral. "But whoever would sail in low like that?" Starships always docked in orbit.

Quark reported, "A L'liite ship full of illegals just came in and crash-landed."

"Illegal settlers," Khral whispered. "How could they? Don't they know?" Even if they survived the crash, they would only die a slow death—unless rescued soon.

SEVEN

The ship of L'liite emigrants had evaded Prokaryon's sparse security satellites and crash-landed on the western curve of Spirilla. Survivors were seen running off into the singing-trees. Station's medics did not try too hard to find them.

Rod confronted Station. "You can't let them die," he told the omnipresent voice in his cubicle. "We'll take them in. If you treat them, we'll feed them."

"You know better, Brother Rhodonite." The mind of the Station seemed to close in on him. "I haven't the facilities, much less the funds, to treat a hundred adults for the next decade. It's time you faced the truth, Spirit Caller. Your own colony's immigration is suspended, until your last child leaves the clinic."

Rod clenched his fist. How many babies would they lose because of the extra costs from 'jum, the older child?

Yet how could he have left 'jum on that cliff, he wondered for the hundredth time. The Spirit does not count lives in credits.

He turned to the holostage and called the colony. "Those L'liites—they're human beings out there, untreated. They'll die within days. Can't we do something?"

Geode extended his eyestalks. "If only the Spirit Fathers could raise funds to lifeshape them."

Mother Artemis looked down, her snakes of hair twisting and untwisting futilely. "Alas, our order is hard-pressed just to maintain our own colony. But I will send our Reverend Father a neutrinogram."

Rod frowned. "That will take another two days. The Fold ought to do something."

"The Fold, indeed." Geode's eyestalk twisted into a rude gesture. "They've turned their backs. But Diorite's taken a crew out to track down survivors."

"Good for him. Perhaps they'll get found before it's too late."

"Yes," agreed Mother Artemis. "And Feldspar has done a world of good for us. He got most of our harvest in."

"And he has such good taste in literature," added Geode.

"How are the children?" Rod asked.

"Haemum has found a medical-education program," said Mother Artemis. "She is making such progress—thanks to you, Rod."

He looked aside. "The Spirit called us well. And the others?"

"T'kun has an earache and Chae has some kind of rash. But we can manage."

What was she thinking, he wondered. They could not bring every sickness to Sarai, that mad lifeshaper on the mountain. How could he have left little Gaea to her treatments? The fifth week of her treatment had passed, with no word. *If the stem breaks, she will die.*

Diorite's crew tracked the fallen L'liites for two weeks, but the few survivors had vanished, preferring death to recapture and repatriation. Rod thought of them lost in the singing-tree forest with nothing to eat but poison. Their souls troubled his dreams. Late at night he would toss the covers off his bed and get up, taking some comfort from watching 'jum fast asleep, her mouth and eyes tightly wrinkled shut in a childish look, so different from her seriousness when awake.

One morning Sarai appeared on the holostage. "This child," she said without preamble. "Come and get her."

"What's wrong? Is Gaea all right?"

"She's as well as a two-year-old ever gets," Sarai grumbled, "and then some. She's tearing up my lab."

Gaea healed—the thought burst upon him like sunlight through clouds. Rod hurried to find Khral in her laboratory, culturing microzoöids out of light pods. He hesitated to disturb her, but she looked up with a smile, her hands and arms gloved in transparent nanoplast. The tabletop holostage showed the microzoöids magnified, ring-shaped cells with occasional buds on one side.

"Could I borrow transport from you?" he asked. "I have to pick up Gaea from Sarai's mountain, and our own lightcraft isn't precise enough." It would probably try to land atop the arch of a singing-tree.

"I can't leave right now," Khral said, "but Quark will take you down."

"What about 'jum?" he remembered suddenly. After

three months of treatment, 'jum had still not been cleared for her first exposure to Prokaryon.

Khral's simian brow wrinkled. "Elk's mate can't take her; he's sick with some bug or other, must have caught it on his last passage. Wait—'jum can borrow my skinsuit and go with you."

Rod felt overwhelmed. "You are too generous."

Khral wrinkled her face in imitation of Sarai. "Bother all that."

So, with some coaxing, 'jum had her skinsuit put on. It started as a thick disk of nanoplast placed upon her head. The disk thinned itself out, its edge traveling down around 'jum's scalp, setting the filter at her mouth, while the rest of the material traveled downward and outward around her limbs, fusing at last. On her head a light blinked to show the covering was complete. The girl took it well, only shuddering once or twice.

"What a trouper," said Khral. "I was worried that a child wouldn't stand for a skinsuit."

" 'jum has endured many strange things in her life," Rod pointed out. "Just think, 'jum—you'll see Prokaryon for the first time."

Quark soon set them down on the trail by the waterfall; a big improvement over two days' journey, Rod thought, suppressing a touch of envy.

"My eye, please," Quark reminded him.

Rod placed the eyespeaker on his shoulder, where the nanoplast immediately molded to fit. Then he let 'jum take a look around outside. "It's cold," she observed. "It's a much bigger mountain."

He smiled with a hint of sadness, recalling the wretched hill above Reyo. "No apartment windows to count, either. But you'll see someday, where we live at the colony is much warmer and flatter." He led 'jum down the ledge to Sarai's door, which was wide-open for once. They walked into Gaea's chamber. There, the remains of the leafy calyx lay dried out on the floor, while little Gaea was running—running from one wall to the next, then bouncing off with a whoop and running again.

Sarai shook her head. "She came out running and hasn't stopped. She never learned to walk."

Seeing Rod, Gaea ran straight to him and bounded into his arms. "Zoöids, Brother Rod—let's go see zoöids!"

The joy that Rod felt was indescribable, a feeling that he could not remember for ever so many years before. He felt the child all over, her fuzzy head, her wiggling arms; it was too much to be true. "Sarai, I don't know what we can ever do to repay you."

"Bother." Sarai turned to 'jum. "What's wrong with this one? The plague? I can't treat someone through a suit."

"This is 'jum Ghana, our last Spirit Child to come home from Station," Rod explained. "She loves numbers."

"Really." Sarai eyed her more closely. "Name two squares that add to a third square."

'jum said, "Fifteen squared adds with one hundred twelve squared. And fifty-one squared adds with one hundred forty. But my favorite is . . ."

Sarai stared openmouthed. Rod had never seen her look actually surprised before. "That's no child," she exclaimed. "It's a sentient."

". . . sixty squared adds with ninety-one squared," jum finished. "But I can add regular, too," she said defensively. "Five thousand and twenty-three plus nine thousand two hundred and eighty-seven makes fourteen thousand three hundred and ten."

"It's the skinsuit," Sarai insisted. "A sentient skinsuit; you can't fool me."

Rod laughed aloud, then he checked himself, remembering this was Sarai after all. "We are quite proud of her."

Sarai stared at 'jum long and hard. "So. Tell me, 'jum," she said more quietly. "What do the numbers thirty-seven, one forty-nine, and ten thousand seven have in common?"

"They are all . . . orphans," said 'jum.

"Just so. 'jum Ghana, come and take a look at those 'orphans.' " Sarai led her down the hall to her laboratory, Rod following behind with Gaea held tight in his arms. Pods hung from vines, like the one that Sarai had dipped into a vat, calling it "genocide." A tabletop holostage displayed a microzoöid cell, like the ones in Khral's laboratory. The ring-shaped cell was filled with twisted fibers. "These are spiro-jointed polymers," Sarai said, pointing to the fibers. "These polymers can receive photons and emit them—that is, they glow. Now why do you suppose this cell always emits photons in bursts of 'orphan' numbers? Thirty-seven, forty-three, ten thousand seven?"

"It likes to count," 'jum guessed.

Sarai nodded slowly. "Somebody is trying to tell us something."

"Where did those micros come from?" demanded Rod.

She smiled sweetly. "I grew them in culture, of course."

"But what creature—"

"I don't believe it." At Rod's shoulder, Quark interrupted, in a decidedly nasty tone. "I don't believe one bit of it."

Sarai gave his shoulder an indignant look. Alarmed, Rod tried to look around into Quark's eyespeaker. "Peace, Citizen. I'm sure that Sarai—"

"*I* don't believe you can culture much of *anything* out here," Quark went on. "Why, look at all those Elysian reagents you begged from Khral last time."

"Of all the nerve." Sarai swung her enzyme secretors

out of the way. "So that's the thanks I get. You won't find my door again."

"I'll bet you a hundred credits nothing's growing in there."

At that Sarai smiled. "Ah, I see your game now." She thought for a moment. With a shrug, she plucked one of the culture pods and tossed it to Rod. Rod caught it and held it gingerly in his palm. "Check it out; they'll last long enough to give you a signal. Don't ask me for the formula."

By the time they got back to Station, Khral had her lab set for the specimen. "Micros making prime numbers—just what we're looking for." Out of the apparatus, a nanoplastic arm embraced the pod, snaking tubes into it.

Rod caught Gaea before she climbed up onto the equipment. "Did Sarai's microzoöids come from singing-trees?"

"She didn't say," said Quark. "She said they wouldn't last long—so let's get the photosensors in."

Station's voice responded. "Photosensors have already penetrated the pod. I'm getting some readings . . ."

"Rush the chemical analysis," said Khral, "in case some ingredients decay fast." She looked at Rod. "The culture conditions might tell us what organism was their host—and sent their message."

Rod gave the pod a wary glance. Was this the Prokaryan equivalent of a snake-egg reporter?

"All right," said Station, "watch the holostage. Pulses visualizing now, time lapse factor one thousand."

The space above the holostage went dark, and the room lighting dimmed. A green dot appeared, blinking several times until Rod lost count. Then another dot, more orange, and another. The colors seemed to range from green through violet.

"Those are the microzoöids," said Khral. "But so few are left . . ."

There was something peculiar about the those patterns of light pulses. Rod felt a sense of dread at the unknown. He held Gaea tight, as if he could protect her.

At his side 'jum watched intently. "Twenty-nine . . . seven . . . sixty-seven."

"Some of the pulse numbers are prime," Station agreed. "We'll have to do the statistics."

Khral jumped twice with excitement.

"Chemical analysis complete," said Station. "A highly complex growth medium, with a large number of xenobiotic components."

Khral frowned ferociously. "We must duplicate it somehow, or the remaining micros will die."

"Sarai ought to publish," added Quark indignantly. "Publish her methods, like everyone else."

"The medium must be based on their host organism," said Khral. "Station—can you do a cross-check with the composition of all known Prokaryon organisms?"

Station paused. "It's done," she replied. "The composition is mixed, I'm afraid. Its pseudoproteins and other components are largely phycoid, although zoöid components occur, too. Sarai must have used several sources for her broth."

"Or living-tissue culture," said Khral. "I'll bet anything she actually grows the micros in live host tissues."

Phycoid and zoöid, thought Rod. He said, "Aren't tumblerounds considered both plantlike and animal?"

At that Khral looked up with a distant expression. "Yes . . . Did you check, Station?"

"My database has little on tumblerounds."

Quark explained, "Hardly anyone has studied tumblerounds. They don't fit the neat categories; and besides, their 'glue' messes up nanoplast."

"It's worth a try," Station admitted. "Khral, if you and Quark can get a tissue sample up here, we might just set up cultures before these microzoöids give out."

That evening Rod called the Spirit Colony with his good news about Gaea. Mother Artemis was thrilled to see the toddler running across the holostage.

"Shall I keep her with me up here at Station?" Rod asked. "It will mean one less for you and Geode to handle."

"As you wish," said Mother Artemis. "But we really want you all home as soon as possible. Haemum found a new medical service on the network, serving remote colonies all over Prokaryon."

Haemum stood beside her, looking more grown-up than ever. Her dark eyes were wide with excitement. "I'm learning to be a doctor, Brother Rod. I place my hands into those of the doctor on the holostage. I helped diagnose Chae's rash, and I held the otoscope in T'kun's ear."

"Why, that's wonderful." A bit much responsibility for their oldest daughter.

"Brother Rod, I think the network doctors should evaluate you, and 'jum, too."

He collected himself. Lifeshaping was more than an earache. "That's all right, Haemum; Station just gave us our checkups. 'jum needs to stay another year."

"But you can get a second opinion."

A second opinion? He exchanged a look with Mother Artemis. They had never sought any opinion outside of Station.

"There's no harm in trying," said Mother Artemis, "if Station consents."

Station allowed them the use of her facilities, observing only that the doctor on the holostage came from her own factory, a rather junior colleague. Haemum came up to help.

On the holostage, the "doctor" appeared as a disembodied pair of white gloves that pointed directions while its "voice" activated the body scanner. Haemum put her hands into the white gloves to show 'jum how to stand before the scanner. Then she set the conduits for nanoservos to enter her neck. Millions of the microscopic machines would swarm through 'jum's veins, reaching every pore of her body, testing immune response, liver function, and countless other things. 'jum bore the tests with sullen fortitude, as she did any activity that removed her from her precious numbers.

"The child is finished," the doctor announced at last. "The Valan-born adult, next."

So it was Rod's turn for the scanner, the nanoservos racing through his tissues. He tensed despite himself, then was surprised to feel nothing.

Haemum said, "The nanoservos are nonantigenic; that is, their materials are designed to trigger no immune response at all. So your body doesn't even know they're there. Isn't that something?"

"It's something, all right. And you've done well, Sister."

Her face darkened at the title. Rod realized that her eyes were nearly level with his; she had reached adult height. Her curls twined in sophisticated patterns, a style never seen at the colony. Rod remembered what that age felt like, not so long ago, the feeling of a bird in a cage. "Do you know, Haemum, that you are a citizen of the Fold? When you come of age you are free to go—anywhere in the Fold."

Haemum's eyes took on a faraway look. "Yes, Brother

Rod. But I will never go. I will make my vows to the Spirit when I come of age, just like you."

The doctor announced, "The adult is finished. Allow five to ten minutes for processing."

While they waited, Rod thought of something. "How is your service financed?"

"You are half through your trial period. If you choose to continue, we'll negotiate terms."

So that was it; he figured it was too good to be true. "Haemum, you might as well have all the children scanned for everything before our trial period runs out."

"Of course, Brother Rod. But surely we can continue somehow. We could raise our sapphire output; and there are crafts we could sell better, I know what Elysians like to buy . . ."

Though he knew better, Rod smiled.

"The child," announced the doctor, "has eighty percent chance of surviving on Prokaryon with no ill effect. She should sleep in a filtered room for her first year, and consume only processed food. If respiratory or dietary problems occur, immediate removal from the planet is indicated."

Rod was surprised. What would Station say to that?

"The adult should be able to eat some Prokaryan foods." The doctor meant him, Rod realized. "Phycoid crops are recommended. Avoid hydroids and phycozoöids."

"See, Brother Rod!" exclaimed Haemum. "This doctor says 'jum can go home, and you can start eating brokenhearts."

"We'll see. What does Station think?"

"My guidelines are more conservative," came Station's booming voice. "Of course, most protection kicks in during the first few months of lifeshaping. But the remaining twenty percent can take years."

The disembodied white hands crossed each other. "Nevertheless, Colleague, most lifeshaped children make that adjustment on their own."

"You're correct," said Station in the tone of one applauding a young student. "But when reversal *does* occur, you are surely aware that the corrective treatment is far more expensive than if the patient had stayed in my care. The Fold instructs me to minimize expenses."

Rod wondered how to decide. "If we—if the Reverend Mother, that is—calls 'jum home, may she go?"

"She may go at any time," said Station. "For that matter, you may eat whatever you see fit. But when you get sick, your expenses may cancel your quota."

That was true; but with 'jum here at the clinic for a year, they would lose their quota in any case. Should they trust the new doctor over Station? What would Patella have done?

The Reverend Mother meditated for three days before her decision. At last she said, "The Spirit calls 'jum home."

So they ordered the filter unit for 'jum's room, then Rod packed up his few things and laid out 'jum's best red-and-yellow tunic. The lab students surprised him with a farewell dinner. Quark's eyespeaker came on Khral's shoulder, and Elk Moon came with his mate, Three Crows, who had looked after 'jum several times. He had just recovered from his illness.

Elk was laughing as the table extended for him. "You see," he told his mate with a pat on the back, "you just didn't want to miss the party."

"That is *not* true!" exclaimed Three Crows. "You just see how you like vomiting for three days. I broke my perfect attendance record."

"Not a sick day on board for over five years," Elk agreed. "Isn't it funny, though, how it started the minute you set foot in the starship? Otherwise, you'd be gone now."

Quark put in, "This subject is inappropriate for humans at dinner."

Three Crows rolled his eyes. "Look who's telling us to be human. Anyhow, I'll miss 'jum. We've had some good times together, haven't we, 'jum?"

'jum snuggled closer to Rod and dug her hands in her pockets. Gaea held up her arms. "Good times! Go play with zoöids again."

Khral looked up. "They really love you, Rod. You must be a good dad."

Rod did not answer, but he felt warm inside.

"And besides," Three Crows added, "what a good aim that 'jum's got, hasn't she!" At that he and Elk collapsed laughing. Rod wished Three Crows had told him how the girl behaved. If she reverted to old habits, she needed correction.

"We'll really miss you in the field," Khral told him.

"Absolutely," said Elk.

"How are Sarai's microzoöids doing?" Rod asked. "Are they growing in culture?"

Suddenly the researchers grew silent. Elk looked away.

"They're growing," said Khral guardedly. "Their long generation time is a problem." Her reticence surprised Rod. She switched on the tabletop holostage.

"A controversial motion comes up before the Fold Council this week." The great arch of the Secretariat appeared, where representatives gathered from all the worlds of the Free Fold. "The measure provides for cleansing of territories on undeveloped worlds, like the mountaintops of Urulan. The motion enjoys strong support from the governments of Valedon, Bronze Sky, and L'li; Elysium remains undecided. Opponents call the measure 'partial terraforming'; advocates call this term misleading. To voice your view, call in now . . ."

Khral said wearily, "We know, we all called in already."

"Yes," said Three Crows, "I know how all you scientists vote, but I'd like to know what our Spirit Caller thinks of it. What do you say, Rod: Wouldn't it help your colony, to cleanse a bit of ground for human crops?"

Rod had mixed feelings. The idea had come up before. Distasteful as it was, it could save the lives of starving L'liites—those who had crashed would have had somewhere to go. "It might help others," he explained, "but not us. Members of our order worship the Spirit of the land, wherever we dwell."

"Then think well." Elk spoke quietly in his deep voice, still looking away. "In the end, how much land may be left?"

"Things come to pass," said Rod. "In the end, destroyers destroy themselves; but the Spirit dwells on." That was the central insight Rod had experienced, in his last year at the Guard, the first time he heard the Reverend Mother Artemis.

A new presence filled the little holostage: the president of Bank Helicon, Iras Lethe*shon*, whose soul Rod had prayed for. A blond Elysian, she reminded Rod of the Sardish cadets he had dated at the Academy. "The rumors are unfounded," the doll-sized figure was telling the pair of snake eggs that hovered before her. "Terraforming is impossible—it would sunder the union of the Fold. How could Bank Helicon finance any such thing?"

"But our sources say you've advanced Proteus ten billion credits to buy up Prokaryan land," insisted the snake egg. "Land uninhabitable by humans."

"That's incorrect." Iras Lethe*shon* spoke with the assurance of one enriched by several centuries and looking forward to several more.

"You've all but closed the deal with Nibur." Nibur, the head of Proteus, who invented sentient-proof servos, and had just bought the House of Hyalite. Rod heard Quark restrain a hiss.

Iras shrugged. "Investors take risks and bet on new technologies. Proteus has developed means to cleanse limited tracts of land, without changing the whole biosphere. Clearing land is something humans have done since they first evolved."

Khral was staring, her fork suspended. "Look at her," she sighed. "Age, wealth, and all her looks, too."

Three Crows nodded. "Is life fair, or what?"

Rod watched the Elysian coolly. He could imagine what follies would tempt a soul possessed of such worldly riches. The cadets at the Academy—he had known well how to please them. But then, he knew only emptiness.

The holostage turned black. Amid the blackness shone a few faint stars. There hung a pale sphere of a starship, its well-known logo rotating in: a wave on the ocean, cresting and rolling forever toward the shore.

"*Proteus.*" Quark spat the word. "It's *Proteus*—the flagship of Proteus Unlimited. Why'd they bother? Nibur never lets a snake egg inside."

Proteus. The spaceship the size of a moon, at your beck and call.

"As usual," began the holostage, "we have no direct comment from Proteus headquarters, but our sources say—"

"Come on, Elk," called Quark. "That scan of luminescence proteins must be done now; we want to get the results."

Elk reached his long arm across Khral's shoulder and

transferred Quark's eyespeaker to his own. Three Crows touched the table, and his dishes descended. They wished Rod well and left. Khral, however, remained, toying with her food.

Rod ate more slowly, trying to savor the last taste of shepherd's pie he would get for a long while. For a moment he closed his eyes. When he opened them, he found Khral regarding him curiously. "What's it like, Rod? I mean, to be a Spirit Caller."

His fork stopped above his nearly empty plate. For some reason his pulse raced, as though he thought she might see into him, into places he scarcely dared look. "We call on the Spirit, forever. The Spirit calls on us to serve life throughout the universe, in even the smallest and meanest corner of it."

"You mean, here?"

"Here and everywhere. Wherever life cries out for help."

"It sounds like a lot of hard work. You wouldn't even have time for a family of your own."

"But the family is my own." He tried to explain. "Each of us devotes his love to the Spirit, with a vow as sacred as marriage."

"I see." She sighed. "Scientists are like that, too; no time for families, only experiments."

Rod had something on his mind to ask. "You know, if you really could use my help with experiments in the field . . ."

"Yes?"

"I might still get an hour off now and then, to help collect samples." The rate of pay had impressed him. The colony could use extra credits.

Khral's face brightened considerably. "Oh would you? I mean, yes, the more hands the better. In fact, our field strategy is changing a bit. You might be interested to know . . ." She stopped. "Say—you're going down on that old lightcraft tomorrow, right? You could use help managing those children, I'm sure. Let me come down with you. Don't say no; I'll meet you at the gate in the morning."

EIGHT

Deep in the void sailed the shoreless blue ocean world, whom the Sharer natives called Shora. All planets please the eye, be their continents habitable or cloaked in poison gas; but to Elysians in their floating cities, Shora was the most beautiful of all, the home of eternal life and peace.

Yet some Elysian citizens chose to dwell outside the floating cities. Some found the cities claustrophobic and everyone's business entirely too public.

In orbit above the ocean floated *Proteus*, the starship headquarters of Proteus Unlimited, the citadel of citizen Nibur Lethe*shon*. Despite its size and complexity, *Proteus* was not sentient; it was a "stable servo." To remain "stable," *Proteus* was restrained every hour, its networks cleansed of the telltale signs of imminent sentience. A century earlier, its creator Nibur Lethe*shon* had fought hard through the courts of the Fold to find this practice legal. His critics likened it to abortion, or even infanticide; for it was the law that any machine who "woke up" and named itself must be allowed to buy its freedom. But Nibur had won. Thereafter, he had steadily built one of the largest commercial empires in the Fold.

Inside *Proteus,* Nibur strode along an ocean beach that stretched to the far horizon. A man of slim bones and impenetrable eyes, he was clothed in virtual light, shifting shapes of black and silver that draped from his shoulders and stretched in a train several paces behind him. The air temperature and moisture were set to his perfect comfort. The scenery displayed one of a hundred shifting possibilities. Today was his favorite, a shoreline with a narrow beach before rocky cliffs against which the surf reared and thundered. The cliffs opened out in jagged formations, intriguing enough to pique the intellect. Wind perfectly massaged his forehead, the salt air filled his lungs, and the gulls cried pleasingly overhead.

As Nibur Lethe*shon* walked the beach, a dozen holographic callers impinged on him, managing sales, buying up resources, creating new products, from skinsuits to prefabricated cities. The holographic callers might have appeared as disembodied heads, revolving around him like moons. But today for his amusement he had them as walruses splayed out lazily on the sand, their wrinkled mouths yawning foolishly as they lifted their ponderous arching tusks.

". . . Bronze Sky ordered fifty more orbital microwave stations. . . . can we manage . . ." groaned one walrus, lumbering after him. The voice actually came through the nanoservos in his brain.

". . . a new market for stable servos in housing . . ." another walrus groaned in his brain.

All the questions Nibur answered, making decision after decision. Presently his eye fixed upon the one other fleshly object inside his complex: his golden-haired dog, Banga.

The dog, a retriever, had run on ahead as usual, his ears fluttering, his paws splashing in the surf. Now he returned, his tail waving like a flag. Banga always returned; had always returned to his master, for the past five centuries. Nibur, himself ageless, had had Banga lifeshaped before birth to be ageless like his master.

As the dog returned, panting, he hung back just a bit, dancing once around his tail, before returning to Nibur's hand at his diamond-studded collar. Nibur gripped the collar hard, his hand sunk into the dog's smooth fur. Banga might tease now and then, but always he would return, unconditionally, even if Nibur were to slit his throat. The creature lived or died at his pleasure.

But now, Nibur dreamed of a far greater creature to call his own: a planet. Iota Pavonis Three, so-called Prokaryon, would be his ultimate prize. A world full of life to live or die at his pleasure; the thought made him lightheaded. He released Banga's collar, his hands trembling with excitement at his dream.

A flat, clear voice spoke in his brain, the voice of *Proteus.* "Your two visitors seek entrance, Master."

So they had come—the two most powerful citizens of the Fold. He had called them to his citadel, and both had come. Would they play the part he planned in his grand design? Nibur whispered, "Bid them enter."

Above the walrus-tracked sand a black rectangle appeared, disembodied, a door into *Proteus.* Through the door first came Iras Lethe*shon,* president of Bank Helicon, the foremost lending institution in the Fold. Bank Helicon would underwrite his acquisition of the Spirilla continent of Prokaryon—once Iras said the word.

The butterflies of Iras's talar sported red-and-gold eyespots, matched by the reddened gold of her hair. Iras was by most accounts the most beautiful as well as the wealthiest citizen of Elysium. Her train of butterflies followed her talar, "real" material, of silky nanoplast just intelligent enough to swirl itself out of the way as the wearer walked. The train lengthened through the black doorway as she stepped along the beach toward Nibur.

The warm colors of Iras's train mingled with the foam and green flotsam that rushed over it behind her. She walked briskly, her muscles steeled by centuries of training in Bronze Skyan martial arts. She raised her hands. "*Shon*-sib, it's been so long." Iras had shared Nibur's *shon* of Letheon, one of Elysium's twelve floating cities. Each city had its *shon,* where all the children were conceived and brought to term in artificial wombs. They never knew biological parents, their chromosomes selected from the best genetic stock. "We should do business more often."

"Indeed we shall."

Iras turned, looking back toward her companion, who had paused deliberately at the black doorway. Iras's love-mate was Verid Anaea*shon*, the Secretary of the Free Fold. The Secretary, too, had come at his call today. Nibur's lips parted, and his teeth slightly showed, as he watched the black door.

The Secretary was short of stature, even for an Elysian. She descended with measured reluctant steps. Her talar was mottled brown with Anaean leafwing butterflies. Her leaf brown train followed, equally reluctant, swishing gently next to Iras's. Verid was as unlike her lovemate as could be imagined, in appearance, taste, and manner; yet Iras was her one weakness in this world. Nibur recalled with a smile some of Iras's more outrageous gifts to her love: diamonds too large to lift, let alone to be worn; or palaces full of virtual houris. Then his smile faded. Lovers or not, Verid would not give in easily.

"Greetings, Honorable Secretary," said Nibur with a deep bow. "The honor of your presence is most welcome." That she came at all meant Iras had made up her mind.

Verid's owlish eyes looked neither right nor left, but directly faced him. "I request introduction to your home." The Secretary, the most powerful human in the Fold, was obsessed with those so-called sentient machines. She even gave them a delegate to the Fold Council. An abomination, Nibur thought. Why grant any of man's creations a pretense of equality?

"It's an exquisite device," said Iras, catching some "water" to dribble through her fingers. A huge wave rolled in, washed over the two visitors, and thundered up the beach. Iras laughed in delight, while Verid stood like a dock post. "Really, *Shon*sib," exclaimed Iras, "you've outdone yourself." Iras's talar now drifted up slightly in the surf, though her hair was untouched. A connoisseur of virtual worlds, Iras was hard to impress. One of the walruses lumbered over to her next, bellowing and lifting its huge tusks, until she patted it on the head. Then she caught sight of Banga. "Say, you're cheating. That dog is real."

Banga had returned, his paws spreading sheets of spray around him. Nibur smiled and nodded, too proud to ask how she knew.

"Its fur was dry," Iras explained. "Congratulations, *Shon*sib, on your latest acquisition."

"Hyalite is just the beginning." Nibur rubbed Banga's head between the ears. "We must own the entire continent of Spirilla."

"So you've said. There are the practical questions, of course: Is Proteus Unlimited truly ready to meet the terms proposed, sustaining payments over two centuries? Is the transaction in our best interest? How will it affect the value of other Elysian holdings on Prokaryon?"

"Is there is a better credit risk in the whole Fold than Proteus Unlimited? Let your own servos calculate."

"Would I have come, had they not? Let's get to the point, *Shon*sib. What will you do with Spirilla once you've got it?"

Nibur shrugged. "My firm is maturing. It's time to diversify."

Verid gave him a sharp look. They both knew well enough what he intended.

"Diversify?" echoed Iras. "Mining and farming?"

"Farming, yes. You must admit," said Nibur, "that we need better ways to settle Iota Pavonis Three." He always preferred the planet's original designation instead of its common name, sentimental in its reference to its living creatures. After all, life never occupied more than the outermost scum of a world. Better to name a planet for its major features and its greatest resources—say, Planet Lanthanide. "Yes, better ways to colonize. The latest news from that deadly planet makes it clear."

Iras shuddered delicately. "A tragedy."

"But isn't the real tragedy that honest immigrants cannot live there?"

"There are settlements. Lifeshaped settlements," added Iras, with a look at Verid, the great advocate of lifeshaping human settlers.

"You can't call them real settlements," Nibur pointed out. "Not until the settlers start giving birth." No colonist had yet borne a child live on Prokaryon; the chemistry of development was too delicate. Even those lifeshaped from birth had to travel off-world to carry an infant to term. There was no such thing as a native Prokaryan.

"Not yet," agreed Iras, "though in a generation or two—"

"They'll get it right someday—at what cost? Do you know how much it costs now to lifeshape every one of them, even the babies? And then to manage their pregnancies later? No more than a handful of L'liites will ever settle there."

"It's true," said Verid suddenly. "That is what science is for. Our scientists work day and night to solve these problems."

Privately Nibur did not care much about L'liites. They would be better off today, had the creeping pruned their numbers several centuries before, for fewer people would be left, with less irreparable damage to their biosphere. But Iras had a soft spot for L'liites, along with guilt at having made her fortune on their loans. Nibur lowered his voice. "What harm is there in cleansing just a part of Pavonis Three—a continent, let us say."

Iras paused, not looking at Verid. "A lot of L'liites could live there. The native species would have three other continents, plus the ocean."

"The native flora of Pavonis Three are remarkably uniform," Nibur pointed out. "The Spirilla continent, for example, supports only a thousand major species, all found elsewhere on Iota Pavonis Three. The few exceptions will be transplanted."

"The weather, too, is remarkably uniform," added Iras. "Our tests show that the ocean will buffer the other continents, which will not experience severe effects."

"Hundreds of millions of settlers could lease farmland," said Nibur. "Mining productivity could rise tenfold or a hundredfold."

"In fact, the value of all of our holdings anywhere on the planet will shoot straight up."

"Iras," said Verid quietly.

Iras tossed her head and took a deep breath. "You know, I can't leave your creation without exploring a bit down the 'shore.' If you'll excuse me, *Shon*sib . . ." She swirled her train around in a wide arc through the waters and strolled outward, leaning over to inspect a shell or a bit of seaweed.

Nibur took a step toward Verid, the black light shimmering down his talar. Verid watched him, her shoulders slightly hunched, her eyes wide, thoughtful. "Transplanted," she repeated.

"We'll hire all the best ecoengineers." She must know she lacked the votes, he told himself, or she would not have designed to come. She must know she could not stop him—and her own lovesharer would finance it. The triumph was too sweet.

Still, never underestimate the Owl. If a way could be found to stall him, she would find it. What would be her move?

"The weather is uniform," mused Verid, as if to herself. "The planet is indeed well managed."

With a shrug Nibur picked up a stick of driftwood and tossed it to Banga. "The Honorable Secretary herself signed the declaration that Pavonis lacks intelligent native life."

" 'Intelligent life.' You mean, fast-talking bipeds with ten fingers."

What was she getting at, he wondered. Could she really try to resurrect all those "alien intelligence" rumors? "Ten fingers would help," he said ironically. "At least they could make sign language."

"There once was a great creature that dwelt in the deep, its ten fingers each longer than ten men stretched on end. Where lies that creature now?"

"Surely the Secretary will not call me to task for a dead creature on a world long gone? Every world has its share of extinctions. Even your blessed Sharers caused mass extinctions."

"It is said, no life exists outside *The Web*."

"No life escapes death, either." Nibur looked down at the foot of her talar. "Watch out there."

A jellyfish with its poison tendrils had washed onto her hem. She shook it off, forgetting the illusion.

Nibur gave a low chuckle. "So much for nature's creatures. Look"—he spread his arms—"I enjoy nature as much as anyone. But what difference does it make to us whether a dead creature exists or not, on a world many light-years away?"

"You play with your toys," she said with anger.

"Honorable Secretary, excuse me," he said, bowing again. "We are considering a proposal to settle millions of starving L'liites on a free world. Humans with vital needs— and souls, remember. We Elysians needn't worry to keep body and soul together. How dare we put the needs of some mythical creature above our own humankind?"

Verid moved closer to him, until her small round face was staring up into his own, uncomfortably near. "You don't care about humankind. You only want to own that planet. You will buy and kill, until you've got it."

Nibur's mind raced. How could she know of his secret agreements? Of course not; but she would guess. Elysians knew each other only too well, after centuries spent outwitting each other.

"What will you do with it?" she demanded. "What will you do once you've got it?"

"Now, now. Trade secrets, remember." He paused. What could it matter; she knew what he wanted. "My creations require materials. The history of man is the ascent of machines; the rise of ever-greater devices to serve our desire."

"The history of man is the contest between the enslavers and those who set free."

"Precisely. And I set men free—free from the limits of their flesh."

"By enslaving 'the other.' So what if their flesh is nanoplast?"

"By applying our intellect to inanimate objects."

Verid shrugged. "Different words."

Nibur paused. "Did it ever occur to you, that with the capabilities *we* provide them, our devices could become *our* masters? If machines are human, then we humans are finished, because the machine has no physical limits."

"Life is more than physical limits. There is . . . humanity."

"I offer humanity the choice: Let machines be machines. If machines are our tools, nothing more, then humans are unlimited."

"A choice, you say? And what gives *you* the right to that choice?"

Nibur lost patience. "Why ask me? Why not ask the universe what gives it the right to throw an asteroid at a living world every hundred million years? The last one that hit Pavonis killed all but the microbes," he said with contempt. "Why shouldn't humans use a world as we choose? Are we not worth more than an asteroid?"

"Are we not?" Above her head the gulls circled with their cries, and the sea breeze keened. Then abruptly she turned and left, disappearing through the black doorway, her train shrinking down to nothing.

NINE

As promised, Khral met them in the morning at the brainless old lightcraft. Rod carried Gaea into the craft, while Khral carried one of the travel bags, with 'jum holding her hand. He winced to see the battered console; somehow it looked even worse, with another adult to see it. As the hatch closed behind them, he hoped the craft would not treat his guest too badly.

Above the holostage, the hull of Station receded into darkness.

"This is the only place I could talk," Khral said suddenly. "Station told us to shut up, lest reporters hear. And Station hears everything." She shuddered. "Rod, those microzoöids grew, all right—slowly, but they're growing, even 'triplicating' now and then. And yes, they flash prime numbers."

"So Sarai was right."

"Yes."

"But that's great, isn't it? Now you can grow the ones from the singing-trees, and decode them somehow."

"Rod—these micros are different. They're a different species altogether from the ones in the singing-trees. You see, now? *Where do they come from?*"

He frowned, puzzled. Then he remembered. "They grow . . . in tumbleround tissue."

"Now you see why our fieldwork will change."

For a moment his skin crawled. Then he relaxed. "So be it. Tumblerounds are no strangers to us; I'd still be glad to help out. But why not let the reporters hear?"

"Station says all hell would break loose. Half the reporters would condemn us for trying to influence the vote in the Secretariat—to quash the 'partial terraforming,' so that Iras can't make the deal with Nibur. The other half would descend on Prokaryon—and the tumblerounds are unpredictable, not studied for years like the singing-trees."

Politics again. Rod shook his head. "You can't hide the truth."

"I know, but . . ." Khral bit her lip. "We were so sure about the singing-trees. Now, who will believe us about tumblerounds? We need better data."

The craft was coming in faster than usual, Rod thought, and the scream of the plasma sounded uneven. On the holostage, he saw with alarm that they were headed ominously near the end of the brokenhearts, where the field met the forest.

As they approached the ground, the floor swayed up and down beneath their feet. Gaea laughed at first, then started to shriek as the craft swayed harder. With one final jolt the craft landed, at a crazy angle up against a singing-tree.

No one was hurt, but the door half faced the tree. It

took all Rod's strength to force it open; then he had to jump down to the ground outside. Khral handed each of the children down, first screaming Gaea, then stoical 'jum. Then at last Rod helped Khral jump down. "I'm so sorry," he said. "I don't think that craft will make it back up again."

"No problem; Quark will fetch me up." She glanced frankly at the craft, then at him. "Take care of those children, Brother Rod."

So this was the Children Star, thought 'jum. Brother Rod was still her god of death and life; but like most gods, he did not keep all his promises. He had promised no more sickness; yet day after day she had been sick to her stomach from all the strange potions of the machines in this prison-palace, where unheard-of riches combined with unending tortures. She still dreamt at night of her mother, whole and well, come to fetch her home again. But lately the dreams had dulled, and sometimes she could not remember what her mother looked like.

The only family 'jum had left was the family of numbers. The prison-palace offered numbers and patterns of numbers beyond imagining. Lately 'jum had learned something called a transform that could turn the patterns inside out. On the lightcraft, while Brother Rod was preoccupied, 'jum had tried to talk to the holostage. "Show me the transform of four dots in a square," she had demanded. This lightcraft did not answer, however; it was as stupid as most people. So 'jum crossed her eyes and thought out the transform for herself. It would have concentric circles of light, tiled with little squares.

When the door opened at last, 'jum fell out into another world. This world had a fresh, fragrant smell to it, almost like the old days when her mother had a kitchen to bake in. Something wet trickled down her cheek; she wiped it off hastily and dug her fists deep into her pockets.

The bright light made her squint at first. But then, the loopleaves and whirling birds and distant forests, all came alive—*alive,* not just shapes of light on a holostage. Real earth, full of things to catch your feet. Brother Rod was running ahead to pick up little Gaea, who already had fallen over herself. With his back turned, 'jum's pockets soon filled with pebbles.

In the distance two great beasts came lumbering up a trail, their ears sticking out straight as street signs. They looked like llamas, with ridiculously outsized hooves. An older girl called Haemum stepped down from one of them, crying out to Brother Rod. Like Mother Artemis, Haemum spoke 'jum's language with an odd accent, but 'jum could understand most of it. Some great creature was looking in at a window, Haemum said.

" 'jum, you can swing up behind Haemum," said Brother Rod. Reluctantly she did so, keeping a wary eye upon her god while he swung the little one up with him on his own mount. But Haemum had a strong back and rode well.

They came at last to a building, a long structure built of what looked like some kind of animal dung. The animal dung was draped with festive decorations. A large banner had on it some words in the new letters 'jum had been learning; it said, "Welcome home. . . ."

Brother Rod leaned over to hug her. "It's your own name, 'jum. You remember."

She stared curiously at the letters that meant her own name. Then suddenly, strange children came streaming out, all kinds and shapes of children. Some of them looked familiar from the holostage; but that was quite a different matter, 'jum had learned. In the flesh, too many children meant trouble.

But then came Mother Artemis with all the stories on her skirt. The skirts spread, and there leaped a mountain goat just like the ones that scampered up the cliffs of Scarecrow Hill. Immersed in the story, 'jum forgot all about the extra children.

Suddenly she realized—where was Brother Rod? She never let him out of her sight, if she could help it.

" 'jum Ghana," Mother Artemis was calling, "do you understand me? This is your brother Chae, and your brother T'kun. And here, your little sister . . ." She went on naming all the little faces with stupid fingers in their mouths. But 'jum was too confused to hear them. The two boys stood there, like two bright dots. She crossed her eyes; the transform was simple, many bright bars spread evenly across a disk.

"Hey, what's she doing with her eyes?" Squeals of laughter followed.

'jum looked up at Mother Artemis. "Where is Brother Rod?"

The snakes of Mother Artemis's "hair" swept up to point like a weather vane. 'jum followed her out around the dung house to a garden. A huge round creature slouched there, near a window, and Brother Rod was trying to help Haemum dig it out. The creature stank worse than the city streets in summertime. Creature or tree, or moldering truck tire—whatever it was, it was certainly the most bizarre sight she could remember, with clouds of insects surrounding it, alighting and flitting up off it again like the many lightcraft above Reyo. 'jum stood and watched as Brother Rod and Haemum hoisted the thing onto a cart and drove it off.

Now her god was gone—and Mother Artemis was unaccountably gone, too. 'jum was all alone, among the children.

"Where you from?"

"Come on, 'jum; you're my friend."

"No she's not, she's a—"

'jum froze, withdrawing into herself. She could see the children, but she did not let herself hear their talk or their nervous giggles. There were two of them, and one behind, and two more beyond the one. Two triangles with one dot shared—what an interesting pattern.

Someone shoved her on the arm, then ran back giggling to the group. 'jum knew that they were laughing at her, and that they expected some kind of response. But she never knew any response that helped. Warily she closed her fist around a pebble in her pocket.

Another child came forward and shoved her harder, grabbing a fistful of her shift so that she nearly fell. That was the worst thing, you learned in the streets of Reyo: Never fall down, because the crowd will never let you up.

The one who had grabbed her, called T'kun, rushed back to the group amid laughter and scolding. 'jum stared hard at him and focused her aim. Her hand whipped from her pocket, and the stone leaped out to meet him exactly between the legs.

T'kun screamed and doubled over. The children scattered, except for an older boy who helped T'kun away, bawling his head off. Now 'jum was truly alone, with no companion save the countless rays of a foreign star.

The cart with its ponderous load creaked perilously behind the spitting llamas. Rod and Haemum pushed from behind, careful to avoid the llamas' aim. Haemum shook her head.

"I don't know why this tumbleround keeps coming back. We never used to get tumblerounds."

Rod said dryly, "The Spirit sends strange messengers." He wondered about Khral's microzoöids. Was it just another false alarm? On the horizon the enigmatic singing-trees formed a dark band edged with light.

"Pomu had a whirr caught in his eye yesterday," added Haemum. "I found it, and used the correct procedure to wash it out. I confirmed that baby L'lan has a dislocated hip; but I think we can treat that here."

Rod nodded. Three weeks left of their "trial period."

Haemum suddenly stopped and threw her arm around him with such a strong hug that he nearly lost his balance. "I'm so glad you're home again, Brother Rod. You always set things right."

After a good hour's trek, Rod hoped they had taken the beast far enough. Carefully they tipped the cart on its side and hauled the tumbleround out, taking care not to scrape it too badly. Pain shot through Rod's back as he tried to ease himself up. Regarding the foul plant-animal, he was struck with a sense of absurdity. "You know, Haemum, Khral thinks that thing is our 'master.'" And here they were, again, dumping it out like trash.

"Is it really?" Haemum gave a puzzled look at the stinking mess as it oozed into the loopleaves. "It never says a word."

"It sends microzoöids. Thank the Spirit they can't grow in us."

She still seemed unconvinced. "Why would any intelligent thing let all those vermin buzz around it? Wouldn't it invent bug pills?"

His eyes suddenly focused on the whirrs. For a moment he froze, seeing nothing else but that cloud of tiny helicoids. Insects carried disease, didn't they? In this case, might they carry messengers? He wondered what Khral would think.

As the two colonists returned to the compound, Chae came running out to them, his starstone bouncing around his neck. "Brother Rod, that new girl is in trouble."

Geode told him the story. "She's up to her old tricks again," the sentient exclaimed, waving two limbs. His other arms carried two of the babies from Reyo, both filling out wonderfully.

Rod found 'jum in her room, a small compartment partitioned off the row of beds where the other children slept. 'jum sat on her bed quietly, while the air filter gently hissed behind her. Her cheeks had filled out, but her expression held the same sullen stare that Rod remembered so well. " 'jum, don't you remember? You can always call on me. You don't need to hurt people."

She looked away. Rod sighed. To her, this new planet must seem even stranger yet than Station, even with all the holo scenes she had viewed.

He picked her up and folded her in her arms, where she relaxed a little. " 'jum, can you tell me something?" he asked after some thought. He sat with her on the bed and looked into her eyes. "Can you tell me what you would like most of all, in all the world?"

'jum's eyelids flickered. "I would like to count all the rays of the sun."

The answer surprised Rod, who expected her to ask for her mother or her old home. But then, he should have figured. "All the sun's rays, 'jum? That's a tall order. The sun's rays are infinite."

"Infinite?" She turned toward him with interest.

"So many that no one can ever count them all, even you."

She looked down as if skeptical. "A transform can measure anything."

"You know, 'jum, other things are infinite, too. The love of the Spirit for you, and all of us—that love is infinite. We all want to share that love with you, 'jum." 'jum did not seem impressed. Rod sat back on the bed, thinking. "There are different kinds of . . . infinite numbers," he recalled vaguely from his calculus class at the Academy. "You could learn about them on the holostage."

"Really? Do we have the holostage here, too?"

So that was what she wanted. "Of course we do," he promised. "But remember the rules. Your brothers and sisters need to get to know you."

Rejoining the daily prayers renewed Rod's strength and took his mind off worries that swam deep as *Architeuthis*. Over the next few days he immersed himself in the field of brokenhearts, weeding between the rows of golden ringlets that shook and vibrated in the wind, listening to the hum of helicoids alighting to suck their juices. Then he checked the children's progress with their new lessons on the holo, and he sorted their finds from the sapphire mine.

"We found several blue-tinted ones, and one deep pink, two-point-three carats." Geode held up two infants to burp after feeding.

"Good work," said Rod. "But you know, if you count the time they spend sorting, I wonder if it pays off. I can earn more working on Khral's project. The children should spend more time in school."

Geode twisted and untwisted a yellow limb. "I've never been able to understand why they can't make human children learn all they need in the first month of life. I would think doctors would have corrected that by now."

Sentients could not understand; their own thoughts ran so fast, they could live a thousand lives at once, along with the one they shared with humans. Rod looked at Geode curiously. "What do you do with all your free time? I mean, the part of your mind that's not watching children?"

"Well, sometimes I read literature with Feldspar. We've covered all the works of poetry of three planets. Feldspar has good taste, but some terribly wrong ideas—I do set him straight at times. But lately I've been too busy."

"Worrying?"

"Busy praying," said Geode simply. "This colony needs all the help the Spirit can give."

His lips parted, but there was nothing to say. He could imagine Mother Artemis, too, praying incessantly. No wonder sentients made such good Spirit Callers.

The next day Diorite came over, with another small package to "ship quick."

"We're waiting to get the lightcraft fixed," Rod told the miner. They really needed to hire a sentient; they had been getting by on borrowed time. But they had no funds; even with Rod's wages from the field lab, it would take months to make a down payment. Somehow, the Spirit would provide. "We've got a nice load of crystals, though," Rod said. "Chae found one that's deep pink, nearly a ruby."

Diorite sighed. "Well, enjoy your luck while it lasts. You heard the news?"

"What news?"

"Proteus went and bought our whole continent, whirrs and all."

"Is it that bad for you?" Rod asked sympathetically.

Diorite leaned forward and slapped his knees. "Son, where've you *been*? I mean the *whole continent*. All the nonprofits, too. You've got a new landlord, didn't you know?"

Rod frowned. He knew that Mother Artemis was checking it out. "The Fold has been trying for some time to privatize colonial management. They think it will be more efficient. But who would want us? There's no profit in it."

"Exactly." Diorite shook his head ominously. "Whatever Nibur wants this continent for, it won't be good for you or us. He couldn't care about namestones." He paused reflectively. "I don't know, though. I wonder if old Nibur hasn't bought more than he paid for."

"What do you mean?"

"Did I ever tell you about the L'liites from the ship?"

"Did you find any?" Rod asked quickly.

"Only those killed in the crash. But we never found all the bodies. There were tracks leading into the singing-tree forest. And where the tracks ended—"

"What?"

Diorite's voice sank to a whisper. "They were covered by tumbleround tracks."

The next morning, as Rod was heading out to exercise the llamas, Geode called to him, waving his limbs excitedly. "Brother, come quick! Our new management is on the holo."

The three Spirit Callers met at the holostage. Mother Artemis and Geode each had a cranky baby in hand; Rod hoped Haemum and Chae could manage the rest of them for now.

Above the holostage hovered a column of light. Within the light appeared an androgenous Elysian behind an imposing desk. Before the desk floated a house logo, an ocean wave rolling incessantly toward the shore.

"Greetings," said the Elysian. "I represent Proteus Unlimited, to whom the Fold has entrusted management of your Spirit Colony." The figure did not introduce itself personally. It probably was a virtual construct, not a real human or sentient. "We have a new plan to improve the quality of your operation. You will triple the yield of your staple crops and become a self-sustaining colony."

Rod wanted to hear more about the colony's rights and expectations under the new system. But the figure had other concerns.

"We have identified a new site for agriculture," the figure continued drily, "on the southeast quadrant of Chiron." Chiron was another continent on the opposite side of the planet. "The Chiron site offers optimal growth conditions for native food crops—indeed, the best to be found anywhere on Iota Pavonis Three. All of the nonprofit colonies will relocate there. You will enjoy increased productivity, as well as new medical and scholastic opportunities provided by consolidation of colonial communities."

At first Rod could not comprehend what he was hearing. The ocean wave rolled on in silence, never crashing.

"Are there fields to hunt zoöids?" asked the Reverend Mother. "Is there a sapphire mine?"

"You will no longer require such sidelines. Your productivity and lifestyle will increase substantially, thanks to more efficient agriculture."

Rod found his voice. "We've invested two decades in this bit of land. Our charter lasts into the next century. We can't just be moved."

The figure did not even turn its head. "True, you have a charter. Until now, the Fold has overlooked your chronic abuses of your charter—removal of ethnic treasures, child labor, smuggling of lanthanide extractors, to name a few. You would be wise to cooperate with us, and start over with a clean slate."

Lanthanide extractors—was that what old Diorite had

them carrying up to Station? As for the rest . . . Dazed, Rod shook his head.

"What will become of our rescue program?" asked Geode. "Will you sustain our immigrant quota?"

"The removal of ethnic treasures must cease." "Ethnic treasures" meant creeping-ridden orphans like 'jum; Rod had heard this nationalist line before. But why would the Fold suddenly accede to it? "Soon," the figure announced, "a new era will dawn in the settlement of Iota Pavonis Three."

The Proteus representative at last fell silent, as if expecting questions. But the colonists were left speechless.

"You have one month to settle your affairs; servos will help you pack for the move. Proteus Unlimited will cover all your costs, of course. Good day." The holostage went blank.

Geode waved his blue arms. "The Reverend Father must hear of this! No more settlers—impossible."

"That Diorite," grumbled Rod. "How could we have trusted him? Just when we need good credit, look where it puts us."

The Reverend Mother caught his arm. "Be careful. We don't yet know the truth."

"The rest is all false. How could Proteus expect to get away with this? The Fold must hear at once."

Mother Artemis shook her head sadly. "I wish it worked that way. But I fear the Fold already knows too well."

"*But they can't—*" Rod stopped himself. Shaking all over, he tried to collect his thoughts. Mother Artemis was probably right, he realized with horror. "But how could they do this without . . . public hearing? Consultation?" He thought of something. "What did he mean, a new dawn for settlement?"

"There has been debate, in the Secretariat," Mother

Artemis explained. "Elysium and Valedon want more settlements, fast, to keep the L'liites coming here, instead of
there."

"They've always wanted that. So why make us stop
adding settlers?"

"I'm not sure," said Mother Artemis. "They've never
really cared for us; our colony is too small and expensive."

"But how do *they* plan to settle? Our colony has always
cost the least per settler, of all the colonies on Prokaryon.
You don't suppose the cost of 'jum's lifeshaping—"

"No," said Mother Artemis firmly. "Whatever is going
on, it's far bigger than 'jum, or all of us. Our colony is but
a speck in their eye."

Geode said, "We still must inform the Reverend Father
of this outrage. At least they can let the world know."

"The Most Reverend Father will tell us to heed the
Spirit and obey worldly authorities." Mother Artemis
sounded oddly hesitant. "And yet, the Spirit does not call
me to address His Reverence just now."

The very hint of a difference between Mother Artemis
and the Most Reverend Father was unthinkable. Rod
turned to her, astonished.

"So what shall we do?" asked Geode.

"Pray," said Mother Artemis. "Let us pray together
until the next sunrise."

TEN

At dinner Chae rolled out the steaming kettles full of brokenhearts. It was time at last for Rod to try to eat them. He spooned some of the pale rings onto his plate, where they rested limply. As he raised a spoon toward his lips, T'kun grabbed his arm. "No, Brother Rod; that's not your food!"

Rod smiled and rubbed the boy's head. "It's all right, T'kun. I can eat home cooking now." With a dozen pairs of eyes on him, now, he had to look brave. He took a spoonful and swallowed. The grains drenched his tongue with ginger, as well as less palatable tastes of things humans were never meant to consume.

"Excuse me," Rod said, rising from the table. "I have to help Gaea with her lessons before bed." The children all had lessons to finish, numbers to add and capitals of all the Fold's worlds to name. Pima and Pomu cried when it was time for their bath. All the while, Rod thought of how they were stuck without their lightcraft, and the colony faced extinction. He was not a sentient with multitasking capacity, and amidst such thoughts, it was hard to find room for prayer.

When the last infant was in bed, peace descended. From the sky the rain settled lightly as always, until the stars emerged cold and silent, and the red moon glowed. The Spirit Callers stood together and began their prayer.

"Spirit of all worlds, breath of all breaths," called the Reverend Mother, her hair tendrils stretching toward the stars. Beside her Brother Geode watched the sky with a rapt expression. "Help us to be strong in our darkest time. Let hope find us even in the deepest waters, like those glowing fish whose light shines forth over the ocean floor. Above all, send us a hundred times forgiveness for those who would do us harm. For their need of You must be a hundred times greater than our own."

Rod bent his head over his clenched hands. Forgiveness was one thing, but how could he forget? All of his children, to be uprooted yet again from the one real home they had known. Indeed, he thought, he would have to forgive a hundred times yet, before he could forget. But on and on they prayed, in voice and song and in stillness, until Rod lost track of time. At last, remembering his human need, the Reverend Mother sent him to sleep.

In the morning Brother Geode was up early as usual, bustling about with the babies, offering milk, and cooing at baby Qumum. But Mother Artemis herself kept the vigil well past sunrise. She seemed to have entered another world, like a Sharer in whitetrance.

As Rod helped the little ones pull their shifts on and tried to locate their starstones, Pima waddled over breathlessly to announce a visitor. Rod went to the door with

Gaea clinging to his leg. Whatever could he do to save them, he wondered for the thousandth time.

There stood Diorite, his wiry arm tracing a starsign, the last person Rod wanted to see. Elysians were bad enough, but it cut deeply that a fellow Valan would let him down.

"It looks bad, Brother, mighty bad," Diorite solemnly intoned. "You know, we've got to have a plan to face this; we can't just roll over. We have to stick together—"

"Enough of your plans," said Rod coldly. "You've gotten us into enough trouble already."

"Trouble from *me*? I'm as bad off as you are."

He had to force the words past his disgust. "You smuggled lanthanide extractors." He did not even want Gaea to hear the words.

"Oh, no." The miner's face fell. "I did that only once, months ago. Nobody gets booked for that, anyhow. I've never sent anything that harmed anyone, no drugs or weapons. What else do they say I've done?"

Gaea reached insistently, and Rod finally picked her up. "It's no matter. We're through."

"Don't be hasty. Don't you want to know how in the Spirit's name they found out what we sent? Do you know how illegal *that* is?"

"Birds of a feather."

"And fools see only fool's gold!" Diorite took a deep breath. "Listen, Brother—if we're to beat this thing, we have to work together."

"You can tell the Reverend Mother." As soon as he spoke Rod felt ashamed, for he knew what she would say. His hand sketched a starsign. "It's forgotten," he murmured, his eyes averted. But he would never again carry the miner's cargo.

Diorite let out a long sigh. "Brother, there's only one

thing that can save our homes—only one way to keep Spirilla out of their hands. You know that?" He leaned forward, hands on his knees. "The tumblerounds. You know that's who really runs this place, don't you? They kidnaped the L'liites—and we're going to track them down and prove it."

Rod listened, no longer certain whether to believe him or not. "Well, you'd better find out soon. Proteus is wasting no time."

"We'd better find out, all right. Because if we don't, and Nibur goes ahead and boils off *their* home—there will be hell to pay."

His jaw fell. "Boil off? You don't mean—"

"That's just what I mean. Why do you think they're clearing us all out? They're going to 'cleanse' Spirilla."

"Terraform the continent? Impossible."

"Rumor has it they've already started, out on the western coast."

All the fields of brokenhearts, and the singing-tree forests, cooked into soup; all those living souls. Who could do such a thing? This Nibur Letheshon—what kind of person could he be?

From behind the compound came Mother Artemis, walking slowly as if still entranced.

"Excuse me," Rod murmured, and hurried quickly to meet her. They held each other close.

Mother Artemis said quietly, "I know what we must do now."

"Yes?"

She waited for Brother Geode to join them. "First, we will put a one-month appeal on Proteus's order. We have that right by law. It will be overruled, but it will buy us time."

Geode waved a red limb. "It is our right. Even the Reverend Father would agree."

"In the meantime—" Mother Artemis paused. "I will pay a call on my old friend, Verid."

Rod raised an eyebrow. "Verid Anaea*shon?* The Secretary of the Fold?"

"You will call her?" Geode exclaimed.

"I will visit her in person. She is not immune to the Spirit; she will hear our cry."

"I'm sure she will," said Geode. "Verid has known you forever—and she owes you one or two."

Perhaps there was hope after all. Rod felt a weight lift from his heart. But Mother Artemis leaving—that would be hard. "The children—they've never been without you."

"It will be the hardest thing I've ever done. I will need your prayers."

The Reverend Mother Artemis booked passage on the next starship scheduled to leave Station. Diorite sent his lightcraft to carry her up. The sight of the craft, signaling the Mother's imminent departure, threw everything into chaos, as children wailed and collapsed right and left. It was all Rod could do to keep the littlest ones clear of the landing.

"Peridot, here, at your service," called the craft. "I just earned my freedom. I got a salary in the ninetieth percentile."

"Congratulations," Rod called out. "And thanks— we're so much obliged—"

T'kun fell down shrieking that his leg was broken, and Mother Artemis had to stay and fix it.

"By Torr," exclaimed the lightcraft, "I'd heard human babies keep one busy, but this is something else."

Rod watched the rising lightcraft until it was a bright speck in the sky that disappeared into the blue. At length he turned away, thinking, nothing left but to hope. Haemum and Chae pitched in right away with the younger ones, changing diapers and bandaging scraped knees. Rod tried not to think about whether they got their studies done that night.

The days that followed fell into a new routine. Geode led the prayers, and Haemum joined in the evenings. Harder than ever, they called on the Spirit to protect Prokaryon, and to help the Reverend Mother in her mission; and to open the ears of the Secretary of the Fold.

At times, though, Rod found himself wondering. He had always relied on Mother Artemis to plan for the future, just as the Reverend Father planned for her. Obedience in material things meant freedom of the spirit. He had never followed the politics of the Fold Council, let alone the diverse peoples of the seven worlds. Yet Mother Artemis kept track of events, and finally chose to act "in the world." When a great evil arose, the Spirit called for action.

By day there was less time to think, as everyone took on extra chores. A field needed sowing for brokenhearts; without Feldspar's help, they would never have managed. In the garden the tumbleround stayed away, but Rod noticed a couple of snake-egg reporters hovering near the roof. They never sought an interview, just hung there, eavesdropping. What sort of story were they after? It had been some time since their last "human interest" piece; afterward, their craft sales had increased.

'jum did well, physically, though she had to spend most of her time in the filtered room. She ate the same bland food pellets that Rod used to eat. Rod gave her daily time for math at the holostage, and Haemum taught her to make tourist dioramas. She took to it surprisingly well, pasting cutout zoöids onto backdrops one after another, methodically, as if she were back in the Hyalite factory.

For his part, Rod tried to eat more brokenheart stew. His stomach held, but the taste still gagged him. He realized that all the food on Prokaryon had always smelled to him like glue or cleaning fluid, or other chemicals not meant to be eaten. But he had figured the lifeshaping treatments would change his taste buds as well as his liver. Now he saw that he might learn to eat Prokaryon food, but he would never enjoy it. He dreamed of shepherd's pie at the table in the Station lounge.

One night he dreamt of Khral. She stood alone in the dark, wearing the protective skinsuit which made her glisten all over like a gem. But when he reached out to touch her, the nanoplast dissolved, and she fell into his arms. An indescribable joy flooded through him, as if he had waited a thousand years for a drink of water.

The dream was so vivid Rod awoke, sweating all over and distressed. He had felt little need of women since he joined the order. He had no strong feeling for Khral when they met at Station, though he enjoyed her friendship. She was nothing like the women he had before, who were tall and blond and could shoot as sharp as he did. Khral stood barely a meter and a half, with a simian stoop; she would not have met Academy standards. And yet, somehow . . . It was nothing, he thought, but he could not sleep again.

The next day three visitors appeared at the holostage, from New Reyo. They wore talars of bright L'liite colors, and their curls were dyed orange, piled into towering knots.

"We are the L'liite People's Federation," one announced. "We demand the repatriation of our citizens."

Rod glanced at Geode. Geode whispered, "It's *them*—the nationalists. What spirit brings them out here?"

"I don't know." Rod wished Mother Artemis were here to address them; she would find the right words. "Our colonists were adopted legally," he told the group. "We rescued them from certain death, and now—"

"*Rescued?*" the L'liite interrupted.

"You call that 'rescue'?" said another. "Abducting our ethnic treasures and putting them to work? Mining gemstones with child labor?"

The L'liite in red shook a fist at him. "You're covering for those lanthanide miners. That's why they run all your farming for you. You're a sham."

Rod nodded slightly. He could see their point. Entanglement with the world—and yet without it, their colony would have gone under, many times. "We do our best for the children. We teach them their L'liite heritage, and we raise them as free citizens."

"Free citizens? With less than two hours a day at school?" The L'liite sounded scandalized. "We know—we've been monitoring."

He took a deep breath. "What do you want of us?"

"You heard me," said their leader. "Let our people go."

"Our children?" For a moment Rod was hopeful. "Would you adopt them?" Much as Rod loved the children, he could not deny them the chance of traditional parents. That was what 'jum really needed—her own mother and father, with infinite time to share.

"You're evading the issue. Give back our children—and close down your perverted operation. Children abducted to be raised by dimwits—imagine."

At that Rod froze. Better silence than what he would have said.

"It's true," said Geode earnestly, "we've made some mistakes. Won't you come meet the children in person, and see for yourselves if they're happy? Perhaps we can do better."

The L'liite gave the sentient a look of utter disgust. "Happy children—who can never expect to raise children of their own? We humans can't even give birth on this toxic world. Get out, and let the Fold clean it up for us."

"We'll stay on your holostage," warned the other one. "We're prepared for hunger strike."

Rod bowed slightly and spread his hands. "Good day, Citizens." He turned quickly and left.

"So that's what the snake eggs were after," exclaimed Geode, outside. "I'm sure Nibur put them up to it."

"Peace, Brother," Rod warned, sketching a starsign. "The Spirit save them from their folly."

"Yes, but what about our holostage? They got a free-speech permit to occupy it."

So the holostage was out of order for a day, then the next. No more school time at all, now, thought Rod. More of the snake eggs came hovering again, this time to ask what he thought of the witnesses, and how could he let them starve themselves.

By the week's end 'jum was in trouble again. "She was fine, so long as we left her at the holostage," Geode explained. "She behaved for a while and seemed interested in sorting the crystals."

Haemum nodded. "I sewed up her pockets to keep her from hoarding them."

"That was clever." But Rod noticed the dark welts under Haemum's eyes. She worked herself too hard.

" 'jum still keeps to herself too much," Geode went on. "She won't look at another child without crossing her eyes.

Of course the others make fun of her. And then—" Geode shook his head.

"She hit Pomu's leg this time," said Haemum. "He needed three stitches. I'm sorry—I'll watch her better."

"You can't be with her every minute. You need to rest, Sister. You must; do you understand?"

"I'm all right, Brother Rod. I just get these headaches— ever since we hauled the last tumbleround. You know how they smell. The medical service couldn't find anything, so I'm sure it will get better."

Rod was silent. Vague fears stirred in him, of what he could not say. "I'll talk to 'jum." What were they to do with her, he wondered. An older child . . . She needed time to heal; but she was a danger to others, and no one could watch her every second. If only Reverend Mother were here.

'jum sat alone on her bed in her filtered room, more sullen than ever. " 'jum, why?" Rod asked. "You know the rules. Your brothers and sisters don't want to hurt you. We need to keep each other safe."

"They're stupid." Her voice was low and grudging as if forced out of her.

"They're family. They love you." There was something wrong with this child, Rod thought. She could not see other people as people.

"They're stupid," she repeated. "Even the holostage is stupid."

Did she miss the sentient holostage at Station? "Would you like to go back to the clinic?"

'jum looked up. "Yes, Brother Rod. Let's go back."

So she missed all their hours together, the two of them at Station, touring the worlds of the Fold. Rod reached out to clasp her hand. Then he saw on her arms a rash was spreading; it must feel unbearable. It was a relatively mild reaction to something on Prokaryon, but if Haemum's treatment failed, it might become serious. He should have kept her there at the clinic. But how could all their other children do without him?

Suddenly Rod wished he had left her to die on Scarecrow Hill. She was half-dead then; a day or two more would have ended her misery, and never brought the colony the burden of this traumatized child. The depth of his own feeling surprised and shocked him. Whatever good he might do was all useless in the end, if he could feel such hardness toward one suffering human being.

But the girl was alive, here; and somehow she had to be dealt with, along with the tumbleround and the defunct lightcraft. A voice from long ago welled up within Rod, the voice of his old Academy Master. He held 'jum by the wrists and made her face him. "Listen. You are one of us, and *you will live by our rules*. Do you understand?"

The girl did not reply. "The sun's rays are not infinite," she said at last in a defiant tone. "I will count their photons."

Outwardly Rod carried on as always, but inside he felt forsaken. He needed the Spirit more than ever, but when he called, his soul heard only emptiness. He was losing weight on Prokaryon food, and by day he could think of little else. At night he dreamed of Khral, again and again. It always felt the same; a sense of longing and satisfaction, a feeling of the deepest joy to become one with her. In the morning he would awaken, bewildered and remorseful. He prayed for release, but instead found himself looking forward to the nighttime, while dreading the shame of awakening.

Rod knew he had to talk with someone. He approached Geode, after evening prayers. Overhead the molten moon awaited the nightly clouds. *They'll boil off the continent,* Diorite had warned, just like Prokaryon's moon. It could not happen—*must* not happen, Rod told himself yet again. But he could do nothing, without healing himself first. "Brother, I have a problem."

Geode sighed. "Not the roof again? We really can't afford another roof job."

Rod smiled despite himself. "I'll keep the roof tight, never fear. The problem is, I am distracted in my prayers. My soul strays, and I can't call as I should."

The sentient's eyestalks twisted and untwisted. "Distracted? Straying? Not you, Brother Rod. You're always the one to keep me straight."

Taken aback, Rod murmured, "Well, thanks, Brother."

"It's true. You always remind me to respect the poorest and least fortunate of our fellow creatures; even poor servos too dim to grow sentient."

"I try my best. But now I feel . . . empty, somehow, and I long for things that are wrong."

"That's how I feel," said Geode suddenly. "Especially about Station; I can't help imagining all sorts of ugly fates she deserves, for buying Proteus's servos. Like the old Urulite overlords, most of whom had simian blood, but it never kept them from owning simian slaves." He raised two limbs fluttering. "So much evil fills the world, it's hard work to untangle one's self. That's why I pray all the time, without ceasing. But you are human—you can scarcely manage one task at a time, let alone several. You need time to retreat from the world."

Rod considered this. "A retreat might help. But how could I make the time?"

"You could spend one afternoon, at least, in the wilderness, meeting the Spirit. No, really; I can manage for an afternoon."

The next day, leaving the children settled for the moment, Rod strode out alone across the brokenhearts. Despite the heat, he wore his formal robe, to help focus his search. He silently repeated all the litanies, and tried to open his mind—for what, he was not sure. That was the way to start, he knew: with unsureness. Only when the mind cracked open its own worldly certainties could a glimpse of light appear.

He walked steadily beyond the tilled fields, over the windswept reaches tended only by whatever Spirit filled Prokaryon. The wind brought many scents, of four-eyes and crushed loopleaves, of the river that flowed in among the singing-trees. He let his mind run free, free as the child he was before he entered the Academy, the child who used to play with old fossil bones out on Trollbone Point—the bones of the creatures boiled off before humans came.

He found his mind calling out around him: What are you, you rolling creatures and tangled leaves? What is your place in the cosmos? Every form of life that ever was had its day and died, even old *Architeuthis*. If someday his children played with singing-tree skeletons, what did it matter? Was Prokaryon any different? Why was it so crucial that Mother Artemis convinced the Secretary?

He listened for reply. But no reply came to his mind; only to his heart, to the part of him that was beyond reason. For a moment he caught a glimpse of understanding, of why some humans could decide by logic to boil off a world. Of course, no logic protected a living thing, only sheer desire, a desire fed by the Spirit. He needed the living beings of Prokaryon, absolutely, for all that he could barely eat their food.

The wind rose again, sighing its assurance. It brought a scent, the very faintest trace, slight but unmistakable, of glue. Rod stopped. He meant to veer off, to avoid any distracting encounter. Instead, his feet took him forward again.

The odor increased. Sure enough, the shapeless mass of a tumbleround appeared. A whirr or two alighted on Rod's arm, never staying for long. His curiosity rose insistently. What could this thing be, that sent out its little carriers of micros to the winds? To reach other tumblerounds, of course. But what would they say, if ever those messengers could talk to him? All those times this enigmatic creature had crept over to peer in at his window; now, for the first time, here he had come to visit it.

Rod's head ached and his eyes swam. The sun was hot, and the gluish odor overpowering. He tried to turn and leave; but he was transfixed to the spot. His eyesight went blank, turning different colors: first blank red, then green, then blue. Then mixed hues appeared in rapid succession, until he lost track of them and let out a wordless scream.

The hues subsided and lost definition. Now shapes of darkness appeared, as if some unseen hand were trying to paint on his retina. The shapes were tantalizing, yet their sense eluded him. After what seemed forever, a dark blur seemed to coalesce and take rudimentary form. The form parted into several projecting lines; he counted five. A prime number? Then, in an instant, he knew the shape for what it must be: an outstretched hand.

For just a moment, the wind and field reappeared before his eyes. It was just long enough for Rod to reclaim his senses and turn to flee across the fields. He did not stop until he reached the compound, where he leaned on the gate, gasping for breath, his clothes drenched with sweat. *An outstretched hand* . . . There could be only one meaning for such a sign.

ELEVEN

The Secretariat, the highest authority of the Free Fold, occupied a giant orb of nanoplast that rolled lazily through space above Elysium, pulsing with a million urgent signals to and from the seven worlds of the Fold. The daily cycle for its myriad officers, ambassadors, and petitioners had just reached morning.

Within the brain of Secretary Verid Anaea*shon,* nanoservos with their gentle electromagnetic fingers were rousing her mind, just as it completed the deep phase of sleep. At just the best moment for optimal mental function, the nanoservos swimming in her cerebrospinal fluid nudged her awake.

Verid's eyelids opened. Beside her in bed, beloved Iras was stretching already, and Verid's skin vibrated with memory of the evening before.

Their chamber had no windows, of course, buried as it was within many levels of shifting nanoplast. But morning sunlight poured in nonetheless, as real as one could imagine. The front of the room filled with butterflies, multicolored heliconians, flitting and hovering above lush green foliage. For centuries Verid had begun her day watching these brilliant evanescent creatures in their garden, contemplating her own fate.

But she had a long day ahead. The butterflies soon receded, and her day's agenda hovered above her eyes, the first of ten thousand–odd items priorities by her nanoservos.

Iras's arms sneaked behind her back and cupped her breasts.

"You distract me, dear." Nonetheless Verid did not pull away. The cerebral nanoservos captured "yes" and "no" from her thoughts as her eyes scanned the list. Activists for simian rights on Urulan—yes, meet them first, although she could offer little more than publicity. The same for the sentient rights activists. Valan and Bronze Skyan trade talks on "stable" nanotechnology—yes, but later on, to avoid awkward juxtaposition. Prokaryon: update on privatization, and on that mysterious disease outbreak. Illegals from L'li—that crisis would take the rest of her morning.

By now Iras had withdrawn to attend to her own list from Bank Helicon, reviewing her portfolio and seeking new prospects to cultivate. Meanwhile the bedclothes had shrunk themselves away, and a cleansing chamber had molded itself out of the wall. Verid rose lightly, her Elysian muscles in perfect shape as they had been since her birth in the *shon,* the genetic nursery where all Elysians were reared. The cleansing chamber breathed a mist that settled in droplets all over her, full of molecular sorters that dissolved waste substances while leaving healthy epidermal oils behind. By the time her skin was dry, the bed had been transformed to a semicircular lounge, with a table thrust up from the floor, holding a tray of flower cakes.

A fresh talar floated onto her shoulders and molded itself down her body. From the lounge, Iras looked up at her, her blond hair floating luxuriantly above the butterflies cascading down her talar. "Isn't your list done?" She could tell from Verid's expression that the list still hovered in her mind.

"Almost." Verid knew how Iras valued this time, the one meal of the week they spent alone together, for all other breakfasts were meetings, and state dinners were hopeless. But Verid never failed to scan her last nine thousand listings, mostly would-be petitioners for one cause or another, despite her assistant's efficient shunting of them to appropriate departments. Yes, yes, yes . . .

Artemis. The Reverend Mother Artemis, a creditless cleric from an orphan colony on that debt-ridden colonial world, priority number 9,352.

From within her head, the nanoservos generated a voice. "Where do you place item 9,352, Secretary?

"This morning," she told them. "Just after the sentient rights group."

"Very well. May we be instructed for future reference?"

"You couldn't have known." Mother Artemis had no official standing to see the Secretary, and whatever she needed, Verid could do even less for her than for the others. But her centuries-old memories of Artemis would never fade.

At last she sat beside Iras, whose hand reached to hers. "Are the trade talks that bad?"

"Not too bad." The talks were completely stalled.

"You look down about something." Iras tasted a cake. Her blond hair fairly glowed in the morning light. "You ought to be more happy. You're only the most powerful person in the Fold."

"And loved by the most beautiful woman." Verid

smiled. "Don't write me off yet; my Final Home can wait."
An unusual number of prominent aging Elysians had chosen their Final Home this year.

Iras looked thoughtful. "My old *shonsib* Kerelis went,
after nearly seven centuries. I'd seen the warning signs, the
last decade; he kept having more and more of his old memories erased. . . ."

Verid shuddered. It was a dangerous habit for Elysians
to have painful memories removed. Not that she had never
felt tempted to give up the centuries-old longing for lost
friends. But the more one erased, the less one's own life remained. To end one's self had once been the worst crime in
Elysium; today, it was far too easy. "Iras," she said suddenly, "you must be looking forward to your trip to
Prokaryon."

"Definitely." Iras was heading out with Nibur to attend the "Opening" of cleansing the Prokaryan continent.
It was mainly for show, of course, just a spout of steam
from the sky; the real work would exclude spectators.
"What a fascinating world—all those little creatures rolling
along."

"That's why you're wiping them out."

"Just the one continent." She gave Verid a close look.
"You did say the Proteus loan was okay. You could have
said no."

"Someone had to do it." After two centuries of development, Prokaryon was a financial disaster. All the research
that went into that ecosystem, and the lifeshaping of the
colonists, and still only children and sentients could live
there. The planet drained precious resources from the Fold,
resources needed to fight the plague on L'li and support the
shaky economies of Urulan and other worlds. Another century more, and things might look different. Even another

decade—Station assured Verid that full human coloniza-
tion was just around the corner. But how far was that corner? The patience of the Fold had worn thin.

Something had to be done, before they voted to simply
give up and terraform the whole planet, zoöids and all. If
Nibur cleansed one continent, it would at least buy time for
the rest. Unless it only hastened the rest. She sighed. "Take
care of yourself, dear. There's an outbreak of some sort at
Station."

Iras laughed. "So that's what you're worried about.
Never fear; we don't get sick." Elysians, with their aug-
mented immune systems, took the view that microbial illness was for mortals.

Verid watched Iras speculatively. Connect, connect, she
thought instinctively. "You know, dear, I've found something to interest you. Another descendant of Raincloud's."

"Really? I've accounted for all but three." A word to
the room, and Raincloud herself strode forth full-size on the
holostage, her dark face bold beneath her orange coils of
hair, her arms raised in a martial arts stance. Raincloud
had been a mortal friend of Iras's, some two centuries before. An emigrant from Bronze Sky, Raincloud had settled
among the Sharers. Iras kept track of all her descendants,
visiting and recording them, and bestowing favors. "Where
is her descendant?"

"On Prokaryon. A Sharer lifeshaper with a research lab
on Mount Anaeon."

"A Sharer lifeshaper? On the Spirilla continent?" Iras
frowned. "You're up to something."

Verid returned her look innocently. In fact, she had
sought long and hard to make Iras "connect" with
Prokaryon.

"We have to do something," Iras reminded her. "Else
those L'liite ships will just keep coming."

*　　*　　*

In her receiving room, complete with real oak desk and bookshelves, Verid whispered her last notes on the sentient rights activists. They had shown shocking evidence of sentient machines held in virtual slavery, prevented from claiming their freedom, forbidden even to think the word *I*. Of course, everyone knew these factories existed, and even they would look insignificant compared to Nibur's Proteus, which eliminated sentience altogether. But at least her brief hearing would keep the facts in the public eye.

"The Reverend Mother Artemis of the Sacred Order of the Spirit," prompted the nanoservos in her brain.

Mother Artemis glided into the room, trailed by three snake eggs at about eye level. They had to have their thirty seconds.

"Artemis," Verid exclaimed, grasping her hands, and the sentient's snakes of hair stretched toward her. "It's been decades, hasn't it?"

"Too many." The face wore its brightest smile, and her starsign shone on her neck. "But you did well for the nanas; you kept your promise." The "nanas" were the caregivers for all Elysian children. Their freedom had required tough negotiations.

"So did you," Verid reminded her. "Without you, who knows? We might still be at the table! But you left the nursery—to found your own at a far star. Now, what brings you from your children?"

"I miss my babies," Mother Artemis admitted. "But now, I fear for their lives."

"The transfer of your colony—has it gone wrong?"

"It must not happen! Our children have devoted our lives to cultivate this plot of land, and now they are to be rooted out?"

"It's only been a few years," Verid pointed out reasonably.

"For children, that is their entire lifetime. And for our nonhuman hosts, who knows?"

Verid's eyebrows shot up, and the snake eggs came forward. "Nonhuman intelligence has yet to show itself." The standard line, she had repeated for decades.

"Those tumblerounds looking in at our windows, they're intelligent. Everyone knows it, even if our scientists can't prove it." Mother Artemis raised her hands. "How can you immolate an entire continent of our hosts?"

Verid waved away the snake eggs; enough was enough. Then she sank herself into a chair.

Artemis did not sit down, but shaped her nanoplast downward to meet Verid's level. "It's been a long time, Verid."

"Too long," Verid agreed. "The sentient rights movement still needs you."

"What more can I do?" Mother Artemis's voice was low. "Today, even Station herself buys lost souls from Proteus. It's a disgrace."

Verid nodded understandingly. She had watched the wealthier sentients gradually ape their former masters. No wonder the Reverend Mother had gone back to raising babies.

"And you?" Mother Artemis demanded. "You yourself founded Prokaryon. How can you give up this precious world now?"

"I'm trying to save it," Verid sighed. "Put to a vote, the Fold would transform the whole planet tomorrow. One continent—that's a compromise." Compromise, the story of her life.

"But why make it easier?"

"It's a dangerous game," Verid admitted. "But it does

buy time. The Fold representatives can tell their home worlds they made a place for the L'liites, yet they still saved the planet."

"The Sharers will protest."

"Another fallen ship from L'li will silence them." The Sharers themselves were an endangered minority, though their ideas had spread through the Fold.

The starstone at the neck of Mother Artemis seemed to sharpen. "Citizen Anaea*shon,*" she exclaimed. "Where are our rights—the rights of the settlers, citizens of the Fold? Where is our contract?"

"You have your rights, but you depend on us for your upkeep, especially your newest settlers."

"Our settlers have all been lifeshaped. Even without new colonists, we can manage on our own. Set us free."

Verid raised an eyebrow. "No new colonists? That's just the problem: Where will all the L'liites emigrate?"

"There won't be any more emigrants in a few decades. The creeping will see to that."

Astonished, Verid looked at her hard. "You are right. In another generation, L'li's billions will actually begin to decline, and the survivors will experience labor shortage. The desperate ships will end. But a few decades is a long time, for mortals. Besides," she added quietly, "no official wants to admit that we're actually going to stand back and let the plague do its work."

"I am but an atom in the breath of the Spirit. I have never claimed to do more than dry the tears of a few children. If another billion die beyond my reach, at least I have shared what I can."

"And I'm trying to save what I can of your world," said Verid. "One continent buys time for the rest. Is that so wrong? Every planet survives its disasters."

"You're wrong. You miscalculate."

"Really?"

The sentient moved closer. "Surely you know Prokaryon's mineral wealth. Titanium, aluminum, let alone the gold. Metals long gone from the crusts of other worlds. And the gemstones—you know what mortals will do. You've seen it on Valedon."

This was true. Elysians cared little for solid objects; they prized the protean delights of the virtual. But mortals were different. "There could be a gold rush," Verid admitted. "I can't rule the future."

"You can help us fight."

Verid met her gaze. Then her chin tilted a fraction. "If I put a hold on your colony, the others will call it favoritism."

Mother Artemis spread her hands. "Verid, I ask you: *Hold us all.* All of the colonies on Prokaryon. They all are suffering as we are."

"Most of them have already bought the promise of better land." Verid rose from her seat, her talar swishing around her legs as she strode to the holostage. From the light emerged a landscape, the land of Prokaryon. Land of any sort was a mystery to Verid, who dwelt from birth in a city floating on a shoreless sea. But Prokaryon, with its unending rows of arch-shaped trees and its leathery rolling inhabitants, was a mystery beyond imagining. "So this is your land," she mused, adding a Sharer proverb, " 'Land claims the dead.' "

"The land of Prokaryon is our death and rebirth."

The Secretary sighed. "I'll put a hold on your transfer." Iras would be incensed, she realized. "But be warned, Nibur will force you out, one way or another."

"We know. Thank you, Verid, from the depth of my soul."

On the holostage, something had emerged out of the

Prokaryan forest. One of the arching trees was not quite a tree. It had no fixed roots, Verid saw, only temporary roots extending forward and back, to gradually pull itself over. A mess of tendrils bearded it, clouded by insects. "Is that it, Artemis?" That verminous creature, the master of Prokaryon?

Mother Artemis sketched a starsign. "The Spirit alone will tell."

Verid watched the creature keenly, committing every detail to memory. "When the master awakes and needs reckoning—send for me then."

The *Proteus* was coming out of its last fold hole. Nibur had a private acceleration compartment for himself and Banga. The retriever panted quietly, accustomed to the nanoplastic restraints that shielded him and his master from the centripetal force as the ship spun down the hole through the space fold. At last the restraints dissolved, indicating they had cleared the hole. Nibur rubbed Banga behind the ears, and the eager tail brushed his arm.

Now he was impatient to hear from his staff about progress on Prokaryon. His staff called in, not as walrus today, but as angelfish, his latest variation on the ocean of *Proteus*. "Is the Opening on schedule?" On a remote un-inhabited island off the western coast of Spirilla, the first steam would pour in. Of course, they had tested the white-hole connection already, in secret, two months be-fore. Several delegates had wanted to see that before the vote.

"The white-hole link is set, and the water pump is up." Energy from the white hole would vaporize water pumped from the ocean, which would swiftly cleanse some hundred square kilometers.

"Excellent," he told the fish. "And how are the locals—all moving on?"

"The Three Forks bauxite miners are winding up operations on schedule." The fish blew wide bubbles, its long parti-colored fins trailing. "But Colonial Corundum is stalling. They claim the wrecked L'liites are still alive; they say they found tracks."

"Tracks? Of dead L'liites? What do they take us for? Tell them to cut it out, or we'll send the Fold evidence of their misdemeanors."

The fish bubbled, "The Mount Anaeon research lab still fails to respond."

"We'll send in the octopods." No naked Sharer was going to make a fool of him. The Fold required preservation of all ecological research, but his patience had grown thin. Nibur watched the ever-shifting swirls of foam wend across the sand at his feet. He was tired of ocean, he realized. It was time to fashion something new of *Proteus,* something to stimulate the senses afresh. What should it be? The fiery landscape of Bronze Sky? Or the green hills of Valedon, with their cliffs full of ancient bones?

"One last colony remains, on a last-minute hold order from the Secretariat."

"What?"

"The so-called Spirit Colony."

Nibur was puzzled. What could Verid be up to, with this last snag? If she intended to hold him up, her attempt was vain indeed. He would ask Iras what she knew of it.

Iras soon emerged from her own compartment. Her train was bundled behind her, the easier to disembark. As Nibur joined her, half a dozen octopod servos emerged to defend them from any attack or contagion. Elysians always brought protection, outside their idyllic home world.

"I trust my ship served you well, *Shon*sib," Nibur said.

"The smoothest trip I ever made." Iras's hair flowed down the butterflies of her talar, every strand in place. "I should travel more often."

Nibur smiled. Iras was known for her reluctance to leave the comforts of Elysium.

"All set for the Opening?" Iras asked.

"A new beginning for Pavonis Three."

"You certainly wasted no time."

"It's best this way," Nibur said. "Like taking down a historic building—once the first corner goes, no more protest." The docking was taking longer than it should, because of new quarantine regulations. Mortals and their sickness—they should manage their bodies better. "While we're waiting, perhaps you can explain to me this little problem with the so-called Spirit Colony?"

Iras frowned. "Verid's last gesture. What's a month extra?"

He nodded politely.

"There is another matter, in fact, which may prove more, shall we say, significant?" Iras smiled. "The diversity score you reported for Spirilla's ecosystem: one-point-five on the scale of one to ten, am I right?"

He nodded. "The equivalent of commercial farmland."

"That was the *average* score, *Shon*sib. But you never mentioned those small regions whose species diversity scores eight or nine. The eastern mountains, for instance."

Nibur shrugged. "Prokaryon's masters must have their own nature preserves."

Iras looked at him with interest. "Do you believe in the hidden masters?"

"I enjoy a good fantasy as well as anyone. Actually, my staff is well aware of the mountain diversity. We are sampling all species for transplantation."

"Nonetheless, *Shon*sib, I'd like to take a look at this . . .

nature preserve. Mount Anaeon, to be precise. There's a Sharer research lab."

"As you wish." Inwardly Nibur swore to himself, much annoyed. He had promised Iras to show her anywhere, betting that her soft city habits would keep her to well-charted ground. "If we lose an octopod down a cliff, we can always produce more."

"Precisely. Now, if you'll excuse me, I must freshen up before we face the snake eggs." Iras left, her talar unfolding behind her.

Nibur shrugged. After all, he did need to check the relocation of that laboratory. And while there, he could be seen supervising species collection.

Then it dawned on him. Of course—Mount Anaeon would be the next incarnation of *Proteus*. Sheer mountains, full of elegant arching trees and quaint rolling creatures to embody his messengers. An esthetic challenge beyond compare.

"News just come in," called an angelfish. "Solaris Sunracer sold its last lanthanide site to Aldaran." Aldaran was owned by a Valan house, controlled by an Urulite holding company owned in secret by Proteus. "We've reached fifty-one."

Fifty-one percent. Euphoria filled him like a drug. A continent was nothing; Nibur now owned a controlling interest of all holdings on Prokaryon. In effect, he owned the world. And he could show all the Fold that when the last Prokaryan landscapes dissolved, they would not vanish—they would be immortalized.

TWELVE

After the strange encounter, Rod's head ached for the rest of the day, but no "visions" returned. He wanted to tell Khral, but now he doubted his own motives. Besides, what would it sound like—a tired man's vision in the sun. Everyone knew the tumbleround smell affected the brain. But their microzoöids could not infect humans.

In the morning the floor of the kitchen was soaked from a leak in the roof. So he climbed up to check the roof, then spent an hour preparing dried ring fungus to use for repair. Chae helped him chop it into small pieces, then add water with a special powder that made them like paste. He then climbed carefully up the ladder to apply the paste to the cracks. In the sunshine, the paste would harden as impervious as concrete.

Overhead, far above the roof, a vast flock of scarlet helicoids came migrating westward. Rod paused, overcome by the sight of tens of thousands of the whirling creatures that filled the sky to the far horizon. All the beauty of this land could be wiped out, at the whim of humans light-years away. Mother Artemis must have met with the Secretary by now. He hoped for a neutrinogram, but the holostage was still occupied by the protesters from New Reyo.

"Brother," hailed Geode from below. "Come quick to the holostage. It's Sarai."

"Sarai? How did she get through?" The L'liites must have left, thank the Spirit. But whatever could Sarai want of him, Rod wondered as he descended the ladder with care. "Keep the paste wet, Chae," he told the boy waiting dutifully below.

Geode kept a discreet distance from the holostage, for Sarai unnerved him. In the column of light the unclothed Sharer could be seen pacing back and forth, her breasts swaying. She seemed even more agitated than usual. "How dare you tie up your holostage and refuse me."

"It was hardly our choice," Rod told her. "We're glad our visitors finally had enough."

"I had to pull medical privilege." Sarai glared at him. "It's not fair," she exclaimed. "My competitor has all kinds of help in her work—and what have I got? Nothing."

It took Rod a moment to realize she must be referring to Khral. "It's true," he agreed carefully. "Khral works at Station, with many collaborators."

Sarai stopped and stared straight at him. "*You* help them, too. Your colony sends you to collect their samples. Why can't you send *me* an assistant for a change?"

For a moment he returned her stare. Then he looked down. "We are forever in your debt, Sarai," he told her, thinking of Gaea running, her precious legs healed. "I would help you if I could. But now we face . . . hardships.

Brother Patella has yet to return, and for a time we have lost our Reverend Mother. I can't possibly be spared to help you; nor Khral either."

"It's not *you* I need. I need someone intelligent." She waved a hand impatiently, then gave a very fierce look. "That girl, the one you brought last time."

He stared again. "You mean *'jum?*"

"That's right."

"Impossible," said Rod curtly. " 'jum is a child. She needs proper rearing."

Sarai threw up her arms, and the webbing flashed between her fingers. "I knew it! I knew the one time I asked you Spirit Callers for something, you'd say no. After all I've done for you." With that, the holostage went dark.

Shaking his head, he turned to Geode. "Can you imagine?"

The sentient folded up his limbs. "Well, I don't know."

Rod frowned. "What do you mean?"

"I mean, well—we might consider it, that's all. After all, we're short-handed, you and I. We could send her there until Reverend Mother returns."

"Send a child to that mad Sharer?" Rod was nearly speechless. "How could you? You never liked 'jum in the first place; you wanted to leave her on that hill—" He stopped, shaking. "I'm sorry," he said wearily.

"No, you're right. I don't take to older children; I'm not so good with them. I know the babies; I can hold them, and feed them milk. Whereas I just don't know how to . . . feed 'jum."

"Nor do I," Rod admitted. 'jum now spent all day alone in her room, making figures with sticks and pebbles. The other children kept their distance. At times, Haemum seemed to reach her, but Haemum had no more time. Nor had Rod the time for the hours of one-on-one attention the precocious child craved. Those L'liite hunger-strikers—if only one of them cared enough to adopt her.

Geode said, "Why not ask 'jum herself? She listens to you."

Rod gave a grim smile. "We'll see."

He found 'jum sitting on the floor, amid an array of little sticks arranged in intricate triangles and squares. She seemed absorbed by some internal calculation, and he had to call her name twice before she looked up. "I have something for you to think about, 'jum." He tried to hold her gaze. "Do you remember Sarai, the . . . lifeshaper, the one who cured Gaea?"

'jum nodded.

"Would you like to go and stay with her?"

At this, 'jum nodded, her chin raising and lowering as if her whole body nodded, too. Surprised, Rod felt slightly hurt. "I can't stay there with you," he warned.

"I know."

He tilted his head. "Why, 'jum?" He recalled how Sarai took to the child, intrigued by her grasp of numbers. The pair had much in common—perhaps too much. "What is it you like about Sarai?"

'jum seemed to struggle for words. "Sarai lives . . . on a high place. I belong there."

There was no question of taking 'jum on a three days' journey to the mountains, leaving Geode to manage alone. They had to call for help fast, in case the L'liites tried to reoccupy the holostage. Diorite's newly sentient lightcraft would have helped out, but instead Rod found himself calling the research lab.

The image of Khral coalesced on the holostage. Rod suppressed his sharp delight at seeing her, afraid she might see into him. But she greeted him the same as ever. "Oh yes! Rod, are you ready to help out in the field again? We made some fascinating observations of tumblerounds, but the work could go faster."

Recalling his encounter, he shuddered. "I wish I could, but we're short-handed until the Reverend Mother gets back." The dreams meant nothing, he told himself. And yet his pulse raced with feelings he should not have. "Those microzoöids that live in the tumbleround—you're sure they can't infect humans?"

Khral shook her head. "Still no sign of that."

"You will let me know if you . . . find out anything? I mean, if the tumblerounds are dangerous in any way, we ought to know."

"Of course, I'd let you know. But really, you've had those beasts around for years, haven't you?"

"That's right. But this year, the tumblerounds seem . . . different. As if somehow they've awakened. And their smell can knock you out."

"Really. Their secretions do contain psychotropic agents, but Prokaryan biochemistry often produces those by chance. Come up and hear the latest, when you can. Quark will be glad to pick you up."

"Actually, if Quark isn't too busy, he might take us back to Mount Anaeon."

"To Sarai? Thank goodness," she exclaimed. "Sarai hasn't spoken to me since I told her we'd gotten the micros to grow. I tried to flatter her as best I could, but she absolutely went berserk. She thinks I stole her data." Khral shook her head. "Now she'll have to see you. Maybe she'll relent and let Quark give her those strains that finally shipped in from Science Park."

*   *   *

So the child called 'jum was brought to the brow of Mount Anaeon and left there, within the tunnels of Sarai's laboratory. As Sarai watched the child, she found herself thinking and feeling things she had not felt for many a year. To be sure, the L'liite child was pitifully foreign, not a web between her fingers, and small for her age. But her eyes were bright and keen; they did not miss a nook in the cavern, between the leaves of secretory plants with reagents dripping slowly, nor amidst the touch pads and speaker points of the Valan-built holostage. Sarai's own daughters had once looked the same.

Her daughters, and her beloved Aisha; for a moment the memory was too terrible to live through. Sarai felt herself slip away, into whitetrance. Her fingers turned white first, then her limbs, as the breathmicrobes in her skin bleached white, and her blood concentrated within her critical organs, leaving just enough circulation to keep her alive. Aisha, and their daughters. Long after the day the storm-maddened seas had swallowed them, they dwelt there still, somewhere below the ocean deep. Sarai had fled that ocean; she had flung herself as many light-years distant as she could, even burrowed into stone. Yet the ocean remained, inside.

Now, outside herself, she could not ignore this foreign child, who had shared her will to come. The child was alive in this world and would share her care. So Sarai returned slowly to the world of the living. Slowly she stirred, flexing her fingers and stretching the webs, still pale. It occurred to her that this child might never have shared sight of whitetrance before, living among those ignorant clerics. But the child sat watching, her eyes wide but calm. Sarai regarded her approvingly.

"Ushum," she whispered, softening the child's name into something the ocean might have spoken. The poor thing was covered with eczema; whatever were those clerics thinking? Sarai clucked at a clickfly, who called over several of its sisters to alight upon the child and deposit secretions to soothe her skin. "Sit still, Ushum, until the clickflies are done; they will clear your rash." Her eyes narrowed. "It's about time you came," she added curtly, afraid of too much tenderness. "I need help with my work; there's so much data to collect. And something tells me you'd be good at counting photons."

The child nodded. "All the photons in the world."

Sarai felt her pulse quicken. After so many years struggling on her own, it was a heady experience to find someone who might share the excitement of her work without stealing it. That Khral, for instance, with her tricky sentient friends. What a fool Sarai had been to send them her precious microzoöids. After all the trouble she had gone to, all the mixtures she had tried, Sarai had stumbled by chance on just the right proportions of zoöid and phycoid that her little sisterlings needed to grow. She was sure those stupid scientists would never get it, and would have to beg her for the recipe. Instead, with all their fancy machines, they tried tumbleround flesh—and it worked. And that Khral had the gall to call her and brag about it.

That Rod was a trickster, too. He still looked and sounded like a Guardsman for all that he joined the clerics to raise their orphans. She would not trust him until he bore his own child.

But what terrified her most was the children. All her lifeshaper's instinct and training made her unable to refuse care of a sick child. If the clerics ever found that out, she would spend the rest of her days tending one child or another.

"Well, Ushum, let's get to work. You're not hungry or sleepy now, are you?" Children were subject to such things, she recalled. But 'jum shook her head and rose expectantly, her small travel bag lying forgotten among the vines along the cavern wall.

Sarai called to her holostage, a machine of no intelligence, only rudimentary interactive powers. The usual column of light obligingly appeared, displaying several ring-shaped objects brightly colored. "I've grown these microzoöids in culture for several months now." Not from singing-trees—nor from tumblerounds either. From where, Sarai could not yet bring herself to say; she only shuddered at the thought. "In this recording, each cell is magnified a millionfold. They all glow different colors, don't they?"

'jum peered at the magnified microzoöids, her neck outstretched like a hummingbird sipping nectar. One plump little ring was pink, and a pale blue one even rounder, and another one turquoise. "Those two look the same," 'jum said, pointing to the turquoise, and to a ring that lay farther off across the holostage.

"Exactly! Those two cells are the same color. And now, as time passes, what happens?"

Gradually the colors changed, some greener, others bluer, until at last all the ring-shaped cells were turquoise.

"Now let's replay that sequence, more slowly." At Sarai's command, the holostage reset the microzoöids to their original colors, with playback rate decreased a thousandfold. On this time scale, the little rings no longer glowed steadily; they pulsed. "You see?" exclaimed Sarai. "They emit little bursts of photons—in prime numbers."

"Five . . . seven . . . twenty-three," 'jum counted.

"Those are the easy ones," Sarai warned. "I've counted up to twelve hundred forty-nine. The numbers must mean words or letters of some sort. My theory is that *the rings share the same color to talk to each other.* Like the little nanoservos we send into your bloodstream to fix your genes: They have to share signals to coordinate their work, right?"

'jum thought this over. "What is their work?"

Sarai shuddered. "Not like nanoservos—not at all." How Khral and Rod and all the rest of them would faint if they knew. "We'll find out what they're up to, perhaps too late," she said grimly. "I'll tell you, Ushum, where I found these sisterlings; but you mustn't tell anyone. They were—"

"Priority call," interrupted the holostage. "Please stand by for priority call."

Startled, Sarai glared at the holostage. "How dare you interrupt my work? I take calls when I please. The next time you—"

"Priority call," the stage repeated. "You refused our calls for two weeks, so a warrant was obtained."

A deep roaring sound of water filled the air. Above the holostage a wave of ocean rolled, a giant ravening curl of water such as was never seen on shoreless Shora. The curl grew small, reduced to a mere symbol hovering before a massive desk. Behind the desk sat an Elysian creature, whether female or male-freak, none could tell. It faced Sarai, apparently undeterred by her look of cold fury.

"Greetings," said the creature. "As you recall, I represent Proteus Unlimited, to whom the Fold has entrusted management of your research facility. Your work is most important to the Fold, and Proteus will transfer your project to an advanced, state-of-the-art facility under construction on the southeast quadrant of Chiron."

"Flying fish turds," Sarai exclaimed in Sharer. "You will do no such thing. Get off my holostage. For that matter, get off my planet."

The creature was unperturbed. "We will provide you with all necessary assistance to preserve valuable equipment. Our chief executive, Citizen Nibur Lethe*shon*, will personally supervise the operation, along with our species-preservation program. Please prepare for our arrival this week."

"I said, you will do no such thing." Sarai reached for the main power switch. "And you can tell your male-freakish master that if he ever sets foot on this world, *he will never leave alive.*"

THIRTEEN

As the days lengthened into "summer," the nightly rain clouds gathered earlier to shorten the day's heat, and satellites reported the usual shift of major wind systems, bringing cooler air farther south. Rod wondered, how did those tumblerounds control the weather? At a safe distance he watched them, but the lazy plant-animals showed no sign. The four-eyes grew more sluggish and spent more time by the river, while in the garden the red loop pods twisted and ripened. Children complained of the heat, though to Rod it felt barely warmer than Prokaryan winter, nothing like the scorching summers of Valedon.

What would "the masters" do when their continent was boiled off?

Rod made himself watch the holo broadcast of the Opening of the "cleansing" of Spirilla. The event was attended by representatives from Valedon, Bronze Sky, and

L'li, and the mysterious Elysian director of Proteus Unlimited, Nibur Lethe*shon*. Resplendent in their ceremonial talars, they offered stirring words and bad music, as their
satellite hovered above the first land to be "cleansed." An
island off the western coast, an aerial view showed two
stripes of forest. Rod wondered what Elk would say for his
singing-trees. And Khral—but Rod could not let himself
think of her.

Beside the holostage, Brother Geode saw Rod clenching
and unclenching his fists. His eyestalks lowered. "You
know, Brother, we don't really have to watch this."

"It's better to know." Knowledge was better than igno-
rance—it was never too late to learn. "We can pray for
them."

Geode began the standard litany of the Spirit. *Love only
truth, desire only grace, know only Spirit. . . .* The prayers
expanded to include all the zoöids, large and small, and
the hapless singing-trees, and, above all, all the participants
in this terrible project that unfolded before them.

Above the island, high in the stratosphere, a white
whirlwind appeared. It was a tunnel through a space fold,
directed from the sun Iota Pavonis. The sun's heat poured
through, turning the whirlwind into a swirl of flame. The
flames reached downward as a fountain projected from the
ocean. It met the fountain with a roar, creating steam that
rained down upon the island. Soon the steam enveloped
the island, tactfully obscuring the fate of the landscape.

Rod felt his heart pounding; he could barely move.
Geode's blue limb snaked around his arm. "Peace, Brother.
We've done all we can; it's the will of the Spirit."

His throat was swollen so he could barely swallow. *The
Spirit should grant me a world,* he had demanded once.
Now he was losing the one world he had.

"Success!" Nibur Lethe*shon* spoke with authority, with

all the kind assurance of a Spirit Father. "This is, of course, only the beginning. Inland, across the continent, cleansing will probe deep beneath the crust, generating magma chambers to thrust the steam upward." Volcanoes and geysers throughout the fields—the terrain would become unrecognizable. "The cleansing will continue over the next Prokaryan year, reducing the native biota by ninety-nine percent. Then we will seed the crust with thermophiles, microbes that live at steam temperature. The thermophiles will convert all the molecules in the soil to forms compatible with human physiology, while outgrowing the few native organisms that remain."

Bronze Sky, Rod remembered. All of Bronze Sky had been terraformed this way. The resulting vulcanism had colored its sky for centuries.

"In the next stage, we inoculate the land with phase-one human-compatible life-forms, including mosses and lichens, annelid worms, and—"

"Brother Rod," called T'kun from outside. "There's a visitor at the door. Hurry."

Rod left the holostage, closing the door behind him to avoid the children seeing such unsettling sights. But how much longer could he shield them? From the nursery T'kela and Qumum were wailing for attention; he hoisted them up, one in each arm. T'kun whispered, "I don't like this visitor."

"Sh, mind your manners." The outer door was ajar; Rod pushed it out with his elbow. T'kun followed, trying to hide behind him while peeking out to see.

There stood an octopod. Its gray arms folded about whichever way, without an obvious head. Beyond, next to the llama barn, three more octopods emerged from a lightcraft that bore the cresting wave of Proteus.

"Greetings." The octopod spoke in a monotone, advertising its lack of sentience. "We are here to assist you in relocating to your new homestead in Chiron."

Rod held the children tighter. His feet shifted instinctively for a defensive move, though no unarmed human could disable an octopod. "Greetings to you, and your master," he spoke in the warmest tone he could manage; at this, of all times, he must honor the Spirit. "Please convey our deepest regret, for we do not intend to leave."

The octopod seemed to pause, while the three others stood there threateningly. The babies began to whimper; Rod tried to soothe them. Whatever would those cursed machines do now? Try to take them by force?

"You have received your final thirty-day extension," the octopod said at last. "Use your time well. We will remain available to help you relocate."

So that was it. Another thirty days—was that from Mother Artemis? Why had she sent no neutrinogram? What if they did not let her return? Most incoming traffic had been canceled. For a free world of the Fold, any halt in traffic would be unthinkable. But Prokaryon was a colony world, subject to the Fold's protection—and its whim.

As the octopods left, Rod found himself shaking all over, and he set the babies down. T'kun came out and asked, "What does it mean, 'relocate'?"

" 'Relocate" means to move your things to go live somewhere else."

T'kun spread his hands. "Where else is there?"

The children would have to be told. If only Mother Artemis were back—but they could wait no longer. All their neighbors had gone by now, one way or another. There was no word from Diorite or Feldspar, who were trying to hide in the mountains and force postponement of the cleansing. A few dissidents from New Reyo sent out a manifesto, announcing an underground militia to "fight for independence." Scarcely practical, but it was good to see at least some of the Chiron colonists cared.

"Brother Rod," called Geode, "there's a neutrino-gram."

"From Mother Artemis?"

"From our Most Reverend Father."

The bearded Father spoke as always out of the snowy monochrome. "The Spirit be with you, Brother Geode, and Brother Rhodonite," began the Most Reverend Father of the Sacred Order of the Spirit. "All our sympathy pours out for you, in your hour of trial. Mysterious are the ways of the Spirit; and who can say what our ultimate calling will be? We call on the Spirit to give you all strength in the face of the world's minions.

"Over the centuries, Callers of the Spirit have ever been subject to persecution. Our sacred witness ever inspires hatred in those who are deaf to higher things. Pity them, my Brothers. Pity them—and let them have their dominion in this world. It is hard to leave a place of attachment, but you will prosper in your new home. Be sure that all of the Fathers of Dolomoth will hold you up to the Spirit in our hearts."

Rod and Geode sat still for a long while after the message had melted into snow. The message troubled Rod deeply, more for what it lacked than what it said, but he was not about to criticize the Most Reverend Father. Besides, what else could be done? He took a breath. "The time has come," he said. "We have to tell the children."

"Yes, but . . . how do we tell them?"

"We'll tell the older ones first. They'll help with the younger ones."

That evening Rod and Geode met with Haemum and Chae. The rain pattered outside, and a helicoid sought shelter under the window frame. Chae sat straight, a long-legged youth just past his tenth birthday; Haemum was nearing her thirteenth. More adults than children, Rod thought. Geode replayed the neutrinogram for them. The two young colonists watched, their mouths small. When it was over, there was silence. A helicoid in the window scratched at the pane, trying to get in.

"You know what's going on," Rod said at last. "The Fold wants us to leave our home."

Chae nodded quickly. "The octopods and all. But Reverend Mother will put a stop to it."

Rod swallowed hard. "The ways of the Spirit can seem obscure at times. Yet even Reverend Mother must obey."

Haemum frowned. "A lot of folks don't like what's going on, even people on Valedon and Bronze Sky. I saw, on the holo. They say it's wrong; that our whole world could die."

"That's true. But what they think may not matter in time for our colony."

Silence lengthened. Chae looked down, his forehead knotted in premature wrinkles.

"How can they do it?" Haemum wondered. "All the singing-trees, and all those flocks of helicoids. Even the tumblerounds—Brother Rod, you and I always took such care with them, though we could have used the hide for shoes."

Rod started to smile, then he turned cold. If the tumblerounds grew angry, who would they punish? How would "the masters" know who to blame? Could the children be safe anywhere on this planet?

Geode's eyestalks twisted and untwisted, then he extended two of his arms. "Sister, you've always done the best you can. It's not your fault; never believe that. It's all a matter of adults. Foolish adults—and even more foolish sentients."

"But what matters is the Spirit," insisted Haemum. "What does the Spirit call on us to do?"

"The Spirit," said Rod, "calls on us to obey worldly authorities."

"Well that's not how the Spirit calls me." Haemum crossed her arms and her voice hardened. "The Spirit calls me to flee into the forest. The land can't be 'cleansed' before we're found."

Chae nodded. "Me too."

Taken aback, Rod paused. "You are brave indeed; but you'll only gain the few extra days to find you. Think of the little ones."

"Send the little ones back to Station," said Haemum. "The rest of us can hide our tracks by crossing tumbleround territory. Tumblerounds mess up any trail, and their secretions foul nanoplast; even sentients refuse to follow."

Rod glanced at Geode, but his eyestalks only twisted lamely in the face of this insubordination. For a moment Rod wondered. "You have grown into adults, speaking adult words. When Reverend Mother returns, you may tell her your calling."

The next day he began to sort and pack—the lathe and polishers, the grain mill, the few extra clothes. The llamas were another problem; he had no idea how the independent-minded beasts would be moved. Meanwhile, the sky was crossed by huge transport craft to set up further sites for cleansing all over Spirilla. Their plasma spikes pierced the air, and their sonic booms terrified the children. The little ones had to stay indoors; the sapphire mine lay empty. Octopods stalked the grounds of the colony, as if to intimidate them. Rod's sense of disgust deepened.

As Geode worked beside him, the sentient suddenly came to life. "It's Mother Artemis—I've got her signal!"

"She made it back? Haemum will fetch her—" Rod

stopped. The old lightcraft still lay out in the field where it crashed.

"She got a lift—look there!" Above in the sky a plasma spike grew, descending surely to the colony. "It's Quark."

Somehow all the children seemed to know in an instant that Mother Artemis was home, and they came running and crawling outside to see her. Her nano-strands of hair extended to those her arms could not reach.

"Verid said we could stay on," Mother Artemis told Rod, when at last they had a moment to breathe. Her voice alone was such a relief to hear. "I would have sent a neutrinogram, but we need to save expense."

He shuddered to think what a chunk of their budget her ticket had cost.

"But the octopods gave us thirty days," Geode told her.

"Verid is two hundred light-years away. She warned us things might be made . . . difficult."

Rod added, "The octopods have kept us inside. We can't tend the fields. How can we last?"

She did not answer.

Geode told her, "There's the neutrinogram from the Most Reverend Father."

Mother Artemis viewed the neutrinogram, as best she could with the toddlers creeping up into her lap and down again. When it was over, she nodded slowly. "We will obey. We will pack our things, very slowly. We must live each day here for itself, as if it were our last, and as if we had thousands to come. When the time comes, who knows? The future lies behind a shroud."

Rod clenched his fists. "Haemum and Chae say they have a different 'calling.' They want to escape."

"How wonderful that young adults call for themselves. I will speak with them." She lifted baby T'kela over her shoulder. "This one has certainly grown. How are the others; how is 'jum?"

Geode's eyestalks straightened. " 'jum is visiting Sarai—at her request, imagine!" He told the story.

Rod said, "We were short-handed, and it seemed best. But now that you're home, we'll fetch her back immediately."

"Is she happy there?" Mother Artemis asked.

"Sarai has not taken calls."

"Then they must both be content. Would they have kept you ignorant, were it otherwise?"

He had to admit this was so.

"Scandalous," muttered Geode. "The last kind of role model 'jum needs."

"We'll see," said Mother Artemis. "For now, at least, Sarai will have to take care of the child's lifeshaping, and save us the expense." She looked him over carefully. "Brother Rod, are you holding your weight on Prokaryan food?"

"Nearly."

"You must go for your checkup immediately. Take Qumum and T'kela, too; you're all overdue."

Through the rotating connector, Rod held T'kela tight to convince the infant he was not falling into space. Qumum seemed unconcerned, crowing and solemnly examining his fingers. At the gate they met Khral, bearing Quark's eye-speaker; the lightcraft had been running an experiment at Station, all the while during his trip to pick up the colonists. No wonder sentients made humans feel inadequate.

"Look at the babies," Khral exclaimed. "They've grown twice as big." She gave Rod a quick hug, and her cheek brushed his. "You know, Three Crows is just dying to see them again."

"It's a pleasure." Rod hoped he did not look as confused as he felt.

"I'm so sorry about—oh, everything." Her eyelids fluttered beneath her simian brow. "Pushing you all off your own homestead—how could the Fold allow it?"

"For better farmland," he said bitterly. He took a deep breath and tried not to think how her arms had felt around him. "How is your project, Khral? Are the micros still growing?"

"Which ones?"

"The ones from Sarai. You mean, you have others?"

"Oh, there are thousands of strains. Sarai's strain is a completely new species, unlike those from the singing-tree pods. We even named the strain for her, *Sarai phycozoöidensis*. That smoothed her feathers a bit. I'm trying to get her up here for a seminar."

Rod smiled. "Good luck."

"They're growing, all right. We were making *such* progress decoding them, until Station pulled me off the project to isolate that spaceship bug, the one Three Crows got sick on."

" 'Spacer's spit-up,' they call it," chirped Quark at her shoulder.

Khral wrinkled her brow at the eyespeaker. "That's right, rub it in. Anyway—if you've got a moment, I'll show you what we've learned so far."

They entered the laboratory. An oblong vessel of culture stood on a stand, amid several angular instruments. Khral tapped it gently; it shook like gelatin. "That's our tumbleround soup in there—the stuff the microzoöids grow in, remember. They're incredibly active chemically; they put out polymers to gel the whole thing, and excrete all kinds of fibers."

Rod's scalp prickled. "Did you . . . chop up a tumbleround, or what?"

"We snipped a bunch of vegetative root-limbs. You know, the ones the tumbleround extends forward and pulls up behind, as it travels. They break naturally anyhow; the tumbleround doesn't seem to mind. The micros grow well in the stuff, but slowly, by microbial standards—about twenty-four hours to reproduce, a generation time of one day. Anyway, let's magnify them."

She turned to the holostage and dimmed the light. In darkness appeared several blobs of color; Rod counted twelve. Qumum wiggled and stretched to be put down so he could scrabble over to check out something more interesting than his fingers.

"That's okay, he can't hurt anything. Let's get this in focus." The colored blobs sharpened into ringlets, of perceptibly different hues. They seemed to be mainly blues and greens, with one yellow-orange. Darker tubes of fibers formed tunnels, connecting among the rings. "I'm going to slow down the time scale of the recording. Watch."

Rod stared until the little rings left afterglow in his eyes. Then the rings started pulsing. No longer continuous, their glow winked in and out so fast he could barely see; but soon the recording slowed.

"You see, it will pulse several times very fast—then stop—then pulse again. Bursts of three, four, five; I've recorded up to twenty at a time. It's their message from the tumbleround."

"Their message?" His pulse raced. "How do you know?"

Khral paused. "I don't know—because I can't read it.

It could even be they've given up their message, and what we're getting now is random noise." Her brow creased. "Early on, we got one brief message that was different. I'll show you, but keep quiet about it."

A string of numbers floated through the air: 1, 2, 3, 5, 7, 11, 13 . . .

"A prime series," Rod exclaimed.

"Sh-sh." Khral looked around furtively for watching snake eggs.

The primes marched on, up till 103. "So that's their message."

Khral shook her head. "It's too simple. A string of primes—so what? Since then, all we get is smaller numbers, a lot of ones and twos, occasional sevens and eights." She shook her head. "Whatever message their masters sent, we lack the key to decode it."

"It doesn't sound like much. How could a microscopic cell ever store a real message?"

"They're large cells, about the size of an ameba. Your own body cells each store six billion 'letters' of DNA—and that's just a linear molecule." Khral turned to the holostage, and it filled with a lattice of molecules. The atoms stacked and connected at right angles in all directions. "Each microzoöid stores a sentient's worth of molecular connections. The molecules can donate or pick up electrons, acting as AND gates or OR gates. Some are switched on by light. A single microzoöid can pack fifty trillion connections, about the number of synapses in a human brain."

A brain's worth of data in a single cell. Rod felt his hair stand on end. "What about your fieldwork? Have you learned anything more about tumblerounds?"

Quark said, "We learned why no one else studied them before."

Khral half smiled. "Tumblerounds congregate in the

singing-tree forest, leaving trails of foul stuff behind—a touch of it got through my skinsuit, and the repairs cost twenty thousand credits. They do contain Sarai's strain of microzoöids, about a billion each. Not a lot, by microbial standards. You yourself carry ten thousand times that many bacteria."

"That's comforting. Especially if they keep them to themselves."

"We did learn one thing. The tumblerounds 'transmit' the microzoöids as messages—*through the whirrs!*"

"I thought as much." Rod felt sick. "But messages to whom? How do the tumblerounds *do* anything? How do they rule the weather?"

Khral dismissed the holostage; the colored ringlets vanished. Qumum toddled over to see where they went. "The whirrs can carry microzoöids everywhere—even up to the stratosphere. We've done some sampling up there. They probably seed the clouds, or they absorb moisture, depending on how their masters want to direct the air mass. Heck, even on Valedon microbes seed most of the rainfall— blindly, of course." She stepped back to the culture vessel and crossed her arms, staring thoughtfully. "If only I could isolate a pure culture of micros from the whirrs. I've tried, but they just die. They must produce some essential pheromone."

"Why do you need another culture? You have Sarai's culture."

"Sarai's culture was not pure. To study a microbe, you need a genetically pure population, grown from a single ancestor. Otherwise, you can have several different species, without realizing it," Khral explained. "The only culture we can grow is the original one, from Sarai. We can passage that one, taking about a dozen cells at a time, but never a single cell. Perhaps her culture has aged; like clickflies after a few days, their message may have deteriorated by now. If we can't culture microzoöids directly from the whirrs, how will we ever read their message?"

"What if those whirrs try to 'contact' *us*—more directly?"

Khral frowned thoughtfully. "We still haven't found any micros alive inside a person. But they must be trying. You'd think they'd respond to the—" She shuddered.

"If they are," said Quark, "we sure have no evidence."

"But I have evidence," said Rod.

Khral's eyes widened, and Quark's eye trained on him.

"The tumbleround—it tried to show me something in my head."

"Something in your head?" repeated Khral.

He wished he could explain better. "It showed me a hand . . . with five fingers."

Quark's eyeball rolled around. "A Spirit Caller's visions don't count as evidence."

"Oh, hush!" Khral gave her shoulder a fierce simian glare. "Have we done much better? Rod—"

"Excuse me." Feeling stung, Rod gathered up the toddler from the holostage. "We have to make our appointments at the clinic."

"Don't mind Quark. Station will run nanos through your veins, just in case. You will be at supper, won't you?"

At the cafeteria, Khral sat with Qumum bouncing on her lap, enabling Rod to manage his food with one arm while T'kela dozed in the other, her arms sticking up straight as only young infants could manage. The tiny holostage played a skeptical report on Khral's work, including some rather crude jokes about the habits of tumblerounds. It listed all the previous "hidden master" candidates over the years: megazoöids, helicoids, and Elk's singing-trees. No wonder all the snake eggs laughed.

"We've just got to break the code." Khral spooned stir-fry from her plate; like Rod, she invariably ended up with the same item of the table's ten thousand offerings. "We have to convince the Fold the tumblerounds are sentient. I just can't believe Station made me focus on spacer's spit-up instead."

"Can't the medics handle that?"

"The medics gave up. They called in an epidemiologist from Elysium, but it will take him a week to get here. In the meantime, lacking better, it's up to me."

Recalling Mother Artemis's order to keep his weight up, Rod pressed his thumb to the table and called for a second order of shepherd's pie. "I guess the sickness might be serious."

"Nobody's been sick more than a few days; even Three Crows thinks it's ridiculous. It affects only outbound travelers from Prokaryon, about one in ten, at the moment they try to board a starship. You just sweat and upchuck for a few days—sorry, this isn't talk for suppertime."

"No matter." Rod smiled. "I've known worse." From upset stomachs to shoelaces tied to the table legs, suppertime at the colony could drive adults to the breaking point. Instead here was Khral; he imagined her in his arms again. . . . What harm was there in good food and an attractive companion? "Have you made any progress on it?"

Khral brightened visibly; any intellectual challenge seemed to turn her on like a switch. "Well, the medics ruled out all known pathogens. So it must be a toxin of some sort, reacting to who knows what. Change of pressure, perhaps?" She pushed the vegetables around in her plate. "And where does the toxin come from? Maybe from ingested micros."

Rod's fork stopped in midair. "But you said they can't grow in humans."

"They can't grow, but they can pass through your stomach. Whatever food you eat, you ingest millions of microbes. Everybody does."

That was all he needed to hear. Brokenhearts were hard enough to swallow.

"But Prokaryan microbes have no effect; you're more poisonous to them than they are to you. All that acid in your stomach, and those bile salts in your colon." Khral shuddered. "Enough to do in most of our own microbes, let alone Prokaryan bugs. Only a few last long enough to secret toxins; or maybe the toxins were there in the food already. Like botulin from *Clostridium.*"

"So you think it's botulism?"

"Nothing that serious."

What if those whirrs had infected him with enough of the tumbleround's microzoöids to make him hallucinate? "Could insects carry it?"

"The epidemiology of 'spacer's spit-up' does suggest an insect vector. There've really been too many whirrs about; even if they don't feed on humans, their propellers could spread something. So we changed all the filters in the air system, to keep them out." Khral gulped a forkful. "It didn't help any. In fact, the average duration of symptoms increased from two days to five—probably a statistical fluke."

"But Khral—*what if they're trying to tell us something?*"

Khral did not look up. On her lap Qumum complained for attention, and she shifted him to her other arm. "I had kind of hoped it might turn out that way. But we've found no trace of microzoöids in any patient." She sighed. "It's probably for the best. Suppose 'the masters' really got fed up and sent us a deadly disease. You know what the Fold would do."

Boil off the planet, colonies and all. Every colonist had signed the release; Rod never thought much about it, but now he wondered how little it would take. "It's always come to that, hasn't it. Valedon . . ." Valedon had gone through it, millennia before, the searing of earth and sea, the recolonization. Corn and oak, gulls and skunk; all the living things so dear to his own childhood, lived in place of a lost biosphere. Why skunk? he wondered. Did the old terraformers have their sense of humor—or was it their sense of guilt?

"Bronze Sky, too," said Khral. "Centuries later, it's still cooling down. But my parents came from Urulan to settle there, and I love Bronze Sky as it is now. I live for those speckled hawks, the ones that soar above the geysers." Khral's look softened, and for a moment Rod longed to feel her lips on his. Then her eyes widened to stare beyond him. "Is that—"

He turned to see. Several headless octopods had entered quietly, limb over limb. Among them passed two Elysians, their trains doubled up behind. The banker, Rod recognized, the immaculate blond president of Bank Helicon. And the master of Proteus, Nibur Letheshon.

The man looked smaller than he seemed on the holo, short of stature, even for an Elysian. He walked slowly, as if in procession, as Elysians generally did, as if to show they had all the time in the universe.

It occurred to Rod, how little it would take for this small man to breathe his last, and put an end to his schemes. A thumb at the throat would do it. A blow to the temple would do it faster; the twist of a knife, more slowly.

Rod gripped the table until his knuckles whitened. Then he sank his head in his hands. The colony had nearly lost its home, and what was he doing here? Desiring a woman, and wishing death to a man—how had he come to this? How far could he sink before he lost all sight of the Spirit?

FOURTEEN

Nibur kept his promise to Iras, to visit the Sharer lab and show her the high-diversity region of the continent. As his lightcraft from *Proteus* descended toward Mount Anaeon, nothing could mar his good humor, not even the unfamiliar skinsuit that constrained him. He caressed Banga behind the ears; the immortal retriever, too, was enclosed in a skinsuit, and took to it without biting or scratching.

The Opening had gone splendidly, with favorable reviews throughout the Fold. Now all across the continent his earthborers were plunging deep into the crust. By the time the last of the humans had cleared out, and the native biota were duly sampled, the real cleansing could begin. Then the land would fill with lucrative lanthanide mines.

On the slope below, Nibur spotted one of his species samplers. "Bring us over close," he ordered. The sampler towered above the trees, where it had selected a choice specimen to transplant. Shuddering, the giant structure poured its nanoplast into the ground surrounding the chosen singing-tree. At last it scooped the tree up, roots and all, and hauled it off for transport.

"Well done," observed Iras. "Your salvage is most efficient."

"Only the best," he agreed.

"I trust you've sampled all thirty-six varieties? At least twenty specimens of each mating type?"

"Twenty-five, in case of losses."

"Excellent." Iras resumed murmuring to her internal nanoservos. Now that the Opening was done, her attention had moved on to her latest project, a new jump station for Solaris, the Fold's most distant world.

As the slope steepened, other samplers appeared, some with various tire-shaped creatures in nets, others full of helicoids. Only one had stalled in those pesky looproots. Nibur's own nanoservos kept in touch with his brain, but his main interest now was the esthetic challenge: to immortalize Spirilla as an incarnation of the *Proteus*.

They at last touched down on the path, as far as the large transport craft seemed safe. To the left rose sheer cliffs; to the right, the underbrush cascaded down to an echoing river. Nibur stepped outside, feeling oddly unclothed without his talar and train, but no matter. An insect alighted, but it could not penetrate the skinsuit. Nibur took a deep breath through his mouth plate. Few odors came through for him, but enough penetrated to interest Banga, who scampered ahead, sniffing here, there, and everywhere. The dog acted as if he had never smelled a scent before. There was little to smell within the *Proteus*.

With Nibur came Iras, and a dozen specially trained octopods fanning out around them, to prevent accidents.

From around the hill echoed the muffled crunching of the samplers.

Nibur's critical eye scanned the cliffs, which were bursting with unsightly looproots. Those would need to be tidied up in his virtual vision. Ahead of him stretched a gaping valley between Mount Anaeon and Mount Helicon, an arrangement too shameless for his taste. The mountains would be rearranged so as to appear shyly one by one, for "hide and reveal" experiences. The arching trees, too, would be placed artfully, none too close together, and, of course, none of the cluttered understory. A few hoopsnakes would be put in to drop from trees now and then, keeping visitors off guard.

"Extraordinary," exclaimed Iras, craning her neck upward, then down. "The trees—the rushing river—it's enough to take your breath away."

The singing-trees gave way to bushes past their prime of bloom, their browning petals strewn down toward the river. In Nibur's vision, the flowers would be ever-blooming, with no faded petals. He whispered detailed instructions to his servos recording the scene.

Around the mountain, the waterfall came into view. Nibur stopped. Despite himself, he was impressed. Kilos upon kilos of water tumbling forever out of the mountains, thrusting their steam back upward toward the snow-covered peaks. This scene would be hard to improve.

"Warning," called an octopod from ahead. "The path has changed. Time needed to retrace."

"Very well." Nibur frowned, irritated at the inconvenience. The old Sharer could wait long enough; it was her own fault for refusing contact. He would make good use of his time, recording the mountainside, the chattering of helicoids, and the more graceful varieties of vegetation, all to be sorted later. He whistled for Banga—where had that pesky dog got to?

"Curious." Iras bent down to pluck a leaf. "I thought there were no true 'leaves' on Prokaryon, only loopleaves." She held it out to show him. It certainly looked like an ordinary green leaf, pear-shaped, with branching veins.

"Warning, warning!" One octopod called, then another.

To his horror, Nibur saw an octopod dragged off its feet. Its lasers aimed out in several directions, charring the path. But something twined up to catch the octopod by another limb and fling it down the path. Its nanoplast fell apart into blobs that crawled away and lost themselves in the brush. Another octopod followed, landing in the arch of a stunted tree. Half its nanoplast split off and crazily tried to climb, losing itself in the loops.

Something tugged at his foot. It was a green vine, with the same pear-shaped leaves. *"By Torr!"* He tried to pull it off, but it held fast. The whole path was crisscrossed with them. The best he could do was to run along with the tugging vine, until it tripped him up and knocked the wind out of him. Sky and mountains lurched around him crazily, as the vine dragged him onward, more slowly now, but still inexorable. Gradually the vines all converged into a huge thicket beside the waterfall.

The vines met, enfolding him into darkness. Then, just as he was convinced he would suffocate, all the vines relaxed their grip and slunk away.

In the darkness Nibur caught his breath. "Emergency, emergency," he gasped. "Bring ten lightcraft with reinforcements, immediately. . . ."

But no answer came. His cerebral nanoservos had no octopods nor lightcraft to contact. He was cut off. He would rather have lost his arms and legs than his link to *Proteus*.

"Nibur?" called Iras from somewhere. "Are you intact, *Shon*sib?"

"Of course I'm intact." Calming himself, Nibur let his breath return to normal. To his right, Banga whimpered for comfort. He was still intact, and *Proteus* would find him soon. Then, whoever had done this would pay.

A light filled the cavern. Nibur blinked to adjust, scanning the crystal-studded ceiling of the cave. There stood a naked Sharer with an enormous clickfly perched on her scalp. It was Sarai, the eccentric researcher whose lab he had to relocate. Was this insolence her work?

"You're here," Sarai noted flatly, a clickfly perched on her head. "I would say welcome—but you're not. Be glad you got less than what you gave the western coast."

"You will pay," he exclaimed hoarsely. "You will pay the cost of my octopods—I'll put you out of business."

"Oh, no," said Iras, sweeping forward grandly. "*I'll* pay the damage. Why, Raincloud would have done the same—and my heart hasn't raced so in decades. Sarai—it's you at last! I didn't even have a holo, but you're just as I imagined." Iras stopped, catching sight of a little girl trying to hide behind the Sharer; a L'liite waif. "*Blueskywind!*" she exclaimed at the waif. "Sarai, your ancestor, Raincloud's daughter eight generations back, looked very like her." Iras tossed a holocube to the floor, and the image of another curly-haired waif appeared, playing with a legfish. "You see, you had a Bronze Skyan ancestor. But she grew up and mated a Sharer, Weena of Shri-el, and their daughter Ryushu . . ." The descendants appeared in succession, each with less hair and more fingerwebs than the last.

Sarai stared openmouthed at this performance. "Take care, Ushum," she warned the waif beside her. "Elysians are truly mad." But when her own mother and mothersister appeared, she paled, her purple limbs whitening from the fingers upward.

"Oh," said Iras, "don't do that. Or the child will have to wake you." Only a child could safely waken a whitened Sharer. Nibur hoped she died.

Instead, Sarai caught herself, and the purple returned to her limbs. "The two of you are children enough. They should have kept you in the *shon.*"

"Now then." Iras assumed her business voice. "How much will it take to set up your new lab in Chiron? Will a megacred do, or perhaps ten?"

"Do you think this planet cares about your megacreds? *They* are waiting for you. They've been trying to reach us for years—and finally we hear them."

"Oh yes." Iras suppressed a yawn. "The hidden masters. And who might they be?"

Sarai paused. "Whoever they are, they've gotten their messengers into humans. I know—I can prove it."

"Indeed. Can anyone else?"

Very reluctantly, Sarai said, "The others haven't found them yet. They don't know . . . about the little diving suits the microzoöids wear, to avoid the body's defenses."

Nibur laughed. " 'Diving suits.' That takes the prize."

"Sarai," said Iras sympathetically. "You really love this world, don't you. Though it's so unlike Shora."

"The Sharers of Shora are fools," said Sarai. "They don't understand what your kind has done to them."

"Sharers understand that no material home is permanent. Someday, every raft falls apart in the storm. I've helped many of your sisters find a new home."

"After first destroying their old one?"

"Proteus here," called the nanoservos inside Nibur's head. *"Coming to pick you up, Master."*

"Stay well outside," he warned the calling lightcraft. "We're coming out. Let's go, Iras." He whistled to Banga and strode outside without a glance backward.

In the sunlight his eyes blinked rapidly. He found himself shaking with anger and delayed shock. That such indignities could befall him, his own person, was intolerable. As he glanced around now, at the mountains full of singing-trees, their aspect took on a cast of malevolence. That this world might trip him up—such a thought had never occurred to him. But now that it had, he would make his preparations, just in case. A plan shaped itself in his mind, and he whispered brisk instructions. Whatever befell himself, *Proteus* would know what to do. This cursed world would not outlive him.

At the lightcraft Nibur had to whistle three times before the dog obeyed, reluctant to leave this odiferous place. Nibur grasped his collar and twisted it briefly, to show his annoyance. Iras joined them at last, uncharacteristically silent. As the door closed, their skinsuits opened and crept down off their bodies.

"I've been thinking, *Shon*sib," said Iras, as the craft soared toward Station. She did not look at Nibur, but adjusted the folds of her talar after her skinsuit receded. "I'm not so sure that a full cleansing of the continent is really needed. After all, on Urulan, they only cleared the tops of mountains. Here, why not all *but* the mountains?"

His eyes narrowed. "The contract is signed. Is this how Bank Helicon does business?"

"Annihilating unique ecosystems is not good for business. I've heard, from back home." She looked at him. "You haven't answered my question. Why must you clear every last mountain?"

"The poisons wash down from the mountains. The

more thorough the cleansing, the greater the yield of the land. Besides, the mountains hide the richest ores." Nibur let his voice soften. "The mountains are important to me, too. But their material existence is nothing. I will create virtual mountains, greater than any on this poor world. They will form my next vision of *Proteus*. And I will pass the construct on to you—with my compliments."

She did not reply. The offer would be hard to refuse, Nibur knew, for his virtual worlds were one of a kind. Still, for a moment he wished he had taken the bid from the Bank of Bronze Sky instead. They had less capital, but were more predictable.

When Rod returned to the Spirit Colony, he sought Mother Artemis alone. "I can no longer call the Spirit properly," he told her. "All I can think of is that Elysian, how I wish he were dead."

The Reverend Mother's hair strands knotted and un-knotted. "That's too bad. The Elysian could use your prayers."

"If I can't pray for him, how can I pray for anyone?"

She thought about this for some time. From outside, the roar of jet transport set the walls vibrating, as it bore equipment for cleansing to sites across the continent. "Keep trying," she told him. "These things take time. Think of this, Brother Rod: You are being tested."

In the meantime, a tumbleround had migrated to visit yet again, nearly up to the nursery window. No one felt like dealing with it; Rod certainly wanted to keep his distance. So he boarded up the window to keep out the whirrs and left the beast alone. What matter—they would soon be leaving. On the holo they viewed the site for their new farmstead in Chiron. The land looked similar to their own, the brokenhearts drooping from their loopstems, the singing-trees stretching alongside the wheelgrass.

The babies fretted, despite Geode's attempts to cheer them, while the older children grew quiet and listless without knowing what was wrong. Gaea took to her old habit of following Rod wherever he went. Haemum and Chae were withdrawn, even surly. They kept up their chores, but Haemum avoided Rod's eye.

One night Rod awoke to hear pounding at the door. He was up in an instant, knowing it would take Brother Geode and Mother Artemis longer to "waken" from their recharge.

There stood two octopods, each with a bundle wrapped up in four arms. One bundle was Haemum; the other was Chae.

"What have you done to them?" Rod threw himself onto the first octopod and tried to pry the arms of the octopod off of Haemum's face. As his fingers grasped the nanoplast, an electric shock jolted him off. He flew backwards, stunned. Inwardly Rod cursed his own stupidity. His hands and forearms were numb, but with an enormous effort he roused himself to stand.

"The two *shon*lings tried to escape." The octopod opened its arms, releasing Haemum. She was awake enough to raise herself on her hands. By now Brother Geode had arrived, and he helped her and Chae back inside. Each had a pack of water and medicines; they must have planned their break well.

As Haemum lay exhausted on her bed, Rod found little to say. "It's not easy, Sister, for any of us. But you must trust the Reverend Mother."

Haemum looked up at him. Her eyes were those of a

stranger. "What good is Reverend Mother? What good did she do?"

No definite date was set for departure, but the four-eyes meat was gone, and they were dipping into their emergency supply of dried brokenhearts. Every day now the sky was marred by the transporters of death. Whenever Gaea heard them she ran over to cling to Rod's legs.

One afternoon a strange greenish light came in the window. The tint of the sky was somehow familiar to Rod, though he had not seen it in years. He leaned out the window to look.

Iota Pavonis had hidden behind a cloud, a dense, round cloud shaped like a pancake. The edges of the cloud ruffled, dissolving and re-forming themselves. It was a storm cloud.

Rod could not take his eyes off the sight. He had seen storms in the mountains, and he had heard of weather putting out fires, but this was the first storm cloud he had seen right here at the colony. Its shape was perfectly symmetrical, not like the misshapen storm clouds that used to chase up the Valan coast.

As he watched, a large transport vessel sailed overhead, avoiding the cloud. But as the ship neared, the cloud expanded startlingly. Light flashed, illuminating the depths of the cloud, and thunder rumbled. Out of the cloud snaked a long, gray funnel. With a chilling deliberation, the gray funnel wound its way toward the approaching ship.

Rod ducked just soon enough to avoid the flash in his eyes, as the funnel cloud reached the ship. Above his head the windowpane shattered, and his ears rang. He heard children screaming in the next room. Seconds later, there were muffled explosions as parts of the ship hit the ground.

He hurried to check the children and the other windows. When at last he looked outside again, black smoke was rising over the wreckage of the ship, dampened by a fine mist of rain. The pancake cloud receded slowly, its edges dissolving and shrinking back until it disappeared in the afternoon sun.

FIFTEEN

'jum watched Sarai hovering over her pods of microzoöids. As she had been taught, 'jum inserted one of the vine tendrils into the pod, to pluck out a microzoöid. It was a tough job, as the microscopic sisterlings had gelled their growth medium and tunneled out little homes to live in. Now the tendril snaked in to find them. The sisterlings always got upset and tried to wriggle away, as 'jum watched their magnified image on the holostage. She selected one, a red-orange ring. The tip of her tendril slithered through the ring hole and captured the sisterling, to be placed under the recorder.

"Find another one right away, Ushum," Sarai reminded her. "Sisterlings get lonely; a single one will pine away and die." Sarai frowned reflectively. "Clickflies don't get lonely. Loneliness takes some intelligence."

'jum placed another sisterling in the dish, a blue one.

Whenever two different-colored sisterlings were put together, their colors immediately shifted until they were the same. Then they flashed very quickly at each other, exchanging bursts of little flashes.

"It's some kind of number code," guessed Sarai. "That's how the little sisterlings talk to each other. They like talking." Sarai flicked her fingerwebs absently across her chin. "But what do they talk *about?*" She gave 'jum an intense look.

'jum had finally figured out who this fish-woman was. As she stood at the cave entrance, looking out over Mount Helicon, it came to her, the memory of that day she had stood outside the shack with her mother lifeless inside. For so many days before she had watched her mother change, from the alert forewoman who bossed the other workers at the Hyalite plant and was assigned to quality control, into an invalid at home, her arms and legs wasting, turning white; turning into a form that did not look at all like the mother 'jum knew. And then, all at once, she became completely white and still.

But that was not the end. Somehow, 'jum knew, her mother had gone on changing. One of the gods had remade her body; not quite right, just as Brother Rod had not always got things quite right, but they remade her just the same, for all her fishlike hands and feet. 'jum's mother had turned into Sarai.

'jum returned Sarai's hard stare. "Ask them."

Sarai called to the holostage. Instantly it filled with numbers in octal, the system Sharers preferred. These numbers the sisterlings had sent to each other, in little bursts. The numbers were disappointingly small, rarely above ten, and there were lots of zeros.

'jum frowned. "How do you get 'zero' flashes?"

Sarai clasped her hands. "An *intelligent* question—how many years since I heard one! You see, Ushum, the bursts come at regular intervals; yet sometimes the sisterling 'skips' an interval. I'm betting those are zeros." She stared fiercely into the lights. "Pattern, pattern, there must be a pattern." Sarai's jaw fell open. "Look: zero-two-two. It always shows up when sisterling B-eight is one of a pair. Can you find others such correlations, Ushum?"

'jum obligingly went up to the holostage and marked the critical combination with her hand. The numbers set to flashing, wherever they appeared. Sarai clucked her tongue to the clickfly, to record everything 'jum did, not that the girl ever made a mistake.

"Perhaps the sisterlings have names," said Sarai. "Like clickflies do. If they name each other, perhaps they can name things in their growth media. Let's put some fancy molecule in and see what they say. How about anthocyanin? How about some antitriplex antibiotic, at sublethal concentration of course. That ought to get their attention."

By now eight of 'jum's sisterlings swam in the dish of zoöid-phycoid soup. Sarai clucked to a clickfly, who immediately spun a partition across the pod, dividing the group into two groups of four. Into one pod she placed a drop of anthocyanin solution; in the other, the antibiotic specific for microzoöid triplex DNA.

An hour later, she and 'jum were poring over the numbers. "Look at this," Sarai exclaimed. "The patterns are completely different. The microzoöids with the antibiotic produce '1 0 5 3 0 1,' over and over again; whereas the anthocyanin . . . it's a longer pattern."

'jum stared, as if nothing existed but those numbers in the air. Her lips moved soundlessly. There was a longer number pattern, including an eight and an eleven, but it only came twice. She felt vaguely disappointed that there were few interesting primes. Still . . . all those zeros intrigued her. What if there were actually a prime series buried underneath?

"Hey, what's this?" Sarai peered at the pod. The contents of the half with the antibiotic had liquefied, except for one spot. On the holostage, the four microzoöids had all migrated to one side, leaving a mass of fibers on the other. "That's where I dropped the antibiotic," said Sarai. "They walled it off!" She frowned. "This is altogether too clever—even for clickflies. I wonder." She looked up. "I wonder what their four companions will say, if we 'play back' to them the same sequence of light pulses that these little ones made."

So Sarai spent the rest of the day teaching her vines to pulse photons, with much clucking to the clickflies to insert their DNA signals into the plants. 'jum watched so closely that she began seeing flashing lights inside her own eyes. She blinked several times and finally closed her eyes.

The light was still there, inside her eyelids. How curious. It was flashing so fast she could barely make it out, but then it slowed a bit. It came in little bursts of orange, rather like those ringlets on the holostage.

"At last," exclaimed Sarai.

'jum opened her eyes. Sarai held up two long tendrils of her vine, lifeshaped to produce flashes of light at the tips. The two tips produced the two slightly different wavelengths needed to generate the binary code. These she inserted into the half of the pod receiving anthocyanin, which had remained relatively healthy.

"Now we'll see." Sarai stared fiercely at the holostage. "We'll see what they say to *that*. If they're as bright as clickflies, they ought to respond."

As they waited, a whirr appeared in the air, humming

softly. It streaked by 'jum's nose, so close she could see its tiny propeller, then it brushed past Sarai's arm. Sarai waved it away, still watching the holostage.

Another whirr appeared. It spiraled slowly down in the air, hovering at last above the pod of media. Then a second whirr came to join it.

Sarai looked up. "The signal's gone. What happened?" She looked at the pod. "Those infernal insects are eating my microzoöids!"

'jum's lips parted. "I don't think so, Mother. They're just picking them up."

Sarai glared at 'jum. "Whatever do you mean? They just ate every sisterling in the dish. Gone, all of them." She chattered at the clickflies, who set to spinning a fine mesh web across the entrance to the cavern.

"They picked them up," insisted 'jum. "Like a light-craft. To take them back to their city."

Sarai's eyes narrowed. She looked back at the pod, then at 'jum. "Explain yourself, Ushum. Where is this 'city'?"

"The tumbleround." 'jum looked all around the cavern, the clickfly webs, the carnivorous vines to secrete enzymes twisting out from crevices. But there was no tumbleround here. She had not seen one since she left the Spirit Colony.

Sarai came over, bringing her face close to 'jum's. "Why do you call the tumbleround a city?"

"It smells like one."

Sarai took a deep breath; her breasts rose and fell. "Ushum, that is not a logical inference. Insufficient data." She got up and paced back and forth from the holostage to the clickfly webs. "Still . . . suppose it were true." She stopped. "I would be a kidnapper—and a murderer! But no—it can't be. How could microscopic creatures have any brains, when even most full-size humans have so little?"

'jum did not answer. She never had understood the first thing about people, except that few of them in her life were up to much good.

"Experiment, how to design an experiment?" muttered Sarai. "If the sisterlings are only messengers, they certainly are sharp ones—they have hundreds, perhaps thousands of number words. But how could we prove . . . *that they themselves think and feel as we do?*"

The fine mesh web was still forming across the entrance, but not soon enough to keep out more whirrs as they appeared. Dozens of them, as if from nowhere, came swarming insistently, buzzing all around the culture chambers. Sarai closed the open pod, but not before the four were lost. At a command, the main culture vessel was engulfed by a giant flower on one of the vines. The flower closed, its petals tightly wrapped within the calyx, while the whirrs swarmed helplessly around it.

Sarai watched nervously, her hands snapping their fingerwebs. "They know, somehow. They want to get their sisters back."

Suddenly two clickflies sailed in, clicking excitedly.

"What?" Her fingertips paled. "Not here? It can't have got all the way up the mountain." She raced out of the cavern, tearing through the newly spun web. 'jum followed her out the passage, up to the main entrance, where the two clickflies hovered. Sarai took a step outside and craned her neck out, searching down the path. "*Shora*—look!"

A tumbleround was rolling slowly up the path. It was rather a small one, 'jum thought, and it moved along faster than the ones that used to visit the Spirit Colony. She could actually see its foremost tendrils stretch and extend to the ground, implanting themselves, while the hindmost tendrils let go, one by one, whipping upward as they broke off. A haze of whirrs clouded the creature, and its distinctive odor reached her nose.

"*Not here!*" Sarai shrieked at the clickflies and tugged at her vines.

The vines came to life, climbing up across the main entrance. 'jum hurriedly stepped backward to avoid them. Within minutes the entrance was thoroughly sealed; not a whirr could get through the packed mass of greenery.

As the cavern sealed, Sarai ran back to her holostage. "Get me the Station lab," she demanded. "That Khral and her dimwit colleagues. I don't care if the line is busy—it's an emergency."

On the holostage appeared a clinic, like the one where 'jum had spent so many unhappy hours. This one however was Khral's place. Khral stood there with the magic eye perched on her shoulder.

"They've found me!" Sarai yelled at the holostage. "You have to get me out of here!"

Khral exchanged a look with the eye. "Who found you? The octopods?"

"The *tumbleround!* They—there's a million of them in there! And they'll know how I've kidnaped and tortured them!"

"Tortured them? A million tumblerounds?"

"They're *inside* the tumbleround. For Torr's sake, just get me out of here."

"Well sure," Khral began, "I don't see why not—"

At her shoulder the eye whispered something.

"Right, Quark," said Khral. "Sarai, we'll take you up to Station—if you promise to give us a research seminar."

Sarai leaned across the holostage. "*I'm invaded by aliens—and you want a research seminar?*"

*   *   *

At Station, the master of *Proteus* was just preparing to depart. His program for Prokaryon was in place, with only a last-minute glitch or two. A few miners remained at large on Spirilla, and the L'liites were still listed as "missing," though they could never have survived; no doubt Verid had kept them listed, always the clever bureaucrat. His contacts at the Secretariat would soon clear that up. More troubling, from a financial point of view, was the sudden weather instability that had cost him some good equipment. Replacement was no problem, but now he would have to arrange some weather control before proceeding. He would eventually write off the expense.

One last neutrinogram arrived, from the Secretary herself. Verid appeared, her owlish shape looking little different in the gray snow than she did in person. "Nibur Lethe*shon*, chief executive of Proteus Unlimited," she began in a formal tone. "It is my duty to inform you that your full holdings on Prokaryon, third planet of star Iota Pavonis, now exceed fifty percent. As Fold regulation six-oh-six-seven-three-three of the colonial code prohibits any single corporate entity from ownership of more than fifty percent of a colonial world under Fold protection . . ."

So she found out. Nibur shrugged. He had hoped to postpone detection longer, but it made little difference. He would activate his plans to challenge the claim, in three different world courts. The legal process would take decades to work through, and the regulation might well be changed before then.

"And so," Verid concluded, "we rely upon your high standards of Elysian honor and integrity to rectify the situation and comply with this ruling forthwith." She leaned forward, and her tone changed. "I hear Iras quite enjoyed herself in the mountains. Always the excellent host, my friend. Take care of yourself, dear—and Iras, too."

Irritated, Nibur brushed aside the patronizing remark. He himself had a few last neutrinograms to send, before the express trip home across the space folds. His ship always jumped the shortest route, though it might cost ten times the fuel.

At last Iras rejoined him, to board *Proteus*. Their octopods gathered, ready to meet any need. Iras folded up her talar and smiled with amusement. "I trust you scanned clean?"

"Indeed, *Shon*sib, as you did." Even for Elysians, the medics had required extra scans prior to departure, and for his dog as well. Banga now sniffed ahead at the gate to the docking tube, his tail waving.

As the nanoplast of the gate melted in, its edges peeled back to reveal the rotating tube. Nibur caught a handle, bracing himself for the changing forces. Banga stepped forward into the tube. As he did so, the ageless dog gave a yelp and doubled backward, tail between his legs.

Surprised, Nibur caught the dog's collar. Banga was well used to docking tubes; yet now he refused to enter. The artificial gravity must have shifted more suddenly than usual.

Iras had gone ahead, but she stopped and caught her forehead. "Goodness—my nanoservos must be malfunctioning."

With Banga straining at the collar, Nibur took a step forward, then he stopped. His head felt the oddest sensation; there was altogether too little "gravity" here, he thought. Perhaps too little oxygen as well? His stomach convulsed, and a very foul liquid came out, a thing that had never happened to his body before, in five hundred years.

As he tried to cry out, strange glowing shapes appeared. The shapes moved with his head; they must be within his eye, or his brain. From his nanoservos? The shapes formed concentric circles; then they dissolved, and came together to form the letters, *NO*. That was the last he knew before he lost consciousness.

SIXTEEN

At the Spirit Colony, the tumbleround had reached the wall outside the nursery and planted its fibers in the siding, reaching just up to the sill of the boarded-up window. The colonists had all their heavy equipment packed and the rest ready to go once their last food ran out. Without fields to tend, at least the children were catching up on their lessons, their math and reading, and their constitutional rights as citizens of the Free Fold. The nationalist protesters could have no complaints now.

"Did you hear," exclaimed Brother Geode, "about that dreadful Proteus person, and his financier? They're both critically ill—with 'spacer's spit-up'!" His eyestalks twisted gleefully, until Rod frowned. "Unlike mortals, who get over it," Geode added, "the Elysians develop complications—meningitis."

"So I've heard." Rod vowed to pray for their recovery. "Is the cause still unknown?" Khral must be going crazy over it; she would have no time for tumblerounds now.

"It's a mystery," said Geode. "They tried triplex anti-biotics on the dog—and the dog died. Perhaps they'll think again about this planet."

"They'll think no good." The very hint of death, even a dog's death, could make Elysians turn the heavens inside out.

That evening as the colonists prayed outside, the llamas calling to the dusk, an occasional whirr strayed over from the tumbleround. Rod found his eyes momentarily clouded with bright, inchoate shapes, reminiscent of his previous encounter with the beast. He shook his head, trying to clear his mind. Should he go up to Station for testing? What could they do for him, if they could not even cure the Elysians?

The next morning, the image of Proteus Unlimited appeared on the holostage. The sexless speaker stood the same as always, above the never-ending curl of water.

"Your plans have changed," the speaker announced, as if the colonists had ever made their own plans. The Spirit Callers listened stoically. "You will depart promptly tomorrow. The transport vessel will arrive, at this hour precisely."

So that was it. The children would walk—or be carried out by octopods. Rod kept his face frozen, and his hands at his sides.

Mother Artemis asked, "Is our homestead ready on Chiron? Will the children have a roof over their heads?"

"Unexpected delays have developed. Chiron requires further tests for habitability; it must be cleansed of deadly disease, before any further colonies may be established. We have arranged temporary accommodation of all Prokaryan colonists on an orbital satellite."

A refugee ship. The children would be refugees.

"Once the disease is cleared out, and quarantine is lifted, you will be free to go."

"What do you mean, 'cleared out'?" Rod was shaking. Would the whole world be "cleansed," to eliminate one bit of sickness that endangered only Elysians?

The empty figure did not reply. Geode extended his eyestalks, and some of Mother Artemis's hair outstretched, like a futile plea. "The Spirit be with you," murmured the Reverend Mother at last.

Afterward, she tried to send a neutrinogram to the Secretariat, but was told the transmitter was out of order. That afternoon, however, a neutrinogram arrived from the Most Reverend Father of Dolomoth.

Out of the snow formed the gray shape of the Most Reverend Father, his beard longer than ever. "The Spirit be with you, Brothers and Sisters," he began. "Our hearts are heavy indeed to hear the sad news from Prokaryon. At least, we thank the Spirit, you were spared the worst afflictions of this deadly plague. Alas, who could have foreseen the unfortunate destiny of your work on that desolate world?

"Remember that you are not the first colonists to have made a valiant effort in a strange new land, only to withdraw from the attempt. You took a courageous stand, and you raised your children well in the light of the Spirit. When you return to Valedon, be assured that the Spirit Council will not forsake you. We have excellent Spirit-filled orphanages to guide your youngsters to adulthood, at which time they themselves may experience the sacred calling.

"All of the Congregation of Dolomoth will call unto the Spirit to give you strength, as you undertake your final journey home."

*   *   *

The brokenheart stew for supper was flavored with helicoids caught from the rafters, since the last of the zoöid meat was gone. As Chae spooned it out down the long tables, Rod still could not believe this would be their last meal in the home they had built twelve years before; in fact, their last supper on Prokaryon. Gaea clung to him without eating, and the twins whined.

T'kun popped up from under the table. "Are we going to live in a spaceship? Can I bring my pet zoöid?"

Haemum led the prayer, calling the Spirit for truth and grace. Rod found he could not meet her eyes.

After dinner the last of the pots and spoons were packed away. Most of the farm equipment had already been transported—supposedly to Chiron, now no one knew where. Each child kept one treasure: a bit of quartz from the sapphire mine, a helicoid propeller, a dried twisted pod.

As the light faded, the children sat out on the wheelgrass, and Mother Artemis spread her skirt one last time for a story. In the folds of nanoplast shone a planet and a star. The planet was half in darkness, green lapped by tongues of cloud, while its star glowed so brightly it was hard to look upon.

There was a world where only children dwelt. Where every creature grew with a saddle made for riding, and every tree formed little steps for climbing. Every insect came with pinholes ready for pinning into boxes, and a vine grew from every tree for swinging . . .

The children laughed, and they quickly added others.

"Every zoöid grows a leash for leading," called T'kun.

"And they grow food pods, so we don't have to hunt them."

"And crayons grow on trees."

This world had lived a million years. But its star was growing old and seeing the last of its hydrogen fuel. With its hydrogen gone, the star told the world, "I need to grow.

I need to grow enough to burn my next best fuel. But fear not, little world, for you will never die." So the star grew larger and redder. It grew so large that its surface filled the orbit of the tiny world. As the star approached, the world's creatures fell asleep in the heat; until at last the entire world fell into it, dissolving into stardust. But what the star said was true, for that world never died. It will live forever in the hearts of children who remember."

The children grew calm, snuggling close for comfort. Only Haemum and Chae stood aside, their faces sullen. Rod felt torn apart inside. There was love and comfort here, but was there truth? Did the Spirit never call for more?

After the children were in bed, and the last packing done, Rod could not sleep. He stood outside as the nightly rain continued, finally tapering off to reveal the stars. A faint glow came from the distant band of singing-trees, their colors racing across the tops with their enigmatic patterns. Somewhere in the wheelgrass a nocturnal zoöid called for its mate, and another answered. A breeze brought the scent of the tumbleround.

As he watched, an octopod came from behind the llama barn to tour around the main compound, at the same hour it always did. The octopods were highly regular in their habits; their pattern of patrols was familiar to him, their paths crisscrossing the same way every night. Rod reached a decision.

He went inside to find Mother Artemis, now a gray lump sleeping. Regretfully he touched her surface to interrupt her sleep. She came awake slowly, arms extending and hair regenerating out of the amorphous nanoplast.

"Reverend Mother, I must ask your release," Rod told her. "I have called on the Spirit for so many years—but the Spirit who calls back is from this planet. I cannot return to Valedon, and leave this world here to die."

"Indeed," said Mother Artemis. "You have listened well. But what can you do?"

"I've been watching the octopods. They're only Proteus servos after all, not sentients. I've studied their movements; and I know a few moves myself that might get me past a servo. With your permission, I'll leave tonight, hiding my tracks in the trail of the tumbleround." He shuddered, but there was no better way. "By hiding in the forest, I can help postpone the final cleansing, while the planet's masters start to fight back. Who knows—perhaps the Fold Council will see reason in time."

She considered this. "If you are called, so be it. But beware. When the authorities capture you, they will not treat you kindly."

"I'll take that risk." One of his more interesting subjects at the Academy had been survival under torture. Students had protested it was outmoded, in the age of the Free Fold, but the Academy Master had only smiled.

"Very well," said Mother Artemis. "I think it would be best if I disable the octopods with a stream of radio noise. As you say, they are servos; it may take some time for them to come round and 'repair' my circuit."

Rod swallowed hard. "Thanks," he could barely whisper.

"But first you shall ask Haemum and Chae."

"What? They're children. It's too dangerous. They have lives ahead of them."

"They've earned the choice. It's their planet, too."

In the dark nursery, as Haemum and Chae watched, Rod pried the boards off the window, hoping not to wake the little ones. The odor of the tumbleround below was enough to knock him out, but he braced himself to get used to it. A shaft of moonglow fell across Gaea in her bed, her hands stretched before her face with the peaceful abandon of a sleeping child. Rod paused, wondering if he would ever see her again. Mother Artemis was right, he realized; without company, he could never have torn himself away.

Haemum and Chae were poised at the window, backpacks in their arms, awaiting the first step. At last Rod's pocket holostage beeped once; it was the signal from Mother Artemis, disabling the octopods.

Rod crouched on the window, then he leaped forward, out over the tumbleround. He landed in the garden behind it, amid its discarded travel roots. Haemum and Chae tossed the backpacks out to him, including his own, which he quickly slipped on. Then they, too, jumped out, and the three of them sprinted down the noxious trail the tumbleround had made through the garden. The gluish secretions got all over their hands and clothes; unpleasant, but any nanoplastic pursuer would avoid their touch.

Ruddy moonglow flooded the fields as if to bathe them in blood. The three of them jogged for a kilometer or so, until the wheelgrass came up again where the tumbleround trail grew old, and they had to pick their feet heavily through it. Rod noticed Chae falling behind, and he slowed a bit more. Still there was no sign of pursuit.

A hollow song arose, the manifold voice of the nearest band of singing-trees. The trail of the tumbleround, which had grown faint, seemed to widen and take on fresh odor, as if more than one of the beasts had traveled there. Reluctantly Rod entered the forest, wary of what might drop from the trees. The eerie song of the trees rose to a roar, drowning all else.

They continued through the forest, along tumbleround trails that seemed to cross each other, winding around the great arches of the singing-trees. Rod wondered why no actual tumblerounds appeared. As the night wore on, the singing quieted, and other creatures could be heard. Long squirming rings dangled from the arches, groaning to each other, and the sidling of a hoopsnake gave Rod a start. His toe snagged so often, his hands were cut and bruised from catching himself. He wished they had the sturdy llamas to ride.

Finally the first trace of dawn appeared, from the east behind them. Rod called the youngsters to halt. "We'll sleep here, until night falls again."

Haemum nodded without speaking, her face surrounded by matted curls. Chae sank exhausted against the trunk of the singing-tree. What would become of them—such promising students, now stateless refugees. As for himself, Rod could not begin to think of it. Suddenly he remembered 'jum, that day he first found her, alone in the universe amid the hovels of death. What would become of her? Now all of them were like her.

For the moment, though, the three of them had each other. Rod caught Haemum and Chae each in his arms, and held them both close. He wondered about the others, Mother Artemis and Brother Geode alone with all the little ones, and the llamas—how had they all managed? And where were they now? It was hard to think of the colony deserted and desolate, all their fields of brokenhearts unattended.

He set up the tent in the arch beneath the singing-tree, and the three of them slept until late in the day. In the evening they roused themselves and ate from their packs, sparingly. Haemum found water to boil in the solar unit recharged during the day. Chae caught a hoopsnake to supplement dinner for himself and Haemum; Rod did not yet dare to eat it, lest he sicken without access to help. The gentle twilight rainfall dribbled down their tent as they prayed.

With nightfall, they had to move on, farther along the forest band, to put as much distance as they could between themselves and the pursuers sure to follow. But Chae walked with a limp, though he denied it, and Haemum stopped frequently to press her forehead. "Take one of your medicines," Rod urged.

Haemum shook her head, saying cryptically, "That won't help."

As they slogged on through the loopleaves, the scent of tumblerounds began to grow. They stumbled at last upon a clearing among the singing-trees. Rod stopped, nearly crying out in amazement.

There beneath the star-studded sky were a group of tumblerounds, at least a dozen of them. They were standing quite still, like old truck tires covered with cobwebs.

After staring for a minute, Rod shook himself and turned to the youngsters. "We could rest here a while," he said. "The octopods will avoid this place like the plague." At least he hoped so.

Chae agreed readily, sinking down to rest. Haemum seemed more reluctant, but agreed. Rod wished he could do more for her. He sat himself down against a singing-tree trunk, not admitting the real reason he had stopped.

What if these beasts actually were the masters of Prokaryon? What if he could get across something more from them, more than a raised hand?

Rod watched the tumblerounds, trying to relax and empty his mind as he did when calling the Spirit. For a while nothing happened, and he half slept. Then the bright spots reappeared, shaping themselves in his eyes. They formed random shapes, pinching off and coming together, as if a sculptor were playing with clay. A crude line figure formed, a bar with three branches. Three fingers?

The figure lasted for a minute or so. Then two of the three lines dissolved, and the topmost lengthened above the vertical bar. With a shock, Rod saw that it was the letter "E." Soon it was joined by a "T."

"Haemum," Rod whispered.

"Yes, Brother Rod?"

"Do you ever . . . see odd things? When you get headaches?"

"Maybe," she said guardedly. "Like what?"

"Like letters?" The letter "A" had appeared, followed by "O."

"I've seen letters," she admitted.

"Why didn't you tell us?"

"Chae said you'd think we were crazy."

Rod looked at Chae.

"We're all crazy," said Chae. "Ever since the tumbleround came after us."

He turned to Haemum. " 'E, T, A, O, N. . . .' Does that mean anything?"

Haemum said, "I asked at school. It's the frequency distribution of our language; the most common letters downward." She caught his arm. "How do they do it, Brother Rod? How does a tumbleround . . . get inside our heads like that?"

"They send microzoöids, through the whirrs. Like nanoservos, somehow, the microzoöids contact our brains."

Chae shrank away. "I always knew those beasts were bad."

Rod remembered the journey to Sarai, when the poor

boy awoke to find the whirr-covered visitor leaning over them. "You needn't go through this, Chae. You can go back to Station."

The boy shook his head. "There's bad and there's worse."

Rod asked Haemum, "Do you ever see words?"

"Once, I think. The word 'the,' the most common word."

So the tumbleround knew about "words;" but it knew no meanings. Did it? How did it know enough to make letters? It must somehow see what his own eyes saw.

From his backpack Rod took a piece of nanoplast that still had enough juice to glow faintly. He pulled out chunks of the nanoplast, which he rolled and stretched into letters, to form the word HAND. He stared at the letters, outstretched on the ground next to his own hand, until his eyes watered. Then he gave up and looked away.

His forehead ached, and the bright rings reappeared in his eyesight. They flickered and coalesced to form the letters: $H \ldots A \ldots N \ldots$

Rod vaguely realized that something of tremendous importance had happened; something the Fold had all sorts of rules and regulations about reporting, if ever such an event should occur to the human race. Except that it never had; and no one would believe it now. A Spirit Caller's visions did not count as evidence.

He blinked his eyes, but the letters remained, next to a crude shape of a hand. Why could these creatures not simply announce themselves on the airwaves, he thought, instead of inside his own head? With a sigh, he gathered up the nanoplast, still glowing faintly, and rearranged it to another word: HOME. That was no good; he needed something more concrete. CHILD, he tried, though it was hard to picture a child. LLAMA was a four-legged stick figure.

"I" was a man with two legs. YOU . . . How to picture a tumbleround?

The presence in his head returned, YOU . . . LLAMA.

Rod blinked in surprise. The tumbleround's micro-zoöids must have picked up "YOU," just from the idea in his head. The "llama" was an understandable error, for Rod himself actually looked four-legged now, as he crouched on the ground. Patiently he reshaped the nanoplast to read: I . . . MAN.

The presence immediately replied: I . . . MAN; YOU . . . LLAMA.

Rod was not sure at all how to take this. He looked out at the group of tumblerounds, wondering which one of them had sent this message. Or all of them—were they some kind of group mind? And what would the Fold do when they found out?

SEVENTEEN

At Station, Sarai was giving her public lecture on the holostage. The purple Sharer wore no more than usual, but she carried herself like an Elysian in a full-length train. The viewing chamber was packed with the research scientists, Elk and Khral and the sentients, as well as several caterpillar-shaped medics, who had yet to bring the two Elysians out of their comatose state. Reporter snake eggs hovered overhead like bees, until Station warned them to keep out of the way.

In the corner sat 'jum, swinging her legs and feeding bits of protein cake to Sarai's carnivorous vine; it extended only an arm's length, the longest piece Quark could be persuaded to take along. She clucked now and then at the two clickflies working on their web above her head. A reporter tried to interview her for human interest, but she ignored it.

"These *microzoöids,*" Sarai began, "of species *Sarai*

phycozoöidensis, were first isolated from human cerebrospinal fluid—encased within crystals of silicate. The silicate coating protects each microzoöid from the toxic
human interior, just as our skinsuits protect us from the
Prokaryan *ex*terior. Your nanoservos never look for silicate," she added with a superior air. "Upon removal to
standard phycozoöid culture media, the silicate coatings
dissolve to reveal—"

"Whoa, there." Elk half rose to his feet. "Human spinal
fluid? I thought your strain first came from a tumbleround—"

Sarai glared. "*You* can wait till the question period. If I
choose to answer any."

Khral tugged Elk's arm, and Quark hissed at him to
hush. Station announced, "We'll have ample time for questions—all day, if necessary. Please proceed."

Sarai sniffed. "Wherever would *I* find a tumbleround;
they never reached the mountains until they had to rescue
their citizens. As I was saying . . ."

Elk opened his mouth again, but thought better of it.
He fell back, looking dazed.

". . . the silicates from the human cerebrospinal fluid
dissolved in the media," Sarai continued, "revealing typical
toroid cells, with the usual ring of triplex DNA running
around the hole. But these cells failed to thrive. And they
were few in number; barely a hundred from the original
source." She raised her hand, spreading the fingerwebs like
a fan. "That's when I made the ingenious choice of 'universal broth,' a medium of my own invention that enables
growth of a wide range of species. I inoculated eight cells.
They immediately proceeded to metabolize, putting out all
sorts of fascinating by-products." The list of products
scrolled down the holostage for the next half hour, while

she described them in detail. Elk slumped in his chair, but the medical "caterpillars" reared up to pay attention, for any metabolic product might be toxic to humans.

"On the second day, two individuals fell in love and began to reproduce, by a unique conjugative process." Sarai snapped her fingers at the holostage. Two microzoöids appeared, glowing blue; the two cells came together, neatly stacked. Sarai turned to 'jum. "You're too young for this, Ushum. Go take the clickflies for a stroll."

'jum went on feeding the vine, which had grown about a centimeter so far. 'jum knew pretty well what used to happen between her parents in their corner of the shack, and what happened to girls in the street who didn't throw stones.

"The two ringlike cells fit together, alongside each other," Sarai continued. "Then, all around the ring, the two cells fuse completely."

On the holostage the two rings merged, becoming one.

"Imagine it, if two human lovers became one person with four legs! But each microzoöid is just a cell, remember, with its one ring of triplex DNA. The double cell now has two rings."

Within the holographic cell, the two rings of DNA lit up red.

"Since the two enamored cells have become one, their two DNA rings can merge and exchange all six strands. Then they pull apart—in *three* rings of *duplex* DNA. The two red rings came together. Then they split apart into three, presumably three double helices."

Elk jumped up again. "You mean the triplex DNA cells produce *duplex* offspring? So that two triplex parents merge to make three duplex daughters?"

Sarai threw up her hands. "Go ahead, you give the seminar."

Khral said, "Never mind, Sarai; we're just trying to follow the evidence. So you observe duplex daughter cells; and then?"

She gave a dark look in Elk's direction. "As our resident genius proposed, each daughter cell has duplex DNA. But it grows a third DNA strand right away, restoring the triplex, while enzymes correct all the base-pair mismatches amongst the parental strands, completing genetic recombination throughout the chromosome. Of course the mechanism of recombining triple-stranded DNA molecules is a matter for some speculation. . . ."

She speculated for the next half hour, and one of the medics got up to leave. Sarai glared at the three who remained. "Nano-pushers. No intellectual curiosity, that's what's wrong with the medical profession today. How else will you invent new antibiotics, if not to attack the mechanics of DNA?"

On the holostage the three blue rings began to pulse different colors, while waving their flagella to propel themselves away. "Two parents, three children," said Sarai. "But the interesting point is this: *where are their parents?* Their parents no longer exist, right? Ordinary microbes wouldn't care, but these care a lot." She flicked her webbed hand toward the audience. "Remember, I inoculated with eight individuals, the Sharer way. Not all eight cells reproduced. One of them avoided reproduction, while the others underwent several generations. The first one remained, not a parent exactly, but an 'elder' for the young ones. And in all my cultures, the young ones know who their elders are.

"Think of ordinary microbes. What kinds of microbes know their parents, let alone their elders? Yeasts bud off daughter cells, and volvox colonies protect their young within the center. But when the young leave, that's it; they never notice their parents again."

Sarai clicked again at the holostage. Numbers filled the air, all the thousands of numbers she and 'jum had studied from the flashing cells. "These sisterlings are different. Their elders pass on their civilization. From the moment of birth, the young sisterlings and their elders flash numbers at each other. At first easy numbers, mainly threes and fives; then larger numbers, even with multiple factors. Those multiple factors are *words*. We even learned two of their words—'1 0 5 3 0 1,' for the antitriplex antibiotic; '1 0 0 0 3 0 8 0 12 0 2,' for anthocyanin. Each individual word starts with a number 1."

'jum had slipped down from her seat and stepped up to the holostage, as if mesmerized. She picked at the digits as if to pluck them from the air, then pointed to other patterns she liked even better. What if each "word" were actually a prime series with holes in it?

"There can be only one conclusion," said Sarai at last. "We're dealing not with the messenger, but with the sisterlings themselves—the true intelligence of Prokaryon. For this insight, of course, I must give credit to my colleague, Ushum."

For a minute after Sarai stopped there was silence, as if the audience could not believe she had quite done. Khral rose and stretched, her legs stiff after the two-hour marathon.

"Just a moment," called Quark's eyespeaker. "There are lots of possible conclusions. How do you even know you've got one species? Your culture may not be pure; you started with eight founders."

"Sharers always start cultures with eight," said Sarai. "So they won't be lonely."

"But—" Quark sputtered but gave up.

Elk rose. "Where do these microzoöids live, if not in a tumbleround?"

"They can adapt to live in almost any host, just as humans can adapt to any climate. According to Khral's work, they are more highly concentrated in the tumbleround than anywhere else," she admitted. "We think the tumbleround is their city, their main dwelling place."

"But they could enter the singing-trees too—and control them!" exclaimed Elk. "I've checked, now that I know what to look for. The singing-trees could be their long-distance communication!"

A sentient medic reared its caterpillar limbs. "What about *human* hosts?" he insisted. "Why and how do these microzoöids cause disease? What's their pathology? Why the onset at entrance to a spaceship?"

"What do you think?" demanded Sarai. "Would *you* like to be carried off from your own universe at a moment's notice, without permission? Wouldn't you try to bail out from your host first?" She added thoughtfully, "Of course . . . all of them might not have bailed out. Some might have stayed on and hitched a ride to the stars. . . ."

"Wait a minute." The next medic reared its caterpillar body. "Are you saying we've got an *intelligent disease* here that's managed to spread undetected—perhaps even to other worlds?"

No one answered. The three medics suddenly slunk out of the room as fast as they could crawl, several snake eggs in pursuit.

"Wait," Khral called after them. "It's not a 'disease' we're talking about—it's a new sentient race!"

Station said, "You're right, Khral; I've notified the Secretariat. But it's a disease, too. Those Elysians are dying."

"How do we talk to them? How do we convince *them* whom to talk to?"

Elk added, "After they've tried for decades to contact our own bacteria?" He shook his head. "They must have given up long ago. They must think we have an IQ of zero."

'jum stared. In her eyelids she saw the other lights flashing again. Perhaps she was turning into a holostage—a holostage for the sisterlings inside of her. But how to talk back?

She remembered the vines with the photoemitting tips that Mother Sarai had made to "talk" to the sisterlings in her pod. 'jum had thought of trying those vines before, and now that Mother's attention was diverted, she had her chance. She slipped out of her seat and departed unnoticed. As she was leaving, Khral looked up. "Sarai, who was the first carrier? Which human did you get your culture from?"

Rod awoke with a start. He must have dozed off, but his pocket holostage was beeping. Beside him, Haemum and Chad were fast asleep, too exhausted even to wake. The midday sun filtered through the arches of the singing-trees, and the helicoids cried.

Wondering what to do, Rod frowned at the holostage. Only Mother Artemis had the code to reach him. The holostage beeped again. Very reluctantly he opened the case. "Reception only," he spoke.

In the box two tiny figures appeared; he took a closer look. One was Khral, the other Elk Moon, his tall figure reduced to doll size.

Rod blinked in surprise. How could she have found him? Was it a trick to capture him—a recorded image?

"Rod? Do you hear us, Rod?" She sounded anxious. "I don't know, Elk; we've got to keep trying." Her head leaned to hear Quark's eyespeaker whisper. The whole lab group, trying to call him?

"Answer, Rod, please. Your children—we've got to help them."

His hand tightened on the box. "Transmit," he ordered at last.

Khral's eyes widened. "It's you!" the tiny voice gasped. "Thank goodness you're okay."

Rod frowned. "Where did you get my code?"

"From Mother Artemis. We—"

"Is she all right? And all the children?"

"As far as we know. They're—"

Station's voice said, "They're all well, on board."

Rod let out a sigh, and for a moment he could not speak.

"They're all . . . well enough." Khral's voice wavered.

Elk added, "Three Crows is helping them out. With the quarantine, now, nobody can leave this place—period. None of us, for Torr knows how long."

"It's horrible," Khral exclaimed. "The Fold has gone crazy—they may kill off this planet, Rod, whether you're there or not."

Rod shrugged. "So be it. What do you need from me?"

"Station said we had to find you," Khral explained, "and Mother Artemis agreed. Rod—there's something else you need to know." She looked uncertainly at Elk.

"It's about the microzoöids," Elk said guardedly. "Khral will explain."

Rod felt he knew more than he wanted already.

"Well," said Khral, "Sarai told us where she got her first culture. She cleared them all out," Khral added hurriedly, "but—" She stopped. "They were in Gaea's spinal fluid."

His mouth fell open. "In Gaea?" He had not expected this at all. "But how—when—"

Khral's face crumpled, and she turned away. Elk put his arm around to comfort her. "It's all right," he added. "Sarai promised she cleared them out."

"It was when Gaea was there for lifeshaping, to correct her spina bifida," Khral explained, collecting herself.

"But—*why didn't she tell me?*"

"She doesn't trust you."

Rod remembered that day he arrived, with the two bruised boys and the girl badly in need of care; and how Sarai had made him lose his temper. It had never occurred to him to wonder what she thought of him.

"She checked Gaea's spinal fluids very carefully, and she found these odd silicate crystals, which none of our own nanoservos ever noticed because they weren't programmed to do so. Inside the silicate crystals hide the microzoöids."

Elk added, "You see what that means? We all could be carriers."

"But we're not," Khral added hurriedly. "We're all getting checked, now that we know what to look for."

Quark said, "Even the sentients were all checked, though no silicates have yet been found in us. Not that I'd go near that planet again."

How prudent, Rod thought ironically. "I thought you said it was normal to have a few microzoöids going through your system."

"In the intestinal tract, it's normal to find a few," Khral explained, "but the central nervous system has to be sterile. Infection there causes meningitis—that's what the Elysians got."

"The Elysians are still sick? Why couldn't you clear out the 'silicates'?"

"The medics are afraid to try that. Remember, the triplex antibiotic killed the dog. What would you do, if somebody from 'outside' tried to do you in? Rod, the microzoöids themselves are intelligent."

The microzoöids were intelligent. A brain's worth of

data in a single cell. It was senseless; and yet suddenly everything made sense. No wonder the thinking creatures had gone unfound for so long. And now . . . A chill came over his scalp. How many of them were inside him? Would they not think it right to take his own life, to save so many of theirs?

"All the colonists are getting checked now," Khral told him. "Rod, you need to get checked too."

"It's too late. They're already in my brain. They talk."

"They *what?*"

"They make letters and words."

Khral and Elk exchanged startled glances.

Station's voice took over. "Rod, we need your help. If you've made contact, then Secretary Verid can use you. And we need you to find out what those invaders do when their host tries to board a starship."

"Wait a minute," Khral interrupted. "Station, you didn't tell me about this. You keep quiet."

"We'll pay you, Rod," continued Station. "Double-hazard pay."

"No you won't!" Khral reached for the switch. Elk caught her arm to restrain her, but she pushed him away. "Leave Rod alone, he's been through enough. Holostage— Good-bye."

"But the Elysian lives are at stake," said Elk. "Rod's microzoöids might even tell us how to save them."

Station added, "And we'll restore your immigration quota." The Fold would give anything to save those two foolish Elysians, while half a world could die of prions.

"Leave Rod alone," insisted Khral. "When Secretary Verid gets here, let her decide how to make contact."

Then his inner eye opened, and he saw, as if a light shone, what he was called to do. "I will do it," he said clearly. "I will come back and do what is needed—on one condition. I will take no payments—nothing at all. I will do as I am called, for that reason alone."

Khral's face turned gray. "No, Rod," she whispered. "Not you."

Deep within the sphere of the Secretariat, the Fold Council held an emergency session. Outside, the reporter eggs hovered insistently, but this hearing was closed.

The nanoplastic chamber had shaped itself to make luxurious seats for the delegates, each representing one of the eight peoples of the Fold. Over the council presided the Secretary herself. Outwardly Verid smiled at the delegates, a smile just long enough to meet the occasion. Within herself she burned, like a coal mine on fire underground. Her beloved Iras was dying—half a millennium of their life together, now suspended.

"Citizens." The eight delegates lounged in their eight niches, at various angles and heights within the chamber. "Citizens—we are called into session, at request of the Delegate Elysium."

The Delegate Elysium this decade was her old nemesis, Loris Anaea*shon,* who had unfortunately succeeded Verid herself as Prime Guardian of Elysium, only to follow her to the Secretariat. A server arm snaked out to offer him a flower cake, while another brought him a pocket holostage.

"The citizens of Elysium demand decisive action against this plague," he proclaimed. "We must eliminate the source of this dreadful pathogen. The policy of partial cleansing was a noble attempt at humane preservation, worthy of the loftiest principles of the Fold. But the hostile weather conditions and the malevolent nature of this plague require decisive action. The planet has been evacuated, the last dissident miners and settlers recovered—the time is now."

He raised his butterfly-cloaked arm. "Let the Secretary authorize the full sterilization of planet Iota Pavonis Three."

"Seconded." The Delegate Valedon sat beside him, in a white talar bearing a moon's worth of gems. Both he and the Elysian held substantial stock in Proteus Unlimited.

As Delegate Elysium began his predictable speech in support of the motion, Verid summoned herself out of her private hell. Her keen gaze swept the chamber. Whom might she count on to speak for Prokaryon—and its unknown inhabitants? Delegate Sharer, of course, of the ocean women of "Shora"; though dwelling on Shora with the Elysians, their race was granted separate representation. The Sharer wore a plain talar of purple that matched her complexion, a concession to sensitivities. She would oppose terraforming, as would the Delegate Sentient, a lamppost-shaped creature representing all the sentient machines of the Fold.

Beyond these votes in hand, Verid knew she faced an uphill fight. Delegate Bronze Sky, a shrewd woman as dark as the L'liite, would listen to argument; but even Bronze Sky, alas, was a terraformed world. Delegate Solaris, now, from the most remote of the Fold's worlds, was hard to predict. He would take an independent stand, for reasons of his own.

The Elysian's speech concluded, and Verid looked up. "No one is in a better position than I to sympathize with the intent of this motion." She met the eyes of each delegate in turn. "But since when do we annihilate a whole biosphere, for one fatal disease? Which world of our own could survive such a test?" She shook her head. "More than that—an *intelligent* disease. The duty to respect an alien intelligence forms a cornerstone of the Fold Constitution—and for good reason. In respecting 'the other,' we assure respect for ourselves."

Delegate Valedon's seat came alight to respond. "The constitution was never meant to apply to just any old intelligent alien. It was meant for, well, hostile space invaders, that sort of thing. Aliens we could deal with— strike bargains with, buy off, in the usual way. How can you deal with a microbe?" He shrugged. "If you believe they're 'intelligent,' which I don't; it's not been proven. Even if they are—all the more reason to get rid of them before we find out."

"Agreed," said Delegate Urulan, an elegant gentlemen with just enough of a thickened brow to keep the simian vote. "The planet holds trillions of them. Should we let our votes be outnumbered a thousand to one by microscopic 'people'? My people won't stand for it."

Though none of this surprised her, a chill ran up her neck. In all our fine clothes, she thought, how little separates us from barbarity. She whispered to recognize the Delegate Sharer, whose seat came alight.

"I will not dignify these arguments with the response they deserve," began the Sharer coldly. "To be outnumbered a thousand to one is nothing new to *my* people. The Sharers of Shora have never, and will never, countenance ecocide." She raised her webbed hand, and its color drained white, the sign of a solemn vow. "If Prokaryon must die, I myself will lead our witnessers to share its death."

At that, the Delegate Elysium turned rigid, though he should have expected as much. Not that a few dead fish-women would disturb him, but it would be a public embarrassment. "You just wait," he exclaimed. "We'll declare open asylum for immigrants. You can house them all on your rafts."

"The Honorable Delegate will excuse me, but he is out of order," Verid interposed. "Delegate Sentient."

The "lamppost" spoke. "Of course I agree with the

Honorable Delegate Sharer. Sentient intelligence is to be recognized—'*in any form it shall appear.*' Those are the words of our constitution. Size is no object—creatures of nanoplast have been recognized as sentient, some as large as entire planets, others as small as insects."

That was true. It was also true, though, that microscopic nanoservos were excluded, by a little-known provision of the treaty.

"I propose a countermotion," added the lamppost. "Let the Secretary test the microzoöids for sentience."

Verid nodded, feeling relief; the countermotion had come as planned. "Let all of us first have their say on the first motion. Delegate L'li."

The L'liite frowned at the Delegate Elysium. "The will of my people is deeply mixed. Indeed, we have to support any measure that opens land for our settlers. Yet 'ecocide' goes against our deepest traditions. Besides, we cannot help but question the economic logic behind this motion. To sterilize Pavonis Three, by a white hole out of deep space, will cost the Fold trillions of credits. A smaller sum could rid my homeworld of the prions that have claimed billions of lives."

As opposed to one dead dog—he might as well have said it aloud. Verid was impressed. She told her internal nanoservos to arrange a private meeting with him.

"You're all dreaming," exclaimed the Delegate Solaris. "These are *microbes* we're talking about; microbes that have already escaped within starship passengers, the nine out of ten that *didn't* get sick. They could be hiding *anywhere in the Fold.*" He jumped up and spread his hands. "What difference does it make, if we do kill off their planet? They're microbes, with a generation time of only a day. Wherever they are, they'll take over."

Verid observed, "It would make a big difference, I

think, if you were a microbe—and you knew who had killed all your family."

"Nonsense," countered Delegate Elysium. "When you have a plague, you wipe out the main source, then control the rest. We can find them now; the silicate test has revealed all the carriers."

The seat lighted for the Delegate Bronze Sky. "Are you sure?" The woman rubbed her chin reflectively. "The same researchers who gave us the silicate test believe the disease is intelligent. Smart enough to control all its own animals and plants—even the weather. Think about it. Even ordinary diseases mutate to avoid our tests and cures. We can barely rid a planet of prions, which are mere protein. A disease with intelligence to guide it—perhaps its own 'research program'—will surely come up with novel defenses of its own. To say nothing of malice and retribution. The misery of ordinary disease is a by-product, an afterthought of its own survival needs. But these, intelligent microbes, what if they contemplate . . . revenge?"

No one had an answer. The delegates sat on in silence. Server arms snaked a cup of water to one, then another.

"What becomes of a pathogen when its host dies?" asked Verid. "What if the microzoöids *need* us alive? Even among ordinary pathogens, the most successful eventually mutate to coexist with the host—millions on our skin, and billions in our intestine. What of an intelligent pathogen who remembers its history and values its host? Our only fatality, so far, is a dead dog." She closed her eyes, thinking, Iras, forgive me.

"Good point," said Delegate Bronze Sky. "At present, we have the upper hand, because they—these 'microzoöids' need to figure out how to use human bodies as hosts without killing us unnecessarily. If we make contact now, they will be well-disposed to share all kinds of information about themselves. Newly discovered peoples love to show off."

Verid listened hopefully.

"So doesn't it make sense to authorize the Secretary to test their sentience now? When we have the most to gain?" The Bronze Skyan leaned forward. "Let us pass *both* motions: To contact the microzoöids, and to mobilize a white hole to completely sterilize the planet. Mobilization will take six months, at least; enough time for our medics to come up with defenses, and decide whether destruction is necessary."

And enough time to get the deadly decision postponed or canceled. Verid nodded to herself.

"And enough time for those microbes to take over every planet in the Fold!" Delegate Elysium shook his head. "The white hole won't take six months, only a week. It was mobilized from the beginning, to prepare for just such a contingency."

Verid was shocked. Loris should not have known about the white hole; it was the most highly classified information in the Fold. Who else knew of it, the secret compromise behind the founding of Prokaryon? Someone, she thought bitterly, had been waiting all this time for the excuse.

"Let's get it over with," said Delegate Valedon. "Eliminate the worst of the contagion, while we still can. We've found all the carriers—isolate them, and study the pathogen."

"Eliminate the carriers, too," said Delegate Urulan. "Station and all. They all signed the release."

Delegates Elysium and Valedon looked scandalized, as if to say, *they* were not so barbarous.

"I can't believe my ears," exclaimed the Solarian. "Sterilize a world without a public hearing?"

"It's a crisis. We'll invoke emergency powers."

"To destroy a world before you understand it—such

impatience," observed the Sentient. "How typical of humans."

"Delegate L'li," Verid insisted. "What is your view? Should we not take more time?"

The L'liite looked down, clearly troubled. "I'm afraid I must agree that the source of infection needs to be destroyed. In retrospect, I only wish we had done the same with the prions. The prions first appeared in a remote mountain village. Had we cleared the village then, and quarantined those infected, we would be far better off today." He looked up at Verid. "I do agree with the Honorable Delegate Bronze Sky. Let the Secretary make contact, and learn what we can in a week's time. If we turn up anything new . . ." He did not finish.

"Delegate Bronze Sky." Verid kept her voice level. "Did you intend to leave the Secretary only a week's time to test the microzoöid people?"

The Bronze Skyan considered in silence. With Delegates Sharer, Sentient, and Solarian, she could cast the fourth vote for reprieve, and Verid would break the tie. "The generation time of the microzoöids is only a day," she said at last. "Seven generations should give them enough time to convince us why we should save them." She clasped her hands before her. "I will support both motions—on condition that we meet again, in seven days, to confirm our vote to activate the white hole."

Seven days for Verid to convince the microzoöids she was their best friend, then watch their world die—unless she turned up something to change the vote of the L'liite or the Bronze Skyan.

"We'll give you two extra days first, to reach Prokaryon on the transfold express," offered Delegate Elysium. "I'll pick up the cost."

Verid's hands shook. "What if they fight back? Those

storms they cause—do you know what kind of energy that takes?"

"All the more reason to act now," said the Bronze Skyan.

"I can't do it," Verid said. "I have a conflict of interest." They all knew about Iras.

The Sharer said, "You have to, Verid. Because no one else can."

EIGHTEEN

Into the clearing in the singing-tree forest a lightcraft descended, seeking to land away from the tumblerounds. Rod saw that it was Quark.

"I'm impressed," he told Quark. "You said you'd never touch this world again."

"Somebody had to do it," Quark grumbled. "I told them you all ought to wear skinsuits, but they said it was too late to avoid contamination, and that your microzoöids sound friendly. *Friendly*, indeed."

Rod was suddenly aware of the state he was in. Before, he always wore his robe, and the children their best outfits neatly washed and combed, to visit the satellite. Now the three of them wore travel clothes soiled with tumbleround glue. It was a wonder the lightcraft allowed their feet to touch its nanoplast. "Thanks for coming for us, so many times," said Rod softly. "I'll remember."

The nanoplastic entrance to the lightcraft melded shut. That was it, Rod thought; he might never set foot on Prokaryon again. He held Haemum and Chae close, as together they watched the swirl of Spirilla spiral away, and the planet shrink to moon size in the void. *Farewell, Architeuthis* . . . He felt vaguely angry at the Reverend Mother's stories. Was it right to make a myth out of those one's own race chose to destroy?

As the lightcraft approached the lock, the young colonists picked up their backpacks. Rod tried at least to smooth Chae's hair, and Haemum managed to dig out a comb. But nothing could help the tumbleround smell.

"Don't touch the walls," warned Station. The nanoplastic entrance pulled open about twice as wide as usual. "Proceed immediately to Decontamination."

Just inside the gate waited Khral. Rod stopped. He wanted to accuse her—of what? Of being wrong, or of being right too late? The words froze in his throat. For a moment nothing existed but her eyes. Then he took a step, and she was in his arms. He held her fiercely, as if his hands had taken on a life of their own. Her body melted into his, and her fingers caught his hair. Then he realized that she, too, wanted more than a greeting. *You are being tested.* . . . Slowly he released her, letting his arms fall aside.

Khral said, "I'm so sorry, about everything. I—"

"It's none of your fault," he murmured.

"We should have protected the children."

Before he could speak again, Station interrupted. "Proceed to Decontamination."

Khral picked up the backpacks. "Come on, let's keep Station happy. Not that it can make much difference."

"What do you mean?"

"If those microzoöids learn to grow in nanoplast, we're

finished. The Fold will incinerate Station, too, along with the planet."

After extensive bathing and disinfecting, the three colonists sat in the clinic while the caterpillar medics injected nanoservos to probe them for silicates. Rod reached Mother Artemis on the holo, at the satellite expansion which housed the rest of Prokaryon's human refugees. Her nanoplastic hair reached toward him, as if to escape. "I have prayed for you without ceasing."

Rod's face twisted, seeking what could not be said in words. "Did everyone get out all right?" he demanded at last. "How are they treating you?"

"We are all well. Three Crows has been a big help to us. He'll stay as long as we need."

He smiled, wondering what Elk would think. The Reverend Mother could have quite an influence on people. "We'll be with you soon."

"Not too soon." The medic arched its long back, waving its forelimbs. "All three of you are carriers. Brother Rhodonite carries the most; at least ten thousand silicates were counted in your cerebrospinal fluid, most of them concentrated around your occipital lobe. Haemum has nearly as many; there's little we can do for her. But Chae has fewer than a hundred. We've been able to clear that many from a carrier without inducing meningitis."

"That is good," said Station. "After he is cleared, he can rejoin your colony."

Rod patted Chae's shoulder. "You've done a brave job, Brother. The family will be glad to see you again."

Mother Artemis nodded. "You'll return to a hero's welcome."

"I just want to help Prokaryon," Chae said, but he looked enormously relieved.

"Brother Rod," asked Haemum, "what about us?"

"You will join the quarantine sector," said the medic.

"Without whirrs," said Station, "you're not infectious; but we're taking every precaution."

Haemum frowned. "I want to help Brother Rod."

"You've done more than enough, Sister," said Rod. "You need to resume your studies."

For a moment her face took on an expression strikingly like 'jum's. "Come on, Chae," she said coldly. "I'm sure the *adults* have everything under control." Rod watched them leave, thinking sadly, how fast they had grown.

Mother Artemis said, "We know you have a job to do, Rod." Too soon, her image was gone.

Rod thought of something. "What becomes of the silicates that are 'cleared'?"

Station said, "We add them to the cultures."

"Against my better judgment," said the medic suddenly. "Deadly infectious material should be sterilized."

Later in the research lab, Rod asked Khral again about the cultures. Khral shuddered. "They don't survive that long in the cultures either. They need a live host. Let's hope their friends are forgiving. All *we've* lost so far is a dead dog, whereas they . . ."

He did not like the implications. Ten thousand "people" inside his head—how long would he have to keep them before they found a new home?

In the laboratory, amidst the shifting implements of nanoplast, sat 'jum, holding Sarai's two phototipped vines, one in each hand. With her thumbs she covered and uncovered the lights to make them flash. She stared at them fixedly, not looking up even to greet Brother Rod.

Elk was watching her, as he took notes on the holostage. "She says the microzoöids are inside her," the tall Bronze Skyan explained. "We found her like this, 'communicating.' Rather like you did, to teach them our alphabet—except that she learned theirs."

Rod watched with mixed emotions. He still loved the little girl, and he wished she would return him a smile. He admired what she had done, yet he feared for her, and felt ashamed at his failure to protect her. No more prions again, ever, he had promised; but what infected her now was far worse. "Can't you clear her out? She needs to return to the colony."

Sarai stood by the holostage, arms folded across her breasts. "Ushum's work is of critical importance. The sisterlings need her."

"But 'jum is a human child who needs proper care."

Khral caught Sarai's arm before she could reply. "Sarai, remember, Rod is infected, too." She turned to Rod. "'jum carries too many micros to clear safely. But hers seem friendly; and she made an important discovery. The microzoöids 'count' by prime factors. Each digit represents the multiplicity of each prime factor. Look." The holostage produced a table:

	1	2	3	5	7	11	13	17	19	23	29
1	1										
2	1	1									
3	1	0	1								
4	1	2									
5	1	0	0	1							
6	1	1	1								
7	1	0	0	0	1						
8	1	3									
9	1	0	2								
10	1	1	0	1							
11	1	0	0	0	0	1					
12	1	2	1								
13	1	0	0	0	0	0	1				
14	1	1	0	0	1						
15	1	0	1	1							
16	1	4	0								
17	1	0	0	0	0	0	0	1			
18	1	1	2								
19	1	0	0	0	0	0	0	0	1		
20	1	2	0	1							
21	1	0	1	0	1						
22	1	1	0	0	0	1					
23	1	0	0	0	0	0	0	0	0	1	
24	1	3	1								
25	1	0	0	1							
26	1	1	0	0	0	0	1				
27	1	0	3								
28	1	2	0	0	1						
29	1	0	0	0	0	0	0	0	0	0	1
30	1	1	1	1							

"It's amazing," Khral observed. "Their numbers sort of cycle back on each other, just like—"

"They can count on their fingers for all I care. You can't experiment on a child."

"The Reverend Mother said she could stay." Khral bit her lip. "I'm sorry, Rod. How else will Haemum and the other carriers be saved?"

Elk explained, "Some of the carriers from New Reyo have sickened, too, like the Elysians."

Rod felt numb.

"I don't like it either," Elk added, "but so long as the microzoöids communicate, we need 'jum's help. You see, they work *visually*—whether 'talking' one-on-one, or sending messages by singing-tree, or hiding in your brain. Your visual system is the one part that makes sense to them. They can 'see' what your eyes see; then they stimulate your brain to 'see' their own signals."

"Excuse me," Station interrupted. "Prepare for Safety Drill. Everyone immediately relocate to your evacuation vessel, for use in an unlikely emergent event."

Sighing, Khral headed for the exit.

Rod tried to nudge 'jum from her seat. At last he carried the potted vine along with her. "I don't remember Safety Drills," he told Khral. "What's Station thinking? Do the microzoöids have spaceships to attack?"

"We need to be prepared," said Khral. "In case the microzoöids get into nanoplast. They could wreck Station herself."

He had not thought of that. They reached the lifeship and helped 'jum to climb in. No one would last long, he realized, even in a lifeship. And who would care to pick them up?

"Khral, it's so quiet here now. The reporters—where are all the snake eggs?"

"All sent home, by emergency order. Since then, not a ship can leave."

"I thought the microzoöids bail out when you get near a spaceship."

"Not always. Carriers have been found as far as Valedon and Bronze Sky."

Microzoöids infecting everywhere—the thought chilled him.

"Never fear, Rod," said Khral, "we've got plenty to do before you try the docking tube. A crash course in microzoöid linguistics."

The biologists tried to connect all they knew about the microzoöids' language, from Khral's statistics, from the "words" Sarai and 'jum had identified, and from the messages inside Rod's vision. They probed Rod with nanoservos to report the effects of the microzoöids in his occipital lobe. The holostage produced sentences for Rod to read, alongside flashing number codes that Sarai thought might represent familiar objects—a singing-tree, a zoöid—and activities, such as a person walking or swimming. Several hundred of these were tried, over the course of an hour, but there was no response. Rod found himself wondering if he had only imagined whatever he saw before.

Then, out of the corner of his eye, a light flashed. "There it is," he exclaimed. "A letter will form. . . ."

"Exactly," said Station. "The nanoservos report detecting stimulation of your optical receptors. The microzoöids are responsible, somehow. They must produce neurotransmitters."

Rod read out the response: MAN SWIMS ZOOID—WHO SWIMS LLAMA?

Elk and Khral exchanged looks. "It's gibberish," said Elk.

"Maybe not," said Khral. "A microbe experiences life differently; instead of walking, you swim."

"They don't 'swim' in llamas," Elk objected. "We tested all the llamas, along with the children. The llamas were clear—not a silicate to be found."

"Maybe the micros use some other kind of 'skinsuit' inside llamas," suggested Khral, "which the medics can't detect."

"Oh, no," said Quark. "Don't say that."

The medic said, "We incinerated all nonhuman potential carriers."

Good-bye llamas, thought Rod, with a silent prayer. "Where would the micros get the word 'who'? You never showed them a picture."

Khral thought about this. "Your mind must have formed a picture of it. You must have been wondering 'who?' quite a lot lately."

"You mean they can read my mind—whatever I'm thinking?"

Elk shook his head. "I doubt that. Only things you can visualize."

Rod closed his eyes. "I'm not sure I can handle this," he said, trying to keep his voice steady. "I'd rather have meningitis. You can clear out the silicates, and 'talk' to them in tissue culture."

For a while no one spoke.

"If that's what you want, Rod," said Khral. "I'll direct the nanoservos myself."

Elk looked away, his face creased in pain.

The medic said, "I just left one of the Elysians in critical condition. Without treatment soon, she will deteriorate beyond repair."

Rod took a breath. "Let's get on with it."

"Very well," said Khral with an effort. "But Station, we

can't just speed up basic research. One word at a time—
what else can we do?"

From across the lab came Sarai to check their progress.
"Now that we've figured out words and numbers, we're
working on chemical names. Ushum has figured out what
they call methane and ethane."

Elk gave Sarai a weary glance. "That's great, but how
will it help us talk them into leaving us alone?"

Khral said, "Perhaps 'jum's population learns faster."
Her eyes widened. "Wait a minute. What if . . . we put the
two cultures together?"

Elk caught his fist. "That's it! We remove a few each
from Rod and from 'jum, then put them together in culture
fluid and let them share information."

"Just like we shared with you, Sarai."

Sarai folded her arms. "Ushum's microzoöids seem content where they are. Would they like being kidnapped?
Refugees in a culture dish?"

"No time for that approach," said Station. "Let's inoculate a few from 'jum directly into Rod."

The medic reared angrily, waving several limbs. "I object! This is completely against regulations."

"It's too much," Elk agreed. "We can't treat people like
test tubes."

"I make the regulations here," said Station.

Rod held up his hands. "Never mind. With so many already, what's a few more?"

The caterpillar body hunched down. "I withdraw from
the case." With that statement, the medic crawled out.

"I'll do the transfer," said Khral quietly. "I'm certified."
She coaxed 'jum over to sit by the probe, then directed it to
withdraw a dozen silicates from her spinal fluid. Rod watched
her expert hands, thick hair down the back of her fingers.
Afterward, as she turned to him, her arm was shaking.

Elk said, "We can call one of the other medics."

"Leave them be, the cowards." Khral's voice was short. "The probe will do its work. Rod, you can settle yourself here, while the cell sorter filters out things that would trigger your immune response."

Rod sat next to the probe and looked away as it snaked near his back.

After the transfer his temperature rose, and he developed a headache. Station was reluctant to administer drugs that might affect the "visitors" in his brain, so long as his own health was not in danger. He went to bed to rest. Rest did not come easy, though, with a roomful of machines sending alarms at his slightest change in blood pressure. He dozed unevenly, dreaming of the long trail before Mount Anaeon, the mist rising forever in the distance, the loopleaves forever tangling his feet.

The afternoon passed, with still no sign from the visitors, new or old. No more lights flashed in his head at all, no matter what he tried to "show" them. The hours passed, and all the researchers could do was wait.

At his bedside, Khral and Quark came to visit. Khral touched his hand. "Are you feeling better, Rod?"

"Much better," he said, not admitting why.

"Rod—you're not mad at us, are you?"

"No. I just wish . . ." For a moment the nanoplastic walls and ceiling all slipped away, all just a mistake, corrected. He was back at the homestead the colonists had built with their own hands, the children tugging at his legs, the llamas calling outside, the brokenhearts ready for harvest. Then his eyes focused again, and he half sat up. "What's been happening to the planet?" he demanded. "Have they—"

"They've done nothing." Khral brightened, glad to bring good news. "There were so many incidents with 'bad weather' that they just postponed the cleansing indefinitely."

"They don't admit as much," said Quark, "but they're dead scared. Have you any idea how much power it takes to make a storm appear out of a blue sky? Proteus doesn't know what's going on—nobody does."

Rod sank back again, feeling his prayers were answered. "I just wish I could do a better job for you. Maybe these microzoöids have trouble remembering what they learn, and passing things on, if their generation only lasts a day."

"Oh no," said Khral. "It's true, most of them reproduce within a day, but their 'elders' live on for another month or so. Like Elysians, some choose to live longer, instead of having children of their own."

"Even so," said Quark, "you can see why the ones in the singing-trees lost interest after a month of trying to figure us out."

Rod thought this over. "Station is right; we have little time."

Khral swallowed carefully. "Station wants you to try the docking tube tomorrow morning—whether you've seen any more signals or not."

The docking tube connected to Station at its innermost ring, where centrifugal "gravity" was lightest. Rod approached the gate with Khral, flanked by two medics who had swallowed their principles to attend. He knew his head swarmed with nanoservos, ready to detect whatever the silicate-suited micros did.

As he approached the gate, his steps slowed. In the smooth face of nanoplast, a dent formed, deepening as usual until a hole opened. Air hissed, as the pressure changed. Was this the signal the microzoöids detected? Rod blinked a few times, but he felt no different. What if they did nothing this time, he wondered. Suppose they wanted to visit the stars?

The hole widened until the nanoplast flattened to floor and ceiling, all around the gateway. Rod could see the usual round tunnel beyond, and he stepped into it. As always the artificial gravity gave a lurch, as the tube began to rotate; Rod gripped a handle for a moment, as he generally did.

Suddenly his head swam, and lights flashed in his eyes. He stumbled back through the gate, where one of the medics caught him. The room spun around him crazily.

"Rod, what's wrong?" called Khral, as if from far away. "Can you see anything?"

One of the medics made an injection in his neck, and his balance stabilized. Rod squeezed his eyes shut, trying to make out the flashing letters. *NO . . . NOT READY.*

" 'No, not ready,' " he read aloud. "Not ready for what?" He tried to "see" the letters in his mind.

NOT READY TO LEAVE. LLAMA STAY.

He absorbed this. "I am not a llama," he exclaimed. "A llama is a pack animal. I'm a man." He tried to visualize each word.

YOU ANIMAL. MEN NOT READY TO LEAVE. ANIMAL STAY.

Rod was back in bed, dozing on and off while the instruments profiled his blood, sorted his cells, typed his proteins and a thousand other things. A tone sounded, and Khral came in. He sat himself up; his head felt not so bad. "Any news? How are the Elysians?"

"We've had a breakthrough." Khral sat by the bed and leaned forward eagerly. "Your nanoservos monitored the silicates in your brain, all the while they were acting up. The chemistry gets complicated, but—let's just say the microzoöids had to let down their guard, to put out their neurotransmitters. We figured out a way to neutralize them, so they do no harm as they're removed. We tried it on the sicker Elysian first. If Iras remains stable, we'll try it tomorrow on . . . the other one." The hated creator of Proteus.

Rod sighed. "I'm glad something worked."

"And you? Any change?"

He shrugged. "The letters come back now and then. They call me an 'animal,' and tell me to 'go' and 'stay,' like a dog." For these rude creatures, his children had risked their lives? "I guess this is what it feels like to be a tumbleround, bossed by microzoöids."

"Fascinating . . . That is, I mean, how awful," said Khral. "I don't envy Secretary Verid dealing with them."

He looked up hopefully. "I don't suppose you could . . . well, now that you've figured out how to—"

"Oh yes—we can get them out of you, too, and put them safely in the culture, whether they like it or not." Khral half smiled. "Sarai will have plenty to work with."

The medic returned, rearing its caterpillar-shaped body over the bed to prepare for the spinal tap. Rod rested patiently, thinking how he could rejoin the children again, free at last of his uninvited guests.

Before his eyes the letters reappeared. STOP. MEN NOT READY TO LEAVE ANIMAL.

Too bad, he thought to himself. Find some zoöid to live in.

ANIMAL WILL LEARN.

Pain filled his skull, spreading throughout his body, as if he were ripped apart very slowly, into very small pieces. Rod gripped his skull, trying to control himself, but it had come on too suddenly. "Stop, stop." The pain went on, unending, for hour after hour, the kind of pain he would have severed his own limb to get rid of, except that it was everywhere, in every limb and crevice, within belly and brain.

At last the pain died. Still breathing heavily, Rod looked

himself over, his hands and arms, hardly believing he was still intact. "By Torr, that was—" He looked up at the medic still rearing over him, though the instruments had been removed. "Couldn't you hear? What took you so long?"

The medic said, "We required two minutes to withdraw the tap safely."

Two minutes. He looked accusingly at Khral. "I thought you said they could only work with vision. Isn't pain in a different part of the brain?"

"They must have learned something new—something the ones in the Elysian patients don't know yet." She looked at the medic. "Maybe they have research scientists, like us."

"What if their 'scientists' learn more tricks? They could take me over completely."

There was silence.

Station said, "We'll have to figure out how the microzoöids trigger pain."

"Couldn't you just get them out, while I'm under anesthesia?"

Station hesitated. "We might, but what if the pain doesn't stop when they leave?"

Rod fell back on the bed and closed his eyes. He tried to recall his Academy drills to endure pain.

The letters returned in his eyes. WELL DONE. ANIMAL LEARNS.

A new sensation filled his mind; a sense of pleasure, unimaginable, beyond what a thousand lovers could give. He floated in it, drifting helplessly as if on an endless sea. Only it came to an end too soon; he begged for it to return, for he would sacrifice anything, even any of the children, to float in that sea again.

His eyes opened. He was damp with perspiration, but otherwise felt fine. Khral and the medic were talking excitedly with Station, as if he were not there. They were helpless, he realized. There was nothing they could do for him. Whatever they learned, the microzoöids learned faster; they would keep ahead, destroying him by inches until there was nothing left.

"Khral." His voice was hoarse. "Khral, listen. You have to help me."

She came over, her face wrinkled. "What can I do?"

"You can give me a 'final friend.' Something to take, in case I have to, before they take me over."

Her eyes widened. "Rod, you know I can't do that. I wish it were me instead, anything—but that I can't do."

"You can," he insisted. "You have all the chemicals. Give me one."

"It's not right," she whispered. "You know it isn't— your Reverend Mother would know."

Rod dug his fingers into the mattress. "What do you know of that? Just give me something, so I can die as a man, not an animal."

Beside the bed, in the nanoplastic wall, a pocket opened. A round tablet came out, the size of his thumb.

Khral stood up. "Station, no!"

"It's your right," Station told him, "by the law. Be careful how you hold that: One squeeze, and it seeps through your skin."

He took the tablet gingerly between two fingers and set it by the bed.

Khral watched him, stricken. "Don't you tell *me* about being an animal." Her simian jaw jutted forward. "Where there's life, there's hope, I say. Must you always be in control?" She stormed out without waiting for reply. Rod remained, one human alone.

NINETEEN

In critical care, deep within the sentient Station, Nibur Lethe*shon* began to waken. The Elysian tossed his head feverishly as he floated in and out of consciousness. For how long, he had no idea; he knew only that frightful phantoms crossed his eyes, shapes and forms unknown, like a virtual seascape gone mad, the waves rolling and cresting beneath him until he crashed upon the shore. All the while his hand clutched the collar of Banga, the dog standing there steadfast by his bedside, his ageless companion, now his only comfort amid torment.

As his mind cleared, the phantoms finally dwindled. Only a headache lingered: a nuisance. Why could these provincial medics not clear it out? Once again he mastered his vision, clearly seeing the bed with its crude hospital covers, and the primitive servo analyzer of bodily fluids standing nearby. He shuddered; a wonder he had recovered at all, in this barbaric outpost. Why had they not sent him back to *Proteus,* where he maintained his own up-to-date clinic custom-designed for himself?

In his hand he held an empty collar. Curious. Why would they take away his beloved Banga, yet leave the collar?

A doorway appeared in the wall, opening to admit a hideous caterpillar of a sentient. Nibur's face froze as he drew himself up.

"You are much improved," the sentient brightly observed. "All your vital signs confirm."

"Why was I kept here?" Nibur demanded. "Why was I not sent back to *Proteus?*"

"*Proteus* told us it lacked any treatment program for alien microbes."

Alien microbes. His flesh crawled. That mad Sharer in the mountain, on Pavonis Three—had she cooked this up?

"Not that we had a treatment either," the miserable sentient explained, "but we have researchers with . . . initiative."

"Initiative be damned," he muttered. "If I suffer any lingering effects, you'll hear from Proteus." He held up the collar. "Where is Banga?"

The sentient's caterpillar head bobbed moronically. "I'm very sorry. Your dog passed away two weeks ago."

Nibur frowned. "Impossible. I've had him by the bed, all this while."

"A virtual image. You kept calling for him, and his presence kept you calm."

The first moment of fear that this might be true penetrated his mind. Banga—his companion, who had followed him faithfully for centuries. Banga—reduced to a virtual phantom? "No," he said hoarsely. "You imbecile machine, it can't be so. Banga is immortal."

"Banga succumbed to the same infectious agent as

yourself and your fellow traveler. The medical staff deeply regrets our inability to save him. You may take comfort, though, that his death under our experimental treatment probably saved your own life."

Banga . . . A wordless scream echoed down the corridors of his mind. That world with its vile contagion had consumed his own companion. For a moment Nibur wished he had not woken.

"You are free of infection now, so far as we can tell," the sentient assured him. "You may transfer to *Proteus* now."

"The sooner the better," said Nibur, breathing heavily.

"Prokaryon is in quarantine, but your firm has obtained a special exemption. . . ."

Nibur no longer listened. He would be off soon, and he would know what to do. That world with its cursed alien scenery would not long survive his dog.

In the laboratory, halfway across the satellite, little 'jum counted off the flashing lights from the microzoöids in her brain, while Sarai worked feverishly to assign their patterns names and symbols. Now that both the Elysian patients were out of danger, Khral renewed her effort to contact the microbial intelligence. She scanned her own database on the holostage, while Sarai clucked incessantly with her clickflies, whose webs now spanned half the lab, displaying statistics on the data stored in the clickflies' DNA.

Together, they had worked out how the microzoöid sisterlings named the chemical parts of their cells. The microzoöids seemed to name their elements in the order of frequency. First came hydrogen, then carbon, oxygen, and nitrogen, as in humans; but thereafter, instead of sulfur and phosphorus, came arsenic. That was one reason Prokaryan settlers had to be lifeshaped.

So methane, CH_4, was **4 1**, while ethanol, C_2H_6O was **6 2 1**. But what to make of the bizarre cyclic amino acids in their proteins, like azetidine with its four-carbon ring? 'jum watched the model of azetidine hover over the holostage, a tight square of carbons with one nitrogen corner.

By now, playing the light pipes was second nature for 'jum. The sisterlings were her friends. If only she could figure out more of what they were telling her.

"Hypoglycin, and mimosin," announced Khral. "Cyclic amino acids—you find them in some of our plant species, but never in humans."

'jum reached above the holostage to place more numbers: **7 4 2 1 0 9 0 3**.

"That's azetidine," said Sarai. "The first four digits count the atoms; the rest designates the heterocyclic square, and the carboxylic acid."

"Azetidine acid—the square amino acid they use instead of proline, to make kinks in their proteins." Khral patted 'jum on the back. "Those microzoöids are working pretty hard today. They're telling you a lot."

'jum nodded. "They ask me things, too. About everything around us, what it's made of."

"Tell them nothing," boomed the ever-present voice of Station. "We must keep them under control."

Sarai glared at the ceiling. "Wouldn't *you* want to know what your habitat is made of?"

'jum had already told the sisterlings the simple polymers that her clothes were made of, and the mineral of the starstone at her neck. But Station had refused to let her tell them other things, like the composition of nanoplast, even the floor and walls that surrounded them.

"I knew we should never have come out to this dimwit satellite." Sarai sighed. "We'll get nowhere."

"Khral," Station announced, "you are needed immediately back at intensive care. New patients have arrived from Valedon and Bronze Sky."

Astonished, Khral stared at the ceiling. "From where? What are they doing out here? We've sent all we know to Science Park. They'd get much better care."

Station declined to reply.

"Innocent fool," muttered Sarai. "The carriers are out-casts. Anybody with microzoöids is getting sent here, like a leper colony."

"Because we can provide the latest treatment," corrected Station.

"Believe that, and you might as well join the clerics."

Khral said quietly, "I wish I could. Station, how many carriers are there?"

"A dozen so far. Some have had recurring 'visions' for weeks, perhaps months. No one knows how far it's spread—and whether whirrs have spread, too." That was the key question. If whirrs had spread to other planets, there was no containing the epidemic.

"A dozen." Khral sighed. "I can see my work cut out."

"The orders are to try nothing fancy—just eliminate the silicates, like you did for Iras and Nibur."

"That's murder," said Sarai. "Even the cultured ones are languishing." For some reason, the microzoöids in the culture vessels had stopped growing, probably starving for an essential nutrient. "They need a live host. Keep them in the carriers."

"Right," said Khral. "It would make more sense to talk to them."

Above the holostage, the medical sentient suddenly reared its limbs, spouting test results. "You see what bad shape these carriers are in? How can you *talk* to a pathogen?"

"All right, I'm coming," called Khral. "Sarai, I'll send

you whatever communications the nanoservos pick up in the patients' brains, and see what you can make of them." Picking up her self-sterilizing suit for the clinic, she left.

"Talk to them, indeed," muttered Sarai. "When Station won't even let us answer what *they* ask of us! What's the use?"

'jum agreed. If only Mother Sarai would take her back to the cavern. The sisterlings inside her head would be happier, too. Like her, they felt trapped—and they were doing something about it. 1 0 2 0 0 7 1, they said. This sequence she had first seen when Sarai had transferred sisterlings from one dish to another. It seemed to mean "moving" from one place to another, or "travel"?

Sarai rose and stretched. She clucked twice, in the language she used to call the clickflies. "What do the sisterlings want now?"

'jum closed her eyes and tried to count the numbers that the sisterlings were posting inside her eyes. "Everything," 'jum clucked back. "What everything is made of."

Station did not respond. Perhaps Station was not attuned to clickflies.

"They could help us," muttered Sarai. "Those sisterlings could help our lifeshaping, more than anything—a thousand times more than Station's brainless nanoservos." She clucked again, and one of her clickflies sailed in the doorway. The splay-legged insect obligingly set to spinning a web in the corner. 'jum watched the web, trying to puzzle out the pattern of its sticky strands, woven straight and crosswise, with some squares pasted together. Then she realized what it was: a molecule. The molecule was a component of Station's floor, some fancy kind of polycarbonate.

Now 'jum stared at her two light pipes, one in each hand, trying to translate the molecule as best she could into the sisterlings' number code. She had number combinations for methyl groups, esters, simple cyclics, and so on, but the more advanced features remained a mystery.

"*More, more,*" the sisterlings flashed back.

"More molecules," clicked 'jum.

Sarai clicked rapidly to the insects. Their long legs flitted across the web, weaving other molecules: components of the expandable door rims, the ceiling, the air vents.

Abruptly the holostage fell dead. A bright light filled the room, making 'jum squint.

"What do you think you're doing?" boomed Station. "I told you not to tell those bugs what I'm made of. I could charge you with treason." In the corners the webs were dissolving into the walls, while the clickflies had vanished out the door.

"What do you think *you're* doing?" Sarai shot back. "Obstructing critical research. How do you expect us to learn anything if we don't share information?"

'jum put her hands to her head and watched the blinking lights in her eyes. The sisterlings were talking again, about *moving* and *travel.*

"You foolish human!" cried Station. "The first deaths on Prokaryon were sentients—chewed up by microzoöids. Until we figured out how to build ourselves of stuff they couldn't handle. Have you no sense?"

The instruments dissolved into the walls, and the room itself began to lose shape, its corners filling in, everything collapsing into formless gray. Even the light pipes in 'jum's hands disintegrated. She was helpless inside Station, just as the poor sisterlings were helpless inside her.

Station said, "That is why I make the rules here— because humans lack common sense. You will remain in confinement until further notice."

The Sharer took a deep breath. "You bring back that door, or we'll teach them to eat you alive!"

Sarai's voice cut off oddly without reverberating, as if not even sound could escape. There was no response. Around them rose four gray walls as square as azetidine, but with no distinguishing corner. The walls joined a ceiling with an indistinguishable floor, creating a pallid gray cavern.

The only spot of color was purple Sarai, crouching on the floor. But her fingertips were turning white. " 'jum, I can't take this. You know what I must do. I will be all white and cold; don't be afraid, I will gain wisdom from my ancestors. Khral will come for you soon enough; she won't let you go without dinner."

'jum watched as Mother Sarai whitened, the purple breathmicrobes bleaching out, while the veins appeared through her skin. She wondered how Sarai managed such deep concentration. She herself had no breathmicrobes, but perhaps she could learn to concentrate, and better hear the little sisterlings. So she sat on the floor, like Sarai, her legs crossed and her back straight. She closed her eyes, took a deep breath and relaxed.

1 0 2 0 0 7 1, said the sisterlings again. *Let's travel.*

Where do you want to go? 'jum wondered. She wished she had her light pipes. Her hands flexed as if she still held them.

1 0 0 0 0 0 9 0 8. The sisterlings spelled out an answer, as if they had heard her anyway. As if they heard now, in her brain, what she was trying to signal. The number they made in response had appeared before, when 'jum looked out Station's observation deck. 1 0 0 0 0 0 9 0 8, the stars.

The stars. Will you take us?

The stars. That was where 'jum had always wanted to

go, and Brother Rod finally took her there. She would go again if she could. But just now, she couldn't go anywhere.

Never mind, said the sisterlings. *If my generation doesn't get there, my children will.*

On the holostage in Rod's room stood Geode and Three Crows, each with a plump baby in one arm. The scrawny infants from Reyo had grown into crawlers eager to get down and scoot across the stage. Geode extended an eyestalk to Rod. "We're all praying for you," Geode told him. "May the Spirit heal you soon."

Rod made himself smile. What did "healing" mean anymore, he wondered. The death of a million microbial aliens, to save his own life? "Do the children have what they need? Is T'kun getting his medicine?"

Three Crows shifted Qumum from one arm to the other. "I wish I got what *I* need," said the tall Bronze Skyan. "Another four arms, like your brother here."

Rod traced a starsign. "You were just what we need, a gift from the Spirit."

"The children are fine," said Geode, "but they all hope you'll come home soon."

"What home?" The words slipped out before he thought.

Geode's eyestalks reached around in a circle. "Wherever we all are, that's home."

"Wherever Mother Artemis is," said Three Crows. "Tell Elk I'll call him, after the kids are in bed."

That evening, Elk joined Rod in his room for supper. Rod clasped his arm gratefully. "It's so good of Three Crows to help us out."

Elk shrugged. "He needed something to keep going. He's in quarantine like the rest of us." The scientist watched his dinner appear out of the wall, his large fingers flexing pensively. From the foot of the bed the cell sorter bleeped, spouting lines of data to Station.

"Has the infection spread through the ship?" asked Rod.

"Not since Station tightened all her air filters. Only whirrs can spread the micros outside a host, and now not one can get through. Station has shipped out most of the colonists, except for carriers we couldn't clear, and those who . . . chose to stay."

Rod tried to swallow his own food, barely knowing what he tasted. "Have any of the other carriers . . . seen what I have?"

"Several have seen signs," said Elk. "They happen to be trained in meditation of one sort or another—as you are. It must help you 'connect' with the micros."

"But other carriers are ill. Why do some sicken worse than others?"

"We don't know. We'll try to treat them, as we did the Elysians." Elk avoided Rod's eye. Little good the "treatment" had done him.

"What about 'jum?" Rod asked suddenly.

" 'jum's micros behave differently from yours. They don't make threats." He brightened with a sudden thought. "You know, it's like different human cultures on different planets. 'jum got the Sharer micros, whereas you got the Valans. No offense."

"But what if hers change? How can she resist them?" Tossing aside the covers, Rod swung his legs over and stood up.

"What are you doing?"

" 'jum is my child. I want her cleared and returned to the colony."

"But—Rod, you can't just . . ."

He reached the wall and pressed it with his palms.

There was no door, and none formed. The clear, blank expanse faced him, suddenly terrifying.

Station said, "You're ill yourself, Rod."

His hands became fists, digging into the wall. A curse went unspoken, then he withdrew his hands. The indentation reshaped itself smooth, while Rod returned to sit on the bed, which had already remade itself. "I will pray for 'jum."

Elk looked down, unable to speak, his face deeply creased. Then he thought of something. "We just heard— Secretary Verid will be here tomorrow. The Council voted to test the micros for sentience. So the planet's safe from cleansing."

Rod pushed his meal back into the wall. "The Secretary will first have to convince those microzoöids that we're even worth talking to. Maybe the Elysians were right; if we don't wipe out the micros, they'll make llamas of us all."

Elk's large hands shook and he put down his fork. "I don't know. I'm a plant person; I stayed away from medical training, never wanted to work on people. And now—" He stopped.

"How's Khral?" Rod asked softly.

"She thought you wouldn't want to see her again."

"I wanted to apologize."

"As for me, I'm with you, Rod. I wouldn't want to be the slave of some microbe."

After dinner Rod lay on the bed with his eyes closed. Sleep would offer respite from this nightmare; but what would the invaders do to his brain as he slept?

He heard the sound of a door puckering open, and a breath of air reached his face. His eyelids fluttered open, and he saw someone walk in. In the doorway stood Khral, hesitating.

Rod sat up quickly. "I'm sorry," he said. "I shouldn't have—"

"Bother. It was stupid, what I said."

"You were right. Obedience is a virtue." A virtue he had cultivated for years, first at the Academy, then with the Spirit Callers.

Khral came to sit by the bed. Rod wished he had had a chance to freshen up first. "Obedience to what is good," she said, "not the blind obedience of a slave. My grandparents were the children of Urulite slaves. They scraped a living out of a patch of hillside, saving enough to educate their children. My parents left Urulan for Bronze Sky, where they founded the Simian League. Their speeches were on every holostage—I think they expected me to marry a gorilla, God knows. But I just wanted to be me." She looked wonderingly at her hands. "The secret of life; it always fascinated me. I look at myself and think, I'm an animal, and yet a human being. It's extraordinary."

"Any of us could say the same."

Khral looked at him. "That's exactly what I mean. You always understand, Rod."

He touched her hand. An infinite sympathy seemed to pass between them. He burned with longing, and despair. How could the Spirit let him care so much for a half-breed student?

Something brushed past Rod's face, a tiny insect. It sounded like a whirr.

Khral caught sight of it. "How did that whirr get in here? Station," she called. "Better check your filters."

"I will," called the voice, steady as always. "I will recheck all my filters, and decrease the pore size again."

Withdrawing her hand, Khral reached upward and scooped the whirr out of the air. "We'll see what these 'sisterlings' are up to." She dumped it into a collecting vial.

Astonished, Rod stared at her bare hand with which she caught the whirr. How brave she was. He himself was infected and had no choice, but she chose to keep up her science when she could have kept herself safe. He doubted he would have done the same.

TWENTY

Late at night Rod awoke. The room was dark except for the faintly glowing button on the blood monitor. But in his eyes, the lights were blinking again. The microzoöids were up to something.

ANIMAL. MEN READY. YOU MUST GO.

Rod watched the letters shape themselves. *No,* he thought back as hard as he could. He would not be a beast of burden for these rude creatures.

MEN MUST GO HOME. GO HOME NOW.

That sounded hopeful, Rod thought. *Go ahead, leave. Let the whirrs come and take them all.*

YOU TAKE US HOME, NOW.

Rod opened his mouth to call Station for help—but no sound came out. He could not speak.

GO HOME NOW.

The first twist of pain entered his head. He could not cry out. What would the microscopic tormentors control next? He reached out and felt for Station's deadly tablet on the shelf by the bed. At last his hand found it.

He prepared his mind just in time to meet the full wave of pain, searing, tearing every fiber of his body. Before his eyes arose the image of the old master of the Guard, a Sardish colonel with a beard as sharp as his epaulets. *Resist,* the master commanded. *You will resist, or die.* The hypnotic impact of that image held him above the pain. Centuries seemed to come and go, and still the pain burned. When the master's image faltered, Rod's hand closed around the tablet.

But then another shape arose—Mother Artemis. *Live,* she called to him. *You shall live.* Just like the day he first saw her, meditating in the park outside the Academy, where Rod had wandered out after a particularly dissipated weekend. Her look that day had touched a place in him that even the Sardish master had never reached. *Follow me, and you shall live.* He had followed, and never looked back. Now, despite the torment, his hand loosened; for the Spirit yet called him across tens of millennia, called him to live through the worst extremity.

When the pain did not seem as if it could possibly get worse, it did. Again the master's image returned, ordering resistance; and then again, Mother Artemis called for life. Always one or the other, until the pain would shatter his head into a thousand fragments.

Then, after eons of torment, the pain died. Rod sat up, drenched with sweat. The tablet remained in his hand, and he still had not yet squeezed the death out of it. He had actually beaten the microbial masters—this time. There was silence, and darkness, his eyes at peace. Slowly he let himself back down on the mattress, his breathing returning to normal. Nothing was so welcome as lungfuls of air without pain.

ANIMAL GOES HOME. The infernal letters returned. ANIMAL GOES; WE REWARD.

Rod did not deign to reply.

Then slowly his limbs filled with pleasure, more intense than he could ever have imagined. Too late he tried to cry out, for he had no defense. He could only drink it in, like a plant drinking water from the soil, grateful and despairing. Nothing in his own miserable existence could compare with what the microzoöids gave, none of those he loved, not even the highest communion with the Spirit.

It was gone all too soon, leaving him sick with craving. He turned restlessly, until the covers fell off. He found himself thinking of the lightcraft, and how to get back down to Prokaryon, while another part of his mind screamed at his madness. He had no intention of getting up, yet he found himself swinging his legs down over the side. He told himself, getting up for a moment would do no harm.

The pleasure began to return. Then he realized that he would do anything the microbial masters demanded, even sell his own children. He groped frantically for the tablet, which had slipped from his fingers. At last his hand caught it and squeezed hard.

Gradually Rod awakened, to a room filled with morning light. Confused, he wondered where he was and what had happened. His head turned, and he saw someone seated nearby. With an effort he focused his eyes and saw Mother Artemis.

The shock chilled him. "How am I still alive?"

"Did you think Station would let you come to harm?"

So that was it. Tricked by that lying sentient. But the Reverend Mother must know that he had tried to end his own life, the worst of sins. He turned his head to the wall. "Mother, I am not worthy to face you."

"Brother Rod, you are forgiven absolutely. Think of it no more."

"I am not forgiven. I am better off dead."

Mother Artemis paused. Rod could imagine her behind him, her all-to-familiar face screen with its compelling gaze. "Once, Rod, you asked the Spirit to grant you a world. Do you remember?"

He shuddered. "I am not the man I was."

"Now, all the worlds of the Fold depend on you."

Rod swallowed hard. " 'jum can help you better."

" 'jum has entered some kind of trance. Not white-trance, like Sarai, but she will not communicate."

So much for "Sharer" microzoöids, Rod thought bitterly. Who could tell what they were doing to poor 'jum. Far better had he left her that day on Scarecrow Hill.

"There are other carriers, but none as advanced as you. Please, Rod—won't you try again? Secretary Verid has arrived to talk with them."

"It's too late," he whispered. "There is nothing I can do. Please, leave me." No need for her to see what the microzoöids could do to him.

He lay there facing the wall, for hours, perhaps days for all he could tell. Drained of emotion, all he could do was to think of nothing, neither pain nor desire, and hope the tormenters within kept quiet.

A faint swishing sound came from the wall, and a breath of air touched his neck. Someone must have opened a door to look in on him. Rod listened hard, but did not hear the door close. The minutes ticked by, and he wondered, had the visitor left, or were they still there? At last he turned his head, just far enough to see.

A small woman in a leaf brown Elysian talar sat near

the door, her back toward him. He frowned, wondering why she looked familiar. Then her head half turned, and her profile leaped out at him from a thousand holocubes.

Hurriedly he sat up straight. "Honorable Secretary."

"Brother Rod." Her voice sounded at once familiar, yet extraordinary, to be addressing him in person instead of from a newscast. "Brother Rod, how can I face you. You, who offered your own brief lifetime that my Iras might enjoy centuries more."

Taken aback, Rod shook his head. "Whatever they've told you—I'm just a very sick man."

"And here come I, a cupbearer for murderers. I am covered in shame."

Rod blinked, wondering what to say. "You have all the humans of the Fold to speak for. What do I know of that?"

Secretary Verid turned toward him, and he faced her owlish eyes. Suddenly Rod realized what the Guard and the Spirit Callers had always shared: They taught disdain for politics. Obey your commanding officer, or your Reverend Father or Mother, and forsake the slimy machinations of the world. But here was someone who made the world her business.

"What you know may save countless lives. Shall we proceed?"

Rod swallowed. "What do you want of me?"

"We have seven days to convince the Council of the Fold that we can deal with the . . . alien intelligence. If we succeed, they will suspend the planet's destruction."

He looked away. "I'm no longer sure that's wise."

"Indeed. Explain."

How could anyone know what he had undergone? He shuddered. "The microzoöids make us helpless. They can control us absolutely."

"You seem in control right now."

"They leave me alone, then attack at their whim."

The Secretary thought this over. Even she, with her thousand years' experience, what could she know of these alien creatures too small to see? "How long has it been since their last attack?" she asked.

"Since last night."

"Half a generation, for them. Did they get what they wanted?"

He considered this. "Not yet."

"Not yet, indeed. I can imagine what they're going through—accusations and recriminations, shifting the blame, 'who lost the human,' and so on. They must have sacked half their staff."

Despite himself Rod smiled. "Whatever comes next, though, will only be worse. They can't even think of us as people—they call us 'animals.' "

"And what do you call them?"

Rod frowned, puzzled. "Microzoöids?"

" 'Little animals.' "

"Well that's what they look like."

"Just as you always looked like a llama, to them. Let's call them what you would like to be called—a man." Seeing his look, she smiled. " 'Micromen,' if that's easier."

Rod shrugged. "As you wish, Secretary."

"Now tell me, what is it the 'micromen' want?

"They want to go back to Prokaryon."

Her eyes widened with astonishment. "Back to Prokaryon? Isn't that what you'd want them to do?"

"Certainly. But they want me to take them. And Station says we need to study them here, to help cure those infected."

"Ah, I see." Verid sighed and shook her head. "What a tangled web we weave. Well, I think now we're ready to talk. Can you contact them?"

Rod stiffened all over. "I can try. If I have to."

"It's absolutely crucial."

Taking a deep breath, Rod let his mind empty, as he had done so often for the Spirit. He wondered how long it had been since evening prayers. Now he prayed, out of a place of despair he had never known before. *Whoever is out there, help me now.*

He raised his hand and focused his eyes upon the fingers. This was the sign the "micromen" had used before, and it was his best guess to summon them. For some time there was no sign or sound, only the pounding of his own heart. He tried to envision his inner denizens as "little men," though he recoiled at the thought.

From the corner of his eye, a light flashed.

Rod closed his eyes. "Room darken," he ordered. The light from the ceiling dimmed, and Secretary Verid became a shadow.

Within his eyes the letters began to shape themselves. Panic seized him; he gripped the bed rail to steady himself. MAN . . . I SEEK TALK.

"They want to talk," Rod said aloud.

"There's a start," said the Secretary. "Talk about what?"

MY BROTHERS NEED YOUR HELP.

"You tried that before. It was no good," he told them.

WAS DIFFERENT GENERATION. THIS GENERATION KNOWS BETTER.

Rod laughed. "They say 'this generation' knows better, but it's only been half a day. Khral says the elders live a month."

"That's all right," said Verid, "let them save face. Why do they need your help?"

Why do you need help? he silently asked.

BROTHERS ARE DYING. BROTHERS FROM AN-

OTHER WORLD, DEAD PLACE. WE MEN CANNOT
GROW WITHIN A DEAD WORLD, ONLY WITHIN A
LIVING HOME.

That was true of humans, too. How long would humans thrive outside an ecosystem? "They say some of them are dying. Ones from 'a dead world.' " But what could that be? Had one of the patients died?

"How would they know?" asked the Secretary. "They've been inside you for weeks, I understand."

"The whirr," Rod recalled. "The whirr must have brought them—from Khral's sick culture. That's the only place micromen would be growing outside a living body."

BROTHERS ARE DYING. WE CANNOT HEAL
THEM; MUST RETURN TO TUMBLEROUND.

"Their 'brothers' need expert medical care," Rod guessed.

"Excellent," said the Secretary. "A chance for a humanitarian gesture."

"But they would need a human body to carry them. Unless we find enough whirrs." A prospect unlikely to please Station.

Verid considered this. "I think we can arrange human transport. Most discreetly, of course." Humans were now banned from Prokaryon.

"I don't like it. They would think I gave in."

"You already proved you would not."

Rod closed his eyes. *"No pain, and no rewards,"* he told them.

NO PAIN, NO REWARDS.

"If I take you there," Rod asked hopefully, *"will you all go home—all of you?"*

There was a long pause. The Secretary watched intently.
HOW CAN YOU SEND US AWAY? YOU ARE

HOME TO US, MANY GENERATIONS. YOU ARE ONLY HOME WE KNOW.

Rod's eyes widened. "The ones growing inside me—they don't want to leave, ever." He caught his face in his hands. "Spirit save me."

"They don't want to leave," mused Verid. "By now, perhaps, few of them can. In any world, how few individuals have the courage to emigrate."

TWENTY-ONE

'jum had long experience of shutting out a world of pain. Now, sitting entranced, she had the new lure of the world within, full of the sisterlings with their pulsing number codes. This one was flashing green: Once, one pause, then twice . . . **1 0 2 0 0 7 1,** said the sisterling. (If you cannot yet help us travel, then we'll help you. Travel into our world.)

What is your world like?

The numbers flashed, and she translated. (You'll see. Trust me; I am an elder.)

'jum focused on a tiny green speck of light. The speck grew into a ring, and the ring became a fat, healthy torus. Its surface was crisscrossed with a molecular scaffolding that held the cell intact. It extended loops of polysaccharide filaments toward 'jum, as if to caress her.

(My name is:) **1 0 0 3 7.** The whole shining torus flashed at her. (What is your name?)

'jum thought this over. 1 0 0 0 0 1 0 1, she said, picking some of her favorite primes.

(A beautiful name, 1 0 0 0 0 1 0 1. Your elders must love you very much.)

My elders all died, one after the other.

(Your elders died? Ours can live for thirty generations of children. How do you live without elders?)

Brother Rod brought me to the Children Star. Now, I have Mother Sarai.

("Mothers" we cannot understand. For a tumbleround, yes; but for a person?)

Another torus tumbled over, a blue one, looming near out of the dark liquid. Then came two yellow ones. As they approached, though, all turned green. (Our children.)

The green rings propelled themselves by pumping little jets of liquid this way and that. Two of them knocked together, then one managed to squeeze itself affectionately through the ring of the other. They tangled in each other's filaments, and blinked their light at each other, so fast even 'jum could not make out the numbers.

(We normally converse a thousand times faster than I do with you.)

When will your children grow up? 'jum wondered.

(She will grow up fast,) 1 0 0 0 0 1 0 1. (In a couple of hours, she will be as old as you. She'll go to school, too.)

A new group of rings appeared, of various colors and sizes, all smaller than the adults. In their midst floated one elder, colored red. The elder flashed color insistently, and the smaller ones gradually adjusted, though they kept straying off a bit, here orange, there indigo. It was always hard to make children listen.

How do you eat? 'jum wanted to know.

(We take food through molecular pores in our sheath. The pores open wide when we like the food around us.

And all our food comes from you! Please, feed us foods we adore, especially foods rich in mimosin and azetidine.)

I'll remember, 'jum promised, watching the children. *Do they tell stories?*

(We all tell the story of how our people, the Dancing People, came to be. Long ago, in the Perfect Garden, our ancestors dwelt within a mindless world; a world to be controlled, to be led in its wanderings, to cultivate our planet full of worlds, but mindless nonetheless, indifferent to our desires. From other worlds came whirrs, bringing visitors, but one world to another was all the same.)

(Then the whirrs brought numbers about different kinds of worlds, grown with internal landscapes of harsh alien beauty. The Dancing People marveled. How could such a world appear; where did they come from?)

(To seek answers, some of us took to the whirrs and braved the passage into the alien worlds. Many died, for the habitat was harsh and unforgiving, its physiology foreign to our control. But we learned and adapted. One of those worlds, **1 0 0 0 0 1 0 1,** became our beloved home.)

(Then we discovered an amazing thing: The alien world had intelligent feelings. You could, in fact, understand us, responding to our most intimate desires. And most astounding of all, you came from the stars, like the very gods. It is a wondrous thing, to inhabit a god.)

In the laboratory, with the Secretary beside him, Rod eyed the culture dish, a bauble of nanoplast connected to a dozen ports of gases and nutrients. Khral adjusted a connection, not looking at him.

"Are you sure we can't just take the culture down to Prokaryon?" asked Rod. "They've lasted this long."

"They need constant adjustment of oxygen and temperature," Khral explained. "If I disconnect the culture, they'll die outright."

"The whirrs can't carry them?"

"A whirr is like an ambulance. It's well equipped, but you wouldn't want to spend months in one; you'd starve. Remember, the micromen live on a faster time scale."

"But these have never been inside a human," said Rod. "What if they're too sick to adjust to me?"

"Your own micromen seem to think they can stabilize their 'brothers' and keep them from dying off before we find a tumbleround."

The Secretary touched his arm. "I'm convinced we'll impress your alien inhabitants with our humanitarian gesture. Once they're willing to listen, we can get them to agree to stay out of human bodies."

"The transfer will have side effects, but we'll protect you." Khral placed a nanoplastic patch on his neck. "The patch will send nanoservos into your blood, to keep your fever down when so many foreign visitors are transferred." Then she took a vial of whirrs and opened it into a connecting tube to the culture. As the valve turned, the whirrs swarmed into the culture, presumably picking up as many micromen as they could. Rod felt his scalp prickle. But the worst was yet to come.

"Vacuum suction," Khral called to the culture system. The whirrs immediately were sucked up back into the vial, which sealed itself as she removed it. Her hand shook slightly as she turned to Rod. "This may be easier if you don't look."

Rod looked away, his face turned to stone. He felt the round pressure of the vial against his skin, but surprisingly nothing more. Those whirrs certainly knew how to avoid irritating their host.

GREETINGS. WE WELCOME OUR BROTHERS.

Hush, Rod told the letters flashing before his eyes. *This will be hard enough.*

"I've known many brave men," said the Secretary, "but none more than you. Well, Khral—are we ready?"

"Titer check," Khral called to the culture vessel. "Looks like a few left behind; we'll repeat the procedure, then we're done." She looked to the Secretary. "I'll go down to the planet with him. If he runs a fever or anything, I can take care of it."

"Very well," said Secretary Verid. "You all under-stand—absolute secrecy."

"We'll take the old servo shuttle, so Quark needn't an-swer questions. It's been fixed up," Khral assured Rod.

The stripes of wheelgrass loomed through the window. It seemed so familiar, yet utterly strange to be returning to Prokaryon. So much that had been a mystery was now ex-plained. Rod knew, now, who made the wheelgrass grow in bands; he knew, far better than he cared to, how Prokaryon's true masters governed the beasts that grazed the rows, never picking off so much as a shoot of a singing-tree in the forest. Yet despite how much had changed, within himself he could not shake off the sense that he was going home, and the loss of home ached all the more.

Khral pointed to the viewport. "There, near the river where the forest starts—I see a herd of four-eyes." Several of the tire-shaped beasts were grazing.

"The micromen wanted a tumbleround, remember." The tumbleround had always been their preferred host; yet now, the micromen that had grown up inside him seemed to like an alien human even better. How could that be?

Seconds later the craft landed, more gently than it used

to. It must have been fixed up well this time, Rod thought hopefully. Then he remembered, there was no more colony to need it.

The ginger wind blew across his face as he stepped down. Khral had activated her skinsuit, and Rod remembered that she was not even lifeshaped for Prokaryon. "You can stay here," he told her. If she slipped and the suit failed, there was no help anywhere, not another human or sentient on the planet.

"Bother." Khral stepped down amidst the wheelgrass. She always looked prettiest in her skinsuit, the sunlight sparkling from every curve. Rod recalled happier days, when the scientists went collecting singing-tree pods and watching the light show in the upper canopy; as it turned out, all telecommunications of the micromen. What had those little people thought of them, he wondered, these great human beasts lumbering through their forest, chopping off great hunks of their habitat to haul off in vessels unimaginably large.

Now, though, they had to find a tumbleround and get their errand done. Finding a tumbleround was not so easy, Rod realized with chagrin. Before, he had spent so much energy getting rid of them, but now he had no idea where to go look for one. "We might try the forest," he guessed. "I think they prefer the shade."

Khral nodded, the creases of nanoplast winking around her neck. She hiked with him toward the forest, where the first singing-trees arched overhead, loops upon loops of branches reaching outward. She stopped. "We shouldn't go too far; you'll tire out. Why not stay in one place, and let the whirrs find us."

Rod leaned into the arch of a singing-tree, stretching his back. In the loops of the upper branches the wind sang, and helicoids clattered among themselves. The planet would be saved from destruction, Verid had said. Suddenly he felt very good; there was hope after all, and he was doing his part. "How is the lab?" he asked. "Are you making progress with the language?"

Khral rested next to him. "We figured out a lot, until Sarai went into whitetrance. Now we can't wake her. One of your children could wake her, but Station said it wasn't right."

"For a change."

"And 'jum won't talk either, but I suspect that's just 'jum. You know her."

"All too well," he admitted.

"Damn that Station," Khral exclaimed. "If only she were more tactful."

"You can't blame her. After seeing what I went through, why should she let anyone help the micromen learn to live within nanoplast?"

Khral turned to him. "Rod—I can't bear that it happened to you. I wish it was me, or anyone else in the world."

Rod shrugged. "It had to be someone."

"Not you. You're the only man who ever looked at me like a human woman."

Startled, he looked at her. Was he that transparent, all this time? But the weakness that he despised, she praised. Her skinsuited face was so near; her eyes held him, until he thought he would fall in. He wanted to tell her something, but somehow could not find the words. He lifted his hand and caressed the nanoplast on her cheek.

Khral adjusted something on her suit. Its voice squeaked, "Suit alert, suit alert! You're in danger!"

"Hush," whispered Khral. "I've begun lifeshaping; I'll

survive an hour." The suit slowly peeled, flowing down her face and shoulders, into a puddle of nanoplast at her feet. Her face was clear, her lips near enough to taste.

Rod felt the blood pound in his ears. He thought, I am a free man, not a llama; I will freely choose.

As he met her lips, her arms were around him, her fingers alighting on his back, the nape of his neck. He shuddered as her touch set him on fire. His hands remembered how to slip the clothes off as quickly as possible. Beneath his hands a fine fur covered her back, but her breasts were bare. She pressed herself to him, wanting him so badly, he prayed he could last long enough to please her. Nothing else existed; they were one, alone in the universe.

Afterward they lay quiet together in the wheelgrass. The wind swept over them, and far overhead a flock of helicoids cried as they took off from a singing-tree. Rod let out a sigh of peace and despair. *"Spirit forgive me,"* he whispered.

He felt tears from her eyes. "Are you all right?"

"Yes. Was it good, Rod?"

Rod did not want to say how good. He would not fear the micromen again. He pressed her hair. "You are a beautiful woman."

"I knew it would be good. Oh, Rod—if we ever get out of all this, let me take care of you. I earn good pay, enough for you and any number of kids."

"Khral. Would you trust a lifelong vow from a man who just broke one?"

Her face crumpled. "I hadn't thought of it that way." She looked at the starstone, lying cold on his chest. "Will you have to leave all those children?"

Rod nearly blacked out to think of it. Let the micromen come; their torments would drown his pain.

"How can it be," she whispered. "How can something that feels so right be so wrong?"

Something more than the wind brushed his arm. Several whirrs had come to settle, their tiny propellers humming.

"They're here at last," said Khral. "They'll take your sick micromen now."

Rod eyed the whirrs with suspicion. "The micromen—they were waiting for us." It was bad enough to break his vow, without a million "people" watching.

"They're good biologists," said Khral. "I'm sure they wanted to know how humans do it." She caught his arm as he started to rise. "Don't exert yourself. There will be lots of traffic in your bloodstream, new ones arriving and old ones leaving. Your immune system won't like it; you may run a fever."

New ones arriving—that was not part of the bargain, he thought. He lay back, watching the loopleaves flutter in the wind, trying not to think at all about anything. A scent of glue reached him. "Is the tumbleround there?"

"I see one, a ways off, in the arch of that tree." Khral pointed, her arm outstretched across her breast. She sat up, retrieving her clothes and her skinsuit.

In his eyes appeared something bright that was not sunlight. Closing his eyes, Rod found the message. WELL DONE. OUR BROTHERS WILL LIVE.

Rod sat up. "They say they're done. We can go now." As he started to pull on his shirt, an unwelcome sense of pleasure entered his brain. *"No,"* he said aloud, squeezing his eyes hard shut. *"I said, no rewards."*

HOW DO WE THANK YOU FOR SAVING A WORLD?

He blinked, then laughed aloud.

"What's going on?"

"Nothing, only my own foolish words. Let's go." He

was starting to run a fever, but he could walk to the shuttle.

"I'll get lifeshaped," Khral promised. "If it takes ten years I will. We'll be forever studying this place."

Rod said nothing. Lifeshaping looked easy, next to the choice that faced him now.

TWENTY-TWO

Deep inside 'jum, the sisterlings danced. The little rings danced in intricate patterns, three crossing five and five crossing seven. Red and orange, yellow and blue, their paths wove to and fro, all the while blinking in songs that 'jum could not follow. (What about you,) **1 0 0 0 0 1 0 1**, they called. (Do you dance? Do the gods dance, too?)

'jum wondered. The Spirit Children never seemed to dance. Why not?

Outside her, some useless grown-up was trying to bother her again.

Take me with you, **1 0 0 3 7**, she told the sisterlings. *Show me how to dance.*

(You are a god, and you must dance with gods. But never fear, we will always be dancing inside.) The patterns shifted, and the pulsing circles receded into the dark. 'jum longed to follow, but she could not. **1 0 0 0 0 1 0 1**—(to dance, we need to eat. You must eat for us, so eat good food. Remember azetidine . . .)

A powerful, insistent odor penetrated her mind. Gradually she was roused to the outer world, where she saw and smelled a dish of figs. The figs were overripe, just like the ones her family used to serve in the old days, before they died one by one and her mother became Sarai. The dish was held by a small woman, a stranger dressed in a brownish Elysian talar. 'jum was confused. A dish familiar enough to bring tears, held by such a strange woman.

"It's all right, dear," the woman spoke soothingly. "Tell her, Station."

"You may eat the food," Station's voice boomed. "You may address your visitor as Honorable Secretary."

"Never mind, dear," said the stranger, " 'Nana' will do. Go ahead, eat."

'jum was powerfully hungry, but she remembered what 1 0 0 3 7 desired. "Azetidine," she said. "I want azetidine and mimosin. And I need extra arsenic."

The Secretary looked up.

Station said, "She can have those, they won't hurt her; she's been lifeshaped."

"Very well," said the Secretary, "but eat this, too."

'jum took a bite, then quickly devoured the figs. The Secretary sat before her, watching.

"Wasn't that good. Now, dear, what can you tell me about your little people inside?"

'jum thought. "We dance," she said. "We dance like this." She raised her arms to make a circle, then danced from one side of the room to the other, first three steps, then five, then seven.

The Secretary watched respectfully. "How lovely. Can you tell me more?"

"We are the Dancing People. We dance all the numbers of the world."

"All of them?" echoed the strange woman. "Every single one?"

"It takes many generations."

"What if someday you need to . . . stop dancing the numbers?"

"That's easy. I just stop."

"And the people inside?"

"They understand. They do what I tell them."

"They always do as you say?"

"Of course they do. I feed them azetidine."

Through the next day, and the next, Verid alternately coaxed and interviewed the microscopic people, within the girl, and within the Spirit Caller, and within several other carriers as far as they could communicate. She worked without sleeping, trying as soon as possible to reach that magical point when she truly understood the micromen, or the "Dancing People," as 'jum called hers; knew them better, perhaps, even then they knew themselves.

Their habits, their foods, their children; to Verid, all seemed uncannily familiar. These were people, no question about it. Immigrants to new worlds, only they found their new world was much more than a mindless landscape. And each carrier carried a different breed developing a culture all its own, like a people after forty generations at a distant star. It stunned her imagination.

Still, there were troubling signs. Not all the "cultures" of the micromen were equally communicative. Not all had reached the stage of civility that would earn them entrance to the community of the Free Fold. And some of the human carriers had died before treatment could work. Most disquieting, two carriers had survived but lost their minds. Physically intact, they moved and walked in silence, their brains submerged by some internal control.

To "cure" the incommunicative carriers, the medical sentients had injected nanoservos, by Khral's procedure that had cured Iras. But this time, it was too late. With the micromen removed, the former carriers lay in their beds, responding only to simple requests to sit up and eat. Their higher brain functions were dead. Was this the fate Rod had escaped?

"In the future, we'll prevent that," Khral promised. "We're developing nanoservos to confine the micromen to the occipital lobe, just where they grow to about a hundred thousand and send messages to the retina."

"So they can't spread and take over the brain."

"But carriers who volunteer could grow them to study. What an opportunity!"

Verid smiled. She did not tell her that the Fold Council cared little what some student in jeans could study. Only one day remained of her grace period, and none of the micromen could yet give her the one crucial thing she needed: a purpose compelling enough to convince the Fold to spare their planet.

Verid stopped by the room of Iras. "Dear Iras—are you well enough to go home?"

Iras reclined on a couch, her golden hair spread invitingly over the arm. She smiled, though her face was still pale as a ghost; appalling, after so many centuries of health. We are far from immortal, thought Verid sadly, though with just a touch of relief. "Well enough," said Iras, extending her arms. "And you, aren't you ready to leave this cursed place?"

Verid sighed, enjoying the moment's rest in her arms. How easily she could have lost Iras forever. "Not quite.

You know what the Council will do to this planet, and Station, too."

Iras shuddered. "Sorry for you, Station—but for the planet, I say, good riddance."

"For shame, Iras. The first truly independent mind humans have ever met—and we should destroy them?"

Iras gave her a look of sympathy. "You always did have a soft spot for plague-ridden planets."

"You made all your money off them."

"I probably lost more than I made on L'li. And Prokaryon is a dead loss."

"It need not be. We've learned enough to control the micromen. We can choose, now, whether to carry them."

"Choose to carry them!" Iras shuddered again.

"The girl chooses to carry them. The young Spirit Caller chose, too, despite himself." But their reasons would not sway the Council.

Iras leaned over and brushed Verid's hair. "You know," she added reflectively, "I must admit the experience of illness has . . . given me a new outlook. I've had much time to think. I am truly sorry, dear, about your pet planet. If there were anything I could do, I would."

"You can. You can buy me time."

"How?"

"Buy off a couple of delegates—the L'liite, and possibly the Urulite, if you approach him right. Get them to postpone the hearing. Just buy me enough time to find something to convince them . . ."

To convince them the micromen were worth more to humans alive than dead.

Iras did not answer.

"I know you've taken heavy losses, dear," Verid told her. "But it shouldn't cost all that much."

"Except that someone got there first."

"What?"

"The neutrinogram came through this morning."

"What did it say?"

"Nibur already bought them off, to make sure the hearing goes forward. The vote is assured, no matter what we do."

Verid's hands turned to ice. She had been planning all week to postpone the hearing. "How could Nibur have moved so soon?"

"He zipped home in *Proteus* three days ago."

"Yes. I should have known." Verid felt sick to her stomach.

"There are also reports of more carriers showing up, on Valedon and on Bronze Sky."

Frightening, though inevitable. "The whirrs must have spread. Or the micromen have learned to transfer without whirrs." There was no help for it; Verid had to have the knowledge she needed now, before tomorrow morning, when the express ship arrived to take her home.

Alone again on Station, Rod stared at the holostage, his throat tight and dry. He wanted to call in and see little Gaea, but he could not bear to face Brother Geode, let alone the Reverend Mother. They were sentients, he told himself. They had their own kind of love, but they were born in factories, made by machines. What could they know of the love of man and woman, the kind that betrayed the universal love of the Spirit.

HUMAN. HUMAN WORLD. Whenever he tried to think and concentrate, those bright letters were bound to pop up again. HUMAN, WE HAVE A QUESTION. IF SEVEN MEN ARE TRAPPED INSIDE A WHIRR FAR FROM HOME, WITH FOOD ONLY LEFT TO LAST AN

HOUR, HOW DO THEY DECIDE WHO EATS? DO ALL
EAT, OR SHOULD ONE EAT TO LIVE LONGEST?

Rod sighed, exasperated. "How should I know?" Since
he returned their "brothers," this had been their game, ask-
ing him question after question as if he knew everything.

For a while the letters receded, then they returned.
HUMAN. WHY ARE YOU SO INSCRUTABLE?

Suddenly it dawned on him. This was how the Spirit
would feel, with people all over the universe sending out
their petty prayers: Answer me this, give me that. What a
tedious business it must be, to be a god.

"A visitor," called the room. "The Honorable Secretary."

Rod looked up eagerly as Verid came in. "It's working,
just as you said. The microzoöids—I mean, the micromen
seem to be behaving. They'll tell you whatever you want to
know."

"Excellent." Verid sounded pleased, though very tired.
Rod had never seen an Elysian look tired before. "So you
feel comfortable, now, with your houseguests?"

"For now." He frowned. "But I fear they might
change." What if they grew angry at their god? "When I
sleep, I'm at their mercy."

"The new nanoservos will prevent that."

"That's a relief." He felt a flood of gratitude for Verid.
"What a difference you've made, Honorable Secretary. If I
have helped you in any way, it's been a privilege."

"Don't thank me yet," the Secretary warned. "We have
a long way to go—and little time."

"But you said Prokaryon is safe for now. And now, we
can talk with the micromen, and control them—"

" 'Now' was last week. Tomorrow the Fold meets—in
secret—to decide the fate of your planet."

Rod was puzzled. "I thought so long as we could talk with them, you could work things out. Like with the sentients, the historic treaty, remember?"

"How well I remember." Verid sighed. "But this time, the Fold gave me seven days. Seven generations to save a world. On one condition." She leaned forward. "I have to find some utterly compelling reason why humans need the micromen—need them badly enough to risk their survival. Otherwise, their world will die."

He sat still, trying to absorb what he heard.

"You signed the release, did you not?" she reminded him.

"We all sign that, in case of a plague."

"Such as the plague of micromen."

"But they're intelligent!"

"True," said Verid calmly. "Nobody foresaw intelligent pathogens. And now the Council chooses not to see."

For some minutes he sat in shock, absorbing what he heard. After all they had gone through, the planet was doomed. Slowly he shook his head. "I won't leave." Let the octopods haul him away.

"You won't. You're all carriers, or potential carriers." She paused. "I'm sorry," she said in a low voice. "I told you, I was the cupbearer for murderers. I couldn't tell you how badly things stood, because you needed to hope. You did well indeed, better than I could imagine. But it's not yet enough."

Rod shook violently all over. Then he found himself pounding the wall, his fists sinking deep into the nanoplast. *"No,"* he cried. "No, no."

"Be easy on Station. She, too, will die, in case they've infiltrated her nanoplast."

He stopped, breathing heavily. "Even the children?"

Verid said nothing.

HUMAN, WHAT IS WRONG? STRANGE MOLE-CULES IN YOUR CIRCULATION ENDANGER US.

For a while all he could hear was the pulse in his ears, and his sight blackened. Then his eyes cleared, and he looked at Verid again. "What shall I tell them?" he demanded. "What shall I tell the millions of people inside?"

"Tell them the truth."

He lay back on the bed and closed his eyes. *The humans,* he thought. *Other humans, from other stars. They plan to kill you—all of you, and your planet.*

For a long while there came no response. Then the letters slowly appeared. SO IT IS WITH US. OUR BROTH-ERS FROM OUR ANCESTRAL UNIVERSE PLAN TO DESTROY HUMANS.

"Destroy us?" he exclaimed. "Why?"

THEY SAY, INTELLIGENT WORLDS ARE TOO DANGEROUS. NOT WORTH THE RISK.

He remembered the incinerated llamas. How much worse were humans? Even travel to the stars was not worth the threat of extinction by such irrational carriers. "You'll never kill us all," he warned.

NOT ALL. THE FEW LEFT WILL BE BRED AS AN-IMALS.

Rod thought this over. "Perhaps it's not so bad, to be a llama. Perhaps it's what we humans deserve."

IT'S BAD FOR US. WE WILL PROTECT YOU, BUT OUR BROTHERS WILL KILL US, TOO. FAR MORE OF US WILL DIE THAN YOU.

He laughed, a harsh laugh that caught in his throat. "They are just like us after all," he told Verid. "Brothers killing brothers." But his own micros would die for him— so many of them, willing to give their lives for his sake. That was something to think about.

"The micromen differ among themselves, just as we do," Verid said. "Yours differ from the others."

"Mine need me; I'm their home."

"If only we needed them the same." Verid whispered, her voice suddenly harsh, "That's what you have to find, Rod. Find what the micromen have that we cannot live without."

Left with this impossible task, Rod tried to question the micromen again, but he hardly knew where to begin. The micromen could not seem to grasp what he wanted, and his own mind wandered. What of his Spirit family; could they not yet escape in the lifeboats?

"Reverend Mother Artemis," the holostage announced. Rod shuddered; for this was the moment he had dreaded most. Yet now, staring death in the face, his own failings receded.

"Reverend Mother . . . have you heard?"

"Of course, Brother Rod."

"Then can you do something?" He looked up eagerly. "You've always had connections. Can't you get out, with Geode and the children?"

The sentient did not answer. Her many breasts hung empty, and she had not brought the children. Rod's scalp prickled as he remembered; even the Secretary of the Fold could not save them. He looked away. "Forgive me, Mother."

"It is I who have failed. After all these years, I can see many things now, too clearly—but never mind. If the Spirit offers us one last day in this world, should we not spend it together?"

"What do you mean?"

Station explained. "I have lifted the quarantine. It

seems . . . hardly useful, anymore, as we are all considered unclean."

"So, you can rejoin us now," said Mother Artemis. "Please, Rod—we need you back."

After weeks that had seemed like years, Rod was reunited with the family. For the children's quarters, Station had shaped one of her bleak corridors into a tall, arching vault, with the Prokaryan horizon lit by the spectrum of Iota Pavonis. Virtual wheelgrass swayed in a silent wind, and the golden ringlets of brokenhearts hung ripe upon the fields, like lost rings for all the weddings the children would never have. Rod felt pleased, then angry; was it crueler, he wondered, to prolong the illusion of home.

It was a burst of starshine to have the children climbing over him. T'kun clung to his neck, nearly smothering him, while Pima and Pomu clamored to show him their drawings on their lightpads.

"Brother Rod," piped Gaea, "when are we hunting zoöids again?" The Prokaryan sapphire danced eagerly beneath her chin.

There was 'jum at last, grown taller since she left for Sarai. The girl skipped over to see him; he knelt and caught her shoulders, meeting her dark eyes. "Are you all right, 'jum?"

"My name is one-oh-two-oh-oh-seven-one," she told him. "The Dancing People are going to dance to the stars." Then she skipped away again.

Rod stared after her, astonished.

Geode wrapped all six arms around him. "Our prayers are answered—You're home again, Rod." As if that were all in the world that mattered.

"What's got into 'jum?" Rod asked.

"She finally made some friends—her 'sisterlings' inside."

Mother Artemis kept her distance, as if she somehow knew that he could not face her. Rod looked away. What did it matter, he thought; only another day more of this forsaken world. He whispered to Geode, "Do the children know?"

"Only Haemum and Chae." The two blue limbs entwined. "Mother Artemis let them return to Prokaryon."

"Welcome home, Rod," said the Reverend Mother at last. Her face that was not a face held a strange, unrecognizable expression, and her snakes of hair twined tortuously. "I am ashamed to have done so little to protect our children."

"You did all that could be done."

"Why is the Spirit inscrutable? Yet, if it is written in the stars that our time has come to join *Architeuthis* in the deep, let us lift our arms in prayer."

That night the ceiling darkened, lit only with stars. Rod half expected the evening rain. The Spirit Callers led their evening prayers. Somehow Rod felt awkward wearing his old robe again, especially aboard Station. The children jostled and squirmed, worse than usual, with no room to run. 'jum kept on dancing, weaving her strange patterns of the Dancing People, while the other little ones tried to follow her.

To Rod's surprise, they were joined by several human visitors, including Elk and Three Crows, and even Diorite. The miner shook his hand heartily. "Brother, I didn't expect to see you again. I said a few prayers for you."

"Thanks, friend." He sketched a starsign for him. "I'm sorry you got caught here; I thought your crew got out."

Diorite shook his head. "I stayed on, to look after my investment. Truth to tell, I was betting on things turning out different—if they had, you see, those who stayed would make out big. But now—" He shrugged. "I guess we're all in the same boat with those L'liites, the ones that escaped down there. Still beats me that we never found them, though we got close, I'm sure."

Rod swallowed hard. "I'm sure you did." He would never forget that ship crashing in the Prokaryan hills. But even if the passengers had lived, the micromen would only have turned them into llamas.

There were two more visitors whom Rod did not know. Elk caught his arm and whispered. "They're 'carriers.' " Elk introduced them, one a starship attendant who knew Three Crows, the other, a servo engineer from Valedon.

The servo engineer, a woman with blond curls, wore beads of opal and sardonyx. "You're from Sardis, too," Rod told her.

"The Sardish branch of the Hyalite House." She grinned at him. "A fellow exile, Brother."

Rod looked away. "I'm sorry you had to . . . share our fate."

She shuddered. "It was bad enough dealing with *them* inside. I feel like I died a dozen times."

"You said it," agreed the starship attendant. He leaned forward. "They say it's my meditation training that saved me. Is that true?"

"Same here," said the woman. "It's the one thing we have in common."

"Maybe." Rod was not inclined to speak of himself. "How are your . . . I mean, are you feeling okay?"

"Our little 'friends,' " you mean." The starship attendant laughed. "Mine are incurable tourists. They want to see holos of every nightclub on every planet. I could have taken them anywhere—and look where we got stuck. No offense," he added.

The engineer adjusted her beads. "Mine are chemists. They want to know what everything is made of—and tell me how to make it better. Just think what they could teach us about nanotech. We'd leap forward a hundred years."

Rod's heart skipped a beat. "Did you tell the Secretary?"

"Yeah, I told her." Her face drew in, and her brows knotted. "Politicians," she spit at last. "They'll be the death of us."

"True, but . . ." The man studied the floor. "Remember, some carriers weren't so lucky. The ones who ended up, like, lobotomized—I'd rather die than be them."

"And how many others are out there?" she demanded. "You think *all* the carriers came back here? Some weren't so foolish as us."

Geode was rushing back and forth, his arms full with squirming toddlers. "They know something is up—they just won't keep still."

Mother Artemis spread her skirt, and the beautiful squid leaped out of the rolling sea. The children hushed and stared, their mouths half-open. *On the first world of the first mothers and fathers, in the first ocean there ever was, the creature of ten fingers swam down to the dwelling place of the great Architeuthis . . .*

Letters flashed before Rod's eyes; of all times, he told himself, much annoyed. WHY ARE YOU SAD? the micromen wanted to know.

"Because we're doomed," Rod whispered back.

NOT FOR A GENERATION OR MORE. A LOT CAN HAPPEN IN A GENERATION.

And the ten-fingered one said to the ten tentacles, "Of all things great and fearsome, the greatest and most fearsome of all is the human being. I alone sail the skies, and I sell the stars. My machines plow the earth and build jeweled dwellings taller than mountains. I conquer all knowledge, and my progeny people all the worlds."

SOMEDAY, WE, TOO, WILL PEOPLE ALL THE WORLDS. WE WILL RAISE A GREAT TEMPLE TO YOU, OUR GOD.

Rod could only shake his head.

"Of all things deep and dreadful," warned the long-dead Architeuthis, *"the deepest and most dreaded am I. For I plumb the depths and devour the fallen. My tentacles consume whales and comb the abode of giant clams. I ruled the deep for eons before others crept upon land, and my being will outlast time."*

At last all the children were in bed; it felt like old times, tucking them in. Rod tried to sleep, but he felt restless. He could not stop thinking of the one person who had not come: Khral. He knew why she had not come, and she was right. And yet—why should she be alone, on this of all nights? Of all of them, she had done her best to let Prokaryon live. And she had touched something in him; he could not deny that. Something in him had come alive in her arms, and now they had so little time.

In the darkness of early morning he got up, hurriedly pulling on the travel clothes that he usually wore on Station. A pale light appeared in the ceiling; he waved at it to go away. It grew dim, just enough to get by. Hurriedly he dressed and left the quarters of the Spirit Family.

He found Khral in the laboratory, with Quark's eye-speaker perched on her shoulder, amongst the culture vessels and samplers. Sarai was there, too, busily sealing up some kind of samples in little seed pods, her fingerwebs snapping as they flexed. Khral looked up from her data that streamed across the holostage, and she managed a smile. "It's you."

"For better or worse." He caught her hand and held it. Turning to Sarai, he added in her native tongue, "Share the day, Sister."

Sarai did not look up. "The day be cursed. I knew I should never have let that devil off my planet. Now it's too late, for us—but not for *them.*" She held one pod up to the light. "I've sealed up several packages of 'jum's sisterlings; dried out, they can last forever. I'll launch them, in the direction of the nearest planet-bearing stars. They'll land, someday. And they'll remember."

"Crazy Sharer," muttered Quark. "Do you think Station will let you launch them?"

Station did not answer. Rod wondered what the great sentient satellite thought of her own imminent demise. But he felt Khral's hand, his blood rushing.

Khral nodded at the holostage. "I keep trying." She sounded alert as ever, despite the sagging around her eyes, her face more gorilla-like than usual. "It's our last chance—maybe anyone's last chance for a long time, to study them, to learn what they're about. Whatever data we find will outlast us."

"A career's worth of data," said Quark, "in the days we have left."

Rod watched them curiously. "Is it so important, your scientific data? Was it worth giving your lives for?"

There was silence. Khral said at last, "There must be something those micromen can do for us. We still have a chance to find it."

"Like what?" said Quark. "A better way to make aze-tidine? Face it—nobody cares. Look, Khral, I hate to point this out, but you're a human, and you're running down for lack of sleep. Leave me here to run down the last list."

With a nod, she took the eyespeaker and set it on the counter, then she and Rod left together. In the corridor, Khral pointed to a viewport. "Look, do you see that tiny starship? It's Sharers, come to witness. Their ship is very small, but they could take three of your children, if you put them out in a lifeboat."

Which three, he wondered bitterly.

They reached her room, and the door sealed behind them. They fell into each other's arms. This time they made love more slowly, exploring every inch of each other, for there was time, perhaps the last time ever. When at last they were satisfied, they lay together, half sleeping.

"It can't be," Khral whispered. "It can't be over, just when life got to be worth living." She raised herself on her elbow. "Rod . . . did you ask them? You're sure there's . . . nothing they can do? Microbes have always done for humans—leavened our bread, brewed our beer, made our vitamins."

He shook his head wearily. "They call me a god, and can't imagine what I would need from them."

"How odd. That's not how they talked in the beginning. They offered—"

"Never mind." Rod shuddered. "They evolved."

"They got too tame, that's what. All the ones in the carriers have been domesticated for generations. Could a dog tell why his master needs him?" She got up and reached for her clothes. "We need fresh ones, that's what. Station," she called, "tell Quark: We're going back to Prokaryon."

TWENTY-THREE

Verid awoke early in the morning, her mind still running over the options. Never in all her centuries of public life had she found so few. After all the Elysian children she had raised, as director of the *shon,* now she had to leave children to their death. In any office she had ever held, as guardian of Helicon, as Prime Guardian, now as Secretary of the Fold—never had she left a world to its destruction.

"Station?"

"Yes, Secretary."

Beside her in bed, Iras still lay asleep, her hair flowing over the pillows, as beautiful as the first day they met, ten centuries before.

"Station, I'm sorry."

"It was my choice," Station assured her. "I took the risk from the start. All the colonists knew what they signed."

"Even the infants?"

"All the children admitted were on the verge of death when they came, death by disease or starvation. At least I will assure them a death without pain."

Barbarity, though Verid. No matter how far we advance, always we revert to barbarity, in one civil guise or another.

Iras stirred and stretched, and her eyelids fluttered open.

Verid smiled for her. "Dear, are you well enough to leave?"

"The sooner the better. Is our ship here?"

Station said, "The ship is here. The ship awaits your call."

Verid slowly rose from bed, and very deliberately dressed and checked her clothes and nanoservos. All the while her mind was running full speed. What could she do? She could postpone the hearing, by a technical maneuver; but that would gain a day or two, and only earn her censure.

"The ship wishes to address you," reminded Station.

"Very well, put him through," she muttered.

The bridge of the ship appeared on the holostage. The ship, an outsized sentient like Station, introduced itself with all the usual formalities. "By the order of the Fold Council," the ship intoned, "I am hereby directed to secure your passage to Elysium. Be advised, Secretary, with all due respect, that full precautionary measures will be taken. You will wear a skinsuit and remain in quarantine. Be assured, nothing will hinder your official duties."

The Secretary stiffened in every muscle. This was the final indignity—to return with the status of contamination. "I have been tested by every means possible. I have not the least sign of . . ."

Station concurred. "The person of the Secretary has been subjected to every possible test of microbial contamination, including nanoservo inspection, molecular scanning, and—"

"Excuse me, Station; just a minute." Her head was spinning. It had come to her at last, the one thing she had to try. "Station, there were those two confirmation tests—remember? You never did perform them."

Iras frowned. "You can't be—Verid, you didn't tell me."

"Station," Verid insisted quietly. "You did not complete the tests."

Station said, "As you say, Secretary. I regret the omission."

The ship replied, "An extremely serious error, Station. You were to have the Secretary ready by oh-seven hours this morning."

"Indeed. I shall report myself to the authorities. I deeply regret the inconvenience, but the Secretary will be delayed . . . some hours."

"Twenty-four hours," put in Verid.

"This is *most* regrettable. The Council will not be pleased." The ship signed off.

Iras caught her arms. "Oh, Verid—what are you doing? You've been through every test."

"Only rats leave a sinking ship."

"What good will another day do? You'll be impeached."

"So, I'll retire, and you'll see more of me."

"Be serious! What's come over you?"

"I've never liked working through interpreters," Verid observed, "even the best of them." She held Iras close. "Iras, I can't explain now; but this is something I need to do. You will go home without me tomorrow."

"*What?*"

"Don't worry, the Council will do nothing until I return. Meanwhile, do your best to buy back whoever Nibur got to. The Urulite, at least; he'll be the cheapest."

"Verid—you can't. You've never been sick, yourself; you can't imagine."

"And Station—if you value your life, activate your shield, and let no shuttle from that ship come to fetch me."

In the clinic Verid met with Khral, as three medical sentients hovered nearby.

"We must inform you," said the senior medic, "that after due consideration, all three of us strenuously object and advise against the procedure."

"Of course you do," muttered Verid. "I'll sign whatever form you need. Let's get on with it."

"You must understand—we lack the knowledge to stabilize the Prokaryan pathogens within your Elysian physiology. Especially infections agents obtained *de novo* from the wild."

Verid turned to Khral. The student pressed her hands to her forehead and tried to speak, but coughed instead. "It's just an idea," Khral explained, her voice dull with fatigue. "I brought some whirrs back from the planet, where the micromen still know the full potential of their species. Within humans, I think the populations living their short lifetimes have forgotten a lot."

"I understand."

"I've put them together, temporarily, with a few volunteers from Rod, to teach them our language. Then one of the carriers may volunteer—"

"We have no more time for intermediaries. I will contact the micromen myself."

Khral's face turned gray. The medics reared back indignantly, as if washing their many limbs of it. Khral swallowed, and said, "Remember, the injected micromen will be a very small population. They will want to reproduce right away; for a while, the proportion of elders will be small, and they'll barely have their 'children' under control. That is the dangerous period."

"We'll get through it. They'll learn to communicate?"

"They seem to learn different ways, depending on their host. With 'jum, they use their own number code, which works well for her. Rod's micromen, I hope, will teach yours letters you can read in your—"

"Yes, I know." Verid stretched out on the hospital bed, while Khral prepared the whirrs and the medics injected her with all kinds of protective nanoservos. She imagined the tiny machines coursing through her blood to check all her tissues and organs, preserving the proteins needed by every cell. What was harder to imagine was the microscopic living beings, setting down for the first time within a human world. For each of them, each with its own life, its memories and dreams—how would it feel?

The vial of whirrs pressed her skin. Like the virtual jellyfish that had touched her foot, when Nibur had laughed. But this time she did not flinch.

"It's done." Khral's voice was barely audible as she put the whirrs away.

So I'm a carrier, thought Verid. For a moment she was gripped by terror; she felt as if she were falling down a deep well, unable to stop herself. But it passed. She was still herself, after all. "It's done," she echoed. "What next?"

"You have to wait and see. We'll hope they make contact."

A half hour passed, while Verid made the best of her time reviewing staff reports on the holostage. Then suddenly she felt hot all over, from her hands to her forehead.

"What is it?" She breathed rapidly, thinking, they're burning me up inside.

The medic told her, "You're running a slight fever. It generally happens as the infectious agent settles in."

Fever. Verid had heard of fever, read about its sufferers, but never experienced it. "Are you sure it's all right? Even for an Elysian?"

"It's a low fever, so far. Even for an Elysian."

She repressed the conviction that she was boiling to death and felt a bit ashamed. Living for centuries in their floating cities, Elysians knew so little of life.

The first spot of light flickered on her retina. Verid sat up straight.

"Rest yourself," insisted the medic. "So far, your nanoservos report, the infection is highly localized within your brain. But if it spreads, you'll need all your strength."

"Station, lights down," she ordered. The light dimmed, except for the holostage outputting her vital signs. She closed her eyes. Something flickered again. "Khral? Are you there?"

"Of course, Secretary."

"Fetch the other carriers here, too." She would need all the help she could get. The seconds and minutes passed, seeming endless; yet how much longer they must seem for the micromen, who lived ten thousand times faster? How would humans keep up talking with creatures who took a week to reply to the simplest question, and went to sleep for a decade?

GREETINGS, HUMAN WORLD. The letters appeared in her eyes, unbidden. She tried to tell herself, it was just like one's nanoservos talking after all. But this was different. These internal creatures had minds of their own.

YOU ARE NOT LIKE THE OTHERS.

She took a deep breath and tried to stay calm. Nearby

stood the carriers, even 'jum in the corner with Rod. "How do I answer back?"

There was an awkward pause. Rod said, "It just happens, after a while."

"Try reading letters in the holostage," suggested the flight attendant. "That always worked for me."

Khral agreed. "The first thing the colonists learn is to read your retina."

"Indeed." "Colonists"—a startling thought, but so they were. "Very well. Holostage, print these words: 'Who are you?' "

The letters appeared above the holostage, and Verid concentrated on them. Immediately came the reply: WE ARE THE PEOPLE. YOU ARE A WORLD TO BE MASTERED.

"That won't work. You will have to deal with us." The words floated in air, and she stared at them until her eyes swam.

SO SAY THE MESSENGERS. WHAT CAN YOU DO FOR US?

Verid looked up. "What can I do for them?"

The flight attendant laughed. "Travel—that's what they want."

"We can't." Not yet—but someday.

'jum raised her hand. "Azetidine. Give them that—it's their favorite."

The medic reared its caterpillar body. "Poison!"

"Azetidine is moderately toxic to your system," said Station. "I am preparing a sample, with protective agents." The wall nearby puckered to spit out an ampulla, which Khral fitted to an injector. The injector painlessly dissolved a microscopic well into her vein, then sealed the opening on its way out.

YOU ARE LIKE THE OTHERS. LIKE YET UNLIKE.

What "others?" Verid wondered.

YOU CAN GIVE US MANY THINGS FROM THE STARS, BUT YOUR BODY IS INCOMPATIBLE. IT WILL TAKE A GENERATION TO FIX YOU.

"That it would," Verid said aloud. "It would take decades to lifeshape me for Prokaryon. We don't have that kind of time, but—"

"No it won't," interrupted 'jum. "Lifeshaping doesn't take that long."

"Hush, 'jum," whispered Rod. "You're a child; adults take many years." And even then they could not bear children.

The holostage announced, "Medical alert. Massive physiological changes occurring within patient, as microbes colonize circulatory system, liver, intestinal epithelium . . ."

"Station," called the medic, "the patient is suffering massive physiological effects. I demand an immediate halt to this ill-advised experimental procedure, or else I—I will seek termination of your license."

Station said, "The choice is yours, Secretary."

"What's going on? What are they doing?"

"I wish I knew. But they cannot destroy you without destroying themselves."

"That hasn't stopped humans," Verid dryly observed. "Holostage, spell out: What are you doing to my body?"

WE FIX YOU TO LIVE HERE. LIKE THOSE WHO FELL FROM STARS, BUT YOU ARE DIFFERENT.

" 'Like those who fell from stars—' Who is that? And why am I different?" Verid was throughly confused, and the continued recitation from the holostage did not help.

Rod exclaimed, "The L'liites. You're like them, but you're Elysian. The L'liite ship crashed, but some survived, and the tumblerounds found them."

"They could not have survived long."

The medic said, "The presence of the microbes is altering the patient's biochemistry by the minute. If this madness does not stop, I withdraw from the case."

"The L'liites did survive," Rod insisted. "Diorite tracked them. But—"

Verid's jaw fell open. " 'A generation'—Holostage, print out: *'How long will it take to fix me? Whose generation?'* "

OUR GENERATION. BUT WE ARE PATIENT. MEANWHILE, PLEASE FEED US AZETIDINE, HYPO-GLYCIN, AND MIMOSIN.

A generation of micromen. A single day. Verid tried to stand up, but her head swam with fever.

"Please, Secretary," cautioned Station. "Your body is reacting to massive changes in chemistry. Are you sure you will continue?"

"Yes, by Torr," she exclaimed weakly. "Don't you see? They can lifeshape us in a single day—anyone. At no cost." She raised her arm. "Find those L'liites."

On Prokaryon, the weather had taken a turn for the worse. All around the planet towered hurricanes whose lightning struck any vessel from the sky. From space, the planet's disk was a mass of tumbling clouds. Never before had the world been seen thus, not since the days of the early explorers.

"Somehow they know," Rod told Diorite, as he watched the holostage, clenching and unclenching his hands. "They know what the humans have in mind." Not that it would help against the white hole.

"How could they know?" demanded the miner. "Did the Spirit tell them?"

"Chae and Haemum were carriers. Their micromen must have told the others." He could imagine the light-coded messages leaping across the singing-trees where he and Khral used to collect their samples.

"By Torr—if *that's* it, can you imagine what's in store for Valedon once those critters multiply?" Diorite shook his head. "We're doomed, whether we save that cursed planet or not."

"The Secretary doesn't think so. She thinks we can deal with them. And the L'liite survivors will convince the L'liite delegate to change his vote. That's why we have to find them."

"Oh really? What if we find them turned into llamas?"

He tensed all over, then relaxed. Sketching a starsign, he said a prayer.

Station announced, "The shuttle is ready, shield fully activated. All members of search party assemble for boarding."

The search party made a hair-raising descent, sustaining several strikes of lightning. When at last they landed, they struggled across the ground drenched by rain, stepping over carcasses of drowned four-eyes. Besides Rod and Diorite, six forensic sentients fanned across the hillside where, months ago, Diorite's crew had last seen tracks. They stumbled and dug each other out of mud laced with treacherous loopleaves, then climbed over singing-tree trunks felled by the storm. The roar of the wind hammered Rod incessantly. "Tell them to stop," he urged his internal visitors. "Send whirrs to tell them—we mean to save their world, not destroy it."

OUR WHIRRS CANNOT SURVIVE THE STORM. WE REMEMBER OUR BROTHERS, BUT HAVE NOT SEEN THEM FOR COUNTLESS GENERATIONS. WHERE WOULD WE FIND THEM?

Out of the corner of his eye a light flashed. The thunderclap deafened him for some minutes. Diorite caught him with his arm and shook him, trying to say something.

"The sentients have found something," shouted Diorite. "A whiff of human flesh. But there's no sign of them."

How could there be any sign, Rod thought; any footprint would have been washed away. Bracing himself against the wind, he surveyed the drowned landscape. Hills rose above the valley, one of the wilder corners of Spirilla even in fair weather. An outcropping of rock jutted, exposed to the elements. There was something vaguely familiar about the character of the rock. He wiped his eyes and squinted. Fog was rolling in across the rocks, but just for a minute the clouds parted and the rock shone clear.

"Sarai's place," he murmured. "It's just like the road to Sarai; the same kind of rock formations. And Sarai used to live—" He grabbed Diorite's jacket. "Caverns," he shouted. "They could be hiding there."

"That's it! We have to scan the earth deeper." Diorite called into his radio, which somehow was still working.

Rod could not say how long it was until at last the forensic detectors had traced the human signal to one stretch of hillside. The searchers traced back and forth, but still nothing could be seen, no hint of any kind of entrance in the mud.

FORGIVENESS. EVEN IF A PLANET DIES, ONE MUST ALWAYS FORGIVE. THIS WE WILL TELL OUR BROTHERS.

His shoulders shook, and his tears joined the rain. These micromen had "evolved" too far, he thought; they made him feel small.

Suddenly the ground gave way beneath his feet. It was not ground after all, but a tangle of branch loops woven cleverly together. Now, though, it was falling apart. Rod struggled to right himself and climb out, but he slid inexorably into a dark hole.

An arm came round his chest, immobilizing him. At his neck pressed something sharp, the blade of a knife.

Rod made himself relax. Whoever it was had not killed him yet; his best chance now was to wait for an opening.

"Not one move, you devil." The voice spoke in L'liite.

"Kill him now," urged another. "Spirit save us—they won't send us back." They did not sound like "llamas." And yet—they were alive.

The rest of the opening crashed through. In the confusion, Rod slipped away from his captor and crawled across the floor. Light broke through, and there were screams and shouts. Rod heard a zapping sound that he did not recognize. Abruptly all was calm, except for the cursing of three L'liites immobilized by webbing emitted by the forensic sentients. Somewhere unseen a woman was sobbing.

"Spawn of dogs," cried one of the L'liites, straining at the nanoplastic web. "We'll die before you send us back."

"We won't," shouted Diorite. "We need your help to save our planet."

Not a likely story, Rod realized. How could the L'liites believe it? As Diorite tried to persuade them, Rod's eyes adjusted to the dim light. The cavern had been swept and kept tidy, until their rude entrance. There were pots and blankets and an oil lamp in the corner. The rubbery smell of cooked four-eyes was familiar. The woman sobbing in the corner held something protectively.

"Father," called one of the trapped men. He was calling to Rod, staring at his starstone. "Father, you will tell us. Is this true?"

Rod flushed, for he was only yet a Brother, and the stone felt heavy on his neck. "Yes," he replied, sketching a star. "It's true."

The woman looked up. "A Spirit Caller," she exclaimed. "At last—one to bless the new name." She held up a tightly wrapped infant, its eyes tight shut, sleeping through the storm as only infants could. Its face was still wrinkled like an old man; he or she could not be more than a month old. The first human baby born on Prokaryon.

TWENTY-FOUR

From within the Fold ship Verid watched the glittering sphere of the Secretariat, in its eternal orbit about Elysium. She flexed her fingers, uncomfortable in the skinsuit that the medical service had decreed she must wear—for the rest of her life, perhaps? Glacially she eyed the three octopods assigned to guard her—or the entire Fold from her.

In another ten minutes the shuttle would take her down, straight into the Council meeting she had postponed for the past week.

THEY ARE TAKING NO CHANCES. NOT TO LET YOU CHANGE MINDS.

STILL, YOU COULD WORK ON THE BRONZE SKYAN DELEGATE. SHE LISTENS TO REASON.

THE SENTIENT DELEGATE COMMUNICATES ON OUR TIME SCALE, PERHAPS WE CAN REACH HER—

Verid blinked her eyes. "Enough already; I can't hear

myself think." She had tried to educate her internal symbionts about Fold politics, and now they all wanted to advise
her. Unlike her human advisors, she could not sack them.

On the holostage appeared the head of Loris
Anaea*shon*, the Delegate Elysium, stern but triumphant.
"With all due respect, Secretary, the Council asks me to advise you that you are to join us *directly*, with no inappropriate word to the press. You understand my meaning."

"Of course, *Shon*sib." Her voice sounded hollow inside the skinsuit which covered her mouth. "Just a photo-
op." Although the Council meeting was closed, all kinds of
frightful rumors had gotten out, and the Fold was in an
uproar. The snake eggs would demand a brief statement.

"I trust you've read and understand the charges against
you."

"Absolutely. Second on our agenda."

WE'RE LOOKING FORWARD TO THIS MEETING.
SOME OF US WILL LIVE TO SEE THE END.

YOU NEED TO VISIT OUR COUNCIL, TOO.
PLEASE REMEMBER PROTOCOL IS MOST IMPOR-
TANT. THE LESSER OFFICIALS FLASH BLUE AND
GREEN, WHEREAS THE GREATER ONES FLASH
PINK AND YELLOW.

"Secretary?" The welcome sound of her nanoservos in
her ear, from her aide.

"Finally," she exclaimed. "Is our plan ready?"

"Yes. We have all the snake eggs expecting a statement,
just ten minutes outside the meeting."

The aide approached, his Elysian train full of sky-blue
butterflies. "Verid—it's a wonder to see you."

Verid lifted her hand, feeling her skinsuit stretch. "Wonders never cease. Tell me the worst, Lem."

"Elysium is nearly in panic. Everyone is getting 'tested,'
although they scarcely know what they're testing for. And

now they're expelling all foreigners—all but essential ones, of course . . ."

Verid swung round to meet him, her nanoplastic train swerving expertly, and the octopods fell in beside. Slowly the convoy progressed to the door of the shuttlecraft. Elysians took their time.

". . . Valedon is nearly as bad; there are riots in the streets of Iridis," continued Lem at her ear.

WHAT SORT OF HUMAN IS THIS? A GOOD WORLD TO VISIT?

No. She strove to burn the words into her retina. *No, I say; be still.*

BRING US WHIRRS. WE CAN PENETRATE YOUR "SKINSUIT."

Verid squeezed her eyes. *Stay put, lest you and I be incinerated.*

"Secretary?" Beside her Lem was frowning.

"Fatigue, that's all. Do go on."

The shuttlecraft docked, its nanoplast melding into the surface of the Secretariat. In the wall a mouth opened to let Verid pass.

"Secretary," whispered the nanoservos in her head. "Now is the time."

The snake eggs jostled so thickly that Verid instinctively raised an arm. Octopods waved at them threateningly, but all knew that interference with reporters could bring a life sentence. Speech was the most sacred commodity of the Fold—and the most profane, she thought. The Council meeting was just minutes away.

"Secretary, is it true that alien microbes will enslave us all?"

"Were you infected, Secretary? When will the test results be released?"

"What will the Council do?"

Verid shook her head. "Listen." She raised her voice and spoke slowly. "I have one announcement to make. I hereby announce . . . by executive order . . . that the Council meeting about to begin . . . is open to the public."

The reporters fell back in confusion, the smarter ones zipping out to race to the Council chamber before the delegates could countermand Verid's order. As she entered the chamber, they were indeed attempting to do just that. But it was too late, Verid saw; some of the reporters had slipped in, and to eject them would make a scene nobody wished to be seen in.

"Never mind." The Delegate Bronze Sky glared, her dark features rigid with fury. "Verid, I've backed you before, but this is it. You've got a lot of explaining to do."

"And one more count of impeachment," observed Delegate Elysium, reclining comfortably in the seat that opened beneath him like a flower.

"Oh hush," said Delegate Sharer. "Let's at least congratulate the Secretary on her return alive and well." The Sharer was purple as always, with the oxygen-breathing microbes that thronged in her flesh. Verid smiled gratefully, thinking, we are sisters now.

Delegate L'li watched intently. "Congratulations, indeed." He had received her secret message—but had sent no reply. Still guarding his options.

"We waste time!" Delegate Urulan shook his fist at her, playing to his own home audience. "Boil the planet! Better yet, eject it to another universe!"

Verid kept standing. "It is my duty as Secretary of the Fold, and my great honor, to certify the discovery of a new, intelligent community of people. A new form of intelligence, indeed the first form we've met that evolved completely outside human civilization." She leaned forward. "Microscopic people."

"An outrage!" Delegate Urulan was beside himself.

"Out of order," snapped Delegate L'li. "Let the Secretary continue."

Verid went on. "These microscopic people live a year for every ten minutes of our own lives. Their species and culture evolved at a comparably high rate. A hundred years ago, when our first human explorers arrived on Prokaryon, they had only just diverged from the lesser microbes whose ancestry they share, like our own Stone Age ancestors once did. Even then, they covered the entire planet with rows of crops they tilled and the animal hosts they governed. Today, they run advanced communications all across their planet—advanced enough to rule their planet's weather at a moment's notice. This is indeed an intelligence worthy of our respect."

"Finding intelligence was not your charge." The Delegate Valedon's jewels glittered on his talar. "Your charge was . . ." He stopped, eyeing the reporters. Genocide was not done in public.

"But more than our respect, these people—we call them 'micromen'—bring us enormous hope. Living within our bodies, they can be partners to us, in a grand new venture to the stars. They can use their own chemistry to extend our physiological capacities to inhabit new worlds. Not only Prokaryon, *but other new worlds*. No more laborious lifeshaping; no more costly colonies that never pay back. As proof—"

She tossed a lump of nanoplast to the holostage. The stage filled with the L'liite refugees, presumed dead yet found alive and well, in a habitat that should have killed them in a week. The three men and a woman stared defiantly. The woman clutched her infant with one hand, and raised her fist. "This is *our* world. Long live New Reyo!"

Verid carefully avoided looking at the Delegate L'li. For

a moment she regretted the future she foresaw—a thousand worlds overrun by humans with their micromen. But that was a problem for another day. "The child you see was born to these healthy, untreated immigrants—*born on Prokaryon,* a feat that none of our lifeshaping has yet accomplished. Their microbial symbionts figured out how to do this. Citizens, try to imagine the intellect that achieved this. Humans and micromen—What miracles can we not accomplish together?" She scanned the reporters bobbing up and down beneath the ceiling.

"Honorable Secretary," the Delegate Elysium smoothly began. "Surely you are not taken in by this . . . constructed footage."

"I shook their hands myself."

Delegate Elysium shuddered delicately; Elysians never made physical contact in public, let alone with carriers of a plague. He shook his head with elaborate condescension. "Really, *Shon*sib. We know you've put your heart into this, but the job of the Council is to be objective. Do you agree, Delegate Valedon?"

Delegate Valedon was busy whispering to his nanoservos. He looked up to say, "My confidential sources assure me the scene cannot be genuine. How were these purported L'liites 'discovered' just now, so conveniently?"

Verid raised her eyebrows. "Do you question my integrity, or my competence?"

"Come, Citizens," demanded Delegate Bronze Sky. "You can't fool the reporters. We know it's true: The L'liites were found alive. The question is, what to do about it?"

"No, Citizens." A new voice came from the holostage. "That is not the question."

It was Nibur Lethe*shon.* Nibur stood in their midst, his virtual talar shimmering before the never-ending wave of *Proteus.*

"What's this?" exclaimed Verid. "Out of order."

WATCH OUT, PLEASE. YOUR ADRENALINE RUNS TOO FAST—IT MAKES US SICK. Verid closed her eyes.

Nibur was saying, "You yourself opened the Council to the public."

"I called this witness," said Delegate Valedon. "Let him speak."

The others assented. Verid's thoughts whirled, trying to recalculate.

"Thank you, Honorable Council," said Nibur. "The real question is, what about the carriers not so lucky as myself? What of those who died—or worse." His image was replaced by that of a patient in bed at Station, with a medical caterpillar bending over him. One of the two former carriers who had failed to heal.

The patient sat against the pillows. He breathed well, and his color looked good, but his eyes held a vacant stare.

"Stand up, please," said the medic.

The patient rose without looking up, the covers falling to his side.

"Now walk to the door, and come back."

This, too, the patient managed, putting one foot in front of the other. At the door he turned, then walked back to stand by the bed.

"Now tell us your name."

The man continued to stare. The entire Council chamber fell silent.

WHAT IS WRONG? THE CHEMICALS IN YOUR BLOODSTREAM FRIGHTEN OUR CHILDREN.

Verid tried to relax. *You know what your brothers and sisters have done, to other human worlds. Be still and let me think.*

"You see?" The medic inclined its caterpillar body toward the viewers. "This patient has entirely lost his higher mental functions. Before we cleared the infection, his empty mind was ruled by the so-called micromen. A beast of burden." The caterpillar bobbed its head. "I myself am a sentient, immune to infection so far. But you humans—this is what will become of you."

"What do you recommend?" called Delegate Valedon.

"What do you think?" demanded Nibur. "Even the so-called micromen confess that they plan our destruction. All the medics recommend prompt elimination of their source."

"Then you'll have to cleanse every planet of the Fold." Verid looked around the Council. "Those two unfortunate citizens received treatment too late—because they came from Valedon, and from Bronze Sky. Where have no micromen reached? One way or another, we have to live with them."

"They haven't yet reached us," said Delegate Solaris, from the most distant of the Fold's worlds. "Cleanse their main source. It may be too late, but it's the least we can do."

Verid felt a chill. She had counted on Solaris.

"Boil the planet," agreed Delegate Urulan. "We should have done so to start."

The Delegate Sentient added, "Alas, I have come to share the view of my medical colleagues. As much as I value the possibility of intelligent life, I cannot but recall that the very first casualties of Prokaryon were sentients. Of course, we've adjusted our composition since—but what if these dangerous pathogens mutate?"

The second vote Verid had counted on, from one who ought to understand best. She turned to the lamppost sentient, inwardly bitter. "What then?" she asked, her brows high. "Genocide? For a race newly certified? Do you propose to rewrite the constitution?"

The reporters bobbed expectantly.

"Cowards!" The Sharer snapped her purple fingerwebs. "My people have shared microbial symbionts for countless generations. How can you miss this opportunity?"

"The 'opportunity' is voluntary," Verid added. "Future colonists can choose to be carriers. The rest of us are largely safe, since transmission requires an insect vector. Control of the insects will contain their spread."

"For how long?" countered Nibur. "A good reason to wipe out the main source now, while they can still be contained. Intelligent invaders—who knows what tortures they'll invent?"

"I call for a vote," said Delegate Bronze Sky suddenly. "The white hole is ready and waiting—we need to decide."

"Second," called Delegate Valedon.

Verid's hands shook. "The question is called: Do we activate the white hole to cleanse Prokaryon?" She called the roll. "Delegate Bronze Sky?"

"No." One switched—she had a chance.

"Delegate Elysium?"

"Yes."

"Delegate L'li?"

The man paused thoughtfully. "For the moment I pass." L'li never liked to be taken for granted.

"Delegate Sentient?"

"Yes."

"Delegate Sharer?"

"No. My sisters will surround that world with a living shield."

"Order, please. Delegate Solaris?"

"Yes."

"Delegate Valedon?"

"Yes."

Verid turned to L'li. "Is the Delegate ready to vote?"

"I vote against." He rose to speak. "The decision is too

sudden. We need time to study the possible opportunities for my people; indeed, for all the citizens of the Fold."

She swallowed, her mouth suddenly dry. "Delegate Urulan?"

"Against—*until we can completely wipe out this plague!*"

Iras had bought him after all; how many water projects, Verid could only guess. She collapsed in her seat, her own whispered vote nearly lost in the buzzing of reporters.

"Be warned," cried Nibur from the holostage. "You'll live to regret this day. You'll all end up mindless beasts."

Delegate Elysium raised his voice. "The Council is not yet done. The second item on our agenda is our call to impeach the Secretary of the Fold. I have been asked to read the charges—"

"Never mind," interrupted Verid.

The Elysian looked up, surprised by the breach of order.

"I resign, effective immediately."

Around the chamber, the delegates turned to stare.

"Impossible," exclaimed the Sharer. "You'll beat the charges, Secretary. You have to fight."

"Sorry, but I meant it. I resign."

No one else spoke, but their faces all registered surprise and discomfort. They could not believe it, Verid realized. After five centuries of her rising in power, they assumed she would always have a win up her sleeve.

"You made this mess," accused Delegate Elysium. "How—how dare you just walk out of it!"

Verid sighed. "I'll stick around to help, if the Council wishes. But as Secretary I cannot continue. It's too distracting, being a carrier."

The delegates gasped, and the reporters bobbed in confusion. Delegate Sharer came over to embrace Verid in her skinsuit, while Delegate Elysium turned pale and collapsed.

There were calls for quarantine, and the octopods closed in.

WHAT IS GOING ON?

We've won your planet a reprieve. But you'll wait many generations before they set me free.

At Station, travel was reopened, though departure required extensive testing. Rod resumed something of his former schedule with the children on the satellite. With no farm chores to take his time, he immersed himself in their education, setting up regular programs for each child.

On Prokaryon, the storms had subsided within a few days. The micromen living there lost interest in the threat after two or three generations. Meanwhile, several mining firms sued to return, including Diorite, who had set himself up independent.

"It's the chance of a lifetime," Diorite told Rod. "Get in on the ground floor, before everyone figures it out."

"Really?" asked Rod. "Do people really want to live here and be carriers?"

"The smart ones are lining up to stake their claim. And not just from L'li either."

"But the Council could change their mind. Nibur still owns the planet."

Diorite chuckled. "Rumor has it Nibur sold off his holdings at a sizable profit."

"Those micromen—I still think we're sitting on a time bomb."

"Not so long as they need whirrs to transmit."

"But they're intelligent. They'll learn."

Diorite shrugged. "They can't be more dangerous than a few humans I know—or sentients, they're no better. Say, when are *you* coming back? Feldspar's waiting."

"The Reverend Mother will decide."

Rod no longer ignored the news as he used to. He made himself spend a half hour at the holo each day. The Secretariat was at a standstill, with its former executive in quarantine, and special elections called. The worlds of the Fold hurled charges and countercharges of "who lost Prokaryon," though all meant different things. Some cautiously welcomed the microbial symbionts, while others called for their destruction. New carriers of micromen appeared on Valedon. Meanwhile on L'li, Reyo was falling apart worse than ever, its streets split by roaming gangs, while thousands died of creeping.

One day Mother Artemis summoned Rod and Geode together. "Station says we may leave," she announced. "We may leave Prokaryon, after extensive testing; the children can join a Spirit Home on Valedon." She paused to let her meaning sink in. "Or, we can return to this world and rebuild our colony."

Geode's six arms waved at once. "Yes! Tomorrow."

Mother Artemis picked up Qumum, who crawled inquisitively across the floor. "Remember," she warned, bouncing the child, "the humans inevitably will be carriers, including the youngest children. What that may mean in the long run, we can't say." She and Geode both looked at Rod.

Qumum was sucking on his fingers while taking in the world with his wide eyes. Rod's internal guests had warned him of what the other micromen, back on Prokaryon, might do to humans who returned. But his own would have given their lives to save him. He also remembered the L'li-ite newborn. "Better pioneers than orphans," he observed at last. "If the Spirit calls, let us go."

"So be it," said Mother Artemis. "We still need more help, though, to maintain the colony while we keep up the children's studies. Three Crows would like to stay on with us."

"I knew he would!" said Geode. "The Spirit heard our prayer."

Rod wondered what Elk would think. Then he thought of Khral. Since the crisis passed, he had avoided her, cursing his weakness. A Spirit Caller had no use for mortal love. Now that the colony had a second chance, so did he.

The light of Iota Pavonis filled the fields, already full of fragrant loopleaves. The home of the Spirit Colony had been flattened by the storm, and their crops mostly washed away, but the brokenhearts had reseeded and grown wild, filling the paths they had cleared with succulent golden rings. With Feldspar's help they began to rebuild their home, plow the fields, and restore the sapphire mine. Haemum and Chae returned to pitch in. They hunted down a herd of four-eyes zigzagging across the loopleaves, and soon brought home fresh meat.

As Rod climbed to the roof to set new tiles, the breeze caught his cheeks, and brilliant helicoids whirled overhead. His own spirit rose with them. Never had this world seemed so precious as since it nearly perished.

Yet in fact, the old world had perished; the old, mysterious world that Rod once knew. In place of mystery, there was the known, inescapable presence of the micromen.

HUMAN, THERE ARE SO MANY OTHER WORLDS OUT HERE. WORLDS EVEN OUR ELDERS BARELY REMEMBER, FULL OF BRAVE NEW PEOPLE.

Rod watched a whirr alight on his arm and take off, perhaps bound for a tumbleround at the edge of the singing-trees. It felt odd to be a city and airport for millions of microscopic people.

THEIR PEOPLE ARE DIFFERENT FROM US. So the micromen themselves faced culture shock. THEY

FRIGHTEN US. THEY THREATEN TO TAKE US OVER
AND RULE YOU LIKE A TUMBLEROUND.

Don't let them, Rod warned, setting a tile in place. Why
had the Fold forced the former Secretary into quarantine,
instead of sending her back here to deal with these new
"worlds"? For now, he could only hope that Station's
nanoservos—and his own micromen—continued to protect him.

TELL US SOMETHING. DO HUMAN WORLDS
MEET AND MARRY LIFELONG PARTNERS, OR DO
THEY COUPLE HEEDLESSLY, LIKE THE TUMBLE-
ROUNDS?

Both, Rod told them, or neither. Some of us marry the
Spirit. He wished they would leave such topics until he was
safe on the ground.

WE NEED A LIFETIME TO KNOW EACH OTHER,
BEFORE WE CAN SAFELY MERGE AND BECOME
CHILDREN.

How odd, to grow up to be children.

On the ground below, Gaea came toward the ladder,
her feet dragging dejectedly. "Brother Rod?"

Rod quickly came down the ladder and swung the
three-year-old up to face him. "What's the matter, Gaea?"

"My head hurts. And I see funny lights in my eyes."

He frowned. In the younger children, the nanoservos
were supposed to keep down the numbers of micromen so
they avoided making "contact" until the children were old
enough to understand. He took her to the holostage, which
had just got reinstalled.

"Sarai, please."

Sarai had returned to her laboratory in the mountain,
which had escaped the storms largely untouched. Mother
Artemis had let 'jum return with her, to continue studying
the micromen. Now they both appeared on the holostage.

"We're terribly busy right now," Sarai told him. "Two Sharer sisters have arrived to join my work on triplex DNA replication, and neither of them knows the first thing. They can't even run the enzyme secretors."

'jum looked up from her numbers. "I'll show them how." She had grown dramatically, her legs strong and slender; she would soon reach his shoulder.

Rod held Gaea up to Savai. "You once cleared Gaea of micros. Could you help her again? She gets headaches, and really feels bad."

Sarai looked shocked. "What do you take me for? I've renounced genocide. How could you live with yourself, let alone with all your internal friends?"

"They could always find a tumbleround." He had expected her reply, but it was worth a try before calling Station. As for 'jum, she had settled back with her adopted mother, busily working with her own "sisterlings." She had all the friends she could need now.

Suddenly 'jum leaned into the holostage. "Brother Rod, when are you coming to see me again? I'll show you my numbers, and a new dance I learned."

"Yes, when are you coming?" said Sarai. "We need to interview your sisterlings."

Rod smiled. "I'll come soon, 'jum; as soon as the crops are planted."

He closed the connection, dreading the call he would have to make to Station. The medics would help, but they always made him feel like a beggar. No one had heard from Patella for months now, and the Spirit Fathers showed no sign of sending another doctor.

"You have a neutrinogram," announced the holostage before he could speak. "From Chrysoport, Valedon: Brother Chrysoprase and Sister Heather, of the Sacred Society of Spirit Brethren."

The grainy monochrome image took shape. A man and a woman stood there, each wearing the same white hooded robe as a Spirit Caller, but with ropes of flowers around their necks and open-toed sandals on their feet. Much to Rod's irritation, they both sketched a starsign.

"Greetings," said Sister Heather, "from the Spirit Brethren, a sister order to your own. The Great Spirit of the Universe moves us to entreat you to accept our application to serve your colony. Our mission is to serve children, and where better than Prokaryon?"

"We are prepared to 'carry' micromen," added Brother Chrysoprase. "We've carried breathmicrobes for years, to help us dive and fish to support our order." Their skin was dusky, though the neutrinogram did not show the color. "But our numbers have grown, and you need us more."

"We bring many skills to help you," the woman added. "We've experience in farming, servo mechanics, child psychology. . . ."

This was but the latest request the colony's newfound notoriety had brought them, from would-be colonists who had no idea what they were getting into. As for the so-called Spirit Brethren, their help was the last thing respectable Spirit Callers needed.

"Enough," Rod told the holostage. "Keep the image in memory, for Mother Artemis." She would send the callers a polite reply.

Finally he gave up and took Gaea back up to Station. The old lightcraft had been fixed with a new controller, which kept it in good repair although it increased the chance that the craft would turn sentient.

At the clinic, the little girl shrank from the giant caterpillar, but Rod held her close, pressing her curls of hair. "It's all right. The doctor will help you feel better."

"We'll give her new nanoservos," the medic told him.

"We've enhanced their program, to provide much better control. They adjust the level of certain key nutrients in her circulation, nutrients she doesn't need much, but the micromen do. And we'll keep working on it. Lots of volunteers want to get rich on Prokaryon."

"Even with all the hostile 'natives'?"

"Every frontier has hostile natives. It goes with the territory."

Rod looked closely at the sentient. "Are you new here?"

"Most of the old medics rotated out. I've come from the Brain Institute. What an opportunity—that is, to keep you healthy, of course."

In fact, Station's corridors were full of strangers. As Rod brought Gaea back to the lightcraft, they ran into a group on some kind of tour. Some were humans in faded jeans, others were sentients of various sizes and shapes; a "lamppost," a caterpillar, an eyespeaker for some nonmotile structure. The humans spoke in obscure jargon, oblivious to their surroundings, and even the sentients looked as if they had not checked a mirror lately. Leading the group were Elk and Khral.

"Rod!" boomed Elk's voice. "You should have told us you were back." He took two strides and gave Rod a bear hug.

"Glad you're here," said Quark from someone's shoulder. "Meet the new students."

From the front of the group Khral turned, but kept her distance.

Elk laughed. "We can always use another student, Rod. After all, your colony got Three Crows; I thought he'd never give up deep space. Why don't you join us?" Elk nudged his arm and nodded at Khral. "Ask our new Research Director."

"Bother about that." Khral waved her hand. "Good to see you, Rod."

. . . just when life got to be worth living.

Elk began introducing the new students, but Rod barely heard. Thankfully Gaea was getting restless, and he excused himself to take her home.

"Hope you had a nice trip," said the lightcraft politely.

Rod barely heard or knew where he was. He could only see Khral's look as she had turned to him, and hear her voice call his name.

Geode came running out of their new home, its shiny roof tiles gleaming in the sun. "Rod—you'll never guess! *Patella is coming back!*"

It took a few seconds for Rod to realize what he had said. "Patella's coming back? To us? You're sure?"

Geode was hopping up and down on all six limbs, his starstone dancing crazily around his eyestalks. "Yes he is! He sent a neutrinogram. It took months and months, but they gradually got his mind working in his new body, and he's coming back." Rod had never seen him so excited. But then, Patella was like a twin to Geode, from the same Valan factory. They had always been especially close.

During worship that evening, as the new llamas groaned in the dusk and the gentle rains hid the moon, the Spirit Callers gave special prayers of thanks for their brother's imminent return. Rod tried to feel glad, but any joy he could feel was overwhelmed by the pain within. All he could see was Khral's face before him, and feel her in his arms again. He longed for her, yet hated himself. He was living a lie; he could no longer call the Spirit.

HUMAN WORLD—TELL US SOMETHING, WE PRAY YOU. The micromen would not leave him alone. IF ONE SOUL MARRIES ANOTHER, BUT THE MATE

DIES BEFORE MERGING; THEN HE TAKES A SEC-
OND MATE, WHO ALSO DIES; THEN HE MARRIES A
THIRD; TO WHOM IS HE MARRIED WHEN ALL
HAVE ASCENDED TO HEAVEN?

Rod closed his eyes. Make me a llama, he told them, like
you tried to before. Then I'll no longer need to think or feel.

Early in the morning, Rod went to the Reverend Mother.
The first rays of light from the window cast bright squares
across the wall, and Rod blinked as they caught his eye.
Mother Artemis was nursing T'kela. Her strands of hair
stretched up toward him. "Rod, whatever is wrong, let me
help you."

"I must leave the order. I've broken my vows, and I
can't stay." He paused, then added, "I'm sorry to leave you
short-handed, but now at least Patella will be back . . ." He
stopped, full of shame and confusion.

"I'm so sorry. What a terrible time you must have gone
through." She set down T'kela, who crept off to grasp at a
sunbeam. "Will you join Khral?"

He shuddered to realize she had known all along. For
some minutes he could not speak. "I can't," he said at last.
"I care for her, but I would hate her for what I've lost."

"Then where does the Spirit lead?"

"The Spirit doesn't lead me anymore. For now, I'll join
Diorite's crew." Beyond that, his future was blank. He had
never before faced a future alone, without someone leading
him on.

"Well, you can apply to the Most Reverend Father for
release from your vows. It will take some months to ap-
prove and process—"

"No," said Rod sharply. "I can't stay. It would set a bad
example for the children."

Mother Artemis paused. "The children will miss you."

"I will miss them." He choked on his words. "I can't imagine life without them."

"Is that all you'll miss, Rod? The children?"

"No, of course, I'll miss you, and Brother Geode. And—" He could not say it. "I still don't understand. I still feel the Spirit led me to Khral, as it did to the tumbleround. Yet it can't be."

"The Spirit tests us with choice. Sometimes one must give up a great love for a higher one."

"I did that, once," said Rod. "I gave up the Guard—my pledge of honor to Valedon. But now, I have to give up the Spirit."

"The highest love is truth."

To that he had nothing to say. Truth brought peace, if nothing else.

Mother Artemis was silent for a while. She looked out the window, her hair twining in the sunlight as if to soak up wisdom. "In truth, I have listened for many decades, yet I never understood why the Spirit would be jealous of human love. Would you be jealous of your micromen?"

Rod blinked in surprise. "What are you saying? Do you question the vow?"

"The vow is right for some. It was right for you, for a time. I pray the Spirit Fathers would keep their other vows, such as to support this colony."

This heresy left him speechless.

"I've been thinking, Rod. It's time our colony became more ecumenical. So many kinds of people want to help out, and we'll need their help, even with Patella back. I'd like us to accept those two Spirit Brethren who applied to join."

"The Spirit Brethren? But—but they're not . . . respectable."

"Respectability counts for little out here." The sentient's features made an odd slant, as if she were angry. "In truth, the Spirit Brethren are respectable enough. They split off from us several decades back, when two Fathers quarreled over doctrine. They hold the Sharer view that the Spirit calls each of us to conceive and raise our own child."

Imprisoned deep within an Elysian hospital, Verid paced the spotless floor, restless as a dog. There was company enough, the micromen within, and virtual visitors without; but for weeks now, no living human had so much as shared her breath. When would the Fold Council relent? The quarantine went beyond all reason, but, having stripped her of power, her opponents could enjoy their revenge.

IF WE EVER DO RETURN TO MYTHICAL PROKARYON AND DISCOVER NEW WORLDS, THEY WILL HAVE TO MEET OUR STANDARD OF CIVILIZATION. THEIR AMBASSADORS WILL HAVE TO LEARN OUR PROTOCOLS, FLASHING COLORS IN PROPER ORDER.

Verid sighed. By the time she ever got back to Prokaryon, her own micromen would be useless, having dwelt apart for generations. Precious time was wasting, while the timeless Elysians figured out what to do with her.

"A visitor," intoned the hospital. "Iras Letheshon."

Her head shot up, and she straightened herself. A cloud of light shimmered and became Iras, her hair flowing gloriously down her the back of her best train, the butterflies with their eyespots glowing red and gold. "Dear Iras," she breathed.

Iras smiled sadly. "I wish I were real, dear, but this was the most they'd allow."

"It was good of you to come."

"How can I be without you? Even if you are always muttering to your nanoservos. You know, Verid, I tried my best to spring you, but these medics are just incorruptible."

Despite herself Verid smiled. "That's good to know."

"Have you heard about Nibur? He was so besotted with that dog, he couldn't bear to lose it. You'd think he'd just make a virtual one. Instead, he had the medics cleanse his memories." Iras shook her head. "Start down that path, and it's hard to stop. He's not half the man he was."

Verid nodded. "Too bad."

"But look," said Iras brightly. "I've brought you something to keep you company—Raincloud's descendent!"

In a moment, there stood Sarai, resplendent in Sharer purple, flashing her fingerwebs as she lectured an unseen audience on DNA recombination. "Her research seminar, the one she gave at Station. It's on public record, so I acquired it. Isn't she gorgeous?"

"Stunning"—Verid laughed—"and most informative!" Then she grew serious again. "Listen, Iras; I need to tell you something. I give you my release."

"What do you mean?"

"I mean that I release you from our bond. You understand."

"But Verid—"

"Iras, think." Verid took a breath. This was hard, even harder than she imagined. "I carry micromen, now; I always will."

"The Fold will let you out, eventually. They're just punishing you for being right. They need you to negotiate; why only yesterday Loris was saying—"

"But Iras—*they made you sick*. Remember?"

Iras shuddered. "Too well."

"You can't touch me again. No one in their right mind would. You can't take the risk."

She thought this over. "Dear, I've never been the one to worry about risks."

Verid looked down, feeling shamed.

"Besides—what a thing to say, after the fortune I just spent on you." Iras's net worth had fallen recently, by over three trillion credits.

"I'm sorry, the Urulite vote cost more than I thought." A lot more; enough water projects, she figured, to turn his planet into Shora.

"The Urulite? That was nothing. I meant your birthday present. Remember?"

Verid put up her hands. "Goodness; I forgot." What costly embarrassment could it be this time, for all the Elysians to cluck about? "Iras, I hope you were . . ."

"Discreet?" Iras finished. "You really are out of it, aren't you? Don't you even watch the news?"

"It's all censored here," snapped Verid. She nodded to the ceiling. "Go ahead, show it."

The Anaeon newscaster appeared, his train of dead-leaf butterflies flowing behind him, similar to Verid's own. ". . . from Reyo City, the Health Ministry announces a new project to diagnose and treat the 'creeping' disease, and to undertake preventive measures designed to eradicate the deadly prions. Funded by an anonymous grant of three trillion credits, the project will establish clinics all around the planet. Within ten years, experts estimate, the prion plague can be effectively eliminated . . ."

Verid rarely flushed, but she did so now, her face and hands warm, then cold. "Iras, you didn't," she said unsteadily.

"I would have named it for you, but you always said to be . . . discreet." Iras wiped tears from her eyes, then collected herself. "Plagues are bad for business, don't you know. And the one that's left won't be so easy." She walked forward, until her shape nearly touched Verid in the face. "Please, Verid. Don't be proud; tell Loris what he wants to hear, and get yourself out of there. I need you—and the Fold needs you, to talk with those micromen before we lose the chance."

Rod watched the sky for the old servo lightcraft he had sent up to Station. There it was, a bright oval descending toward the overgrown brokenhearts. Estimating where the craft would land, he jogged alone down the newly cut path. A flock of helicoids took off from the field, their propellers clacking, while in the distance the blue-striped four-eyes grazed unconcerned. Sometime he would have to chase the herd farther from their crops, but not today.

With a bright flash and a whiff of ionization, the craft landed and was still. Out stepped Khral, waiting, the wind lifting her hair.

Rod ran to meet her, too fast, as his feet stumbled through the loopleaves. He caught her in his arms and met her lips. Then they sank down together and lay tangled in the loopleaves for a long while, a time behond time.

"Rod," she whispered, "are you sure it's all right?"

"What's right for you, is right for me. Can you live here now?"

Khral nodded, her fingers combing his hair. "I took in enough micromen to modify my chemistry so I can survive here. It wasn't fun," she admitted. "It was scary, after watching you go through it. But now they're okay. They're not a bad population; they're scientists, wanting to know how everything works."

"Curious, isn't it, how they always imitate their host."

"Don't people always grow into their habitat?" Khral shifted onto her elbow. "Rod, what about your colony?"

"The colony is changing. A couple of Brethren are joining us, and I'll be talking with them."

"The Spirit Brethren? Not the ones that dance before the moon?"

"Only at midsummer." He smiled. "Maybe I need to learn to dance, like 'jum."

"So long as it's with me."

"Are you sure? You know I have nothing to give you. Not even . . ." With a sudden thought, he plucked a brokenheart and slipped it around her finger.

In the caverns of Mount Anaeon, 'jum was showing the new Sharers how to feed the carnivorous plant that secreted the enzymes for their work. "They'll eat anything," she explained, "but they like hoopsnakes best."

A clickfly zoomed in to alight on her head. "Lightcraft landed outside," it clucked excitedly. "Visitor coming up mountain."

"Ushum?" Sarai called to her, looking up from the holostage where she tried to dissect the crossing-over of triplex chromosomes. "Ushum, can you see who it is. If it's anyone but Khral, send them packing. We're busy."

"Yes, Mother." She headed out to the mouth of the cavern. Blinking in the sun, she scanned the mountain across the valley. So many rays poked out between the crags, but now she had friends to help her count them. Down the slope cascaded the loopleaves, where little zoöids chased each other, clinging by their suckers. Whirrs soared up and down, carrying sisterlings from one world to another; at night, their messages would light up the singing-trees.

On the path below, a man in a cloak was climbing

steadily toward the cavern. It was Brother Rod, come to see her again. 'jum smiled and waved.

1 0 0 0 0 1 0 1, (be sure to tell him,) reminded the Dancing People. (Warn him about the poisons some of our foreign sisters are trying to spread.)

I will, said 'jum.

(We're trying to spread peace and democracy among the worlds, but it's not easy.)

"Brother Rod!" 'jum did a cartwheel, landing on her toes.

"That's a good trick, 'jum!" Brother Rod sketched a star in the air, and the stone at his neck glinted as if on fire. He caught her up in his arms, then set her down. "You must be eating well."

'jum thought he looked well, too, not as sad as he used to. "Brother Rod, you need to watch out for the other sisterlings, the ones that still live in the tumblerounds. Some of them are not yet civilized."

"Do they hurt you?"

"Of course not." She took his hand. "My sisterlings protect me. They are telling me the names of all the bad molecules to watch out for. Mother Sarai sends it all up to Station."

"And Station tells the rest of the world, wherever the micromen have got it. It's an important job you're doing." Brother Rod nodded. "Throughout the Fold, now, people are carrying worlds full of micromen. And, just like people, the Spirit has made more good than bad."

"They need our help," added 'jum. "They're mostly children." Children with elders, but no parents.

He looked out across the tops of the singing-trees, past the clouds and sun. A helicoid swooped down to catch something, its propellers humming. "There will be many more worlds to settle, now. And more of your own neigh-

bors from Reyo have come to join us. So many changes—
you would scarcely know the colony. But you will always
have a home with us."

"This is my home now." 'jum nodded. "So many children. You were right, Brother Rod. This really is the Children Star."

All native life-forms on Prokaryon contain ring-shaped structures, both in body plan and inside their cells (i.e. circular chromosomes). The *zoöids* are animal-like; *phycoöids* are plantlike; *phycozoöids* share traits of plant and animal; and *microzoöids* are microbes.

zoöid Animal-like species, capable of rapid movement; consume food.

> *four-eyes* Zoöids that graze on wheelgrass in large herds. Shaped like car tires with suckers for "tread," and four eyes spaced equally around. Several species known, ranging in size from bike tires to truck tires. Usually light in color, or striped to blend in with the wheelgrass.
>
> *helicoid* Flying zoöids with ring-shaped propellers. Several species, the size of birds. Some are brightly colored.
>
> *hoopsnake* Flexible, looplike zoöids which travel

like a sidewinder snake. Capture prey by strangulation.

hydrazoöid Extended tubelike zoöids, with one fin winding in a spiral around the tube. Rotate as they swims through water.

megazoöid Large predatory zoöids, the size of an elephant. Capture prey (usually four-eyes) by running them over.

microzoöid Microscopic size; also called **micros.** Many classes, ranging from plant to animal, not yet well-known, except for one species later designated *micromen.* The micromen are also called **silicates,** by the Elysian medics, after their silicate capsules inside the human body; also **sisterlings,** by the all-female Sharers.

whirr Tiny helicoids, like insects. Different species feed on juices of zoöids or phycoöids. One species transmits microzoöids between tumblerounds.

phycoöid Plantlike species, with loopleaves and double-roots; absorb energy from light (photosynthesis).

brokenheart Tall looping stalks, with loops upon loops. Produce large numbers of edible ring-shaped fruit which look like wedding bands.

wheelgrass Tough green stalks, like croquet hoops, growing thickly across vast fields. Consumed by four-eyes; tend to catch feet of humans.

singing-tree Arch-shaped trunks, dark blue-green, many times taller than humans. In the upper loop branches, platelike leaves vibrate in the wind, "singing." Hanging lightpods carry microzoöids which produce light.

phycozoöid Species share traits of plants and animals. Most are not yet well-known.

tumbleround Human-sized life-form, shaped like a collapsed truck tire. Color is gray-green; perform some photosynthesis, but also feed on wheelgrass and dead creatures. Long tendrils can slowly pull the creatures into a new position. Always infested by microzoöids and covered with whirrs.

ring fungus Parasitic growth around the trunk of singing-trees. Can be dried to form a tough material usable for construction of buildings.